shy girls can't date

fake date

shy girls can't date

fake date

MILLY ROSE

MILLY ROSE

TOP

One

I turn up the volume on the kitchen speaker. As if given more energy, my head bobs and my hips sway. Whenever I'm baking, I have the same playlist on. Everyone in my family knows not to mess with the stereo when I'm in the kitchen. And that's most mornings because I have a sweet gig baking desserts for Morton's Café.

A few days a week, I work there as a server. Baking desserts is something extra I do a few mornings before school. Everything I earn goes into one fund, earmarked for attendance at a Parisian patisserie school.

I don't know how the French would feel about me dancing while I bake. Although, I doubt I'd ever be that brave. No one outside of my family and my best friend knows I get my groove on in my kitchen. If there were ever an occasion I needed to bake at the café, I don't know how I'd function. I'm far too self-conscious to have anyone watch me shimmy at the counter, or bob in front of an oven.

This part of me stays at home, where I'm safe to experiment and have fun. At my workplace, I'm just a server. At school, I'm just an invisible student.

Sometimes, I wish I could leave school now and be a full-time baker. But there's one perk of still being at school. It's five days a week in the same place as the gorgeous boy next door. Seeing him before and after school just wouldn't be enough.

Ever since his family moved to Victoria Falls, my heart hasn't stopped fluttering. I've easily replayed the moment we met a million times. That day, I was so scared to go over to their house and introduce myself. I was carrying a tray of brownies, and because my hands were trembling, I was sure I'd drop them on my shoes.

My mom made me stand by her as she rang the doorbell. My anxiety lowered when his wonderful parents welcomed us inside. I swear, my jaw almost fell to the floor when he descended the staircase. I'd never seen a more beautiful boy.

"Hi, I'm Lewis," he said, waving at me.

After every syllable caught in my throat, my mom made our introductions and offered up the brownies I'd made.

I couldn't keep my eyes off Lewis as he took his first bite. His sky-blue eyes lit up like the sun was rising for the first time. A pink hue highlighted his cheeks as his grin stretched.

"Man," he mumbled with a mouthful of brownie. "That's the best thing I've ever eaten."

My heart pumped into overdrive.

His eyes locked with mine as he asked, "You made these?"

I swallowed my leaping heart and managed to squeak, "Mm-hmm."

As my mom chatted with Lewis's parents, Lewis snagged another brownie and waved goodbye, wandering into the back of the house. This is the part of the memory where my imagination takes over.

If only I were more confident, I would've followed Lewis into the back room. My mom wouldn't have minded. She always encourages me to chat with more people my age.

Most times when I reimagine this moment, Lewis stays in the front room with us. He asks me more about baking, and we discover our mutual love of zen activities, which require mindfulness and quiet. We then find a private place to sit and enjoy each other's company.

Ahhh.

Just thinking about it puts me at peace.

I always get my baking done as early as possible so I can catch a glimpse of Lewis before school. With the white chocolate, raspberry swirl tart out of the oven and resting on a cooling rack, I hightail it toward the staircase. I detour through the back room and give our lazy and spoiled golden retriever, Brandy, a good dose of pats.

"Hey, girl," I whisper. "I gotta go upstairs and see Lewis."

Her head tilts to the side, and she emits a quizzical sound.

I giggle. "I know. What am I doing here? I might miss him."

I leave Brandy and head upstairs. From my bedroom window, I gaze into the corner of Lewis's bedroom, where the most I can see is his desk and a poster on the far wall. It's a movie poster from his favorite action franchise, Wasteland Gang. I've forced myself to watch the first three in the series so I can wow Lewis. So far, we haven't had that conversation outside of my head.

As if willed into existence, Lewis steps into frame. He closes a textbook and the laptop on his desk, and slips them inside his backpack. The thumping of my heart plays like drums as I stand motionless. Honestly, I wouldn't be surprised to find myself drooling. He moves away from the window, but not from my thoughts.

I breathe out slowly, and envision him standing in my bedroom. His hand scuffs through his buttery blonde hair, the way he does at school. I always imagine he's deep in thought when he does this. There's so many layers to this boy I want to discover.

The conjured Lewis kicks back on the edge of my bed and smiles. "I always love looking at that poster."

I sit down on the edge of the bed, taking a whiff of his cologne that's been burned into my memory. I gaze at the poster of Paris and drift into the fantasy of snuggling close to Lewis.

"One day we'll get there," I whisper.

Beep, beep, beep.

The alarm on my phone shatters the illusion. Lewis evaporates from the space, and part of my soul goes with him. But one day, he'll be here for real.

It'll be the day he remembers how romantic our first meeting was and runs over here for another tray of brownies. It's not like I'm not always prepared.

I smooth down my school uniform, grab my backpack, and head downstairs. I drop my bag by the kitchen doorway and move over to the counter to slice and package the tart for delivery.

"*Mmm*," Mom says, sniffing her way into the kitchen. "Maddy might have to pay you double for these. You outdid yourself."

I grin. "That's what I'm trying to do."

"Are you ready to package them up and get going?"

"Absolutely."

Before taking me to school, Mom drives me to Morton's Café. It's always a good pick-me-up when my boss, Maddy, praises me for my baking skills.

When we later arrive at school, Mom lists off the errands she has to do downtown. I'm barely listening as I pan around the parking lot for Lewis sightings. As he walks by, my heart leaps into my throat. The air gets thinner, and time moves slower.

My senses return to normal function, and I rush a goodbye to my mother. I leave the car and suck in a breath of bravery as I move onto the path toward the school gate. Every day, I time my arrival perfectly so I can follow him into school. Every day, my obsession with him grows. And one day, he'll realize he feels the same way about me.

If I'm going to talk to him, I have only a few moments to accomplish the mission. Once we're in the hallway, he'll be joined by his friends, who also ignore my existence. I'm not deterred when he's in a social setting. I love seeing him interact with people. Not only does Lewis light up, but he makes those around him better. He has no idea of the positive impact he has on my wellbeing.

My heart flutters, and my pace quickens. Just hi. No one died from saying hi.

I curl my fingers around the straps of my school bag. My brave breath morphs into fear-soaked pants. The thumping of my steps echoes in my ears. I have a few more feet to gain in order to reach him, and then what? Look like a red-faced fool who puffs hello?

I skid to a stop, gritting my teeth. No way. I'm not starting our relationship on such an awkward note.

Relationship?

Did I actually just go there? Yes, I want to be with Lewis Allen. He's perfect. But we need to be friends before we rush into anything romantic. The fact he doesn't acknowledge his classmate who lives next door doesn't bode well for us.

I linger behind him, entering the school foyer. Ahead, Lewis meets up with his friends, Parker and Tyler. Their chatter is fast, but their pace is steady. They congratulate him on the latest news about his photography. His work has been nominated for another prize.

As I listen to their praise, it's like fireworks spark in my chest. I went to the last exhibition Lewis took part in. His work is so exquisite. I've even seen him in the local park, crouched and patiently waiting to snap the perfect macro nature shot. Those are the moments that make me love him the most.

I envision myself by Lewis's side, holding his hand as he chats with his friends. I watch myself brush back my cinnamon brown hair, distracting Lewis from his conversation. The boys take the hint, and fall back, giving Lewis and I privacy as he kisses my cheek. His bright blue eyes look deep into my soul, and I caress the side of his face. His honey-blonde hair is silky to the touch, and I melt in his presence.

Laughter erupts from the boys, breaking my illusion. The crowded hallways of Ashworth Academy try to separate us, but I use all my might to stay close to the boys. I get lucky when they stop in the hallway so Tyler can stuff his backpack into his locker.

Okay, maybe not too lucky. I'm stuck in the middle of the hallway. There are too many students rushing around on either side of me. I could move to the opposite side of the hall, but then I'll be too far away from Lewis. Ugh. This is awkward.

As I turn my head from left to right, checking if I can make it across, I hear Tyler's locker snap shut. I look over at the boys to check if they're moving.

Parker Kelly leans against a locker, gazing around the hallway. He looks my way, but his eyes are vacant. It's like he's looking through me.

Like I care. It makes no difference to me if I don't exist to Lewis's friends. Lewis is the only one I care about. He's the only guy I want thinking about me.

One day, he'll be the only guy to hold me.

To kiss me.

Ahhh.

Just imagining it sends a thrill of goosebumps across my flesh.

I giggle, soaking up the good vibes, and get back to reality. My eyes wander along Lewis's school tie. We all wear the same school uniform, which includes a tie and blazer, but there's just something irresistible about the way Lewis fills it out. As my gaze lifts, my lips wet when I take in his solid jawline. When I take in the rest of his face, Lewis smiles and waves in my direction.

I blink hard, certain it's another daydream pulling me away from real life.

When my eyes open, the cutest smile lines crinkle around his eyes, and his grin expands with an adorable laugh. My heart swells and my knees almost give way.

This is it.

This is our moment.

He's finally seen me for who I truly am.

His perfect girl.

Oof.

Someone pushes past me in the crowd, and I stumble to the side. As I regain my balance, Yvette Anderson struts ahead of me. Her fingers pump in a flirtatious wave as she strolls by Lewis and his friends, who are practically drooling.

My heart sinks as Lewis's gaze follows Yvette.

He waved at her?

I clutch the space on my chest over my cracking heart. The boys continue along the hallway, following in Yvette's direction.

When a hand lands on my shoulder, I jump in shock.

"Hey, it's just me," my best friend, Josie, says, spinning me around to face her. "Are you okay?"

"Oh, yeah, fine."

Her eyebrows raise with skepticism. "Tell that to your tone."

I sigh. "It's just... I thought Lewis was waving at me."

Josie's eyes widen as she smiles. "Really?"

I chew the inside of my cheek, trying not to frown. "But it was at Yvette Anderson."

Josie groans, throwing her head back. "I'm so sick of her. On the bus ride here, she was literally the only topic anyone talked about."

I roll my eyes. "It's the same thing every few months. Why do people keep giving her attention over this drama?"

"Well, you know people love to discuss anyone in the Ashworth family."

"She keeps calling herself their cousin, but I found out her mom is cousins with Mrs. Ashworth."

Josie smirks. "So, she's not even related to the Ashworth side of the family?"

"No, she's a second cousin looking for fame."

"I don't think it matters how far removed she is," Josie says. "She's a relative on the Scandinavian side. She's tall, skinny, and blonde. Apparently, she thinks she's God's gift to men."

A gag reverberates in my throat. "As if."

Josie giggles, following behind me as I move toward my locker. "Let me guess, your Lewis would never be interested. He was just waving to be friendly."

"That has to be it. Sure, he can see how pretty she is, but he'd never be with someone so shallow and vapid."

"Well then, you might want to make sure you're on his radar while Yvette's still single."

"He knows I exist."

"He's lived next door to you for over a year, and you still haven't walked to school with him, or taken the same route home."

"I get driven to school most days because of the café. And sometimes his friends drive him to school."

Josie clicks her tongue teasingly. "Excuses, excuses."

"Hey! At least my crush is at the same school."

"Well, mine *was* at this school." She huffs, planting her hands on her hips. "And we got a heck of a lot closer than you and Lewis ever have."

"Sure, sure," I tease, opening my locker.

"It would be nice to hear about you and Lewis getting together," Josie says, leaning against a locker. "Purely so I don't have to hear about Yvette anymore."

I snort. "So, my happiness doesn't factor into it?"

"It doesn't outweigh the unbearable Yvette gossip."

I nod, shoving my backpack inside the locker. "It's an endless cycle every few months. The girl can't do long term relationships, or be single. It never takes long for the story to turn into who she's dating next."

"At least when she's off the market, our ears get a break."

"But not our eyes when she turns the cafeteria into a makeout scene."

"*Eww.*" Josie grimaces. "Don't remind me."

"Maybe you can't handle the gossip before class, but how about you feel sorry for me?" I say, hitching my books under my arm. "I'm the one stuck with her as a chemistry partner."

Josie giggles under her breath. "I don't know how you got so lucky."

"I only get through it by staring at my guy."

"*My guy,*" Josie teases. "Do you get any work done during chemistry, or do you spend the whole time in fantasyland?"

"As if you don't ignore your classes and daydream about Wyatt the whole time."

Josie plays with her dark brunette curls. "At least I knew the real him. I bet not many of the Hollywood types surrounding him can say that."

When the bell rings overhead, I hug my lovesick friend, unable to determine which of us is more pathetic, and make my way to class.

My first two classes are a total drag, but now it's chemistry. On its own, it's one of my favorite classes. Lewis being there puts a cherry on top. I enter the science lab, and glance at his workstation. His seat is empty, but his lab partner, Parker Kelly, is here. He leans back on his stool, talking with Jared at the table behind him. As I approach, it's the same conversation I've heard all morning.

"Have you heard if anyone's made a move on Yvette yet?" Jared asks Parker.

Parker smirks. "Why do you think I'm here so early? I'm not missing another opportunity."

"You'd better get in line," Jared says with a hint of laughter.

I sit down at the table across from Parker. Seriously, these boys are all the same.

"Don't you worry. I have everything figured out this time," Parker says.

Jared splutters a laugh. I peer over my shoulder to see him leaning over his workstation to nudge Parker. "You're too late, man."

Parker's brow furrows. "Huh?"

Jared nods toward the front of the room. "See for yourself."

At the same time that Parker's head pivots, I turn toward the front of the classroom.

The wind is knocked out of me.

Hand in hand, Lewis and Yvette walk between the aisles of lab desks.

"What the…" The words slip from Parker's lips.

With her sleek white-blonde hair, porcelain complexion, and pale pink, pouty lips, Yvette Anderson captivates the class. My eyes stay on Lewis. He can't take his eyes off her as he proudly walks her to his workstation.

Lewis and Yvette stand by the desk as Parker stares at them with an open mouth. "Ah, what's this?"

"Yvette needed some help with her chem notes, and we want to keep working on it together," Lewis tells Parker. "Do you mind switching seats with her?"

Nervous laughter puffs out of Parker. "Are you serious?"

Yvette leans into Lewis, and my heart splinters into jagged pieces.

This can't be happening.

Lewis and Yvette?

My Lewis?

She can literally have any guy at this school, and she has to take him?

Why is she doing this?

She's ruining my life!

Mr. Thompson walks into class and notices Lewis and Yvette standing in the aisle. "What's going on here?"

Lewis turns to him. "We were just hoping to change lab partners."

"During the last week before spring break?" Mr. Thompson replies, ambling toward them. "I hardly think so."

On cue, Parker and I let out sighs of relief.

When Lewis and Yvette give our teacher sad-puppy eyes, Mr. Thompson adds, "I'll consider changes to lab partners after spring break. For now, please return to your assigned seats."

Lewis gives Yvette an optimistic smile, and they part ways. There's a gloominess to Yvette as she plonks down on the stool beside me.

I've never been so relieved for class to start. Mr. Thompson announces today's lesson plan, and I hastily open my textbook. I swipe through the pages, finding the right chapter. Deciphering graphs and diagrams would be a great distraction, if not for the sniveling and sighing coming from Yvette.

What's her problem?

She held hands with the most beautiful boy in the school. She can't wait forty minutes to do it again?

The nerve of her!

With no self-discipline, I steal a glimpse at Lewis, and my stomach flips.

Somehow, Yvette has trapped him under her spell. But he's better than this. He's better than being with her. He can break free of her black magic and finally see clearly.

Finally see me, who's always here waiting for him.

The corners of my mouth drag down, and I'm left feeling like a warped candle. I can't shake the sense of loss, even when Parker turns my way.

"Whoa," he murmurs.

I break away from staring at Lewis, and cower under Parker's scrutiny.

Okay, focus. I glue my eyes to the page, following along with Mr. Thompson's voice. But my focus breaks every time Yvette sniffles, mumbles, and sighs.

Fed up, I side-eye Yvette, who whimpers and wipes under her eyes.

She sniffs again, glancing at me. "Sorry, I'm a bit of a mess at the moment."

I shrug, muttering, "It's okay."

"Usually, after a breakup, I have my friends to talk about it with, but..." She pauses to sniff again. "Well, one moved away, and the other refuses to talk to me."

I nod, not having any other way to respond.

"It's just easier having girls to talk to," Yvette says, squirming on her stool. "You know what I mean?"

I clear my throat, refocusing on my textbook. "Mm-hmm."

Yvette flicks her white-blonde hair over her shoulder and sighs. "At least Lewis is being an absolute angel. I've never had a guy listen to me so intently before."

My stomach folds in on itself as my back grows rigid.

Did she really just say that?

He's supposed to be my sweet and sensitive guy.

Not hers!

"He turned up at exactly the right time," she says with a giggle. "I never noticed him before. Now I can't understand how he was never on my radar."

Ugh. She stole my guy and doesn't even understand how great he is.

She's infuriating.

"He should be on my radar," she murmurs. "Shouldn't he?"

I gulp, making myself cringe, and slowly turn to her. "So... You and Lewis? You're dating?"

Yvette cups a hand over my mouth, muffling a giggle. "Uh, no. I mean, not yet. Ah, I don't know if anything's there. He's just a great guy, you know. Maybe I just need a friend right now."

Warmth spreads through my veins, and I sit taller. "Yeah, just being friends sounds like a great idea."

Yvette lets another giggle slip out. "Although, who am I kidding? When am I ever *just friends* with a guy?"

And just like that, my mood sours, and I hunch over my stool. Thank goodness it's a theory lesson, because there's no way my rage will let me hold a test tube or beaker without shaking.

Two

Josie meets me outside the cafeteria. She holds up her phone, and there's a dumbfounded look on her face. "Is this text for real?"

I pout and fold my arms. "Saw it with my own eyes."

Bewilderment fills her eyes, and her head slowly shakes. "Lewis and Yvette? I know I joked about it, but I didn't think he'd actually be interested in her."

"I don't know if they're just friends," I say, barely believing myself. "But, how many friends hold hands?"

Josie latches onto my folded arms, smiling. "I like holding your hand."

I smile, unfurling my arms. "I mean boy-girl friends. Hand holding seems romantic, doesn't it?"

Josie links our arms and walks me into the cafeteria. "Well, what makes you think they might be just friends?"

"Something Yvette said. I don't think she's really into him. Like, he was just around. She thinks something more might happen only because she's never been just friends with a guy."

Josie gives me an optimistic smile. "Maybe this will be the first time? Lewis wouldn't actually go out with someone as shallow as her, would he?"

I suck in a hesitant breath. "I never thought he would."

Josie hugs me closer as we approach our usual table. "See, we've gotta think positively. It's not over yet."

I sigh as I sit beside her. "Ah, you're right. It's just, Yvette's never single for long. It was such a shock to see my guy on her radar."

"Let's not lose hope. He can still be your guy."

As if on cue, we both turn toward Lewis's table. The only reason we sit here is because it has a perfect view of him and his friends at lunch. My jaw clenches when Yvette approaches his table.

Josie clutches my hand for support. My heart misses a beat when Yvette stands by Tabitha Jones. Until recently, Yvette and Tabitha were inseparable. Then their ringleader, Camila, left town. Now, Tabitha sits at Lewis's table because she's dating his friend Kai.

Yvette gingerly touches Tabitha's shoulder and tries to spark a conversation. From here, it's hard to decipher what's going down, but Tabitha seems more interested in staring at the floor. When Tabitha's shoulders stay uninvitingly rigid, Yvette takes the hint and steps away.

I squeeze Josie's hand, hopeful the icy reception prompts Yvette to take a hike.

Josie turns to me with worry when Yvette rounds the table toward Lewis.

We stay silent, eyes glued to the scene as Lewis and Yvette chat. There's hair twirling, hip popping, toe digging, stance shifting, and readjusting of blazers and ties. All clear signs of flirting.

I stare so hard, everything goes white. I take an extra-large inhale, worried I'll black out at some point.

I blink, watching the two lean in. I swear, time and space morph into slow-motion.

Their lips connect.

Kissing.

Lewis and Yvette are kissing.

What?

No!

I grip my chest, and my heart crunches, struggling to survive. With strained lungs and a scratchy throat, a gasp whooshes out of me.

"Oh, Kylie," Josie whispers, leaning her head by mine. "I'm so sorry."

My vision blurs, and I blink until it's clear. There's wolf whistles and cheers as Yvette and Lewis seem unable to disconnect their mouths. I pan away, unable to stand another second of this spectacle.

I land on Parker, and as if in pain, he turns away from his friend. His eyes drift around the cafeteria for a distraction. My breath hitches in my throat when his eyes connect with mine.

I gulp deeply, feeling a sweat bead roll down my spine.

His expression changes. The hurt dissolves and is replaced with pensive theorizing.

I rear back in my seat, alarmed by his striking interest in me. Why is he looking at me like that? Is it just to ignore his best friend canoodling with the girl he likes?

I avoid his gaze and pick at my unappealing sandwich.

That has to be it. He needed somewhere to look, and I just happened to be it. But, boy, did he need to stare so intensely?

I shiver, chilled by his gaze.

"Are you okay?" Josie asks, rubbing my upper arm.

"Yeah, just cold for some reason."

"I'm so sorry this has happened. And that you had to see in close range."

"I think it's better that I saw it first-hand. I wouldn't have believed it otherwise."

"But you could've stayed in fantasyland."

"Not if Yvette insists on babbling about herself during chemistry." My head falls into my hands. "Ugh. I can't deal with her telling me about how wonderful Lewis is. I already know that. I know it better than she does."

Josie rubs a circle on my back. "It's only two more days until spring break. You can get through this."

I lift my head and stare at her with dread. "It'll be even worse after spring break. Lewis and Yvette asked Mr. Thompson if they could be lab partners, and he said they could switch after the break. How am I supposed to deal with them all loved up during class?"

"But this is Yvette we're talking about," Josie replies as upbeat as possible. "She's never been with a guy for very long. Maybe they'll spend too much time together and break up before school comes back? Or maybe they won't see each other at all and break up because they forget each other exists."

I retch. "What if she goes over to his house? I don't want to see them from my window."

"Doesn't Lewis spend most of his breaks and weekends with his friends? I thought you said you rarely see him at home."

"Yeah, but he never had a girlfriend before."

"Okay, we saw them kiss, but this doesn't mean they're official."

"It's Lewis." I deadpan at her. "He wouldn't randomly kiss a girl. This is real."

The rest of the school day is a blur, and somehow, I find myself walking home from school. The only thing keeping me semi-alert are supportive texts from Josie.

I've never been pessimistic about my chances with Lewis before. When we were both single, anything could happen. But now, as I picture him walking beside me, I feel hopelessness. Yvette has her perfectly manicured claws in him, and I don't stand a chance.

He shouldn't want her.

He should be pining for the girl next door.

When my hand starts cramping from texting, and it's the second time I almost run into a utility pole, I tell Josie I need a nap and slip my phone into my pocket.

As I approach my house, a car pulls in ahead of me and parks on Lewis's driveway. It's Parker Kelly's car. Recently, Lewis's parents banned him from driving because he had crashed his car. He only had his license for a month, and before then, Parker had always given him a ride from school or anywhere else in town.

I don't really know what their friend group gets up to outside of school. Sometimes, I get a glimpse, because they hang out at the café where I work. And oftentimes, they make their way to the local skatepark. It's always awkward to act like I'm not staring or eavesdropping on them.

Speaking of awkward, I shimmy past Parker's car as the boys chat. I keep my head down as Lewis gets out of the car. As I step onto the path leading to my front door, I hear the name "Yvette" mentioned.

I can't help myself.

I turn and peer over my shoulder, focusing on the car.

Lewis smirks as he closes the door, and then waves and walks to his door. I don't know why, but my eyes stay glued to the car door. Particularly, the face looking out.

Parker's eyes transfix mine. His brow lowers as if he's calculating something.

When heat prickles my face, I swiftly turn away and move toward my front door. As I fumble with my keys, Parker's car reverses onto the street. I exhale hard as I hear it drive away.

"Hey honey, how was school?" Mom calls from the living room.

"Fine," I mumble, kicking off my shoes.

She makes her way into the entryway, tilting her head with concern. "I know that tone."

I drop my backpack and shake my head. "No, really, I'm fine. Just thinking over a math problem that has me stumped."

Mom's lips press into a line, not buying it. "Hmm. Okay. You're sure everything's fine?"

I deflate my chest and let my shoulders relax. "Yes, especially because I'm home now."

Mom smiles. "Okay, honey."

I pick up my bag and take it upstairs with me. It is true. Now that I'm home, nothing can hurt me. There are no rumors about Yvette. No sniffling Yvette, sitting beside me. Or, no Yvette sitting across the room and kissing my dream guy.

I move into my room and walk to the window. I lean against the windowsill and fixate on the desk in his bedroom. My veins electrify when Lewis walks into view. I bite into my lip, anticipating what he might do next.

He smiles, and sweet dimples indent his cheeks. As he laughs, I notice the phone held to his ear, and take in his nervous body language.

Is he...

Is he talking to *her*?

I swallow the influx of saliva pooling in my mouth.

Please, let it be anyone but her.

He continues to laugh, scrunches a hand through his hair, and paces his desk.

Oh my gosh. I'm done for.

Whenever I've watched him on the phone, he's calm and cool.

Oh my gosh. What if he invites her over?

Then everything really will be ruined.

There will be no fantasizing about us being in each other's houses because Yvette will be marking her territory. Right now, home is the only place I have left that's safe from her.

I can't watch her paw at him here.

I just can't.

Beep, beep. Beep, beep. Beep, beep.

I turn to my bed, where I dropped my phone. It's ringing, and I see it's my sister calling.

As I lift the phone and hit answer, a heavy sigh pours out of me. "Hey Tess."

"Whoa. What's wrong?"

"Huh? What do you mean?"

"You sound so down. What happened? Was someone mean to you at school?"

I huff. "Why do you always jump to that conclusion?"

"Because I spent four years at Ashworth Academy. I know how horrible it can be to get through a day there."

"Sis, I don't go to school with the same people you did."

"It doesn't matter. Every grade has mean people."

I frown, ready to hang up on her. "Is this really what you wanted to talk about?"

"No, I just called to check in with you. And I was serious when I said you sounded down. Tell me what's happened."

"You know the boy next door?"

Tess chuckles. "Oh, yes. Your long-running crush."

"Well, one of the popular girls has her eye on him."

"Uh-oh."

"Well, it's not just her eyes." I take a beat, sickened by the memories flashing before my eyes. "First, they were holding hands, and then..." I gag on the words. "I saw them kiss."

"Oh, Kikki, I'm sorry."

"What's worse is she's no good for him," I reply. "She's a serial dater. He deserves better than someone who'll eventually dump him."

"Then why are you so worried if you think they'll break up soon?"

I fiddle with the buttons on my blazer, too afraid to answer.

Tess sighs. "Because you're worried he might be the guy who lasts with her."

Another heavy sigh gushes out of me. "Exactly."

"I hate that you had to see all of that."

"And I'll have a front-row view of them in chem lab."

"What do you mean?"

"She's my lab partner, and he sits at the bench across from us."

"You should stay clear of them," Tess orders.

My heart sinks. "What?"

"You don't want this girl knowing you're into him too. If she's popular, she'll have friends who'll help destroy you."

"Actually, she had a falling out with her friends. That's why she always tries to talk to me in chem lab."

Tess sucks in a fearful breath. "Kikki, be safe. You know better than to get lured into a popular person's trap. They love tearing down people like us."

"Don't worry, sis. I've taken all your warnings to heart. No one's ever messed with me or Josie."

"Good, because it would break my heart if anyone ever hurt you."

"Don't worry about me. I'm okay."

Tess pauses for a beat before replying. "Look, don't hate me for saying this, but maybe this is a blessing."

I chew my lip, waiting for her to elaborate.

"Having this girl go after the guy you like might be the best thing for you."

I almost drop the phone. "What? How can you say that?"

"Well, he's popular too, isn't he?"

"Yeah, I guess."

"Well, maybe he's not the best fit for you."

"You don't want me to like someone who other people like to be around?"

"I'm just saying..." She pauses for another beat. "You don't really know him. In your head, it's all sunshine and rainbows, but in real life it might be a nightmare. This girl might be saving you from heartbreak."

I scoff, outraged. "I can't believe you. You know how much I like him."

"Kikki, I just..."

I cut her off. "Tess, I gotta go. Talk to you later."

I've never hit the *end call* button faster.

I drop the phone onto my lap, my hands trembling from the rush of adrenaline.

I appreciate that she's looking out for me. She had a really hard time in high school. But telling me to give up Lewis is crossing a line.

I flop back on my bed and frown at the ceiling.

I shouldn't take it as a sign, right? This isn't the wake-up call to end my crush on Lewis?

My heart throbs, and I'm called to my window.

I pull myself off the bed and trudge toward the window. Lewis is leaning against his desk, texting. I close my eyes, imagining a text pinging on my phone.

Beep, beep.

I almost jump out of my skin when the notification pings. I creep toward my bed and gingerly pick up my phone.

My shoulders droop and my heart sinks.

It's from Tess. *"Please don't be mad at me. I love you."*

I sigh and text back. *"Love you too. I'll never be mad at you."*

I drop the phone and sheepishly smile. How could I be mad at her? She has my best interests at heart. But I can't take her advice. I can't quit on my crush. Just, perhaps, I'll have to keep it a secret from my sister.

Three

Today at school I convinced Josie to join me for lunch in the library. It was weird spending a lunch break without staring at Lewis, but my heart couldn't take another sighting of him and Yvette kissing.

I've kept my head down most of the day, keeping away from crowds and tuning out the gossip. But my day is about to end in the worst way.

Chemistry.

It's always been one of my favorite classes. Learning the theory and doing the practical experiments actually helps me become a better baker. Lewis being in this class is a bonus, not the top priority.

But if he and Yvette become a fully-fledged item, or worse, become lab partners after spring break, I'll have no favorite class.

Oh geez. Should I just turn around and go to the nurse's office instead? It's the last class of the day, anyway. It won't matter if I skip out early.

Behind me, thunderous footsteps quake the vinyl floor and a voice calls out, "Hey, wait up!"

"Huh?" I turn around, not expecting anyone to be calling out to me. I stumble backward when Parker waves at me.

"Hold up," he calls, meeting up with me. "Don't go inside yet."

I hug my books, shying against the wall outside the chem lab. "Umm, okay?"

"So, what are we going to do about this?" he asks, stepping in close to me.

I hug my books higher until they touch my chin. "About what?"

"Our current problem."

I squint at him. "Huh?"

"I've seen the way you look at him," he whispers desperately. "It's how I look at her."

I swallow roughly, sliding against the wall. "I... I... I think you've got me mixed up with someone."

"Don't give me that," he says, keeping his voice low. "We need to do something about it."

"About what?" I say, pushing space between us. "I can't do anything about them being together."

Parker grins. "No, that's where you're wrong."

I roll my eyes and turn into the classroom. "You're crazy."

Parker follows, stepping way too close behind me. "Won't you just hear me out?"

"I don't know what you're talking about," I whisper harshly, filing behind my workstation.

Parker places his books on my desk and leans over them as he talks to me. "We can put a stop to what's happening between them. We just need to work together."

My brain doesn't compute. I scrunch my eyes closed, shaking my head.

"Kylie?"

I open my eyes and stare at this ridiculous boy. "What do you mean, work together? Like, lab partners?"

He smirks. "No. That's what I'm trying to avoid."

"Hi, Parker," Yvette says, placing her books on the desktop. She looks from me to him with a grin. "What are you doing over here?"

Parker smiles. "Just trying to get Kylie's attention."

Yvette clasps a hand over her chest and gasps. "Really? How cute!"

I retch, looking between the two of them. "Uh, no. He was just leaving for his own desk."

I narrow my eyes at him, baffled by his words. Outside, he basically confirmed he's into Yvette. Why on earth would he suggest he wants to talk to me over her? Worse, I don't want Yvette telling Lewis that something flirtatious happened between me and Parker. I don't want Lewis thinking anything could happen between me and any other guy.

I am a one-man woman!

Parker grabs his books and pushes off the desk, maintaining eye contact with me. "I'm leaving, but I want to talk about this later."

I scoff, shaking my head as he walks over to his desk.

Yvette latches onto my arm, leaning in and whispering, "What was that about? Are you and Parker...?"

"No way!" I reply much too loudly.

She releases my arm and rears back. "Oh, okay. Sorry."

I slouch on my stool, and flip through my textbook. "Don't be. I didn't mean it to come out so harsh."

"I just thought I was picking up on a vibe."

"I honestly don't know why he was over here. I've never talked to him before."

She nudges me playfully. "Maybe he thinks you're cute."

I splutter a laugh. "Yeah, right."

She shrugs. "Why not?"

I shake my head and don't respond. Hello, Yvette, because you're in the room. Every boy is absolutely gaga over you, you vapid beauty queen.

Soon, any interest Yvette has in me evaporates when Lewis walks in the lab. She sits tall, grinning and waving as he strides across the aisle.

His smile sends me melting.

And, I hate that it's aimed at her.

My chest rises and falls in slow motion as he moves toward our desk. I freeze as he leans his elbows on the space in front of me. A citrusy, woody scent wafts off him. I want so badly to curl my arms around his neck and let him take me away. My lids lower for a nano-second, imagining him scooping me up, but then the illusion shatters.

"Hey gorgeous," Lewis says in a breathy tone.

My eyelids flutter open, and my lips drag into a frown. Lewis's eyes sparkle as he leans in to touch Yvette's silky, white blonde hair.

Yvette gushes and giggles as my insides contort.

"Okay, students," Mr. Thompson says, marching into the room and dumping his laptop case onto his desk. "Everyone to your desks so we can begin class."

Thank goodness.

I swallow hard and force myself to sit taller as Lewis walks across to his workstation. Unfortunately, Parker catches my eye.

His eyebrow arches, and he nods subtly at Lewis. Urgency fills his stare, but I have no interest in indulging him.

I turn toward the front of the room, and follow what Mr. Thompson writes on the board. It's particularly difficult today with Yvette continually giggling beside me.

Ugh.

Spring break cannot come soon enough.

Once Mr. Thompson finishes writing the lesson plan and hands out the experiment instructions, I leave my workstation for the equipment cupboard. Before I can open the cupboard door, Parker slips in beside me.

"Can we talk now?" Parker whispers.

My shoulders bunch up as I recoil from him. "What? No."

He looks around at the other students leaving their tables, and moves in close again. "What about after class? Do you have anything planned after school?"

"I'm going straight to work."

"At the café? Can I drive you there?"

My forehead creases with confusion. "Why are you asking me this?"

"Because I have a plan," he whispers insistently. "And it only works if you're on board."

"Parker, we've never spoken more than needed in classes. Why are you trying to involve me in some kind of plan?"

"Because it'll help you get together with Lewis."

My mouth opens, but nothing comes out.

What do I even say to that?

It's crazy. Isn't it?

He grins. "You want that, don't you?"

I glance back at my workstation and find Yvette missing. She's over at Lewis's table, shamelessly flirting.

Parker hangs a thumb in their direction. "We can stop them before they get more serious."

I've decided. "You're crazy." I take the equipment I need and move back to my workstation.

"So, that's a no on the ride?" Parker calls out.

When other students' ears prick and start looking back and forth at us, my face flashes with hot embarrassment.

"No," I say as loudly as my awkwardness will allow.

I move back to my table and organize my equipment. It doesn't matter if Yvette takes ages to get back over here. I'll be working on my own, no matter where she sits.

Parker puts his equipment down at his table, and I can't help watching from the corner of my eye.

He nudges toward the front of the class, and says to Yvette and Lewis, "Mr. Thompson isn't paying attention. Why don't you two work together?"

"Are you serious?" Lewis asks.

Parker shrugs, backing away from the table. "Go for it. I'll work with Kylie."

Every molecule in my body malfunctions. I want to close my mouth, but my shock won't allow me to move.

Parker slides behind me and plonks down on Yvette's stool. "Hi again."

With rampant force, my heart pounds into action. "What are you doing?"

"I told you. I want to talk."

I nod my head toward Lewis's table. "You said you'd stop them from getting closer, but you just did the opposite."

"One class won't hurt. Besides, when Mr. Thompson finally wakes up, he'll make Yvette and I switch back. I just need a few minutes to make my pitch."

I rearrange my equipment for the experiment. "Look, I don't have time for games. I just want to get started with this class."

"Well, let me help you while we talk," Parker says, swiping the vial of sulfuric acid.

"I don't want your help, and I don't want to talk."

"If you at least act like you like me, I can get you closer to Lewis."

I rub my temples. "Why are you saying this stuff?"

He leans in, lowering his voice. "Because I want to be with Yvette. If we act like a couple, we can hang out and get between them on their dates."

The wind is knocked out of me. I tap my chest, coughing. "Act like a couple?" I whisper hoarsely. "Yeah, you are crazy."

"It'll work. We have to try."

"Look, can you just go back to your table?" I whine. "This is my favorite class, and I don't need you ruining it."

"Wouldn't it be even better if Lewis was *your* lab partner?" he asks, making a final plea.

I blink at him, taking a moment to imagine Lewis and I at the same workstation after spring break.

"Parker Kelly," Mr. Thompson calls from his desk. "Back to your station, please."

Parker slides off the stool, standing too close for comfort. "Are you sure I can't drive you to work?"

I shiver, wishing he'd step back. "My mom is picking me up from school."

He nods and moves behind me and toward his desk. Unfortunately, I take in Lewis's desk just in time to witness Yvette kissing his cheek.

Yuck.

Yvette feigns embarrassment as she sits beside me. "Sorry about that. Did you have fun chatting with Parker?"

"Umm."

"He seems into you. Or am I reading it wrong?"

I busy myself by following the experiment instructions. "Uh, I really didn't know what he was saying."

"Oh my gosh," she gushes. "You're smitten, aren't you?"

Yeah, but just not with the guy you think.

It's a sweet relief when class is finally over. I managed to breeze through the experiment and quickly scribble down my findings before the final school bell rang. I needed to get out of the lab before Parker could talk to me again.

I let Yvette copy down my notes while I cleaned the test tubes and beakers. Parker made one more attempt to get close to me at the equipment cupboard, but I made a quick getaway.

I was out the front of the school as soon as Mom's car pulled up.

"You're out early," Mom beams. "I thought you liked to stay back after chemistry."

"The experiment was too easy. I finished early."

"You're getting too smart for your own good, Kikki."

"Uh, Mom, can we get going?" I ask, keeping an eye out the window for incoming Parkers.

"In a rush to get to work?" Mom jokes, pulling off the curb.

"Something like that."

Not that work is actually an escape from Parker Kelly. He and Lewis are in the same friend group as my boss's niece, Jamie. She doesn't work every day at the café, but she usually pops in during the afternoons. It's a coin flip whether her friends join her or not.

My stomach twists.

I really hope Parker doesn't come into the café. He was so determined during class. I really hope something better has distracted him and he forgets all about me and his wacky plans. Their friend group will probably be at the skatepark. It's a few blocks away from Main Street, where I work, and it's where I've seen Lewis take his macro photographs of nature.

I can't believe Lewis actually likes skateboarding. He totally has to be there for the photo ops. On weekends when I've watched them, I imagine Lewis ditching his board and walking over to me. We sit under a shady tree, enjoying the birds chirping and the softness of the grass, and cuddle together. By watching how patient and still he is with his photography, I can just tell he'd be into being quiet with me.

Initially, the café is bustling. By the time I'm able to look at a clock, my shift is drawing to an end.

I wipe my brow after taking a load of dirty dishes into the kitchen.

Phew. I made it. No Parker Kelly sightings.

"Hey baby," I hear Maddy say when the front door opens.

Oh no. That means Jamie has walked in.

I force my body to stay calm.

Silver lining. Lewis might be here.

I perk up and move out of the kitchen. As I move out from behind the counter, I pan across the boys entering the café behind Jamie. Gloom hunches me over when Lewis isn't part of the group.

The door closes behind the final boy. Parker. Heat prickles on my cheeks when his eyes fix in my direction.

Why must he keep staring at me?

I'll keel over if he tries talking to me about Yvette and Lewis again. I don't want any of his friends hearing us and thinking I'm interested in him. If they mention anything to Lewis, it'll ruin everything.

Jamie moves behind the counter with her aunt, and they work on making milkshakes for the group. As the boys chat, I keep my head down and take cleaning products to my section.

It feels like an eternity before the milkshake machines stop buzzing.

Finally, their group is loaded with their orders, and ready to head back out.

My back loosens as the door chimes with their exit.

"Parker, you coming?" Kai calls as he follows Jamie and Tyler out of the café.

"No, I'm going to stay and kill some time," Parker says, sitting on a tabletop. "My mom texted me to pick up my brother from his robotics club. I'll probably just go home after that."

Kai waves, leaving for the door. "Your loss."

When his friends leave, Parker swivels on the table and leaps off in my direction. "Hi Kylie."

"Hi?" I drag out the word, dropping my cloth and spray bottle on a table. "You want to order something?"

"Yeah, I was wondering if a new girlfriend was on the menu?"

I give him a disgusted look. "Excuse me?"

"C'mon." His eyebrows wiggle. "I wanna make a deal with you."

I back away, taking my cleaning gear to another booth. "Pass."

Parker laughs. "Why?"

"Because you're up to no good."

"No good?" He clutches his heart, feigning distress. "I'm here to give both of us a second chance."

"Ugh. You're giving me a headache."

"Okay, here's the deal. We pretend to be a couple so we can get close to Yvette and Lewis."

With no way to hold it back, loud laughter erupts out of me. I clasp a hand over my mouth, noting the few customers inside turning my way.

Parker smiles. "Good to see you're not totally uptight. I didn't know you knew how to laugh."

I drop my hand, frowning. "Rude."

"I dunno, I only see you in classes, and you're always so serious."

"Because I like to do well," I reply. "Having fun is for outside of class."

Parker beams. "Okay, so you're in? We're all going to Logan's Point on Saturday, which is always fun."

I wince. "Logan's Point? Not exactly my scene."

"So, which is it?" Parker teases. "Fun Kylie or uptight Kylie?"

I huff. "Just because we don't have the same definition of fun doesn't make me uptight. Anyway, shouldn't you be leaving to pick up your brother?"

"I lied." He smirks. "See, I'm good at it. This can work."

I scoff. "You think I'm a liar? I don't want any part of this."

"All you have to do is stand by me and nod. I'll take care of the rest."

"No way."

"It'll help you to get closer to Lewis." Determination surges through him. "I know you want that. I saw your face when I suggested it in class. Besides, when you talk to Lewis, you won't have to lie. You'll get him by being yourself."

I roll my eyes. "He's with Yvette."

"But it doesn't have to stay that way."

"I don't want to be with him if he wants her."

He gives me a doubtful look. "Are you sure about that?"

I turn away because I'm definitely not sure.

"I didn't think I'd want to be with Yvette after seeing Lewis macking on her, but I do."

"Hey, Parker," Maddy says, moving toward the booths. "What are you still doing here?"

"Oh, nothing," Parker says coyly. "Just trying to convince Kylie to date me."

Maddy's mouth falls open, and smile lines crinkle around her eyes. "Oh my gosh, really? This is so dang cute!"

In revulsion, I swipe the spray bottle and cloth and move further down my section.

"Why won't you give this a shot?" Parker asks, following me.

I huff, scrubbing harder than necessary on a tabletop. "Because it's ridiculous. I'm not interested in dating you, Parker."

He smirks. "Yeah, that's kinda the point."

"You really want Yvette thinking you're into another girl? It makes no sense. I don't want Lewis thinking I'm into anybody else."

"So you'd prefer him to date Yvette without any distractions?"

Exhausted, I plant my hands on my hips. "How would us dating help break them up?"

"It'll help more than doing nothing." Parker slides into the booth, resting his clasped hands over the freshly cleaned surface. "Yvette was asking Tabitha to double date with her and Lewis."

My stomach somersaults. "She's already talking about going on dates with him?"

Sincerity fills Parker's expression as he sits in the booth. "There's still tension between the girls, so Tabby didn't give Yvette an answer. If we act fast, we can get in on the double date before Tabitha caves."

Queasiness rises through me, and I awkwardly swallow it down. "That's your plan? Go on double dates with them? I don't think I could stand the torture. Chem lab is barely tolerable, and their relationship isn't even official yet."

Parker sits forward, ensuring he's captured my attention. "Think about how much worse it'll be after spring break if they become lab partners. I know I don't want to see that. We can't admit defeat. This is our best shot. You've gotta do this with me."

Wincing, I rub a hand over my face. "Just let me finish my shift. Then we can talk about it."

Four

"So, I never noticed you liked Lewis before," Parker says, scuffing his shoe against the Main Street pavement. "Is it a recent thing?"

I clear my throat as the heat of embarrassment coats the back of my neck. "Uh, no. I've liked him since he moved to town."

Parker's eyebrows raise. "He's lived here for like a year and a half."

I shrug, shying my face away from him. "Yeah."

Parker shakes out his shoulders. "Okay, no biggy. Maybe you just never had pressure to make something happen before. Do you really want to be with him?"

I turn my body toward him and look him square in the eyes. "Of course, I do. He's the only boy I want."

Parker grins. "Okay, let's make this happen."

"Are you sure you can get Yvette's attention? No offense, but every boy in our grade has his eye on her."

"Oh, Kylie, you underestimate me."

I snigger. "If you say so."

"So I have a crush on her because she's beautiful," Parker replies. "So, what? Like your crush didn't start because you think Lewis is hot."

I scoff, folding my arms. "My crush is more than that."

Intrigue flashes on his face. "Enlighten me."

"Okay, so, yes, I thought he was cute, but that's not what made me fall for him," I reply. "It was because... Uh, don't worry. It's stupid."

"No, it's not. If it's your crush, it's not stupid."

I pinch the bridge of my nose, squinting as I turn away from him. "He liked my baking, and that's what did it."

"Your baking?"

I throw a thumb back toward the café. "I bake some of the sweets at Morton's Café."

His eyes light up. "You make them? Wow, you're really good."

"Thanks." I blush. "Anyway, I bake for most occasions. When Lewis's family moved in next door, I took dessert over for his family."

"Whoa," Parker drags out the word. "You've liked him since he first moved in?"

"Mm-hmm."

"This is an epic crush." He holds out his pinky. "I swear, I'll help you land him."

I giggle. "A pinky swear?"

"Hey, if your crush has lasted this long, it needs a happy ending."

I link my pinky with his. "I'll pinky swear to that."

When we let go, Parker snaps his fingers. "I've got step one of our plan."

I clench my teeth, wincing.

"Stop looking so scared, would ya?" Parker teases. "Tomorrow at school, bring something you baked and give it to me in front of Lewis. It'll drive him crazy jealous."

My heart flutters with hope. "You think so?"

Parker swats a hand. "Are you kidding me? Your desserts are incredible, and we'll use them to remind Lewis that you once made them especially for him."

A twinge of nerves hit me. "You think he's forgotten?"

Parker nods. "Yeah, but don't take it personally. His memory's like a sieve. That's why I do most of his chemistry homework."

I give him a doubtful look. "*You* do his homework?"

Parker grabs his hips. "Is that so hard to believe?"

"Ah, yeah," I say, dragging out the words. "I've shared classes with you since middle school. I never thought of you as academically gifted."

Parker laughs. "Well, thanks. I wouldn't call myself a nerd, but I can remember enough to pass my classes. It's just chemistry that seems to take twice as much effort because your partner affects your grades."

I sigh. "Tell me about it. Try working with Yvette."

"Well, if we successfully break them up, I'll take her off your hands."

"It'd be a dream to sit with Lewis, but I can't imagine working overtime to compensate for his grades when I'll be busy staring at how beautiful he is."

"Don't make me gag," Parker jokes. "How about this? If you promise to put your all into this plan, I promise to keep helping Lewis with his homework so your grades don't tank."

I rock on my heels. "You'd do that?"

He sends me a wink. "I just need you to play my girlfriend for a week. What do you say?"

I chew on my lip. "You really want Yvette that bad?"

"I've seen how you look at Lewis. You want him badly, don't you?"

Undeniably, I nod.

"I feel about her how you do about him. I saw it in your eyes. That's why I think this will work." He pauses for a beat, vulnerability coloring his face. "That is, if we work together."

"But how would this work?"

Parker laughs, running a hand down the back of his neck. "I don't exactly know. I've never had a fake girlfriend before."

I let slip, "Have you ever had a real girlfriend before?"

He twitches awkwardly. "Well, no, not exactly." He clears his throat, standing taller. "But I've had dates before. You know, like school dances."

I nod hurriedly, hoping it'll help dissipate his nerves. "Yeah, right, of course."

"Look, I just think this will work best if we get the ball rolling on this relationship, ASAP," Parker says. "I really don't want Yvie and Tabitha to make up before we get our chance."

"I don't think we need to worry," I reply. "Yvette is constantly complaining that she doesn't have any friends."

Parker tilts his head. "She is?"

"In chemistry," I elaborate. "She's always muttering about losing her friends. That one moved away and the other's not talking to her. I don't know why she's constantly whining at me."

Parker snaps his fingers in front of my face. "Kylie, wake up. This is your moment to strike."

I frown, rearing my head back.

"She's begging for a friend," Parker says enthusiastically. "Why don't you get close to her and use what she tells you to your advantage?"

I grimace. "Umm, because that sounds slimy."

He nudges me. "I'll tell you what Lewis says."

"I don't want to go behind his back."

"You basically are behind his back because he doesn't know you have a crush on him."

I fiddle with the hem of my T-shirt. "He doesn't?"

Of course, he doesn't.

He doesn't live in my head with me.

"But he can," Parker says optimistically. "I can help him see you."

My stomach sloshes. "By dating me?"

He shrugs. "By saying aloud how amazing you are. If I start talking about how cute and talented you are, Lewis will take notice."

My face flushes. "Cute? Talented? Me?"

"When I'm through, those are the words Lewis will think of when he hears the name Kylie Green."

I shiver at the thought.

Parker grins. "I need to talk you up so Lewis will dump Yvette for you."

I wave my hands and back away. "Okay, this is crazy. He'd never do that. Who'd give up Yvette to be with me?"

"Would you stop," Parker says, moving toward me and clasping one of my wrists. "This won't work if you put yourself down. Why can't you be with Lewis? If you stop isolating yourself by being so freaking shy, you can get his attention. I promise."

"How can you promise that? School's almost over."

Parker winks, grinning. "That's because you're my girlfriend, and my girlfriend will be hanging out with me and my friends during spring break."

I gulp. "You want me to hang out with your friends?"

Parker smirks. "You rock climb, hike, and canoe, right?"

Dizziness sends my head spinning, and I lean against a shop front to keep me upright.

Parker rubs my shoulder. "Chill. You don't need to be an adventure pro."

I chew my lip. "But it would impress Lewis if I were?"

He lifts his hand off me. "It wouldn't hurt."

I push a hand into my feeble stomach. "Then I guess I have to try."

"Good, because I don't want to come back after spring break and sit across from the lovebirds. It'll be hard enough watching them cozy up when we're all hanging out."

"And you really think we can get through that?" My teeth clench as I take a beat. "Together?"

"I'm counting on it."

I pout. "What if I'm a disappointment?"

"You can't think like that. Us double dating will be the best plan of action."

"It's going to be so hard."

"Think of the positives. We'll be the closest people to them because we'll be with them the entire time they're dating. When they inevitably break up, we'll be the first people they run to for a shoulder to cry. It'll be sweet."

I recoil. "Sweet?"

Parker huffs, rolling his eyes. "You know what I mean. We'll be right there for them. Lewis will want to be with you, and Yvette will want to be with me."

"And it's that easy?"

Parker shrugs, his optimism unwavering. "They got together out of nowhere. It can happen again."

"I think it happened because you and Lewis have been drooling over Yvette since she was dating that footballer meathead."

Parker grins. "Exactly. And if I can get him to drool over you, he'll want you even more than he wanted Yvette."

I burst with bashfulness. "No way."

His eyebrows wiggle. "Trust me. I know my best friend."

I bite my lip and cautiously nod. "Okay. I'll trust you."

"Will you come to Logan's Point with us? If it's an epic fail, we can call it off." Queasiness ripples through Parker's expression. "I just really don't want to see my best friend and the girl I like cozying up together. I'd like to pull them apart any chance I get."

"I feel like I'm joining you purely to annoy Lewis."

He chucks my chin. "I'll just show him a better girl."

Something about that makes me feel icky. Clearly, I'm not the better girl. Parker's using me to get the better girl.

"Are you okay?" He takes a step back. "Looks like you're about to hurl."

I shake my head. "I'm good."

Who cares if he's using me? The deal is, I get to use him to get the better guy.

I hold out my hand. "We've got a deal."

"Sweet." He lifts his hand, but hesitates on clutching mine. "Can we stipulate how long we do this? I know I just said you could throw in the towel after one day at Logan's Point, but I really don't want it to be over that soon."

"Me neither." And I mean it. "I want Lewis."

He lifts his hand higher. "So, are we in it until we break them up?"

I latch onto his hand. "Yes. Until they break up."

He eagerly shakes my hand. "You got it, Green. But can we add one more thing to this deal?"

"What's that?"

"No one can know this relationship is fake."

"No one?" I try to pull my hand back, but his grip on me is tight. "I can't lie to Josie."

"This could all unravel if anyone finds out."

I shake my head. "No, I need Josie to know."

"There's only one day of school left. Can't you hold out on her?"

"Parker, we tell each other everything."

He frowns. "She's trustworthy?"

"She's the best."

Parker loosens his grip. "Can't you wait to tell her until school's out tomorrow? That way there's less risk of it getting on the gossip train."

"I can't make that promise."

"Ugh." He gives my hand another shake. "Just promise she's the only one you tell."

I smile. "That I can do."

With our agreement in place, Parker drives me home. When he pulls into my driveway, he asks, "So, what color is your bikini?"

Instinctively, I fold my arms over my chest and gasp. "What?"

"You'll come to the lake with us, right?" Parker says matter-of-factly.

"Hmm, yeah." My shoulders tense. "But I don't own a bikini. I just have a black one-piece."

Parker's lip upturns. "Seriously?"

I shrug. "I swim laps."

"You won't get Lewis's attention with a one-piece," he says bluntly. "You need to get a bikini before Saturday."

I swipe the loose hair off my forehead and huff. "Okay, I'll go shopping tomorrow after school."

"Get blue," Parker insists. "It's Lewis's favorite color."

I open the car door, nodding. "Okay, thanks for the tip."

He playfully salutes me. "No problem."

Before I leave the car, I ask, "What should I bake for tomorrow?"

Parker taps the steering wheel, mulling over the question. "What are those small cake things with the gooey chocolate inside?"

"Do you mean the cookie dough cups?"

"Yeah, that's it. Lewis buys three whenever they're at the café."

My heart flutters, and I bounce out of the car. "Okay, great."

"*Ha*, you finally seem happy about this plan."

"He loves something I bake. How could I not be happy?"

Parker waves. "See you tomorrow, girlfriend."

My mood lowers. "I don't think I'll ever get used to hearing that."

"Don't look so grossed out. We have to sell it, you know."

Squashing my repulsion, I wave back. "Bye, boyfriend."

Parker chuckles, reversing the car out of the driveway and giving me another wave before driving away.

Oh boy. What did I get myself into?

I move into the house and find Mom on the phone in the living room.

"Oh, she just walked in," Mom says into the phone. "I'll put you on with her." Mom lowers the phone. "Hi honey. It's Tess."

"*Ahhh*." I struggle for an excuse to avoid the call before Mom places the phone in my hand. She walks away, leaving me to speak with my sister.

I lift the phone and ensure I have a chipper tone. "Tess, hi."

"Hey Kikki. I just wanted to actually talk because I know you were peeved yesterday."

"It's cool. I was just in a bad mood because I've had a crush on him for so long."

"I know. It was safe to crush on him from afar."

And now I'm going to be up close and personal with him thanks to Parker. "Mm-hmm."

"I get that you're heartbroken. I've been there before. But as someone who's been through my share of torture when it comes to love, I just want you to see the possibility of this being a blessing in disguise."

I'm glad we're not on video chat because my eyes roll so hard. "Yeah, maybe."

"Was school easier today?"

"Yeah. Josie and I spent lunch in the library." And then I had the weirdest proposition of my life.

Tess sighs with relief. "Good call. You don't need to make yourself suffer."

"That was the plan," I say, thinking over my deal with Parker.

"Are you excited for spring break?"

"Yeah. We were talking about doing things differently this break."

"Oh, yeah? What are you and Josie getting up to?"

"Umm. I'll let you know when we finalize everything. We just have a bunch of ideas at the moment."

"Well, tell her hi from me. It's too bad our breaks don't line up."

"Mmm. Yeah, bummer." I check the doorway to see if Mom is in the hallway. "I gotta go. Mom's calling me."

"Okay, Kikki. Glad you're feeling better."

"Yeah, thanks. Bye, Tess."

After goodbyes and I love yous, I hang up on my sister, exhausted from lying.

I venture into the kitchen to check whether I have the ingredients for cookie dough cups.

Mom walks in when I'm scouring the pantry. "Who drove you home tonight?"

I almost drop the container of flour. "Huh?"

"I peered out the window," Mom says. "Who's car was that?"

"Just someone from school."

"Looked like a boy."

I shove the flour back on the shelf before the container explodes on the floor.

"Kikki?" Mom presses.

I clear my throat and turn from the pantry. "You remember Parker Kelly, don't you?"

"Oh, sure," Mom says with a happy smile. "I haven't seen him since you were in middle school."

"Yeah, well, it was him."

"Why was he driving you home?" Mom asks with a mixture of intrigue and giddiness. "Do you two hang out often?"

I shake my head. "No. He was just at the café. He's at the café a lot because he's friends with Jamie."

"Uh-huh," Mom drags it out, waiting for me to draw the dots.

I shrug. "He offered to drive me home."

Mom chuckles. "Well, that's adorable."

I turn away before I blurt out something I'm not supposed to. I pull the flour and sugar containers from the pantry and set them on the countertop.

"You're baking?" Mom asks.

"Yeah, for Parker," I say, wishing the heat in my cheeks would dissolve. "He drove me home for cookie dough cups."

Mom sits on a counter stool, resting her chin in her hand. "Oh, really?"

I busy myself with getting the vanilla extract and baking soda. "We were talking in chemistry, and then kinda kept talking during my café shift."

"Well, I remember him being a nice boy. You've just never talked about him before."

"Haven't I?" I say coyly. "Well, he and Lewis are always around. It feels like I know him."

Well, I know Lewis, but I have to pretend I'm interested in Parker.

Before Mom can ask another probing question, the front door opens.

"Hello, hello," Dad's voice calls out.

"In here," Mom calls, and I continue gathering ingredients.

Dad walks into the kitchen and lets out a whistle. He puts his briefcase down on the stool by Mom, kisses her cheek, and then smiles at the array of ingredients. "Are you baking, Kikki?"

"For a boy," Mom says with a giggle.

"*Mom*," I groan.

There's nothing more humiliating than talking about boys with your dad in the room.

"A boy?" Dad asks, shook.

"Parker Kelly," Mom blurts.

I click my tongue, looking up at the ceiling. "Mom."

"Parker Kelly," Dad says, moving to the fridge and grabbing a soda. "That's a name I haven't heard in a while. How are his parents?"

"I wouldn't know," I murmur.

"So nothing serious has happened?" Mom asks.

Ugh, this is the worst. "No, we're just talking."

"Okay," Mom says, raising her palms. "Just seems like if you're baking for him, it must mean you like him quite a bit."

Dad tilts his head, taking me in. "Is something serious happening?"

I dip my head between my raised shoulders. "I dunno. Umm, he asked me to join him and his friends at Logan's Point on Saturday." I pivot between my parents, who exchange glances. "Can I go?"

"Logan's Point?" Dad says, his intrigue piqued. "That's different for you."

I shrug. "I know. Is it okay?"

"I think it'll be okay," Mom says, checking with Dad. "It'll be good for you to get out of your homebody routine."

"Is Josie going with you?" Dad asks.

"I hope so." I'm going to need all the moral support I can get.

"Who'll be driving?" Mom asks.

"He didn't say, but I assume Parker."

"Has he been driving for long?" Dad asks.

"Why are you guys interrogating me? Is it okay if I go or not?"

Mom and Dad share another look and then both let out a laugh. Dad puts an arm around my shoulder, while Mom says, "Of course, honey. We trust you."

"Just make sure Parker comes to see us before you leave," Dad says.

I gulp. "You want to talk to Parker?"

Dad moves back over to Mom. "Yeah, we haven't seen the guy in ages. He was a good kid, but I don't know what he's like now."

I pull out a mixing bowl and move around the kitchen for the rest of my utensils. "He's still a good guy."

"Arnold," Mom says. "She wouldn't be talking with him if he was a dimwit."

Dad chuckles. "That's true. So what are you making?"

"Cookie dough cups." I chew the inside of my lip, thinking about Lewis. "They're his favorite."

"*Yum*," Dad cheers. "My mouth is watering already."

I side-eye him. "They're not for you."

Dad scoffs. "How many does the boy get?"

I snigger. "The whole dozen."

Mom cups a hand over her mouth as her shoulders jiggle in a laugh. "Oh, she's smitten all right."

Mom was right. She just had the wrong boy.

<h1 style="text-align:center">Five</h1>

Never have I felt more pressure to bake.

The first time I baked for Lewis, I had never seen him before. It was just a, "welcome to the neighborhood," gift for his family. The fact he was the most gorgeous boy I'd ever seen was an after-the-fact bonus.

Now, baking cookie dough cups specifically to gain his attention, while his eyes are on one of the most beautiful girls in school... Yeah, the pressure is on.

It's Friday morning, and I find Parker at his locker. "Umm, Parker?"

"Hmm?" Parker turns from his locker, and his eyes light up at the sight of the bakery box in my hands. "Oh, awesome!"

I awkwardly keep the box lifted between us. "Umm, do you want to take it?"

Parker's gaze moves left and right. "He's not around."

I pull the box closer to me. "Oh."

Parker turns back to his locker, pulling out two books and then shoving his backpack inside. He hitches the books under his arm and slides a hand under the bakery box.

"But what kind of boyfriend would I be if I didn't hold this for you?"

I bite into my lip, unnerved by the statement.

Parker suggests we wait by his locker for Lewis to walk by. I got to school earlier than normal because my anxiety was running rampant. It's weird to have arrived before Lewis.

We keep our eyes peeled, knowing the man of the hour will enter the hallway soon.

My knees buckle when I spy the blonde Adonis.

"Yo!" Parker calls out.

Lewis's head tilts with curiosity, noticing me standing by Parker.

Whoa. He's noticing me.

When Lewis reaches us, Parker lifts the bakery box lid, revealing the array of treats. "You're into cookie dough cups, aren't you?"

Lewis's mouth falls open as he stares at the neatly packed cakes.

Parker swivels the box away from Lewis. "Unfortunately, Kylie brought them for me, not you."

My knees knock together as I fight off full-body convulsions.

"What?" Lewis asks, confused. "Why did she bring them for you?"

Parker wiggles his eyebrows, enjoying teasing his best friend. "Jealous your baker neighbor likes me more?"

Lewis's confused expression turns to me, and I squirm under his gaze.

I hate this! I don't want Lewis thinking I like Parker more than him. All I've wanted is for this boy to notice me.

This is the worst way for this to happen.

"Wait." Lewis's confusion morphs into curiosity. "You made these?"

Parker nudges him. "She always makes them. She bakes for Maddy's café."

"Whoa," Lewis says, impressed. "Well, they're amazing."

I look at Parker for reassurance, and then say to Lewis. "Take one."

Lewis plucks one from the box. "Don't have to tell me twice."

Parker smirks at his friend. "It doesn't worry me if you take them. Kylie's already promised me more."

Lewis sniggers with a mouthful of cake. "How come?"

Parker sends me a wink. "Why don't you tell him, Kylie?"

"Uh, I..." My chin drops as Lewis stares at me, waiting for an answer. "Umm, we, ah..."

Lewis's eyebrow raises as I malfunction in front of him.

I turn away, mumbling, "Nothing."

Lewis chuckles, grabbing another cake from the box. "Whatever. I'll catch ya later, man."

"Hey," Parker calls after him. "She said you could take *one*."

Lewis strolls down the hallway, and Parker shakes his head, closing the bakery box.

"What was that?" he whispers harshly. "Why didn't you tell him we're dating?"

My shoulders bunch up toward my ears. "I don't know. I couldn't." My stomach contorts and twists. "Parker, I don't think I can do this. I don't want him thinking we're together."

"But you know this is our one shot. Don't you want to be there when they break up?"

I frown, hugging my middle. "Well, yeah."

Parker roughly pats my upper arm. "Then get it together. He needs to buy it."

I blow out a breath and swipe a hand across my clammy forehead. "Okay. I'll try."

Parker takes two cookie dough cups out of the bakery box and then slides the box into his locker. "I'll make sure he sees me eating these, and I'll take the box into the cafeteria at lunch. Do you want to meet here before going into the cafeteria?"

"You want to walk in together?"

Parker hooks a finger under my chin. "Yeah, I want to walk in with my girlfriend."

I tug my head away from his grasp. "Can you stop calling me that?"

He huffs with frustration. "Kylie, are you in or not?"

"I'm just not used to it. Does it have to sound so official? Can't we just be hanging out?"

"Yvette doesn't want a double date with people who are *just hanging out.*"

"Oh, gosh." I sigh. "I can't handle the idea of spending time with her."

Parker takes a bite of the cookie dough cup and winks. "Hopefully, I get most of her attention."

"Hey, I thought Lewis was supposed to see you eating those?"

He shrugs, grinning. "I'll try to resist the other one. They're just too good, Kylie."

I smile modestly. "Thanks."

"What's your first class? I'll walk you."

"Oh, that's okay," I rush. "I have to meet up with Josie, anyway."

With his books shuffled into the nook of his left arm, he lifts his right arm into a wing. "Are you sure?"

I chew my lip, feeling a confusing flutter in my chest. "Yeah, I'm sure. I need to talk to her."

He frowns. "You're not talking to her about us, are you? I mean, the *real* us."

"I told you she's trustworthy."

"If you say so."

"I do." I backtrack toward Josie's locker. "I'll see you at lunch."

He gives me a salute. "See you then, GF."

I cringe, turning around and hurrying amongst the surging crowd.

I find Josie, ambling her way through the hallway. "Hey, do you want to go to the mall this afternoon?"

She opens her locker, amused by the idea. "Yeah sure. Do you have anything in mind, or is this a smoothie and window shopping situation?"

I grit my teeth with hesitation. "Umm, I want to buy a bikini."

Josie's face elongates with surprise. "Get out. Since when do you buy bikinis?"

I bite into my lip, my face coloring with deceit.

Josie's stare intensifies. "Whoa. What's going on?"

"Remember that text I sent you last night?"

"Umm, yeah. The one that made absolutely no sense."

"Because I couldn't find the words to tell you what happened. I still can't believe what's going on."

"You're starting to scare me. Your vibe is way off."

I hang a thumb over my shoulder. "I baked for Lewis and he just ate one of my cookie dough cups."

Josie lights up, grinning widely. "Oh my gosh. You did a grand gesture for Lewis?"

I swallow hard, feeling unbalanced. "Yes, but not exactly. Lewis thinks I baked for Parker."

"Parker Kelly? What, why?"

"Umm, because I... Because he and I..."

Josie blinks at me, waiting for more. "What? You and he, what?"

I throw my hands up. "I think we're dating?"

Josie throws her head back, laughing so loud it turns every nearby head.

I grab onto her shoulders, shushing her harshly.

She slams a hand over her mouth, her eyes watering from the hysterics. Stifling her laughs, she whispers, "Sorry. It's just the silliest thing I've ever heard."

I nod. "I know. But he asked me yesterday at the café."

"What? Are you for real?" She looks from side to side. "You're dating Parker Kelly?"

I rub the ache in my chest and force out the words. "It's fake."

Her face screws up. "Fake? What the heck are you talking about?"

The bell overhead rings, and I groan at the intrusion. "I'll tell you everything at lunch. Meet in the library?"

She shrugs, looking at me strangely. "Yeah, okay, I guess. Are you sure you don't want to skip class and talk about whatever's going on with you?"

"Sure, speed up my anxiety further by skipping class," I joke. "No way. I'll just get myself together so I can explain this properly."

"Good, because this is the first time I haven't understood something you've told me. A bikini, baking for Lewis, and something fake with Parker? Maybe you should see the school nurse."

I give her my best smile. "I'm fine. I promise."

Oh gosh. This is going to be harder than I thought. How am I supposed to get through this when I can't even explain it to my best friend?

I blow out a breath and make my way down the hall. I just need to keep my head down and get through my classes. Hopefully, without hearing or seeing anything to do with Lewis and Yvette.

Thankfully, my first two classes go without a hitch.

On my way to history, Parker walks past with Lewis. He scoops his arm around my waist and pulls me into a hug.

"Uh, hi," I stammer.

Parker chuckles, looking down at me. "Hi."

"Umm, I need to get to class."

"Oh, I know," Parker says with a grin. He spins me back toward history class and winks. "See you later, Green."

I give him a hesitant smile and cautious wave.

When he catches up with Lewis, Lewis throws his palms up with confusion. "What was that about?"

Parker shrugs. "Just saying hi to Kylie."

Lewis throws a questioning stare my way, and then continues along the hallway with Parker.

A shiver runs down my spine.

Lewis Allen looked at me.

What does that mean?

Was he jealous?

Oh my gosh, what if he's jealous? Does that mean he wishes he was holding me instead?

I internally squeal and rush to history class.

Thoughts of Lewis bubble inside me, all the way up to art class. As per usual, I need to be careful that my sketches don't resemble him too closely.

After the bell rings, I leave my sketchbook and supplies in one of the art room cubbies, and leave for lunch. In the hallway, I find Parker leaning against a wall, holding the bakery box. When he spots me, he pushes off the wall.

"Hey. How was class?"

"Uh, fine," I say warily. "Were you waiting for me?"

He grins, nodding. "Yeah, I've got Spanish across the hall and saw you go in earlier."

"Oh, okay."

"Did you forget?" he asks teasingly. "We said we'd walk into the cafeteria."

My stomach flips. "Oh, right."

He winces. "You look ready to hurl."

I swallow hard. "No, I'm okay. Just nervous."

He holds out his winged arm. "Just stick with me."

With little choice, I link arms and let him lead me to the cafeteria. On the walk, the passing student body makes me anxious, and I slip my arm away from Parker's.

He stops, getting a read on me. "Are we good, Green?"

I rub my lips together, taking a beat. "This is big."

He holds out his hand. "We gotta do this right."

I shiver before latching onto his hand. He gives me an encouraging smile, and walks me into the bustling cafeteria.

"We got this," he whispers from the corner of his mouth. "Just play it cool."

Cool? Is this his first day meeting me?

He squeezes my hand for extra assurance, and we approach his lunch table.

"Whoa, Parker, what's going on here?" Tyler asks, leaning over the lunch table as he gawks at us.

Like ricochets, every other head at the table turns in our direction.

Kai's eyes almost bug out of his head. "You and Kylie? Since when?"

Parker lifts our clasped hands. "Since now, I guess."

Jamie tucks her calf under her butt to sit higher on her seat. She scrutinizes us, saying, "I haven't even seen you two talk before."

Yvette combs her fingers through her hair, the urge to gossip too overwhelming for her. "Well, I saw Parker talking to her yesterday in chemistry."

Jamie's eyes narrow as if she's putting invisible puzzle pieces together. "During dinner last night, my aunt said something about you two. I told her she was crazy, but maybe it was for real."

Kai turns to Jamie. "What did Maddy say?"

Jamie pivots her gaze between me and Parker. "That Parker was asking Kylie out."

Parker plonks the bakery box on the table and slings an arm around my shoulders. "Is it really that hard to believe?"

Lewis tilts his head, getting a read on his friend. "Is that why she brought you cakes?"

Tyler sniggers, sitting back in his seat as he stares at me. "You baked for him?"

Jamie swats a hand. "She basically bakes in her sleep. It's not that special."

Parker scoffs. "Have you eaten them before? I think it's more than special."

Kai's girlfriend, Tabitha, clears her throat. "It's just a bit weird because, Parker, I thought you liked..."

Parker shrugs, interrupting, "I kept my feelings quiet because I wanted to make sure Kylie liked me back."

My gut cramps and my vision doubles. I can't bear to look over at Lewis. I want him to know I only have space in my heart for him. This charade is only pulling us further apart.

"There's no way. I'm not buying it," Kai says, slinging an arm around Tabitha. "Tabby's right. Parker, you've been drooling over someone else all semester. Now you want us to believe you're into Kylie?"

"Agreed," Lewis pipes up. "It's out of nowhere."

Phew.

Lewis sees me. He really sees me.

Parker squeezes my hand. "Well, you guys need to believe it because Kylie's coming with us to Logan's Point."

"Tomorrow? Kylie's coming with us?" Jamie asks, side-eyeing me like I'm not really here. "I didn't think she was into that stuff."

Parker inflates his chest. "What can I say? I'm *that* irresistible."

Yvette giggles and claps. "Yay. Another girl amongst all these dudes."

"Kylie," Jamie says bluntly. "What's really going on?"

I want to back away, but Parker keeps a hold of me. Plus, I think my shoes have turned into cement blocks.

"I... I..."

Subtly, Parker tugs on my hand. He wants me to spit out more than one syllable. To say something to win them all over. But it's impossible. How will my heart ever let me say I'm into any other boy than Lewis?

Tyler laughs. "She looks terrified next to you, man."

Tabitha narrows her stare at me. "Kylie, why don't you leave if you don't want to be here?"

Kai smirks. "Parker, are you holding her hostage?"

Jamie slouches in her seat. "I knew my aunt was crazy. This isn't real."

"Uh, fine." Parker huffs, exasperated.

Parker's arms snatch around my waist, and he pulls me in until I slam against his body. Without a moment of warning, his lips push against mine.

My eyes pop wide open, shocked at this insidious act. When Parker's lips meld around my bottom lip, I swiftly close my eyes. If I push him off me, it's game over.

But...

All I can think about is Lewis's eyes on me as I kiss his best friend.

Parker's lips nestle against mine, and I find myself smiling at the taste of chocolate in his kiss. I move my lips, slipping against his as I concentrate on picking out the lingering ingredients from the consumed cookie dough cup.

In the middle of my back, Parker's fingertips press into my blazer with perfect pressure. As he tilts his head in the kiss, my toes curl and cling onto the sole of my shoes. Scared I'll lose my balance, I run my hands up his arms, eventually hooking my hands behind his neck.

Parker's lips fit against mine like missing puzzle pieces, and I get woozy at the thought of this being real. How can something so ludicrous feel so freaking amazing? When I kiss him back, his bottom lip lowers. With an elevated heart rate, I slide my hands away from his neck. I open my eyes as we pull out of the kiss.

"Whoa, that was a kiss," Yvette blurts.

Smile lines crinkle around Parker's eyes from his crush's approval.

My expression grows blank.

Kai laughs, clapping. "What a show, Parker."

My chin drops, as the weight of what we did drops on me.

"Maybe she does like him," Tyler jokes, tapping on the lunch table.

Adrenaline surges through me.

Jamie exhales loudly. "*Okay*. Maybe not so crazy."

I.

Am.

Mortified.

Parker's hand grazes my arm, and I flinch. My stomach sours, and something tries leaping up my throat. I wipe my forehead and teeter in a dizzy circle.

Parker's hand clasps my shoulder. "Hey, are you okay?"

As my vision doubles, I take in all the faces at the table gawking at me.

Since when did I become a sideshow act?

I didn't sign up for everyone to judge me and make me prove anything.

I spin on my heels and hightail it between tables, weaving my way to the bathroom.

"Kylie!" Parker calls after me.

I hear his footsteps following, but I don't slow down.

"Hey, stop," he calls again, this time reaching out and grasping my shoulder.

I bump him off. "Don't."

"Wait," he insists, moving alongside me. "I'm sorry, okay."

I make it to the rear wall of the cafeteria and slam my back against it, folding my arms. "You're sorry?"

He digs his hands into his pockets, looking down at his shoes. "I just wanted them to believe us."

My heart pounds so frantically I feel it in my throat. "You stole my first kiss."

Parker lifts his gaze, sending me pity in his eyes. "Huh?"

"You have no idea how many hours I've spent dreaming about my first kiss." I swallow hard, clearing the anguish in my voice. "It was supposed to be with Lewis. How could you?"

"Look, it was an impulse. I'm sorry. I didn't plan it."

I stomp my foot. "Kissing was *never* part of the plan. I didn't sign up for this."

Parker turns away, and I catch a flex in his jaw. "It's not like it was a real kiss."

"Lewis doesn't know that. I hate that he saw us kissing."

"It's not like he's not kissing someone else."

My heart hurts. We take a beat, staring at each other as our chests rise with leftover adrenaline.

Parker takes a long exhale and runs a hand through his hair. "Look, he's kissing Yvette, but he won't know what a real kiss is like until he has you. You just have to think of our kissing as fake."

I chew my lip, considering his words.

"It's the only way we'll get through this," he adds.

I sigh, pulling myself off the wall. "Okay. I know you're in the same boat as me. It must've killed you when Lewis and Yvette kissed right in front of you."

He nods, trying his best not to frown. "I just have to keep reminding myself it's not real until she's with me."

My mind rewinds to Parker's lips on mine. Tentatively, I tap my fingers against my bottom lip.

"How much better could a real kiss get?" I whisper. "That was pretty dang good."

A nervous laugh puffs out of Parker. "Really?"

I rub my lips together and nod. "My toes curled. I thought that was just something they said in the movies."

"Wow." Satisfaction flashes across his face. "Good to know. I was winging it. It was my first kiss too."

"Are you serious?"

He nods, faint pink streaking across his cheeks.

"I just..." I pause, fidgeting in my stance. "You said you had dates to school dances. I just thought that meant you'd had kisses before."

"Uh, no. Does that make me lame, or something?"

I giggle. "Not to me. I'm the one who's been dateless this whole time."

Parker smiles and pats my shoulder. "At least you can get some practice before being one-on-one with Lewis."

My knees knock. "Yeah, right."

His smile spreads with sympathy. "Don't worry. The nerves will eventually pass."

I nod despite my skepticism.

"Lewis will be lucky to kiss you," he says, dipping his gaze. "You're really good at it."

I hover a hand over my mouth. "No way."

He looks up, biting his lip. The corners of his mouth tug upward, and he nods.

My cheeks flash hot pink, and we both let out nervous laughter.

Parker throws a thumb over his shoulder. "Think you're ready to go back to the table?"

I push my hands into my stomach. "Oh gosh. I don't think so. That was humiliating. And then I ran off like a big baby. I don't think I could handle facing whatever they have loaded to say to me."

"Whatever they say, I'll throw it back at them. I know how to handle my friends."

"Is teasing each other all you guys do?"

Parker chuckles. "Pretty much. Whether we're on skateboards, playing video games, or eating lunch, we're always ribbing each other."

I sigh out. "I'm not used to them. It's a lot, especially knowing I'll be hanging out with them without the escape of classes."

"You'll be fine. Going to Logan's Point is just a way for you to hang with Lewis, and for me to get time with Yvette."

"This is all becoming too much. I need to go to the library and meet up with Josie."

Parker throws an arm out in front of me. "You can't do that. I need you."

"I need to talk to my best friend. This is a lot."

"Can't you just stay until we make a solid plan to double date with Lewis and Yvette?"

I gulp. "You need me for that?"

Parker rolls his eyes. "I can't very well make a double date without my girlfriend by my side, can I?"

"Ugh. Let's just make it quick."

"Can you at least act like you're happy to be by my side?"

I fake a smile and let Parker put his hand on my back as we walk back to the lunch table.

As we approach the table, Jamie and Kai leave toward the cafeteria exit. Tabitha also moves away from the table, meeting us in the aisle.

"Oh good," she says with a hopeful smile. "I was coming over to bring you back to the table."

I turn to Parker with an uneasy look. I'm not sure how I'm supposed to respond.

Tabitha gestures at their lunch table. "I was talking to the others, and we know we should apologize. It just got a little insane, you know? We were just surprised to see you two together."

Parker curls an arm around me. "We were talking about how happy we are to be a big joke to everyone."

Tabitha's face falls. "We never should've pressured you guys into proving your relationship." She motions to the table again, summoning invisible support. "We all feel icky about you having to kiss in front of us."

I lean into Parker, feeling woozy again.

"I'm sorry you guys felt like you had to do that." She locks eyes with me and displays a sympathetic smile. "I would've made a run for it too."

Tabitha's genuineness puts me at ease, and I stand taller. I pull away from Parker, but he hooks me closer.

His chest puffs, and he stares down at Tabitha. "Maybe you should've thought about that before you started grilling us."

"Whoa." Tabitha lifts her palms, taking a step back. "I'm trying to apologize."

Parker gestures at me. "Yeah, after you humiliated her."

"Parker," I murmur. "It's cool."

"It's not cool," Parker doubles down. "Why don't you just give us space before I say something I'll regret."

Hurt creases Tabitha's face, and she backs away, toward the cafeteria exit.

"What was that?" I whisper harshly. "She was only being nice."

Parker turns to me. "You can't be friends with her. She and Yvette are on the outs. You need to be besties with Yvette. That's the only plan that matters."

My stomach gurgles, and I frown, hugging myself. "I don't like this."

He swipes a thumb across my jaw. "It's time to toughen up."

"Ugh." I grimace, jerking away from him. "I don't want to be mean to anyone."

He clutches my hand, tugging me toward the table. "You don't have to be. Just focus on being nice to Yvette."

Parker yanks harder on me when I barely move behind him.

Nice to Yvette?

This would be a challenge.

"Come on, girlfriend," he teases. "Stop acting like you don't want to be holding my hand."

I huff out my frustrations and move in step with him. He grins, squeezing my hand tighter.

Tyler's the only one still sitting at the lunch table. He doesn't acknowledge us. Instead, he's glued to a video on his phone.

Lewis and Yvette stand off to the side, whispering and giggling to each other. Parker hurries our pace, needing to break them apart.

"So, Logan's Point," Parker blurts, gaining the couple's attention. "Do you two want to come with us?"

Yvette claps gleefully. "Almost like a double date."

"Except we'll be meeting up with everyone else." Parker looks at me, smiles, and then turns back to the other two. "We were thinking about asking you guys to join us on an actual double date. Like dinner at Alto Burgers?"

Lewis practically salivates. "Oh, man. I can't get enough of their double sizzler burger."

I'll put that fact in my permanent memory bank.

Parker looks at Yvette. "Are you in?"

Yvette shrugs. "Not exactly the cutest date location, but sure, why not."

"Where would you like to go instead?" Lewis asks.

Yvette's eyes sparkle with excitement. "What about Fratelli's?"

Lewis sniggers. "The super snob restaurant?"

"It's not snobby," Yvette argues playfully. "It's elegant."

I glance at Parker, who seems to be putting the information in his memory bank.

He subtly turns my way, winks, and then addresses the other two. "Why don't we try a burger joint first?"

I can tell he wants to take Yvette to Fratelli's on a solo date, and I'd much prefer to go to a place where Lewis is actually comfortable.

"Yeah," I pipe up. "A good burger sounds amazing."

Lewis smiles and nods, happy I've agreed with him.

My heart flutters so hard it might actually lift me off the ground. I mumble a giggle, grounding my shoes against the tiled floor.

Parker slings an arm across my shoulders. "So, we're on for tomorrow morning?"

"Okay with you?" Lewis asks Yvette.

She smiles, shrugging. "Sure. I don't care who drives me."

Of course not. She changes her boyfriend so often, she's used to random guys driving her around town.

Honestly, what must her parents think?

"Lewy, I have a craving," Yvette says in a horribly whiny voice, yanking on Lewis's hand. "Come with me and buy me a candy bar."

Like a puppy, Lewis follows Yvette to the vending machine on the far wall.

"Wait!" Parker calls through cupped hands. "There's a box of cakes here."

When the two don't answer, Parker looks at the bakery box sitting on the lunch table. It's empty apart from a few crumbs.

"Oh," he murmurs. "Dang it."

"At least they were a hit," I say nervously.

He gives me an agreeable smile and then gets back into scheming mode. "Tomorrow, I'll pick up Yvette first, and I'll be late to pick up you and Lewis. That way we'll be in a rush, and you and Lewis will have to share the backseat."

I tap my fingers against my bottom lip, grinning. "You think that'll work?"

"If you help tell Lewis to get in the back quick. We need to be fast enough so Yvette doesn't get out of the front seat."

I clasp my hands in front and rock on the balls of my feet. "I'd love to sit next to Lewis."

Before Parker can respond, he's yanked backwards. Kai has him by the collar, and when the two come face to face, Kai is seeing red.

"What gives, Parker?" Kai seethes. "Tabby said she tried to apologize to you and Kylie, and you chewed her out."

"I was protecting my girlfriend," Parker fires up. "Just like you're doing now."

Kai gestures at me. "I'm not attacking her."

"No, but you were involved in making her feel uncomfortable," Parker argues. "If we wanted to kiss in front of everyone, we would've done it before saying hello."

Kai groans, rolling his eyes. "Tabby was coming over to make things right."

Before Parker gets out another syllable, I slide between the boys. "It's okay. It was just a misunderstanding. Everything's cool now."

Parker rests a hand on my shoulder. "Kylie, I..."

I cut him off. "No, really, everything's fine. Kai, I'm sorry for how things went down with Tabitha. I really do think she was being genuine. It was just a lot when we kissed. I got overwhelmed with everyone looking at us."

Kai glances at Parker and then shifts his gaze back at me. "If we're all hanging out tomorrow, I want things to be easy. I've already had to deal with Jamie and Tabby not getting along. I don't want to go through it again."

"I'm sure it won't," I reply in a rush.

Parker squeezes my shoulder, and I watch him stare down his friend. "As long as no one harasses Kylie, we'll be fine."

Kai nods at Parker. "Say you're sorry to Tabby."

Kai walks away, and I bump Parker's hand off me.

Parker spins me around to face him. "Stick to the plan. You've gotta be friends with Yvie, not Tabby."

I shake my head. "It's not worth jeopardizing your friendships. I don't want you and Kai at war because of this silly fake relationship."

"Don't worry about it. Kai and I are fine. We've said worse things to each other about dumber stuff."

"You should apologize because it looks like you argued with your friend because I came into your life. And I don't want everyone to hate me."

Parker nods. "Lewis might not want to date you if Kai thinks you're meddling in the group."

"You should also want to apologize because Kai's your friend. And because Tabitha was being nice."

Parker bats a hand. "Yeah, yeah." He grabs my hand and pulls me over to Kai and Tabitha. "Tabby, I'm sorry I came off so harsh. It's just that Kylie was really upset, and I lost my cool."

Tabitha swallows hard, nodding. "I get it. It's cool. I just hated the idea of my mean girl rep spreading around the school again." She smiles at me with kind eyes. "I was really sorry about how everything went down."

I nod. "I know. It's fine. It wasn't just you."

"So, we should get back to Lewis and Yvie," Parker blurts, hanging a thumb over his shoulder. "They want to plan a double date with us."

Surprise filters across Kai and Tabitha's faces.

"Oh really," Tabitha utters. "Did they already know about you two before today?"

Parker nudges me. "Yvie had her inklings, right, babe? I can't help myself in chem lab. I make any excuse to go over to their table."

I smile, replying, "More than anything, Parker is one persistent guy."

Parker and I distance ourselves, waiting for Yvette and Lewis to make their way back.

"Should we go to them?" I suggest.

"Yeah. I could say I need a craving filled because everyone ate my girlfriend's cakes."

An exhausted laugh pours out of me. Somehow, I'm less disturbed this time by him calling me his girlfriend.

One step away from the table, and the bell for the next period rings.

"It's okay," Parker says, patting my back. "We've still got chemistry class to get between them."

"It's so weird that we've organized a double date with them."

Parker grins. "We're one step closer to breaking them up."

"Out of what, a million steps?"

"Have a little faith, Green." He slings an arm around me, walking me out of the cafeteria. "What class do you have now?"

"English. You?"

"Social studies. I can walk you part of the way."

"Okay. The charade continues."

Six

After I part ways with Parker, I take my usual seat in English class. Josie and I used to share so many classes together, but this year, it's like the administration staff went out of their way to separate us.

Our teacher begins the lesson by discussing the poem we're currently analyzing. I try to follow along, but I can't stop overthinking the cafeteria situation.

All Parker's friends think we're a couple.

I'm going to Logan's Point with them tomorrow.

Lewis and Yvette agreed to go for burgers with us.

Is this seriously my life?

Beep, beep.

I check that the teacher isn't looking in my direction, and subtly pull my phone from my pocket.

It's a text from Josie.

Oh crap.

It's the third unread text from her. With all the craziness happening at lunch, it never occurred to me to check my phone.

"Hey, where are you?"

"Is everything okay?"

"What happened? You never came to the library?"

My stomach jitters with queasiness. With trembling fingers, I quickly text a reply. *"Sorry. I got caught up in something."*

I'm pathetic. I still have no clue how to tell her what's really going on. And how do I even tell her it all ramped up to a kiss?

Oh my gosh, I still can't believe that happened.

I kissed Parker Kelly.

And I didn't hate it.

Why didn't I hate it?

Ugh. All I gotta do is keep my head down during English class, then it's on to chem lab.

How do I even function in chemistry with Parker posing as my boyfriend?

Do I need to act differently?

If Lewis was my boyfriend, I wouldn't be able to stop staring at him. I'd be waving, sending him love notes, and blowing kisses.

Eep. Do I have to do that with Parker?

No. No way.

I'm not doing anything that will make being with Lewis less special when we're finally together. All the giddy stuff can wait for the right guy. Besides, I know Parker won't be able to stop staring at Yvette either.

Ugh. I just want today to be over.

After English, I keep my head down on the way to chemistry.

"Are you trying to ditch me?" Parker asks, jogging to catch up to me.

I keep my head down. "No. Just walking to class as per usual."

"Remember when Lewis and Yvette walked into class, hand in hand?"

I seize up. "I don't want to do that."

"Why not?"

"Because it's not just for Lewis and Yvette to see. It's the whole freaking class. I'm not doing it."

Parker groans. "Ugh. Fine. But I'm still walking in with you."

I shrug, hurrying my pace. "Fine."

"Do you have to act like you're running away from me?"

"I'm just going to class."

I bustle my way into chem lab with Parker's footsteps hot on my heels. When I get to my workstation, I can't help glancing over at Yvette cuddled up with Lewis across the aisle.

Parker moves to his table and says, "Can you now see why I didn't want to swap with you?"

Lewis gives him a confused look.

Parker motions at me. "If I sat with Kylie, I'd get zero work done."

Lewis laughs, hugging Yvette. "That's true. We'd probably be in the same boat if we got our way."

Yvette giggles and moves her way over to our table. "Bye, boys."

Mr. Thompson has us working on another experiment similar to yesterday's lab. When Parker and Lewis are chatting, I make my way to the equipment cupboard. Knowing Parker, he'll probably want to hug me in the aisle or make a big show of carrying my equipment tray. After the horror in the cafeteria, I've had my fill of people staring at me.

When I'm back at my workstation, I do my best to ignore Parker as he ogles me across the aisle. As usual, Yvette is useless while we set up our experiment. As I organize all the pieces, she spends her time twirling her hair and waving at Lewis.

At least that comes to an end when Parker joins Lewis with their equipment. While they set up their equipment, Lewis actually pays attention.

Ahhh. Love that about him.

As Mr. Thompson meanders around the workstations, ensuring all the setups are correct, I take the time to reread the instructions.

Parker moves over to our workstation, inspecting our setup. "Not bad, Green."

I follow his eyeline and then tighten the metal test tube holder, making sure it's secure. "Thanks. Did you come over to get tips?"

"No. Just to get a better view."

I look up and find him smiling at me, ignoring the setup.

Yvette nudges me. "Oh my gosh. That's just the cutest thing I've ever heard."

I smile at Parker, impressed. Okay, maybe he does know how to get Yvette's attention.

Mr. Thompson nears the table in front of ours, and Parker retreats to his workstation.

Yvette leans closer to me. "So, that was some kiss in the cafeteria."

I underline a number in my notebook to hide the nervous twitch in my hand. "Oh, was it?"

"Totally. Especially when you didn't seem to want anything to do with him yesterday."

"Oh, well, just playing hard to get. You know how it is."

Yvette giggles. "Oh yeah, I've played that game before."

The thought of playing games when it comes to love gives me the ick.

I glance over at the boys, and ask Yvette, "Is that what you're doing with Lewis?"

"No. I kissed Lewis before you kissed Parker." Yvette sighs, leaning her cheek against her palm. "I think it'll be so cute if we go on a double date. The boys seem excited about it, don't they?"

I sneak another peek at the boys' table. Parker grins and gives me an eager wave, while Lewis seems deep in thought.

I turn back to Yvette. "Parker seems excited."

"That's what I like about Lewis. He doesn't put all his cards out on the table."

"But at least with Parker you know what he's thinking."

Yvette shrugs. "Where's the fun in that?"

Dang. Is Parker going about this all wrong?

Yvette gasps and clutches my shoulders. "Oh crap, Kylie. I'm so sorry."

"What?" My eyes bulge as I look at the experiment, horrified that something went catastrophically wrong.

"I just talked badly about your guy," she apologizes, releasing my shoulders. "I totally didn't mean anything bad about it. I think you two are awesome together. And me and Lewis are awesome. And together, we'll all be awesome."

If she uses awesome one more time, my head might explode.

"Forgive me?" she squeaks.

I fake a smile. "Already forgotten."

"*Eep.*" She squeals, pulling me into a tight hug. "You're the best."

I wriggle out of the hug and glance at the boys' station. My shoulders sink as Parker gives me a thumbs up.

After we get approval from Mr. Thompson, we get underway with the experiment. It's the best part of class because Yvette gets bored and quietly doodles in her notebook. Unfortunately, something in my process isn't working. I redo my calculations three times, and struggle to run the experiment.

I slouch, fearing I'll need to ask Yvette for help.

What has the world come to?

"Are you stuck?" Parker asks, leaning into the aisle.

I huff and brush my hair back. With a pout, I nod.

His smile is effortless, and he slides off his stool. At our workstation, he oversees what I've done. Then he views my notebook, running a finger under my handwriting.

"Ah. That's where you're tripping up." He grabs a pen. "May I?"

I shrug with nothing to lose. "Sure."

He leans in closer, writing in my notebook with his left hand. His breath tickles my earlobe and the nape of my neck, spreading tingles down my arm. I focus on his crooked handwriting and appreciate the logic behind his corrections.

"Thanks." It comes out hoarse, so I roughly clear my throat. "Uh." I tap the page, nodding. "Yeah, that looks good."

Parker drops the pen and pecks my cheek. "Glad I could help."

He moves away from the table and I'm left stunned. The touch of his lips lingers on my skin. My fingers gently raise to touch the spot, but I'm interrupted by Yvette.

"Do we have the answer now?" she asks eagerly, gripping my forearm. "Geez, maybe he's the one I should've asked for help with chemistry."

"Yeah, maybe you should have," I mumble under my breath.

She shrugs with a laugh. "I just thought Lewis was the smart one."

Yvette stands and sashays over to Lewis.

Beep, beep.

I glance around the room to make sure Mr. Thompson isn't lurking, and pull my phone from my school skirt pocket. There's a text from Josie.

"YOU AND PARKER KELLY MADE OUT IN THE CAFETERIA?!?!?!?!"

My heart explodes with thunderous beats. Every vein inside me sizzles with electric jitters. I swallow hard as the churn of my stomach increases in speed.

As I stare hard at her text, more messages rapid-fire into our text chain.

"What the heck, Kylie?"

"You and Parker? This makes no sense!"

"I was certain this was a lie, but everyone is talking about it. Like eye-witness accounts."

"KYLIE!!! Explanation???"

With a headache burrowing into my skull, I reply with, *"Tell you everything at the mall."*

She texts back, *"You bet you will!!"*

A hand slides under mine, pushing my phone toward me. Parker is by my side, covering my phone with a cupped hand.

"Thompson's on the prowl," he warns.

I pocket my phone, eyeing our teacher wandering around the workstations.

Parker sniggers. "I didn't take you for someone who texts during class."

"It was Josie," I mutter. "She heard about our kiss."

"Oh. Was she surprised?"

"Shocked, more like it. Exclamation points everywhere." I cup the sides of my face. "Oh, how do I explain this?"

"You didn't tell her about us?"

I shake my head and check no one is within earshot. "I wanted to. I tried to. I just didn't know how."

Parker moves back to his workstation before Mr. Thompson strolls by and gives him a lecture. He taps Yvette on the shoulder, warning her to move back to her own seat.

I never thought about anyone other than Parker's friends seeing us kiss.

But now that I think about it, when Lewis and Yvette kissed, they were on full display for everyone to see at the very same table.

Oh gosh, this is the worst outcome. I don't want the whole school talking about me and my supposed boyfriend. The thought of my best friend hearing the gossip without me explaining the context is mortifying.

The rest of the class rolls by. I was too stunned to finish my notes, and I even let Parker pack away my equipment. Yvette gushed about him being a great boyfriend, but I was too comatose to respond. Parker even has to coax me off my stool. Seriously, I could stay glued to this seat until spring break is over.

In the hallway, we bypass Parker's locker, and then he walks me to mine. At best, you could call what I'm doing a trudge.

"It's not so bad," Parker insists, placing a hand between my shoulder blades. "School's over now. By the time we're back, this whole thing will be done."

A pout is my only response as I drag my backpack from my locker.

Parker laughs, taking my backpack and squeezing me in a one-armed hug. "Cheer up, buttercup."

"Oh my freaking..." Josie can't finish the sentence, moving toward us, stunned. "It's true?"

My chin drops. "It's not..."

She cuts me off, holding up her phone, which displays an image. "This photo is doing the rounds."

My eyes narrow as I take in the image. It's in chem lab and taken from the table behind mine. Parker is standing by me with his hand on my back.

Like he is right now.

In panic, I bump him off me, freaked by people staring and pointing at us.

Josie lowers the phone, confusion contorting her facial features. "You two are together?"

I still can't get over the photo. "Who sent that to you?"

"No one," Josie replies. "Well, Kimberley, who sits next to me in biology, got it in a group chat. She showed me and asked me how long you two had been together. Imagine not being able to answer that question about your best friend."

"Josie, I..."

She cuts me off again. "I thought you were into..." She stops herself, pressing her lips together as she glances at Parker. "Uh, I just didn't understand what you were telling me this morning about Parker."

"I said it was fake..."

Parker grabs my shoulder, cutting me off. "Not here," he whispers harshly. "Not in the school halls."

"How does fake explain the whole cafeteria seeing you two make out?" Josie blurts.

"*Shoosh.*" Parker pats the air in front of her. "Can we please get out of here so we can explain?"

Josie folds her arms. "I'm ready to hear it."

I gesture towards the foyer. "Josie, let's go. Besides, it was just a peck. It's been totally blown out of proportion."

Her brow furrows. "Don't you think any kind of kiss between you and Parker is a big deal?"

I frown and nod.

She leans in close, whispering, "You gave up your first kiss?"

My eyes instantly water.

She gasps and tugs on my hand. "Let's get out of here. Parker, are you driving us?"

"Yeah, sure," he says, hurrying behind us.

We get into Parker's car, and it feels totally weird to be riding shotgun with Josie in the backseat. This only happens when my mom drives us somewhere. Now, supposedly, it's my boyfriend driving us.

"Okay, where to first?" Parker asks, pulling the car into the strip mall parking lot.

"We need to get to the smoothie bar for this debrief," Josie says.

"Okay, I've crashed your shopping trip," Parker says. "How about smoothies on me?"

"Deal." Josie slides out of the backseat, dragging her backpack behind her. "You have so much explaining to do. I feel like I've fallen into an alternate universe."

I move onto the sidewalk, and Parker locks the car, leaving our bags in the trunk.

He mentions to Josie, "You could keep that in the car, you know."

She hikes her backpack over her shoulder. "I know."

I suck in a ragged breath, and tension ripples through me with every step to the smoothie bar.

Inside, Josie blurts her order at Parker and then gestures at us. "Look at you two. There's barely a gap between you."

I take a large step to the side. "Better?"

Josie shakes her head. "How exactly did I end up playing third wheel?"

I smile at Parker. "You know, you could leave so Josie and I can talk."

Parker steps closer and slings an arm around me. "And what kind of boyfriend would that make me be?"

Josie's mouth falls open. "Boyfriend? You're labeling this?"

I stammer nonsensically. "Ah, umm, we, uh…"

Parker hugs me closer and winks at Josie. "Kylie could do a lot worse."

Josie's palms raise and her jaw moves with questions that can't come out of her mouth. I mean, I get it. She wants to ask about Lewis. She wants to know how I could possibly replace my obsession with him. Valid because it's incomprehensible.

Josie's head shakes, and she slowly backs away to a table. When she sits, I tell Parker to order me the same, and step toward the table.

He grabs my wrist, tugging me back. "Are you trying to ditch me, girlfriend?"

"I need to explain to Josie what's going on."

"Do you even know what you'll say?"

"I'll figure it out. Look, I appreciate the ride here, but you really don't have to stay."

"But a good boyfriend makes nice with his girlfriend's friends."

I retch. "You don't need to lay it on so thick. She's finding out the truth."

"That doesn't mean she'll buy it. I'm gonna make sure she sees me as boyfriend material. Otherwise she'll blow this."

"No, she won't."

"I doubt it," he replies smugly. "She could barely contain herself in the school hallway and almost outed us in front of everyone."

"So, you want to stay?"

He pecks my cheek. "I'm staying, girlfriend."

"Do you have to keep calling me girlfriend? It's not exactly natural sounding."

"Maybe I need to work on a nickname for you."

"Or, you could call me Kylie."

"Mmm. I'll find something cute to call you."

"Okay," Josie calls out through cupped hands. "I get it. You two can't handle being apart. But can you hurry up and order so I can get this story?"

I leave Parker so he can order our smoothies. I edge toward Josie's table with a deep inhale.

Here goes nothing.

Seven

When our smoothies arrive at the table, Josie fires up. "I want to know how this happened. I'll believe whatever Kylie tells me, but I don't know you, Parker. I want to see if you're lying because I won't stand for you hurting my best friend."

"I won't hurt Kylie. You have my word."

Josie smiles with discern. "I haven't started grilling you yet, Parker."

He glances at me with a chuckle. "Oh, boy."

I sit forward and give Josie puppy-dog eyes. "Are you peeved at me?"

She sits forward, whispering, "No, of course not. I'm just confused." She swallows hard, glancing at Parker. "I just thought you liked someone else."

"Oh, Lewis," Parker blurts. "Yeah, I know all about that."

Josie blinks at him, sitting back. "You do?"

Parker gestures at me. "Just like Kylie knows about my crush on Yvette."

Her jaw drops. "What? This is sick."

"Josie, I..."

She cuts me off. "Not only is it sick, it's beyond twisted. Why are you two doing this?"

Without much thought, I snatch my smoothie and busy myself with sucking through the straw. I don't stop until my skull aches from the chilled liquid.

Josie smirks. "A brain freeze ain't getting you out of answering my question."

Parker laughs. "Should I take this one?"

I lift a hand, squinting until the ache subsides. "Okay, the truth is, Parker and I were talking yesterday during my café shift."

"And during classes yesterday," Parker adds. "Although, she didn't want to give me the time of day."

"Can you blame her?" Josie teases.

Parker smirks. "*Hey.*"

"Anyway," I say, "We continued chatting after my shift, and we found a lot of common ground. And when he drove me home..."

"You drove her home?" Josie blurts.

Parker laughs. "Let her finish a sentence."

I shrug, blurting, "Well, let's just say, we decided to get closer."

"Get closer?" Josie's lip upturns with perplexity. "This makes no sense. Although, it does explain why your texts last night made zero sense."

"We got closer because our crushes started dating," Parker admits.

"That's no reason to start dating."

I clear my throat, and croak, "Remember how I said it was fake?"

Nervous laughter rolls out of Josie. "What, like some sort of fake romance?"

"You can't tell anyone," Parker rushes.

Josie deadpans him. "That's what this is? A fake relationship?"

"It's to get Lewis," I blurt, feeling ridiculous as each syllable leaves my tongue. "It's my last shot."

"How..." she falters. "How would this make Lewis want you?"

"Because I'm going to show him how amazing she is," Parker says. "It was a real promise. I'm going to protect Kylie from getting hurt. We'll both end up with the people we want."

She side-eyes him. "And you want Yvette?"

He nods. "And I'm going to be with her."

Josie huffs. "Wow. That's a lot to take in."

"See why I could barely explain myself?" I shrug. "I need Parker to get through this. I won't be with Lewis without him."

Josie lowers her voice. "You both realize how nuts this sounds?"

Parker and I share a look and then let out a chuckle. "We know," we reply in unison.

Josie nods. "At least you're on the same page."

"We are," I reply.

Josie's eyes narrow. "So, this morning, why did you mention buying a bikini?"

"Umm, we're going to Logan's Point tomorrow," I say, squirming against the queasiness rippling through me. "Do you want to join us?"

"Umm, we don't do Logan's Point. Seriously, what universe is this?"

"She's going with me and my friends," Parker explains. "She's getting closer to Lewis."

Josie smiles at me. "Well, that's something I want for you."

Hope rises inside me. "So, you'll come with us?"

"It's not just couples going." Parker wiggles his eyebrows. "My friend Tyler is single."

The idea sends a thrill down my spine. I sit up tall, beaming at Josie. "That's perfect! You should come."

Josie backs up in her chair, palms lifted. "Umm, no. You know I only have eyes for one guy."

"Who?" Parker asks.

"Wyatt Hayes," I reply.

"What?" Parker snickers. "He doesn't even go to our school anymore. And I doubt he's ever coming back. Tyler's a good guy, and he's in town."

"Ugh. I don't care about Tyler," Josie complains. "And I want to stick to my regular spring break plans."

"Come on, Kylie would love her best friend to come," Parker insists.

Josie looks him up and down. "Why do you care?"

"Because I'm doing my best to be a good boyfriend."

Josie takes him in, seemingly impressed.

"What do you say, Josie?" I ask.

She bites her lip. "I can't do Logan's Point. The stories I hear just fill me with too much anxiety. Do you really have to go there to be with Lewis?"

"She does," Parker answers for me. "This isn't her last shot. It's her first shot. Lewis doesn't know she exists."

"Hey, that's not true," I whine.

Parker crooks an eyebrow. "I'm sorry, he never talks about you. Except for today, when he ate your cookie dough cups. And then he kept asking me why I kept finding you in the hallway between classes."

My heart swells. "He was talking about me?"

He nods. "This is why you need me." He looks at Josie. "And this is why she has to go to Logan's Point."

Josie meets my gaze. "You know I support you in getting your dream guy. I just want you to be okay."

"I'll be okay," I reply. "Being with Lewis will make everything okay."

"Did I pass your test?" Parker asks Josie. "Am I good enough to be in a fake relationship with Kylie?"

"Well, you're both clear on what you want." Josie exhales slowly. "I'm just really worried about you both getting your hearts broken. Just because you hang out with Lewis and Yvette, doesn't mean they'll break up to be with you."

"But it's a shot," I reply.

Josie nods. "It's a shot."

Parker gestures across the street. "I guess it's bikini-buying time."

"*Eww.* Could you be more lewd?" Josie clicks her tongue. "Kylie doesn't have to wear that to be seen."

Parker folds his arms. "Umm, yes, she does."

Josie narrows her stare. "Because why? You'd only date a girl who'd wear a bikini?"

"No, because any guy looks at a girl in a bikini. And we need Lewis to look at her."

"Can you two stop talking like I'm not here?" I interrupt.

"Sorry," Josie replies. "Parker, do you really think you can act like a convincing boyfriend?"

"Don't worry, I've got this down."

"Have you ever had a girlfriend?" she asks.

"No, but that doesn't mean I don't know how to treat a girl right." He looks at me and smiles. "I'll hold the door open, pay for our dates, and be polite to her parents."

"Okay, that's a good start," Josie says, standing from her seat. "I want full updates on all these shenanigans."

"Why don't you just come with us?" I ask, following her to the door.

"Because between you pretending to date Parker and trying to catch Lewis's eye, there'll be no room for me," Josie replies. "I'll be left on my own."

"Or hanging with Tyler," Parker adds.

"Ugh." Josie frowns. "Don't go there again."

We get onto the sidewalk, and Josie gestures ahead at the number six bus pulling up. "Whoa. That's my line. I gotta go."

"I can drive you home," Parker offers.

Josie wraps me in a hug. "Don't pick out anything too revealing." She pulls out of the hug and points at Parker. "I've still got my eye on you."

Parker gives her a salute. "Yes, ma'am."

"Bye, Josie," I wave as she rushes to catch her bus.

A chill runs down my spine as we cross the strip mall toward a store that sells everything beach aesthetic. It would be so much easier if I were making this purchase with Josie by my side.

"Are you okay?" Parker asks.

"Yeah, I'm glad she knows. I don't want her to be confused about my feelings for Lewis."

"I guess you're right. It would've given her mental whiplash if she thought we were a real couple, and then next week Lewis is your boyfriend."

Sparks ignite inside me. "Do you really think I could be with Lewis in a week?"

He grins, wiggling his eyebrows. "Why not?"

I giggle and take a large slurp of the smoothie to lower my rising body temperature.

Parker opens the store door, and I freeze.

"Why don't you wait outside?"

Parker rolls his eyes. "*Geez*, Green. I'm gonna see you in it tomorrow. Suck it up."

"I can buy it on my own."

"No way." Parker takes my smoothie and puts both our cups in a nearby trash can. "If I leave you alone, you might chicken out."

"I'm more likely to chicken out with you standing over me."

Parker walks me inside. "I won't stand over you. I'm here to support you."

"The weirdest support ever."

"Don't you want me to point out something that would make Lewis drool?"

I recoil. "How do you know what he's into?"

He smirks. "Because it's the same thing any guy would be into."

I step away from him and toward a rack. "Ugh. Whatever."

Parker laughs, following me. "Decoded, it just means buy something skimpy."

"That's exactly what Josie said *not* to get."

"And you're both single with unrequited crushes."

I keep my head turned, hiding the sting left by that statement.

"You do know you're going up against Yvette, right?"

I hold on to the rack for balance as a dizzy spell takes hold. I ground my feet and exhale hard. "I know," I say flatly. "And I'm better than her."

"Whoa. There's the confidence you've been hiding. How so?"

"Because I don't have to flash my body to get a boyfriend."

Parker gives me an uneasy look. "Except Yvie is dating your crush, and your boyfriend is fake."

My eyes roll. "I mean, I'll get Lewis in a non-superficial way."

"And all I'm saying is you need to get his attention with something flashy and then you can win him over with your personality." Parker pulls a blue bikini from the rack. "This would work."

"*Yikes.* Would you look at how tiny the material is? Just looking at it gives me anxiety."

Parker puts it back on the rack. "What about the one next to it? The darker blue?"

"There are no straps. It's just a boob-tube. Umm, no way."

"Are you here to buy a bikini or not?"

I move ahead, thumbing through the racks. I feel the material of a baby blue two-piece with thicker straps. It doesn't have two little triangles, like Parker's selection. This one actually looks like it'll hold in place.

I pull it from the rack and show Parker. "How about this one?"

He shrugs. "It's blue."

"It's not one-piece, so I think it's a happy medium."

"Are you sure you don't want to try my pick first?"

I back away to the fitting room with my selection. "I'm sure."

With my new purchase, Parker takes me home. When he parks outside my home, I unbuckle my seatbelt and tell him, "Ah, my parents want to talk to you."

Surprise fills his expression. "You told them about me?"

"They asked me who I was baking for. Plus, my mom saw your car yesterday."

"Oh."

"My dad wants to make sure you're still okay before you drive me out to Logan's Point."

"Another grilling," Parker mutters. He unbuckles his seatbelt and opens his car door. "Okay. Let's get this over with."

"Are you okay with this?"

He winks. "I got this. Parents love me."

When I get my backpack out of the trunk, I shove the shopping bag inside.

"Hiding your purchase from your parents?" Parker teases.

"No. It'll just be weird to walk into the house with a bikini when I'm introducing you to my parents."

"Relax, I've met them before."

"They knew you in middle school. This is a reintroduction."

"It'll still be a piece of cake."

"How does nothing faze you?" I ask as we walk to my front door.

"Because usually things don't turn out to be such a big deal."

I roll my eyes. "We live in different worlds."

When I push the door open, the distinct sounds of eighties pop echo throughout the house.

"Oh no," I utter, wanting to stop Parker from stepping inside the house.

"What's wrong?" he asks, expecting me to welcome him in.

I wince. "Ah, this mightn't be the best time."

"Is that Kikki?" Dad calls from the kitchen.

"Ah, yeah," I call back, letting Parker follow me inside.

With no further warning, Dad sashays his way into the hallway, boogying toward us.

"*Dad,*" I whine.

Parker laughs at my dad's dance moves and waves. "Hi, Mr. Green."

"Parker!" Dad cheers. "Long time no see. Damona, Parker's here."

"Parker?" Mom calls over the top of the music.

When she makes her way into the hallway, I cringe. "Guys, can you cut the music?"

"Why would we do that?" Dad says, snapping his fingers as he twists to the beat. "It's Friday afternoon. Work's done for the week. Plus, the two of you should be celebrating. No school for a whole week."

"I hope you're a fan of old-school pop," Mom says, patting Parker's arm. "There's always music pumping in this house."

Parker turns to me with raised eyebrows. "Oh, really?"

"Just don't dare try to change the music while Kikki's baking," Dad jokes. "When she's baking, it's her way or the highway."

"Kikki?" Parker questions.

I cover my eyes. "Oh, boy."

Dad clutches my hand in an attempt to make me do the twist with him. "Yes, that's right. Kikki."

"Dad, stop," I whine.

"Oh, stop acting embarrassed," Mom teases, swatting a hand. "Parker doesn't care if you dance in your own home."

Umm, this is high school. Anything can and will be used against you.

"Well, I happen to think this song is a banger," Parker says, bopping in place.

"Excellent," Dad says, spinning on his heels. "Come join us in the kitchen."

As he and Mom shimmy toward the kitchen, I wince at Parker. "Sorry about them."

Parker laughs. "Are you kidding? I've never seen a pair of parents happier and more carefree."

"You're not just saying that, and then texting everyone about what happened here?"

"And why would I do that, Kikki?"

I hiss. "Don't call me that."

Parker smirks and runs a thumb along my jaw. "Why not?"

"It doesn't leave this house," I warn. "Even Josie doesn't call me it, because she knows I'm not the same person outside of my home."

Parker's hands land on his hips, and his gaze wanders the deserted hallway. "And who are you at home?"

I shrug, dumping my bag in the foyer. "Someone who's not scared."

"Okay then," Parker says, stepping into the hallway.

"You're doing it wrong," I say, holding back a laugh.

"Huh?"

I move in front of him and dance along the hallway. "When the music's on, you must dance."

Parker whistles. "Slick moves, Green."

I turn, dancing backwards down the hall. "Let's be real, even when the tunes are off, there's still dancing in this house."

Parker two-steps toward me. "I never would've guessed you live in such a fun house."

"Home is fun," I reply. "It's away from the nightmare of rumors and ridicule of high school."

"Ah, so that's why you're not scared here."

"Precisely. It's always safe."

We dance our way into the kitchen, where we meet my parents at the counter.

"How are your parents, Parker?" Mom asks, stirring lemons and mint into a pitcher of iced tea.

Parker sits on a counter stool. "Yeah, they're good, thanks."

"I saw your dad on the golf course a few months back," Dad says. "I hope he's worked on his backswing since then."

Parker chuckles. "He doesn't get out there as much as he would like to ."

"Well, I'm sure your mother appreciates that," Mom says. "It's a sport that keeps people away from home for far too many hours."

Dad leans back in his chair. "It's not my fault. It's my buddies that drag it out."

Mom smirks. "Sure, sure."

Mom pours from the pitcher of iced tea and hands out the glasses.

"How long have you had your driver's license?" Dad asks, his tone gaining seriousness.

Parker sits straighter, picking up on the tone change. "Four months, sir."

Dad laughs. "Sir? Ah, I like this boy."

Parker glances at me, and then back at my dad. "Is that all you needed to know?"

"You've driven Kikki home twice without crashing," Mom says. "That's a good sign. But Logan's Point is another thing. Mountains Road can be tough."

"My friends and I drive over the mountains all the time," Parker says earnestly. "Trust me, Mr. and Mrs. Green, I can handle it. I'll keep Kylie safe."

Dad points a finger gun at Parker. "You'd better."

He nods hurriedly. "I will."

"Lewis from next door made a real mess of his car," Dad says, frowning as he shakes his head. "He only had it a month, I think."

"Yeah, it was a bit insane," Parker agrees.

"Insane?" Dad says, semi-amused. "He didn't brake before a crosswalk and jerked his car into a sign post."

"We ran into Sheriff Lennon and his wife at the grocery store," Mom says. "Apparently, from the tire marks on the road, they could tell how fast Lewis was going and how hard he braked at the last minute."

"It was just the car that got damaged," I pipe up. "There were no other people around, and he didn't get hurt."

"Kikki, that's my point," Dad replies. "Imagine if anyone had been on that crosswalk. What that boy did was immensely dangerous."

"Well, I'm driving Lewis tomorrow," Parker says. "There's no way he's getting behind the wheel. Plus, my parents make me drive my brothers around all the time. They have plenty of faith in me."

Before the conversation can continue, Brandy barks to be let inside.

"Brandy's calling out for attention," Mom says, walking out of the kitchen.

"We forgot about her when you kids came home," Dad says, his shoulders jiggling in a silent laugh. "I'm surprised she didn't revolt sooner. It's the longest she's been outside in ages."

"We have a very spoiled dog," I tell Parker.

"You have a dog?" Parker says, straining his neck to view the doorway.

Brandy scampers into the kitchen, bounding toward my stool. "Hey girl," I say, scratching behind her ear.

I turn to Parker to introduce them, and find him with a lowered chin and mouth ajar.

"Are you okay?" I ask. "Do you not like dogs?"

Parker slips off the stool and pats Brandy. "No, I love them. She just looks so much like my dog."

"You have a retriever?" Mom asks with a happy grin.

"Had," Parker replies. "He died a few months ago."

Mom and Dad awe in condolence.

There's a pain in my chest as I whisper, "I'm sorry, Parker."

His smile is small as he keeps his eyes on Brandy. "It's okay. The vet did all he could."

"Doesn't make it any easier," Dad says.

Parker looks up and nods with appreciation. "No, it doesn't."

Brandy barks and jumps on her hind legs for attention.

Parker laughs, scratching her back as she lands back on all four feet. "Were we not paying enough attention to you, girl?"

My lips pout, watching the melancholy in his eyes as he's reminded of his dog. "Maybe you can help me walk her sometime?"

"Really?"

I nod with a heartfelt smile.

He grins at me. "Okay, sweet."

"Is your family looking to get another dog?" Dad asks.

"Eventually," Parker replies. "It just seems too soon."

"I get that," I say, running Brandy's floppy ear between my fingers. "Would you get another retriever?"

"Definitely. I couldn't imagine having a different breed. My mom..." He pauses and his Adam's apple bobs as he searches for the words.

"Yes, son?" Dad prompts him. "Your mom?"

"Uh." He falters again at the sentence. He pats Brandy, and his body relaxes. "She had golden retrievers growing up."

"Oh, that's lovely," Mom says. "And she wanted to carry on the tradition with you and your brothers?"

Parker doesn't take his eyes off Brandy. "Something like that."

"Brandy's only five, so hopefully she's around for many more years," I say.

Parker smiles at me. "I have no doubt."

"She's got another ten years in her, honey," Dad says. "Don't you worry about that."

Parker pushes on his knees, standing from Brandy's side. "Thank you so much for having me over, but I'd better get home."

"I'll walk you out," I say, getting off my stool.

Mom and Dad say their goodbyes to Parker, and we make our way to the front door.

"Seemed to go well," Parker says softly.

"Yeah, I think you got their approval."

"I'll see you tomorrow. Remember, I'll be late to pick you up."

I nod. "I know the plan. I'm sharing the backseat with Lewis."

Parker winks. "That's my girl."

"*Eww.*"

Parker and I share a laugh, and I wave him off before closing the front door.

I wander back into the hallway where Mom meets me.

"I'm so glad you brought him over."

I blink hard. "You are?"

Mom cups the side of my face. "He seems like such a nice young man. I'm so happy for you two to spend some extra time together."

I squirm in place. "Really?"

Mom smiles. "Of course, honey. Why wouldn't I like a boy who entered our home by dancing?"

Wait, she likes him? She approves of him?

She thinks Parker is boyfriend material?

How do I tell her this isn't a long-term thing? And how will I explain when I get a new boyfriend so soon after this farce with Parker?

I clear my throat, and stare at the hallway flooring. "It might not last that long."

Mom's eyes fill with worry. "Why would you say that, honey?" She runs her hand down my hair. "You're a wonderful girl. Don't doubt yourself so early in the relationship."

"Oh, no, I don't mean…" She thinks I'm insecure about being with Parker?

"Come on," she says kindly, walking me up the hallway. "Let's get dinner ready."

In the kitchen, Dad is preparing the vegetables while singing along with one of his favorite David Bowie songs.

He turns to me and waves a carrot and vegetable peeler as he talks. "That Parker's okay. I'm still wary about his driving capabilities, but he doesn't seem like a hopeless case."

Mom moves to the sink to scrub her hands. "I was just telling Kikki how much I liked him."

Before they go into full-on Parker praising mode, I say, "Can you not tell Tess about Parker coming over?"

Mom double-takes at me. "Why would you say that?"

I shrug. "I dunno. I just don't think she'd be happy about it."

"Tess would like him if she met him," Dad says.

"It doesn't matter who he is, I just don't think she'd like the idea of me hanging out with any guy."

Mom gives a sympathetic smile. "Tess won't be jealous, honey. I know she really wanted to go on dates in high school and it didn't really work out for her, but she'd never want to hold you back."

That would be how I'd describe my sister if it were opposite day.

"Tess can be very risk-averse," Dad says diplomatically. "Are you asking us not to say anything until you decide to keep seeing Parker?"

A lightbulb shines in my head. "Yes. Just hold off."

Mom and Dad nod in agreement. "Okay, we can do that," Mom says. "As long as you don't keep anything from us."

I grin. "Deal."

By the time Mom and Dad expect me to give the greenlight, I'll be with Lewis. And once I'm with Lewis, Tess will just have to deal with it.

There's nothing anyone can say that would keep me from seeing him.

While dinner's cooking, I chill on the couch with Brandy lying by my feet.

Beep, beep.

I lift my phone, and there's a text from Parker. *"So my parents were asking about you when I got home. My brother Kurtis heard about us at school and was sent the photo from chem lab."*

Goosebumps coat my skin. *"What did you say about me?"*

"I said you were cool, and we were hanging out."

"So you kept out the girlfriend stuff?"

"I told them I thought you were more into Lewis than me."

I almost drop the phone. *"Are you serious???"*

"My mom thought I was putting myself down and tried to pinch my cheeks. I should've just said we were dating."

A laugh tumbles out of me, and my cheeks hurt from grinning. *"Your mom sounds cute."*

"She overdoes it sometimes. She keeps trying to tell me how special I am and that you'd be crazy not to date me."

"She'll relax once she sees Yvette on your arm."

"Here's hoping!"

Eight

"Have you got everything, honey?" Mom calls out from the living room on Saturday morning.

My stomach jitters with nervousness, which has lingered since last night.

"Yeah, I think so," I say, stuffing my beach towel into my tote bag.

I descend the stairs, almost missing a step when I'm hit with a dizzy spell.

I'm going to Logan's Point with Lewis and his friends.

This isn't a daydream.

This is real life.

I land on the first floor, renewed with giddiness. *Eep!* How'd I get this lucky?

I bite inside my lip, remembering the pretense of dating Parker. For now, I can ignore that part. I flick the ties of my blue bikini that run behind my neck and giggle. I can't believe I'm actually wearing this and Lewis will see. What if he dumps Yvette today?

I giggle again, and Mom meets me in the hallway.

"Well, you look happy this morning," she says with delight. "Excited to see Parker again?"

So much for ignoring that part.

I swallow hard. "Something like that."

"Did you pack the Tupperware container?"

I pat the tote bag. "I've got everything. Is it okay if I wait outside?"

A nervous laugh puffs out of Mom. "Did we embarrass you too much yesterday?"

Yes. "No, it's just that Parker texted that he's running late. I think he wants us to get in the car as soon as he pulls up."

"Us?" Mom asks.

I gesture toward the house on the left. "Lewis from next door is coming with us. He's probably waiting out front already."

Mom nods. "Okay, you can wait with your friend."

My friend. I give Mom a hug, thanking her and saying goodbye.

"Have fun, Kikki," she says, waving me out the door.

I step off the front porch as Mom closes the door behind me. I try not to dwell on the fact she's probably spying from the front window as I move down the footpath.

I smooth down my white sundress and summon the courage to glance over at Lewis's front yard. After a substantial stomach flip, I turn my face.

The air drains out of my lungs as I view the empty yard. Standing curbside, I clutch my elbows and allow myself to pout. The only way I got through my anxiety-ridden night was by convincing myself I'd get one-on-one time with Lewis while we waited for Parker to show up.

It was a long shot, but something deep inside me said it was gonna happen.

As I wait, alone, I swing my body back to face my house. Maybe I should just go back inside and wait. Do I look totally desperate waiting outside? Will Parker tell me I did the wrong thing and I've actually turned Lewis off?

As I admit defeat and walk back toward the house, my ears prick to a door opening.

"Bye, Mom," Lewis's voice calls out.

I slowly backtrack to the curb.

Lewis emerges from his house and takes his porch steps two at a time. He hitches a backpack over his shoulder, and his gaze slides my way.

He smiles and puts his hand up in a wave.

My heart palpitates.

That's at me.

He's waving at me.

"Hey, Kylie," he says, making his way toward me.

My knees buckle. Oh my gosh. He's coming over here. Whoa. How am I gonna stay upright?

"Umm," I stutter. "Hi, ah, umm, hi Lewis."

"Ready for today?" he asks, searching the quiet street.

"Yeah, I've never hung out at Logan's Point before."

"Really?"

"No. I've traveled through the town on the way to the city, but my family's never stopped there."

"Well, we don't go into the town," Lewis replies. "It's not the best. But just outside of the town has the best hiking trails, rock climbing spots, and the lake is great for rafting."

The freaked out look hits my face before I can stop it. "Rafting?"

Lewis chuckles. "We're not going near those spots today. We swim at this cove. There's no fast current, but there is a cool waterfall."

My heart swells. "Wow." I imagine Lewis and I standing under the waterfall, having our first kiss. As my toes curl in my shoes, my voice turns breathy. "I can't wait to see that."

As I break out of fantasyland, Lewis's attention is back on the road. I shuffle weight between my feet and sink into the awkwardness.

How the heck do I jumpstart the conversation again?

Lewis pulls his phone from his pocket, and it's like I'm officially put on mute.

We stand a foot apart, in excruciating silence, for what feels like an eternity, until Lewis lowers his phone.

He lets out a weighted sigh, and jokes, "Has Parker forgotten where we live?"

I laugh a little too hard, but who cares? Lewis Freaking Allen is talking to me.

I smooth the hair from the side of my face. "Ah, yeah. He must be taking the scenic route."

"Maybe he's lost on the way to Yvie's house. He said he lived close to her, but they're in different neighborhoods."

My mouth runs dry. "Have you been to her house before?"

"She had a party a few months ago that me, Parker, and Tyler went to," he replies. "Did you go to that?"

"Ah, no, I must've missed that one."

"You didn't miss much," Lewis says, searching the road for Parker's car. "She was still dating that deadbeat footballer. I ended up leaving early."

"Oh, well, you could've come over to my house," I say, instantly blushing. "I could've baked you something to boost your mood."

He grins. "I'm sure that would've worked. You're a wicked baker." He eyes my tote bag. "Did you bring anything today?"

I pat the bag. "I never go anywhere unprepared. I always have snacks."

Lewis's laugh plays like music. "I'll remember that and stick by you today."

Eep! My heart bursts with giddiness. The stretch of my grin hurts, and it takes three attempts to get a word out. "Umm, yeah, that'll be cool."

"I bet Parker will have something to say about that."

The tension in my smile eases. "Oh, yeah, maybe."

"It's so cool the two of you are together," Lewis remarks. "Yvie won't stop talking about our double date. I think she's more excited about getting burgers than hanging out at the lake today."

"I thought she didn't like burgers."

"It's the four of us hanging out that has her excited."

"Oh, okay. Cool."

"You two have been getting close during chemistry, right?"

"Who? Me and Yvette?"

"Yeah. She said you two talk all the time."

If you mean she talks *at* me, then yes. "Mmm, yeah, I guess."

"It's awesome my best bud is dating someone my girlfriend gets along with."

Oh boy. He thinks I'm friends with Yvette. How long do I need to play along? Surely once they're broken up, he won't want us hanging out with her. I just hope that doesn't do anything to ruin his friendship with Parker.

Okay, maybe I can play nice with Yvette for the boys' sake. Although, how my sanity will last is beyond me.

Finally, Parker's car appears on our street and pulls in at the curb. My gut plummets as Lewis's smile grows at the sight of Yvette through the car window. He pulls on the door handle to help her out, but the door doesn't budge.

"Huh?" Lewis mutters.

Yvette's window lowers, and Parker leans across her to tell Lewis, "Get in the back."

"What?" Lewis recoils. "Why's the door locked?"

"I dunno," Parker blurts. "Just get in the back so we can get going."

"Parker, unlock the door," Lewis insists. "Yvie and I wanna sit..."

"We're late," Parker interrupts. He nods at me. "Kylie, sit behind me. Kai's gonna go berserk if we turn up any later."

Lewis groans with an eye roll. "Fine." He leans over with pouted lips to kiss Yvette, but the window raises before he gets the chance. "Hey!"

"My bad," Parker's muffled voice calls from inside the car.

My shoulders jiggle as I walk around the back of the car, suppressing my laughter with all my might. Good one, Parker. I didn't want to see that either.

"Hi Kylie," Yvette says in a chipper tone as I buckle myself in the backseat. I mumble, "Hi."

Once Lewis closes his door, Parker takes off from the curb.

Lewis grunts, flailing forward and then back. "Whoa, dude. Take it easy."

"Whoops," Parker blurts. "My bad."

Lewis shakes his head as he buckles his seatbelt. "What's with you today?" Lewis then looks at me and chuckles. "Oh, I get it."

I suck in a breath, feeling a tightness in my chest.

He knows? He's already figured out Parker's ridiculous plan?

Lewis laughs, slouching in his seat. "Are you nervous, bro?"

Parker shifts in his seat. "Huh?"

"Did you get too in your head about making a good impression on your girlfriend?" Lewis jokes.

I sink in my seat and cup a hand over my eyes.

"I'm good, bro," Parker mutters. "Don't you worry about me."

Lewis chuckles to himself and stares out his window. Soon, the car falls into silence.

Yeesh. Awkward silence.

I swallow hard, budging my head to the right to look at Lewis. It's a monumental effort. Sharing a backseat has heavier connotations than standing in our front yards.

As the drive continues with nothing but the stereo filling the silence, there's finally movement from Yvette. Unintentionally, I hold my breath as her hand snakes around her front passenger seat. Her hand angles behind her, signaling to Lewis.

Lewis grins, clutching her hand and massaging the top with his thumb.

I stare intently at their linked hands, and the low thump of my heart drowns out the music. With all my might, I wish for them to let go. In a moment of panic, and with no better options, I kick the back of Parker's seat.

"Huh?" he mutters.

Parker's head turns and he double-takes when spotting Yvette's arm fished between the front seats.

Suddenly the car swerves, and their hands break apart.

"Whoa!" Yvette gasps.

"Whoa is right," Parker blurts. "That thing came out of nowhere."

"Geez, can you take it easy, Parker?" Lewis grumbles.

"Hey, I'm not the one who had his driving privileges taken away," Parker teases.

Lewis straightens in his seat, frowning. "*Ha, ha.*"

Great. Now the silence is ten times more awkward.

I stare ahead, watching Parker fidget in his seat. He cranes his neck, and I notice him gaining my attention with the rearview mirror.

"Hey, did you bake anything for today?" he asks.

"Yep," I reply. "I made snickerdoodles and red velvet cupcakes."

"Oh, yum," Yvette mumbles. "I hope they're as good as what you brought to school yesterday."

Lewis sits forward, smirking. "I already told Kylie I'm snagging them before you get to them, Parker."

"*Ha*!" Parker snickers. "If you can't stop drooling over Kylie's baking, maybe you picked the wrong girl."

"Hey!" Yvette squeaks.

"I can appreciate how good Kylie's snacks are without dating her," Lewis says.

"Yeah, but if you want to be first in line, you should be her boyfriend," Parker replies.

Oh, gosh. All the blood is rushing to my head.

"Umm." Yvette flicks her hair off her shoulders as she leans over the center console to eye Parker. "He's happy being my boyfriend."

Parker's teasing laugh sizzles out of him. "And do you bake, Yvie?"

She sits back. "No. I have other talents."

Parker can't help himself. "How come Lewis doesn't talk about them as much as he does Kylie's baking?"

What is he doing? Why is he antagonizing her so much?

"Unlike you, Parker," Lewis interjects, "I can compliment both girls."

"What are you trying to say?" Parker asks, shifting in his seat. "You think you can make both girls happy?"

"Probably with a lot less effort than you."

"What do you say, Yvie?" Parker says, the fun coming back into his tone. "Is it good to know that your boyfriend's contemplating making another girl happy?"

Yvie retches, crossing her arms. "Ah, no."

Lewis leans forward to touch Yvette's arm. "That's not what I meant."

"And what do you think, Kylie?" Parker asks, tilting his head at the rearview mirror. "Would you want to share a boyfriend?"

With irritation at his friend filling his expression, Lewis's stare lands on me.

Fear and embarrassment inflame my face. I raise my hands to cover, but there's a tremble in my fingers. When Yvette turns to look at me, another wave of humiliation crashes over me.

"Kylie?" Parker asks, moving to view the mirror again.

I rotate to face the car door, overwhelmed by everyone's attention. Oh my gosh. They're not gonna stop until I give an answer. I gotta come up with something fast.

Without overthinking it, I fake a sneeze with a mighty hunch.

I inhale hard, lowering my hand and turning back to face front. "Sorry," I mutter. "I couldn't think straight. I could feel that sneeze coming on."

Yvette huffs, swatting a hand. "Whatever. Parker, you're being so dumb. Lewis doesn't want two girlfriends."

"Good," Parker replies, "because there's no way he's getting my girlfriend."

My heart rate lowers as the conversation dies and Lewis settles back on the seat beside me. I glance over at him with a kind smile. He sighs and smiles back.

Okay, I'll take that as progress.

The car zooms through Mountains Road. Parker takes the twists and turns like a pro, proving he made all those swerves and jerks earlier on purpose. After a few ascents and declines, the car turns onto a dirt track. Soon, we're driving alongside the dazzling lake and shadowed by a canopy of trees.

Parker drives the car across a patchy grass area, where we spot Tyler sitting on the hood of his car.

Once parked, Parker opens his door and asks, "Are you the only one here?"

We all exit the car as Tyler replies, "Yep. Should've known you'd all be taking your sweet time."

"See, we didn't have to rush," Lewis grunts, punching Parker's arm.

"*Ouch*," Parker whines, rubbing his arm. "How was I supposed to know? Kai told me what time to get here."

Before the boys can get into another argument, another car approaches the area. It parks and Kai gets out of the driver's seat. Tabitha leaves the front seat, and Jamie and her boyfriend Milo emerge from the backseat.

"Whoa." Tyler smirks. "You actually convinced Milo to come along?"

"He's here with Jamie," Kai grunts. "I'm not babysitting him."

Milo rolls his eyes. "I don't need babysitting."

Kai and Milo are identical twins, but telling them apart is easy. Kai's hair is cropped short, and he has a scar by his eye. Milo's hair is thicker and longer, and he wears glasses. Not to mention the confidence absolutely drips off Kai, whereas his brother has an awkward, somewhat hunched, posture. Although, when Jamie's by his side, I swear Milo stands taller.

Parker's hands land on his hips. "So, what gives? Why are you guys so late?"

Kai hangs a thumb at Jamie. "Blame her. We couldn't get her out of the café."

"It's Aunt Maddy's fault," Jamie complains. "She forgot to organize for the new girl to come in."

Unable to fight it, I gulp. Usually, I fill in for Jamie when she goes out with her friends. Is she going to blame me for not taking her shift?

Her boyfriend, Milo, wraps her in a hug and kisses her forehead. "We got you out in time. It's cool."

Tabitha smiles, nodding. "We all pitched in so Jamie could get out of there while Maddy called up her replacement."

Jamie sighs. "Honestly, my aunt can be such a scatterbrain."

Phew. No death stares from Jamie.

Yvette giggles, staring at Parker. "Well, we were late because Parker got lost on the way to my house. I thought you said you'd been there before."

Parker shrugs, and a faint blush highlights his cheeks. "I have. I guess I got my routes mixed up."

Yvette chews on her fingernail, grinning at him. "Maybe you're the scatterbrain."

Discomfort seeps into Lewis's body language. He shifts over to Yvette and places an arm around her.

I share a look with Parker. He rattled him. Lewis is totally marking his territory.

As the four of us stand in front of the four of them, Tyler idly stands in the middle, like some kind of weird, double-dating referee.

Kai grabs Tabitha's hand and tugs her forward. "Shall we?" he says, and they move toward the cove.

Jamie's eyes shift my way, and then she motions at Milo to follow. I bet this is weird for her. It used to be just her and the boys. Now she has all these other girls to contend with, and two happen to be reforming mean girls.

I'm supposed to be playing best friends with Yvette, but it sure would be easier if I got to hang with Jamie instead. Even though we've rarely talked while we've worked together, making nice with a tomboy would be easier than dealing with Miss Perfect.

We move toward the cove, and it takes my breath away. The water is turquoise blue, and the backdrop is a magnificent cliff face with a gushing waterfall as the centerpiece.

As the group sheds clothing to get down to their bathing suits, nervousness bubbles inside me. I clutch the straps of my dress, scared to let it fall to the ground. Am I really letting everyone see me in a revealing bikini?

Nerves are clearly not affecting Yvette. She's stripped down to a hot pink bikini and is anchoring a hand on her hip. Her body sways without a care of who might be staring.

To save my sanity, I avert my eyes from the real-life Barbie. I double-take at Jamie as she rubs sunscreen into her shoulders. She's wearing a navy one-piece and a pair of black shorts.

I nudge Parker and murmur. "Jamie's not in a bikini."

He raises an eyebrow. "So?"

"So, you said I needed a bikini to get noticed." I gesture at Jamie while her boyfriend rubs sunscreen further down her back. "She's got her boyfriend's attention."

Parker snorts. "You can't compare yourself to Jamie. She's one of the dudes."

Parker whips off his shirt, and heat steams out of my pores. My eyes roll down his torso, and it takes a moment to realize I should avert my eyes.

"Do you need sunscreen?" Parker asks.

"Huh?"

My eyes draw to his thumb, which points at the sunscreen sitting on a rock.

"It was Kai's idea," Parker whispers. "He wanted a reason to touch Tabitha, and we agreed it was a killer idea."

He backs away, giving me a questioning stare.

I shy away, hugging my middle as I shake my head. "I'm good."

He backs away, and the image of Parker's hands on my shoulders gives me confusing tummy flutters. Seriously, will my body heat stop rising?

Parker brushes past Lewis and Yvette and pumps the sunscreen bottle.

"Ugh, I got too much," Parker complains at the wad of white lotion in his palm. He steps close to Yvette. "Do you need your shoulders done, Yvie?"

There's something flirty in her smile as she moves her hair off her neck.

"Nuh-uh," Lewis interrupts, draping an arm around Yvette. "Apparently, you have a girlfriend too."

Parker puts up his defenses. "Hey man, there was nothing suss happening. She's just so pale, I thought I'd help."

"I'll help her," Lewis says bluntly.

Yvette's grin becomes more devilish as she releases her hair and watches Parker move toward me.

He gives a mischievous grin and moves in close to my ear. "You can't blame me for trying, can you?"

I shake my head with a laugh. "You're shameless."

He lifts his palm between us. "Well, as you can see, I've got way too much. Can I rub some on you?"

This time I force my eyes away from his shirtless body. "Umm, no, I'm okay."

"Oh, come on. Help a guy out."

I laugh out of nervousness and tap my forearms. "Just slide some on my arms and I'll rub it in."

He shrugs and does as instructed. I keep my gaze low when he moves onto rubbing sunscreen on himself. Doing my best to stay cool, I take a while to spread it across my arms, shoulders, and neck.

"Little help?"

I look up, startled. "Huh?"

I'm greeted by Parker's back, and he points at the middle. "I can't reach that spot."

"Ah," I stammer. "Umm, yeah, okay."

I'm struck with another bewildering tummy flutter as I slide my hands along his back.

Just pretend he's Lewis. Just pretend he's Lewis.

Uh-oh. That just brings up a new problem. Imagining my hands on Lewis causes them to tremor.

"Everything okay, Green?" Parker teases.

"Yep," I say, patting his back. "You're all set."

"Thanks." He turns around. "And you're sure you're good?"

I lift my palms and nod. "I'm good."

He winks. "Time to get in the water then."

I grit my teeth and tug on the straps of my dress.

Okay. Here goes nothing.

Nine

I suck in a breath as I lower, knee-deep, into the water. It's colder than I expected. The others run into the water, splashing and hollering, and I wonder if their bodies experience temperature in a different way from mine.

An awkward shiver rings my internal alarm. I hug my midsection, hating that I'm still exposed above the water. I want to get deeper, purely to cover my bikini-patched body. But, boy, not being a waterbaby is holding me back.

My jaw clenches, I hold my breath, and tense my muscles. Inch by inch, I lower. An ache niggles between my shoulder blades as everyone else swims several feet ahead.

In a deeper section, Parker and Tyler are trying to dunk each other underwater. They laugh and yell as water splashes around their chaotic wrestling.

In a mess of hands and elbows, Tyler manages to push Parker off, who flops backward.

Tyler whips water off his hair, and in a mocking tone says, "Why don't you find your girlfriend?"

Parker spits out water and squints as he wipes his brow. He looks around his immediate area, and after concluding I'm not with the others, spots me.

I gulp, feeling every pinprick of insecurity.

Parker waves me over, but I can't do anything but stare at him.

His head tilts questioningly.

When I still don't budge, he glides through the water toward me.

My anxiety competes with the water temperature over what can give me the most chills.

"Hi," he says with a cheesy grin.

I hug my middle and stammer, "Umm, hi."

He blinks at me, peers over his shoulder, and then wiggles his eyebrows. "What ya doing?"

"Acclimatizing."

"You're cold? The water's beautiful."

"If you say so."

He motions behind him. "They're starting to talk. Why don't you dive in and join us?"

"It's not that easy," I protest, but I'm thwarted by Parker. He scoops me up, making me yelp. "Parker! What are you doing?"

"Helping you out," he jokes, carrying my body against him.

My core heats up at the others flicking their heads in our direction.

"Put me down!" I squeal.

"Are you sure?" Parker asks, backed by a mocking laugh.

My body tenses. "Do not throw me in the water!"

"Ready?" he teases, swaying my body like he's ready to hurl me further into the lake.

I loop my arms around his neck. "Don't!"

He throws his head back with laughter and stops swaying me. He lowers us into the water, gradually submerging my body. I suck in an apprehensive breath, taking in the water temperature at a faster rate.

He smirks. "Not so bad, is it?"

I pull my arms from around him and put all my effort into not letting my teeth chatter.

"Oh man, Green, you can't be serious," he says in disbelief. "It's a beautiful day. The water isn't cold."

"I just don't do open water," I defend. "I swim laps at the town pool. It's heated."

He pulls on a lock of my hair. "Who knew you were so precious?"

"I'm just unaccustomed."

"*Ha.* That's one way to put it."

"Hey, lovebirds!" Jamie calls through cupped hands.

I double-take once I realize she's talking to us.

She waves us over. "Are you going to join us or just keep flirting?"

Flirting? Us? Me and Parker?

Umm... No.

"Coming!" Parker calls back.

I give him a questioning look, and he replies with a shrug. "Apparently we can pull off being a couple without even trying," he says.

"Umm, yeah." I fake a laugh. "I guess so."

Parker hoists me against him, and I toss my arms around his neck as my legs wrap around his hips. My eye line is a little higher than his, and it feels weird looking down at him.

"Ah, what are you doing?" I murmur. "Everyone already believes we're together."

Parker smiles, and sunlight dazzles against his brown eyes. "Yeah, I know."

With the surrounding noises muted against the calming sounds of the water, we stare at each other for a beat too long. The way his smile highlights his face, along with his unwavering eye contact, fills me with a desire I don't understand.

This moment is perfect, but the guy isn't.

Something in the way his jaw flexes sends an extra zing through my heart. I know he feels the same way I do. We're putting on a show in order to gain the attention of the people we really want. So, if I'm thinking about doing this, he must be too. Right?

I trace my fingertips against his jaw and take note of the pout on his lips.

Okay. Here goes nothing.

I lean in, angling my head, and press my lips over his pout. He kisses me back, and I relax against him. He holds me in the water, and I want to hate how normal this feels.

Why did I choose to kiss him? We'd done enough to prove we were together. This is so unnecessary.

I run my hands through his hair, kissing him harder.

In the back of my mind, I focus on where Lewis might be. How good is his view of this? Is he wishing he's in Parker's position?

Is he dying of jealousy?

Before I can delve further into fantasyland, and turn Parker into Lewis, Parker pulls back. The spell is broken, and I blink at the blushing boy.

"Dang," he whispers.

I wipe my mouth. "Sorry."

"Don't be."

He releases me, and I slide against him until my feet hit the muddy sand below. I turn to the others and find Jamie laughing at us.

"Flirting it is then," Jamie jokes as she swims to the rocks with Milo.

From behind me, Parker pulls his arms around my middle and rests his chin on my shoulder.

As my body lifts in the water, I grab onto his forearms as he moves us toward the group. "Let's join the others, Kikki."

I groan. "Don't call me that."

He pecks my cheek. "Admit you love it."

I roll my eyes. My gaze wanders to the right, and I find Lewis gawking at us. A blush sparks on my cheeks, and I sink lower in the water. I'd hide my entire head if Parker weren't holding onto me.

How long has he been staring?

Did it work?

Is he actually jealous?

I give Lewis a smile and then rest my cheek against Parker's.

Okay, maybe faking a relationship does have some perks.

"Kylie, is this your first time at the lake?" Tabitha asks.

"Yeah, it is. I can't believe how beautiful it is. I feel a little dumb for not coming out sooner."

Tabitha bats a hand. "I never came out to Logan's Point before dating Kai. This cove is my favorite place out here."

"I tried telling you to come out to Logan's Point more often," Yvette pipes up. "My cousins, the Ashworths, totally approve of coming out here. They call it the perfect place to let off steam."

Tabitha practically shudders when Yvette brags about being related to the Ashworth siblings.

Lewis pulls an arm around Yvette. "Good thing it didn't take much convincing for you to come out here with me."

Parker nudges me and, from the corner of his mouth, says, "Remember which one you're supposed to be friends with."

Not wanting to get between two warring former best friends, I choose to keep conversation around the stunning nature. "I kinda want to swim to the waterfall."

"We can do that," Parker says, and then swims toward Lewis and Yvette. "Kylie and I are swimming over to the waterfall. Wanna join?"

"Cute," Yvette cheers. She grabs onto Lewis's shoulder. "Let's go."

Oh boy. I'd really prefer to swim without dealing with Yvette squealing the entire time.

Swimming a lap is my speed. The thought of splashing, tackling, and jumping off rocks has my anxiety spiking. I swim ahead of the others, needing the breathing room. With every stroke, I'm deliberate with my breath and concentrate on the hum of the waterfall.

On the approach, the water bounces off the rocks with a cool temperature. It's not unsettling like my first experience of getting into the water. It's calming and renewing. I breathe out with relief and take in the white noise of rushing water, muting everyone in the cove.

Soon, Parker passes me, grabbing onto the rocks at the base of the waterfall and pulling himself up. In a rush, Lewis passes on my other side and pulls himself onto the rock base. It takes me a moment to realize they're racing. Before I can take them both in, they backflip off the rock base, Parker narrowly beating Lewis into the air.

The splashes rain over me, made worse by Yvette shrieking behind me. So much for the serenity.

The waves from the boys hitting the water shoves me against the rocks. Unflatteringly, I spit out water and wipe my face.

Parker makes his way over to me with a cheesy grin. "So, who won?"

"If winning means whoever hit the water first, it was you," I reply. "If it were who looked most insane, the jury is still out."

Parker raises a fist in the air, cheering. "Beat ya, Lewis!"

"You hit the water first because I got more air," Lewis says, bobbing against the waves. "I say getting more air wins."

"Not according to Kylie," Parker replies.

Lewis shrugs. "So?"

Ouch. Why does that sting so much?

Yvette giggles. "Yeah, more air totally wins."

"Rematch?" Parker suggests.

Yvette swims to the side. "I'm not judging. You two make too many waves."

Lewis laughs, following Yvette. "Guess that means I'm the winner."

Parker scoffs, pushing off the rocks to swim behind them. "You're so deluded."

Even though staying by the rushing water sounds like a dream, I follow the others so I'm not labeled a loner weirdo.

As the boys continue to bicker, we move near the rock formations on the edge of the cove. Jamie, Milo, Kai, and Tyler sit along the rocks, chatting.

Tabitha gets out of the water and positions herself on a smooth rock. "Time for some sun."

Tyler looks up at the sun rays beaming down on Tabitha. "Girl, you're gonna burn there."

Tabitha puffs a laugh. "I lotioned up. I'll be fine."

"Sun tanning is okay if you don't care about your skin," Yvette remarks, wading in the water. "I couldn't do it. I mean, my skin is so pale. I need to be careful because I don't want wrinkles when I'm older."

"What are you saying?" Tabitha asks, reclining on her elbows. "That I'll be a raisin when I'm old?"

"Oh, no," Yvette says in a squeaky voice. "I didn't mean you. I just don't want wrinkles."

Tabitha's eyebrows push together as her glare intensifies. "And you think I'm going out of my way to get wrinkles?"

Jamie sighs loudly, getting up and moving further down the rocks. "So much drama since girls started hanging around."

"Well, we're not tomboys," Yvette blurts, "so we care about how we look."

"Hey!" Milo shouts, standing in front of Jamie. "Not cool."

Sitting on the edge of a rock, Kai deadpans at Lewis. "You gonna say something, bro?"

"Ah," Lewis drags out the word, pivoting between Yvette and his friends.

The poor guy. Imagine having to defend such a shallow girl. Of course, he has no words to say.

Kai grunts and turns to Tabitha. "Are you okay, babe?"

Tabitha nods and lies down to get the sun she craves.

Parker blows out a breath and swims further into the lake. "Well, that was awkward."

I swim away with him and ask, "What would you have said if you were in Lewis's position?"

"I wouldn't have needed to say anything."

"How do you figure? Your friends were clearly annoyed at how she spoke to Tabitha and Jamie."

"She wouldn't have said it if she had been with me."

"Don't tell me something stupid like you'd kiss her so much she couldn't talk."

Parker laughs. "No. I mean, at the moment, she sounds super insecure. If she were with me, I'd make sure she has confidence."

"That's a nice sentiment, but I think Yvie has a long road to go. Insults fall too easily out of her mouth."

"But she always backtracks," Parker defends. "I don't think she says anything mean on purpose. I think it's a nervous tick."

Bless this boy and his rose-colored glasses.

Back at the lake's edge, Kai backflips off a rock formation and splashes into the water. Jamie follows soon after, cheering about how Kai barely made any air.

"*Oof.*" Parker wades by my side. "Here come the competition rounds."

"Just between those two? Or do you all get involved?"

"Well, Jamie and Kai are always trying to one-up each other. We all get involved, but they're usually the two left standing. They just can't let the other one win."

"So they'll be too wrapped up in their own competitiveness to try to get me involved in anything?"

Parker wiggles his eyebrows, which I now know as a sign of no good. "Don't you want to impress Lewis?"

My jaw clenches. "Will Yvie do it?"

"If she did, it would be hot."

I glimpse her in her hot pink bikini. I shudder as she giggles and splashes water at Lewis.

"I bet you can make him say, 'Yvette who?'" Parker says.

I laugh and splash a handful of water at him. "No way."

He laughs and splashes me back. "I'm serious."

I glance over my shoulder. "Should we join them? Isn't the whole reason I'm here to get between them?"

"Yeah, we can head over."

Parker leads the way, and he crash-tackles Lewis. Yvette shrieks, flailing in the water to avoid any wayward elbows.

"Yvie, calm down," I say flatly. "They're nowhere near you."

"Oh my gosh," she says, swimming toward me. "Like, I know my hair is already wet, but it's just a natural reaction to scream when water flies at it."

"Mmm. Sure."

"So, you and Parker keep stealing the show."

"The show?"

Her eyes light up. "Those kisses."

"Oh yeah." I steal my courage to say something in the same tone she uses. "I almost feel bad. Like, I see other girls kissing their boyfriends and it's like their toes don't even curl."

Yvette's eyes widen as she takes in the statement.

I gasp and touch her shoulder. "Oh gosh, sorry. I didn't mean to say you and Lewis have bad kisses. I just mean, me and Parker have really good kisses. I was hoping no one got jealous of us."

"Uh-huh." Her mind ticks over. "Well, maybe me and Lewis just don't want to put everything out on display."

Oh.

Yeah.

Right.

She has made out with every single one of her boyfriends in every square inch of our school.

This girl is not shy.

"That's so nice," I say with the fakest nicety. "I wish Parker and I could hold back like that. I don't know how you two do it."

Her tongue clicks as her chin drops.

"Okay, who's jumping off the cliff?" Kai calls out through cupped hands.

Jamie leaps in the water. "I'm in!"

Kai cheers. "*Woo*. I can always count on James."

Tyler pulls himself out of the water, calling out, "What are you all waiting for?"

I give Parker an uneasy look. "Jumping off a cliff?"

Parker points to a spot in the middle of the cliff face. "There's a ledge right there where we jump." His eyebrows wiggle. "You ready?"

"Heck no!"

"You already swam to the waterfall. You know how deep the water is."

"Doesn't mean I want to plunge into it."

Parker holds onto my forearms, tugging me through the water. "Come on, Kikki. You'll love it."

Lewis and Yvette pass us, ready to join the others toward the cliff edge.

We all move out of the water. Jamie kisses Milo, who doesn't follow her up the dirt track. Kai waits for Tabitha to leave her tanning location. And Tyler impatiently waits for everyone else.

"Are you gonna jump?" Lewis asks me.

I gulp, not waiting to say no.

"She can't wait," Parker boasts. "Ain't that right, Kikki?"

I glare at him, nudging him in the ribs.

Yvette giggles. "Aw, cute. You already have a pet name for her."

Murmured laughter circles around the group as they make their way up the dirt track.

I grab his arm and drag him backward. "I told you," I whisper harshly. "Kikki doesn't leave my house."

Parker sniggers. "Oh, come on. It's cute."

"No, I don't want everyone calling me it."

"They won't. It's a boyfriend name for you."

"No, it's not. It's my family's name for me." I glance ahead at the group. "Besides, I don't want Lewis calling me it."

"You're safe. He won't call you something he heard me say. It's a territorial thing."

"Can you just cool it with the nickname? It's too weird hearing it outside of my family."

He pecks a kiss on my forehead. "No can do, Kikki."

"*Parker*," I whine.

"Come on," he says, tugging me forward. "We're lagging behind."

I resist. "Do I really need to do this?"

"Do you want to skyrocket Lewis's interest in you?"

I pout. "I hardly think he'll care once Yvette jumps in that skimpy bikini."

"Hey," he coos, hooking a finger under my chin. "You've got this. Besides, everyone's going up. If you don't, you'll look weird."

I hang a thumb at my side. "Milo's not."

Parker grabs my shoulders, pointing me in the direction of the path. "Milo doesn't have to, he has Jamie to protect him. You have to forget about those two. You're here to impress Lewis, not copy their relationship."

I huff in frustration. "Fine."

Parker pushes me up the incline, and we meet up with the others. "You'll be fine. We've done it hundreds of times. No one's ever gotten hurt."

Jamie laughs, turning to face us. "Unless you count one of Kai's concussions as getting hurt."

I gulp. "One of?"

Jamie bats a hand. "Oh, yeah. He only got one of the concussions at the lake."

I backtrack, but Parker grabs hold of me again. "Don't scare her, Jamie. Kai's the daredevil. No one else takes it as far as he does."

Tabitha grins, adding, "Unless Jamie's trying to one-up him."

Jamie raises a hand. "Guilty. But our rivalry has gone too far to stop now."

"Who's going first?" Tyler asks.

"Kai, let's go," Jamie says, stepping up to the cliff edge.

Kai scratches the back of his head. "Ah, I was gonna jump with Tabby."

Jamie nervously shrugs it off. "Oh, yeah, right. That's cool." She beckons Tyler closer. "Come on, Ty. Let's do this."

Without batting an eye, Tyler counts them down. "Three, two," and he leaps off the cliff before saying one. Jamie jumps off, spinning her body as she cheers on the way down.

My heart pounds in my throat, waiting for the splash below. With hands clasped to my chest, I near the edge and spy them below. In the water, Tyler and Jamie high-five and cheer on the next people to jump.

Kai grabs Tabitha's hand and beckons her closer to the edge. "Come on, baby. Let's do this."

Tabitha squeals, readying herself, and the two leap off the edge.

I press my hands onto my chest, gasping for breath. "How are they all doing this?"

Parker rubs my shoulders. "Once you take off, you'll have so much fun."

"The adrenaline rush is addictive," Lewis agrees.

I give Lewis a thankful smile. Okay, everything will be fine. My guy is here. We'll remember this moment forever, even though we're not together yet. One day, we'll laugh about how I came here with Parker just to get his attention.

My nerves lower. When Lewis finally finds out how much I'm absolutely crushing on him, he will swoon and call me adorable.

Lewis gives me a heart-melting smile. "Okay. Who's next?"

Ten

Jamie and Tyler jog back up the dirt track, while Kai carries Tabitha on his back.

"I'm about to jump again if you guys don't get moving," Tyler warns.

I share a look with Yvette. We've both been holding up the line because neither is eager to jump.

"Okay," Parker says with a clap. "Lewis and I will go, and then you girls can follow. Deal?"

Not pleased with having to jump with squealing Yvie, I nod anyway.

Lewis pecks Yvie's cheek. "See you on the other side."

The boys take a running start, and as competitive as the race to the waterfall, they spring off the cliff edge. They hit the water with an almighty splash.

Below, they cheer and encourage us to follow.

"Ready?" I ask Yvette.

On shaky legs, Yvie moves beside me. She clutches my hand, and I don't hate it as we scuff toward the edge.

Parker and Lewis wave from below. Before I can wave back, Yvette has a meltdown.

"No, I can't do this!" she shrieks, stumbling backward.

She yanks on my hand and then flings it away. I let out a shriek as I teeter against the loose dirt and rocks below. As my body sways back and forth, I eye the lake below. I can't exactly make out what they're saying, but there's hollering and cheering.

I still haven't caught my balance, and in a moment of impulse, I step off the edge. Rushing through the air, my hands flail above my head. In a panic move, I clutch my chest before hitting the water.

All noise mutes as I surge into the lake. Water rushes into my nose and down my throat. I thrust my limbs in a scramble, making my way to the surface.

Spitting out water and coughing hard, I barely hear Parker as he approaches.

"You jumped solo?" he questions.

I cough again, taking in the impressed faces of both boys.

My voice is raspy as I rush to say, "Yvie pulled away and made me lose my balance."

Concern brightens Lewis's eyes. "Is Yvie okay?"

My stomach drops. I'm the one who jumped, but he's worried about her.

The defeat is hard to shake. I flail in a bad attempt to tread water. My hair mattes over my face and I desperately gulp for air.

"Hey, hey," Parker coos, pushing his way toward me. "Don't panic."

Anxiety pumps through me as Parker nears my thrashing limbs. He manages to clutch my hands, steadying my wild movements.

"I got you," Parker says, hoisting me against him. "Wow, Green. You really did it."

My arms hang over Parker's shoulders as I cough.

"I didn't think you had it in you," he teases. "Maybe next time you can try it without inhaling a mouthful of lake."

My brow furrows. "*Ha, ha.*"

Lewis swims past us, gesturing up at the cliff. "I'm gonna check on Yvie."

Parker looks up, asking, "You wanna do it again?"

I cough again. The remnants of lake water irritating my throat. "No, I'm not feeling so great."

"Well, you did great," Parker says, moving us toward the shoreline. "How about we take a breather?"

I nod against his shoulder, letting him carry me through the water.

When we reach the rocks, I'm careful not to slip on the wet surface. With everyone leaving the water after their jump to run back up the cliff, water has seeped into every crevice of the smooth and jagged area.

Out of the water, goosebumps litter my skin and I shiver my way across the rocks.

Parker laughs as he plucks our towels from the mess of dumped bags. "I can hear your teeth chattering from here."

I can't respond as my arms instinctively bunch over my chilled chest.

"Here," Parker says, smirking as he whips my towel around me in one smooth action.

As I cinch it tight around me, I manage a garbled, "Thank you."

Parker mumbles another laugh as he gathers his towel around his waist. "No problem."

As we sit on the shady patch of grass, I drag my tote bag closer. "We can't forget the snacks."

"Mmm," Parker purrs. "I knew I was fake dating the right girl."

The comment leaves an uncomfortable niggle in my stomach. "Are you sure you want to sit with me? What about Yvette? Aren't you missing a shot with her?"

He shrugs, watching the others milling around Yvette. "She has everyone fussing over her." He turns back to me and smiles. "Besides, if I don't sit with you, you won't have anyone."

My heart flutters. "I'll be okay on my own."

"No, it's okay. The longer we're away from everyone else, it will increase Lewis's suspicions. I want to make sure he's jealous."

"Jealous of what?"

He nudges me, grinning. "Of me getting to spend alone time with you."

I splutter a laugh. "Yeah, right. He's probably annoyed that everyone won't leave him alone with Yvette."

"Trust me, he'll be thinking about you," Parker murmurs. "You jumped off the edge, and his girl wouldn't."

"He'll really care that much?"

Parker smirks. "He will because I'll keep rubbing it in."

I click my tongue. "*Parker.*"

"How can I not boast about my awesome girlfriend? It'd be suspicious if I didn't."

I swallow hard, watching Lewis wrap his arms around Yvette's bare torso as the others chat and laugh with them. "Don't make a big deal of this in front of everyone. It's too embarrassing having everyone's eyes on me."

"But you want Lewis's eye on you?"

"Well, yeah."

"Look at Yvie. She loves the attention," Parker comments. "He's not dragging her away anytime soon."

"Are you going to be okay sharing her with everyone else?"

He wiggles his eyebrows. "I'll make do just fine."

Ick.

I turn my gaze away from the others. Instead, focusing on the gentle breeze, scent of wildflowers, and the cozy warmth of the midday sun.

Parker reclines against the base of the tree, and his eyelids lower. When he stops motor-mouthing, it's actually peaceful in his presence. Delighting in the serenity, I run my fingers between the blades of grass and let the wind blow-dry my hair.

For a moment, my imagination takes over, and Lewis is reclining beside me, playing with the wet locks of my hair.

If only it were real.

Parker opens his eyes, letting his gaze run over me.

I smile, knowing how close I am to my dreams coming true.

Footsteps sound from the right, and I look over my shoulder at the dirt track. I smile and motion in that direction. "Oh, it's Milo. We should call him over."

Parker's lip upturns. "Really?"

I nudge him. "Don't be mean. Milo's cool."

"Uh, no, he isn't."

I roll my eyes. "Whatever. I think he's a nice guy."

Parker lifts his hands in defense. "I already promised Jamie I'd make more of an effort with him. It'll be much easier if you're with me to do the heavy lifting."

I wave Milo over, who gives me an apprehensive smile.

I pat the tote bag. "Making friends is easy when you have baked goods."

"Do you want to pass them over, sweetie pie?"

I recoil. "Sweetie pie?"

He shrugs, laughing. "I was trying another nickname. You don't like when I call you Kikki. I thought sweetie pie would be cute because you bake sweet things; including pie."

I lift a hand to stop his ramble. "How about you stop with the nicknames?"

"Can't do, Kikki Green."

"Ugh." I push the tote bag closer to him. "You're impossible."

He laughs, pulling out the Tupperware container. "You love it."

"You know I don't."

"Hi," Milo says, somewhat alarmed as he joins us. "What's up?"

I pull the Tupperware away from Parker. "I was wondering if you were also hungry?"

"Wow, you baked for the trip?" Milo asks, impressed.

"She bakes for every occasion," Parker answers for me.

I nod, lifting off the lid. "It's true."

"Ahem," Parker blurts, leaning across me to snag a cupcake. "Doesn't your boyfriend get first pick?"

I flash him a fake smile. "Of course, honey bunny."

He chokes on a mouthful of cupcake. He pounds on his chest, forcing it down his throat. "Okay," he says hoarsely. "I see what you mean about the nicknames."

Milo looks between us like he's solving a riddle. "How long have you two been dating?"

"Not long," I mumble, pinching a snickerdoodle.

"It took a lot of convincing and chatting in and between classes," Parker adds.

Milo breaks a cookie in half. "You two seem really close, but I was asking Jamie about you because I've never seen you guys hang out. She said she hadn't either." He shrugs. "It just seemed weird because she's friends with one of you and works with the other."

"It was on the down low," Parker replies. "You know what it's like."

Milo exhales slowly, slouching. "True."

"Are you and Jamie still good?" I ask.

A giddy smile sweeps across Milo's face. "Really good." He takes a bite of the snickerdoodle and his eyes light up. "Oh crap. These are crazy good."

I blush. "Thanks."

Milo gestures at the cliff. "You left me so stunned when you jumped. I can't believe you did it."

"Me either," I admit.

Parker cuddles into me. "Who knew she was so adventurous?"

I nudge him away. "Not me."

Jamie jogs toward us, targeting Parker. She twists her knuckles against his scalp, asking, "Have you been giving Milo a hard time?"

"Ouch," Parker complains, ducking away from her. "No, you maniac."

Jamie laughs and settles down by Milo. Her eyes light up at the cupcakes. "*Ooh.* Are those your red velvet ones?"

I nudge the Tupperware closer. "Yep. Have at it."

Jamie leans against Milo, making him recoil. "Dang. You're soaked."

"Duh. I was just in the water." She puts down the cupcake to wring out her hair. "Some of us have been jumping off cliffs, you know."

Milo winces as she flicks her wet hair at him. "Yeah, and I've dried off."

Jamie rolls her eyes and then smooches his cheek. "Stop being such a baby, Milo."

Milo muffles a laugh and then gestures at me. "We were just talking about how adventurous Kylie has been today."

Jamie's cheeks balloon as she nods with a mouthful of cupcake. She swallows and says, "I know. I totally thought you'd chicken out." She snaps her fingers. "Come to think of it, I owe Kai five bucks now."

My chin drops. "You were betting on me?"

"I can't believe Kai bet Kylie would do it." Parker laughs. "Maybe you're the new daredevil now."

I laugh. "Hardly."

Milo peers over his shoulder at his brother, who backflips into the water. "He clearly has more faith in you than in me."

Jamie hangs an arm over his shoulder. "No, he knows you too well to bet on you."

Parker snickers, leaning over to take a snickerdoodle. "Yeah, I wouldn't take that bet either." He sits up, giving me a wink. "But, as for Kylie, I'm always betting on her."

"*Ick.*" Jamie grimaces. "That was so sickly sweet I might barf."

Soon enough, the rest of the group joins and devours the snacks. My heart sinks when Lewis and Yvette don't join. Everyone congratulates me for jumping off the cliff on my first time up there. I smile and nod my thanks, but can't help keeping an eye on the water. Lewis and Yvette are swimming together, and I wish someone would call them over.

"So, no one could make Yvie jump?" Parker asks.

"She was hysterical," Tyler says with his lip upturned.

"Welcome to life with Yvette Anderson," Tabitha teases.

Kai snaps his fingers. "Hey, the fair is coming to town. Are we all going?"

Tabitha blows out a breath, side-eyeing the waterfall. "I think I'll hit my limit if I'm there with Yvie."

Jamie nudges Milo. "We're in, right?"

Milo half-smiles. "I guess."

"I've got nothing better to do," Tyler adds.

Kai pulls an arm around Tabitha. "Lewis will want to bring Yvie. We can't just exclude them."

"Maybe we just go in two groups?" Parker blurts. "Me, Kylie, Lewis, and Yvie can go in my car. Maybe we'll all meet up somewhere on the fairgrounds."

Kai looks at Tabitha. "Does that work?"

She nods. "The buffer room sounds good to me."

Parker nudges me. "Do you wanna come with me to tell Lewis and Yvie?"

I nod, and Parker latches onto my hand, leaving for the water. As we approach, it takes a moment to spot them. Parker leads me across the rocks, readying to call out to his friend and his crush.

He halts, making me run into his back. I peer around him, seeing Lewis and Yvette swimming to the base of the waterfall.

Tiptoeing across the wet, slippery rocks, Yvette leads Lewis by the hand behind the waterfall.

I glance at Parker and then back at the waterfall. Through the haze of the water, the couple comes into view.

My heart sinks.

Oh no.

They're not...

Yvette throws her head back, giggling as Lewis wraps his arms around her waist. They cuddle under the rush of water flowing overhead.

My mouth runs dry and everything goes out of focus, except for these two.

Like magnets, their lips press together with unbreakable force.

No.

No, no, no.

Did I do this? Did what I said about Parker and I kissing push her into doing this incredibly romantic display?

Suddenly, I'm yanked by the hand and spun to the side.

"Don't look," Parker whispers as my face lands by the nape of his neck. "I can tell it's upsetting you. Don't do it to yourself."

"If I don't look, it doesn't mean it didn't happen," I whisper back.

"But it won't hurt as bad."

At that, I look up at his face, and he gives me a sympathetic smile. Oh my gosh. He was saying it to himself as much as to me.

Great. Now my heart hurts for him too.

"I'll break them up," he whispers. "I promise."

I grab his hand and intertwine my pinky with his. "*We'll* break them up."

I know I shouldn't, but I glance back at the waterfall. Out from under the rush of the water, Lewis and Yvie are hugging. Yvie's head rests on Lewis's shoulder, and her stare points toward us.

Wait. It's not at us.

It's at Parker.

Whoa. Was she counting on him watching?

She kissed Lewis for Parker's benefit?

I blink hard to ensure my eyes aren't playing tricks on me. Yvette cuddles into Lewis, no longer looking in this direction.

A shiver runs down my spine.

I whack Parker's arm. "Did you see that?"

"Ugh. I told you not to look."

"No, not the kiss. The look. Yvette was looking at you."

"Huh?"

"I think she was checking if you were watching?"

Parker grins. "Do you mean, like, to see if I was jealous?"

With a growing smile, I nod my enthusiasm.

"Whoa."

"I kinda told her how amazing your kisses are and that I felt bad for all the other girls."

Parker laughs in shock. "You did what?"

"I just wanted to give her a taste of her own medicine."

Parker slings an arm across my shoulders. "Looks like it did the trick, Kikki."

"Ugh. Is that nickname really sticking?"

"I can go back to sweetie-pie, if you like?"

I cup a hand over my eyes. "I literally don't know which one is worse."

We move toward the rest of the group when Lewis and Yvette make their way over from the cove. Parker scoops up their towels and motions for me to follow. We meet the two who thank us for the towels.

"I didn't expect it to be so icy under the waterfall," Yvette says, shivering under the towel.

Lewis blushes. "Worth it, though?"

Yvette sneaks a glance at Parker as she answers, "Yeah, of course."

Parker nudges me, and I'm prompted to say something.

"Ah," I falter. "It sure is romantic here."

"I'll say," Lewis replies. "I never thought of it like that until today."

"That's probably why you didn't kiss me like they did," Yvette says, looking away.

Lewis is caught off guard. "What was that?"

Yvette wrings out her hair, keeping her gaze downcast. "I don't like feeling jealous."

"I'm not surprised," Parker says. "Kylie said your eyes practically bugged out when you guys were talking about me and Kylie kissing."

Lewis looks at Yvette for clarification. "Huh?"

"What?" Yvette shrugs. "They're kisses are hot."

Baffled, Lewis gestures at the waterfall. "What was that back there? Wasn't that hot?"

Yvette flicks her wet hair off her shoulders. "Yeah, but we're catching up."

Wounded, Lewis glances at Parker and then back at his girlfriend.

Oof. Could she cut him any deeper?

Parker wraps his arms around me and kisses the side of my head. "If I'm good, it's only because I'm with this beauty."

There's silence as both Lewis and Yvette stare at me.

My skin crawls. I seriously hate this sideshow thing I have going on.

"No way," Lewis says, grabbing Yvette's hand. "Parker is not a better kisser than I am. Have you seriously been thinking about him?"

Yvette shrugs.

"Look," Parker says awkwardly. "The rest of the group were talking about going to the fair tomorrow night. We just came over to see if you two were into the idea."

Yvette's eyes run up and down Parker. "Sounds like fun."

"Yeah, man," Lewis says, yanking on Yvette's hand. "Sounds good."

Lewis leads Yvette toward the rest of the group. We head over as Tyler stands with his bag and says his goodbyes.

"Ty, can you take Yvie and I home?" Lewis asks, grabbing his bag.

Tyler shrugs. "Sure, man. You're not going home with Parker?"

"No, I just need to get home earlier," Lewis says in a rush.

Yvette winces. "Good. I can't wait to wash my hair."

"I can..." Parker begins.

"It's all good," Lewis interrupts. "We'll see you guys tonight, right?"

Parker lifts a hand in a confused wave. "Yeah, sure."

Yvette wiggles her fingers in a wave. "See ya later."

I watch them leave with Tyler and mumble. "See you guys."

It's not long until everyone else starts packing up and I get into Parker's car.

"Wow, Lewis must be super peeved at you," I say, buckling my seatbelt.

Parker gives me a doubtful look.

"He clearly wanted Yvie away from you."

Parker grins as he reverses the car onto the dirt road. "Well, I am the superior male."

My eyes roll. "Oh, brother."

Parker laughs. "What? No good?"

"Can you be serious for a minute?" I ask. "If he didn't want to ride back with us, won't it make tonight awkward?"

He shakes his head. "It won't be a problem. Lewis and I argue over the dumbest stuff, and it's never affected our friendship."

"But you were both single then."

"Kylie, it's cool."

I'm not so certain. Whatever happens, I need to make sure these boys remain friends.

On the way home, Parker continues to chuckle over Yvette lusting after him and his best friend's jealousy. I can't believe this scheme is actually working.

Could Yvette already be thinking of breaking up with Lewis? If she wants Parker, I'm more than happy to hand him over.

When he pulls up in my driveway, Parker asks, "What are you wearing tonight?"

"To Alto Burgers?" I ask, confused. "I dunno, like a T-shirt and denim shorts."

His eyebrow raises. "On a date?"

"It's a burger place."

"But you're going up against Yvette."

I sink into the seat. "Oh right, Victoria Falls Barbie."

He pats my arm. "Wear a dress."

"I don't want to stand out. It's a pretty casual place."

"You need to stand out. You're getting Lewis's attention, right?"

"What are you wearing?"

He smirks. "A T-shirt and jeans."

I scoff, folding my arms.

He shrugs. "It's different for guys. Besides, I've clearly gotten Yvie's attention. Tonight, you need to work a little magic."

I huff. "Can't baking be enough?"

"I got into Yvie's head during the car ride this morning. She knows Lewis loves your baking. Now, get him drooling over how you look, and you'll steal his attention from her."

My skin chills with uncertainty. "How do you always make things sound so simple?"

He chucks my chin. "You've gotta have faith, Green. Optimism always wins out."

I exhale slowly, opening the car door. "Okay. I'll try to get it together."

Eleven

With a huff, I end my call with Josie. I rambled about every thought and feeling I had, making her head spin. Just like on Friday morning at school, Josie repeated that I wasn't making sense. But I needed to purge.

At the lake, so many things were perfect. The kiss, the sitting under a shady tree, holding hands, and even the cliff jump.

It was just the wrong guy.

Thinking about sharing all those moments with Parker makes me want to rip out my hair. I hate that I'm having all these giddy moments with him instead of Lewis. Now, leaning against a window on the second-floor landing of my house, I stare at the fence between mine and Lewis's homes.

It's crazy I'm putting on this facade. And I have to do it again tonight. Can't I just skip all this pretending? Can't Lewis and I just be together now?

I sigh against the window frame.

All I want is time alone with him.

No Parker.

No Yvette.

Below, I spy Lewis taking out the trash.

Normally, this is as far as it goes. I stare at him until he returns inside. But now we've talked. We've shared a car ride. He's seen me kiss another boy, and his stare lingered.

Goosebumps roll down my arms, and I dash away from the window. I rush down the staircase and race to the front door.

"Kikki? Where's the fire?" Mom calls out.

"I'll be right back," I reply, pulling the front door open.

When I step off the porch, I spot him walking away from the trash cans.

Before I chicken out, I jog to the fence line. "Lewis!"

He looks up and around before landing on me. "Oh, hi."

Catching my breath, I blurt, "How are you getting to dinner tonight?"

He gives me an uneasy look. "I'm not going with Parker. Nothing personal, but..."

"I'm not going with Parker either," I blurt. When surprise hits his face, I add, "I just mean, he texted. He'll be late. *Again*. He thought I should meet him there. I was just wondering if you..."

I trail off when my gut tenses, warning this is a bad idea.

"Oh, do you want to go there with me?" Lewis asks.

Yes! Just you and me!

"Well, there's a bus that heads to Main Street at six-thirty. We could take that," he suggests.

A squeal escapes me before I can catch it.

Lewis laughs. "Glad to see you're excited."

I blush, looking down at my shoes before I embarrass myself further. "Sorry. Just glad not to get there on my own."

"No sweat," Lewis says. "It'll be cool to head over together."

My heart swells, and I bite my lip in anticipation of another squeal.

Lewis Freaking Allen and I are going on a date together.

Granted, it's to meet up with our actual dates. But, for now, I can forget that part.

"Okay, cool," I say, hoping to sound casual. "I'll see you later tonight then."

"Meet out front at six-fifteen," Lewis says, "and then we'll walk to the bus stop?"

I contract every muscle inside me to halt the need to squeal. It doesn't take fifteen minutes to walk to the bus stop. I'm getting *extra* one-on-one time with him.

"Okay," I say in a higher pitch because I'm on the cusp of squealing. "See you then."

I turn on my heels and pace to my house, struggling to keep the squealing excitement inside me.

When I shut the front door behind me, I bundle my hands into fists and jump in place.

"*Yes!*" I shriek, punching the air as the delight takes over my body.

"Kikki?" Mom asks, backtracking down the hallway.

I skip toward her, kiss her on the cheek, and keep moving toward the staircase.

"What's going on?" she asks, bewildered.

"I have to get ready for my date," I call, racing upstairs and letting a trail of giggles spill out of me.

In my bedroom, I scoop up my phone and call Parker.

He answers. "Hi?"

"Don't pick me up tonight," I blurt.

"What?" Panic reverberates in his voice. "But you promised to come tonight."

"Yeah, I'm still going," I reply. "I'm just going with Lewis instead."

He sighs into the receiver. "Okay, slow down. Can you start at the beginning?"

"I just organized to take the bus into town with Lewis," I explain. "I told him you'll be late, and that you told me to meet you there."

"I have to be late tonight?"

"I don't really care, to be honest. I'm going with Lewis. Nothing else matters."

"*Geez*, Green, I'm impressed."

I mumble a laugh. "Thanks."

"So, what's happening with Yvie?"

"I have no idea. She doesn't live near us, so I assume she's meeting us at dinner."

"I'll call her. See you tonight, Kikki."

"Don't call me..." I don't finish the sentence, because he's already ended the call. "Okay, bye then."

I fling the phone onto my bed and wander over to my wardrobe to find my cutest dress.

No brainer, right?

Anything blue.

With blow-dried hair, a fresh face of makeup, and a light spray of perfume, I'm ready to join Lewis for our bus ride into town. The caramel color of my wedge sandals and clutch purse perfectly accent the cerulean blue of my dress.

I say goodbye to my parents before skipping out the front door.

Lewis lets out a whistle as he walks down my front path. "You look great."

I clutch my chest, blushing. "Oh my gosh, really?"

"Sure. Parker won't be able to take his eyes off you."

My bliss decreases. Does he only care about Parker not looking at his girlfriend?

"Are you okay?"

I snap out of my thoughts. "Yeah."

"Looked like you were frowning."

"Oh, no, I'm okay."

We set off down the sidewalk, and Lewis says, "I know what's got you down."

How could he possibly?

"It's Parker, isn't it?" Lewis asks.

"Huh?"

"You're peeved he's not taking you to Alto Burger tonight," Lewis guesses. "I totally get it. It's date night. You'd want your boyfriend by your side."

I tilt my head, making sure he catches my smile. "It's okay because I have good company with me."

"Well, thanks. Why haven't we hung out before?" Lewis asks. "I mean, we live next door to each other."

It takes me off guard, and I almost trip over my own feet. I let out a nervous laugh, and reply, "Yeah, that's what I was thinking."

"I guess it took you dating my best friend to make it happen."

"Yeah, I guess."

"I think it's worked out for the best, don't you? Not only does Yvie want to double date, but she also wants to replace her friend who left town."

Repulsion fills my veins. "I'm nothing like Camila."

Lewis raises his palms defensively. "Oh, I know. I mean, she wants to upgrade her friendship."

"Oh." I blush. "Thanks."

A breathy laugh sings out of him. "No problem."

"Oh, I wanted to congratulate you," I rush before I chicken out, "on your photography nomination. I went to your last exhibition. You're really talented."

"You were there?" He blushes, rubbing the back of his neck. "Thanks. How come I didn't see you?"

I shrug. "You were with your friends."

He nudges me. "Well, you're in the group now."

"Umm, I was thinking, maybe you and I hanging out is super important," I say before my lack of confidence shuts me down. "Yes, I'm dating Parker, and yes, Yvie and I want to be friends, but I can't really be friends with either of them if I'm not friends with you. You're the glue holding the four of us together."

"You think?"

"Absolutely. Maybe you and I should hang out more?" My voice cracks, shattering my illusion of confidence, but I push through. "What do you think?"

"I'm up for these double dates. I don't know if you know this, but this is the first time I've had a girlfriend. It's cool I get to do all this with my best friend by my side. Smashes my nerves."

"You're nervous?"

"I just want to be good at this," he admits. "I have a lot to live up to with a girl like Yvie."

I frown, swallowing something sour. He deserves so much better than a superficial girlfriend. I hope, once this is all over, he can see her as a fake first girlfriend.

"Sorry," he mumbles. "Did I make you uncomfortable?"

I shake out of my thoughts. "No."

"You don't have to worry about Parker, you know. He doesn't expect you to be anything you're not."

I nod, knowing I'm more on the same page with Parker than he is.

An easy laugh tumbles out of him. "You already hooked him earlier today. Jumping off that cliff. Man, that was impressive. I can't believe you actually did it."

I place my hands on my hips in an attempt to appear brave. "Really?"

"Yeah. Everyone chickens out on their first time."

I smile, holding back a laugh. "Did you?"

He rubs the back of his neck. "I'm surprised Parker didn't already tell you. He never lets anything go."

"I've noticed that."

"But I'm no chicken now. You saw my backflips, right?"

I giggle. "Sure did."

"Good, because I didn't want you thinking you're more of a daredevil than me."

I fan my face in disbelief. Lewis and I are actually chatting. "I would never."

He motions ahead. "We're almost there. You're not going to gloat while we wait for the bus, are you?"

"I would never." I bat my lashes as I grin. "Even if I'm acting more like a part of Wasteland Squad than you."

Impressed, Lewis's eyes widen. "You watch those movies?"

I clasp my hands and giggle, picturing the movie poster on his bedroom wall. "They're only my favorite action movies."

"Wow. You're not like other girls."

Oh my gosh. Are Lewis and I flirting?

Beep, beep. My phone vibrates with the notification sound, but I have zero interest in checking it. I mean, why would I? I'm in the presence of the most beautiful boy in Victoria Falls.

"Was that your phone?" Lewis asks.

I shrug. "Yeah, but I don't need to check it."

Lewis chuckles. "Wow. I can't stand knowing I have an unread text."

Oops. Does he think I'm weird now?

I pull out my phone and say, "Well, just checking it won't hurt, I guess."

Lewis gives me an approving smile. It's so hard to look away from him for the sake of my stupid phone.

It's a text from Parker. *"You're not going to be happy."*

My brow furrows as I reread his message. I reply with the only response that comes to mind. *"????"*

"Yvie's taking the bus."

I suck in a ragged breath, but quickly dismiss the irrational fear. *"So? She'll be on a different route from us."*

"Apparently not."

Ahead, the number twenty-two bus slows to a stop. Three passengers disembark, and...

Oh no.

One is Yvette.

With a beyond chipper grin and lifted on tippy toes, she waves madly at us.

Beside me, Lewis's chest inflates. His shoulders seem to broaden, and pep livens his steps.

My stomach drops, and I fall into a dawdle as Lewis meets up with his girlfriend. When they hug, I'm ready to hurl on the sidewalk.

Crap.

This is why he wanted to get to the bus stop early.

For her.

Lewis greets her with a hug, and it feels like my insides are disintegrating.

"Kylie?" Yvette says with surprise, pulling out of Lewis's arms. "I thought you'd be going with Parker."

Lewis rolls his eyes. "He's running late again."

"Oh, that's so weird," Yvette says, screwing up her face. "Why would he offer to drive me then? He wanted me to be late too?"

Lewis's back stiffens. "Parker texted you?"

Yvette shrugs. "I only just replied. I don't know when he asked. Maybe he thought I'd be late. I mean, *this* does take a long time to perfect."

Lewis chuckles, kissing the side of her head. "You're already perfect."

Okay, now I'm really gonna puke.

"Well, I'm glad we all get to hang out. Thank you, guys, for agreeing to take the bus," Yvette rambles. "My parents want me on this whole no-dating kick, so I didn't want them to see a guy picking me up for dinner. They think I need a break, but what do they know? So, if anyone asks, I'm hanging with Tabby at the mall. Like, they don't know Tabby and I are barely talking, but, whatever."

Lewis hangs an arm across Yvette's shoulders. "Any way I get to see you works for me."

Is he serious? She just mentioned she dates too much—that her parents think she dates too much—and he breezed past it?

How do I wake this boy up?

Like a true third-wheel, I sit with this couple on the bus stop bench. *Great.* Our bus better not be late because I can already tell this will be the longest ten minutes of my life.

Lewis and Yvette snuggle and whisper like they're in their own world. Sickness rolls through my stomach as he looks at her like she's the only girl for miles.

I'm such an idiot. How could I have thought he was into me on our walk over here? Of course, he was doing anything to see Yvette again. I will never beat her for his attention.

After an agonizing wait, the bus pulls up at our stop. I let the loved-up couple board first, dawdling behind. I take a seat adjacent to theirs and slouch down. As the bus moves toward town, Yvette continues to giggle as Lewis's arms wrap around her.

I'm ready to scream when he starts giving her butterfly kisses against the nape of her neck.

Before I yell at them to stop it, I pull out my phone and let my fury out in a text to Parker. *"I'm never traveling to a double date without you ever again."*

He replies, *"Is she on the bus with you?"*

"Yes. I'm such an idiot. I was starting to believe Lewis wanted it to be just the two of us."

"Don't be hard on yourself. It was a ballsy move trying to get alone time with Lewis. It should've worked."

"But it didn't. He wants to be with her. I'm just a tag along."

"I'll try to drive Yvie home tonight so you and Lewis can take the bus. It'd make no sense for her to take two buses home again."

"It didn't make any sense for her to leave so early to meet up with us this way. I thought Barbie needed hours to plaster on all the makeup."

"Don't spiral. You need to perk up tonight. I'm getting in the car now so you're not left alone with them at Alto's."

"Good. I need you to stop them from being so cuddly. I'm already having trouble keeping my stomach contents down."

"Remember what I told you at the lake? Don't watch. It's not worth it."

"It's hard."

"I know."

I put the phone down so he can drive to Alto Burger. This is a development I certainly didn't expect. I'm on the bus with Lewis, but I'm dying to see Parker. The situation is just so topsy-turvy. Usually, if I were going to complain to someone, I'd be texting Josie. But Parker gets this. With him, I have someone who sees this situation in my perspective. And, without him by my side, being around Lewis and Yvette is unnerving.

We get off the bus and walk along the path toward the front deck of Alto Burger. The decking spans the entire length of the restaurant with timber flooring, and the railing is decorated with twinkle lights. Picnic-style tables and bench seats fill the outdoor space, and like always, it's crazy crowded because everyone loves the chill vibe and the view of the mountains.

Lewis leads as we maneuver our way across the deck and stops three tables deep.

"I thought you were running late?" Lewis asks.

I peek around him and find Parker sitting on top of a table with his feet resting on a bench seat.

Parker stretches his arms to the side. "Aren't you gonna thank me for snagging us a table?"

My body relaxes with relief at the sound of his voice.

He jumps off the table and says, "My dimwit brother said he needed a ride, but then hitched with a friend. Anyway, it made me ready earlier than I expected."

"Oh, is that why you texted me?" Yvette blurts.

Parker's smile twitches as he takes in the heated stare from Lewis.

I stand at Lewis's side, staring at Parker like he's a life preserver. He moves over to me, ignoring the others as kindness eases any hesitation in his expression.

Parker presses on my shoulder. "Can I talk to you for a minute?"

"Aww," Yvette beams. "It's so cute how you two miss each other."

Ugh. I can't stand her voice for another second. I grab Parker's wrist and step backwards. "Yes, you can."

Parker looks over his shoulder at Lewis. "Make sure no one steals our table."

Clutching her hand, Lewis walks Yvette over to the table. "No problem."

We backtrack, and Parker asks, "How was the trip over?"

My chest rises with hot breath. "Ugh. I can't believe Yvette showed up. She ruined everything. Lewis and I were actually talking."

"Really? What about?"

For a moment, hope lightens my mood. "He asked why we never hang out. Like, he wants to be friends with me."

Parker grins. "That's awesome."

"I even said to him that me and him being friends was super important. That I couldn't be friends with Yvie or you if Lewis and I didn't hang out. Like, the dynamic wouldn't work."

"And he agreed?"

I nod heartily. "I thought so. I really thought he was into spending time with me. Then Yvie got off that stupid bus and wrecked everything. Once she was around, I was totally invisible to him. It was brutal. Ugh, and she does not shut up."

Parker laughs.

I deadpan him. "I'm serious."

He strokes a hand down my shoulder, swallowing the laughter. "Okay, I'm sorry. Look, it sucks that happened. I really thought you had a clear shot with him. But I guess they organized the bus trip once they left the lake with Tyler."

I sink into my pout. "Mm-hmm."

He tilts his head. "Are you gonna perk up?"

I fold my arms. "I dunno."

"Do you think pouting will win over Yvie's giggle?"

I retch, dropping my arms to my side.

"We should get back over there," Parker says.

I nod but can't help dawdling my steps.

Parker slides a hand on my back, which I want to think it's for support, but it's probably just to hurry me up. His hand can press as firmly into my back as he likes. Nothing is making me excited to get back to that table.

Twelve

Just a few feet from the table, we witness Yvette snuggling into Lewis. When her head nuzzles against his shoulder, a fiery rage boils inside me. My blood fizzles and pops in my veins as the confusing mess of anger and insecurity writhes inside me.

I just can't stare at them and feel second best. I don't want them to awe at me and call me cute like some kind of pet. They need to know I'm on their level. I'm a girl worth chasing. I don't deserve to be invisible.

As my emotions peak, Parker's hand presses into my back. He turns me toward him, and there's an intensity in his eyes. My brow furrows to question him, but before I utter a word, my body takes over. On instinct, I lift onto my toes as he leans in and plants his lips on mine.

For a moment, I struggle with resistance, but then my arms snake around his neck. My lips twitch with friction, and I let him set the pace of our kiss. Our chests press together as he holds me upright so I don't stumble on my tippy toes.

My anger dissipates, and I ease into the solace of being on the same page as Parker. This kiss isn't for us. It's for our audience of two.

We want them to watch.

We want them to get jealous.

We want them to want us.

Gradually, my arms roll off his shoulders, and my hands slide down his chest. My eyes open as our lips part and my heels touch the ground.

"Wow," he mumbles. "How come you're so good at that?"

I blush, giggling. I wish he'd said it louder or waited until we were back at the table to say it.

He takes my hand and walks me to the empty bench seat across from our observers.

Yvette's eyebrow raises as she takes us in. "I thought you two were making out when you were out of view."

Parker shrugs, resting an arm across my shoulders. "Maybe we were."

Lewis sits back, looking away from us. "Can we please stop talking about who's kissing who?"

I sit a little taller. "Agreed."

Lewis turns his face back and sends me a smile.

I relax, smiling back at him. That is until Parker's fingertips massage my upper arm. I want nothing more than to fling him off, but I know it'd make our kiss for nothing. But can't he just let the moments between Lewis and me breathe? We're not like him and Yvette. We need to take in our moments and let our feelings grow naturally.

Lewis leans into Yvie. "You wanna order?"

"I never come here," Yvette says, lip upturning. "I don't even know what they have."

Lewis stands, taking Yvette's hand. "Come to the counter with me and we'll check out the menu."

Lewis and Yvette leave for the counter inside the restaurant, and I slouch with a huff.

Parker lifts his arm off me. "You're down again."

"You're touching me too much."

"So? I'm your boyfriend."

"But Lewis and I were having a moment. Don't touch me when that happens."

"I'm trying to make him jealous."

I groan. "And I'm trying to get him to like me."

"Okay, fine." He huffs, hiking a leg over the bench seat. "I'll give you some breathing room. What are you ordering?"

"I want the whadda burger."

Parker hums. "That's my favorite thing on the menu."

"Really? Mine too." I smirk. "Do you think we'll look too coupley if we order the same thing?"

"Hmm, maybe. Maybe you should order a double sizzler burger, like Lewis."

"Ugh, I was joking. Besides, the double sizzler isn't that great."

"Don't let Lewis hear you say that."

"If you don't think we should order the same, why don't you get the same as Yvette? I think she's ordering a lettuce leaf."

Parker gives me an unimpressed look. "*Ha, ha.*"

I nudge him off the bench seat. "Just order me a whadda burger. You're paying because we're on a date."

He exhales in shock. "Wow, look at you calling the shots."

I fold my arms and give him a smug smile. "Think of it as paying me back for all the baking I'll be doing."

He gives me a salute and heads towards the counter. "Okay, girlfriend."

I roll my eyes but can't help smiling as he makes his way inside.

Even though the deck is crowded, I manage to find some peace as I sit alone at the table. I look out at the dusk sky and admire the muted colors of the mountainous backdrop.

Lewis and Yvette make their way back to the table before Parker.

"Is Parker still inside?" Lewis asks.

I nod. "Yeah. I wanted to stay outside and soak up the view."

Lewis grins, viewing the mountains. "It's awesome. This is seriously one of the best places in town."

Yvette clears her throat. "You're only saying that because you haven't been to Fratelli's."

"What did you order, Yvie?" I cut in.

"I got the eezy-peezy burger."

I rub my lips together, suppressing a laugh. This place is known for its gourmet-style burgers, and she got the plainest thing on the menu. Lewis has to be disappointed.

"Is Parker ordering yours?" Lewis asks.

"Yep. I'm getting the whadda burger."

He smirks. "Copying Parker?"

"Heck no. He's copying me."

At that, Lewis laughs.

"What's so funny?" Parker asks, slipping into the space beside me.

"Just your girlfriend," Lewis says, smiling at me.

Oh gosh. Did it just get hot out here?

"Oh, I already knew that," Parker says, like it's no big deal.

I don't care. I keep my shared gaze with Lewis, feeling every flutter and sizzle of electricity inside my chest.

Yvette combs her fingers through Lewis's hair, remarking, "Some girls need to be funny."

My heart short-circuits as Lewis's eyes break contact with mine, giving Yvette his full attention.

"I dunno, it might just be me," Yvette says in a breathy voice, "but I spend all my time laughing at my boyfriend's jokes."

Lewis grins. "Do I need to make you laugh more?"

She snuggles into him. "Haven't you noticed how easily I laugh?"

My eyes roll hard. Who hasn't heard that ear-piercing giggle?

Parker and I sit in silence, watching Yvette and Lewis attempting to make us lose our appetites with their flirting. I could thank the heavens when our meals hit the table.

"Aww, cute," Yvette says, picking up her no-frills burger. "It's so small, I love it."

Lewis playfully nudges her. "You're the only person to come to Alto Burger and be glad they got a small burger."

Yvette leans over to view Lewis's burger. "What's so special about yours?"

Lewis lifts the top burger bun, revealing the two layers of grilled beef patty, with layers of cheese, ketchup, pickles, and lettuce. "This is the best burger in history. It puts yours to shame."

Yvette grins. "Whatever."

Lewis side-eyes her. "You've got no idea."

"Okay, let me try it then."

Lewis lifts the burger, and Yvette takes a bite. My insides clamp down, because it's both adorable and romantic. Dang it. I wanna share food with Lewis. I want to tell him why my burger is far superior to his.

"Mmm." Yvette closes her eyes as she savors the bite. She pushes her plate away, swallowing. "Wow, I don't even wanna try mine."

Lewis laughs, hanging a thumb toward the counter. "Do you want me to order you another burger?"

"No, I'll just have another bite of yours. I'll be full after that."

My eyes roll hard. *Give me a break.* Choosing to tune them out, I lift my burger to take a bite. Parker does the same, obviously struggling with listening to them as well.

I keep biting, hoping that the more burger I shovel into my mouth, the less I'll be able to hear. With plump cheeks, I drop the last half of my burger on my plate. Every chew is an effort, but it distracts me from the nauseating sight across the table.

Yvette cackles. "*Eww,* Kylie. Do you even know how to eat around other people?"

My eyes stay glued to my plate, unwilling to give her the satisfaction of eye contact.

"You'd know why she can't stop eating if you'd ordered a real burger," Parker says. "*We* ordered the best thing on the menu."

Yvette reaches across the table. "Let me try."

Before Parker can hand her his burger, Lewis catches her hands. "Umm, no. You don't want to try that."

Yvette shrugs, leaning against her boyfriend. "Whatever you say, babe."

Babe?

BABE?!?

With tension expanding between my shoulder blades, I pick up my burger. I still need to swallow the remainder of my last mouthful, but I take another bite, regardless. Zoning them out, I focus on chewing and swallowing until there's no burger left on my plate.

Yvette sniggers. "Are you gonna lick your plate clean?"

She needs to stop commenting about me, or I'm going to snap.

Parker finishes his burger, pushing his plate aside. "I'm telling you, it's the best burger in Victoria Falls."

"Is that so?" Yvette says in her breathy voice.

"No, he's wrong," Lewis says flatly.

"My boyfriend says you're wrong." Yvette's tone turns into a baby voice. "And my boyfriend would know."

Parker shifts on the bench seat. "Oh, is that so?"

"Yep," Yvette says, going up another octave. "He's only been in town a year and knows it better than you."

"And how do you know what I know?" Parker asks in a flirty tone. "You don't know my secrets. I know parts of Victoria Falls you've never heard of."

"Well, if they're all like Alto Burger, I won't be impressed," Yvette teases. "You need to step up your game."

"Do you really think your boyfriend will take you to fancy places?"

I lift my head to catch the look Yvette gives Lewis. "He will if he wants to keep me around."

Lewis rushes in to kiss Yvette. Yvette wraps an arm around Lewis's neck, kissing him back with some of the grossest sounds I've ever heard.

Parker sits back, jolted by the change of events. His head turns my way, and I swear he's gone a shade paler.

When they pull out of the kiss, Lewis says, "Does that tell you I'll take you any place you want?"

Yvette giggles, practically jumping onto Lewis's lap. "Oh, baby, you're gonna do just fine."

Inadvertently, I shudder with disgust. Parker gradually exhales, and he gently touches my back in a gesture of support. Needing more from him, I snatch his hand and intertwine our fingers. I give him an apologetic look, which I hope conveys I'm unable to let go of him.

"Like, I hope you two aren't jealous or anything," Yvette says, glancing our way before turning back to Lewis. "I mean, I just know what I want and need out of a relationship. I know you guys are newbies at relationships, so don't compare yourselves to us."

What the heck? Why is she baiting us?

"I don't know if you've noticed, Yvie," Parker says, "but Kylie and I are doing fine."

Yvie mumbles a laugh under her breath. A move I know too well, hearing her snide comments in class. "Like, you two are doing fine," she says in a mocking tone, "but it's like baby steps. It's cute, but it's not really on the same level."

What the heck? She's lying! I know for a fact she was jealous of us. I saw it at the lake.

Yvette looks at Lewis, prompting him to agree. "I mean, that's what we think, right, babe? They're totally adorable together."

I clamp down on Parker's hand. His jaw flexes as his head swivels, edging his mouth close to my ear.

"Ouch," he whispers through a tight mouth.

I don't relent. As I crush his hand, my eyes widen as I stare at him.

He doubles down on a disapproving glare, begging me to release his hand.

Fed up, he stands from his seat and reefs me up by the hand.

"Excuse us a minute," he says flatly, and hikes a leg over the bench.

As I turn to follow him, Yvette pipes up. "Aww, it's so cute how you two need privacy to talk. I've never been like that with any of my boyfriends."

Ugh! Why won't she ever shut up?

Parker jerks me away from the table, and I fumble behind him as we weave around the packed picnic tables.

"What the heck is up with you?" Parker hisses as he tugs me behind the south wall of Alto Burger.

"I was about to burst," I say, with no regard for the volume of my voice. "I couldn't stand another moment of listening to her."

Parker rubs his hand. "It didn't mean you had to break my hand."

I slouch. "I'm sorry. I didn't mean to take it out on you. The feelings had to go somewhere."

"Can you get it together?"

"No. I told you, I can't listen to her anymore." I grunt. "How can you? She's insulting you too."

"We rattled her today. She's trying to save face."

I retch. "I can't deal with these stupid games."

"We're faking a relationship. We're playing one big game."

I sniff hard, feeling a sob welling in my throat. "I want Lewis. I don't want to deal with her."

"This is a team effort," he says softly. "It's the first day, Kylie. You promised we'd do this until they break up."

I fold my arms and swallow my sadness. "I guess it's harder than I realized."

"This doesn't work if I don't have you by my side. Yeah, it sucks we have to witness everything they do and say, but we gotta roll with the punches."

I roll my eyes. "Don't tell me to be optimistic again."

"Optimism is the only way to get through tough stuff." He pauses for a beat, looking off to the side. "Trust me."

"It's just been a long first day, okay. I'm not throwing in the towel. I'm just hitting a limit."

Parker nods. "We won't stay out much later. Then we won't be hanging out with them again until tomorrow night at the fair. There's plenty of time to mellow out before then."

I exhale slowly. "I guess so."

He puts an arm around my back and walks me back to the decking. "We got this. One little meltdown isn't gonna stop us."

I smile, choosing to appreciate his optimistic take. "Totally."

When we get back to the table, Yvette is standing and pulling her purse strap over her shoulder. "I gotta go. The last bus to my place comes in five minutes."

Thank goodness.

"I can drive you home," Parker offers.

"No way," Yvette replies. "My dad will go ballistic if he sees me getting out of a boy's car. I promised to take a break from dating."

Parker smirks. "I'm not your boyfriend."

Yvette chews on a fingernail. "They won't believe that."

Parker slicks his hair back. "Because I'm so irresistible?"

"No, because I'm never single," Yvette replies. She leans over to peck Lewis's lips. "Call me when you get home."

He cups the sides of her face, kissing her with extra effort. "I will."

Parker motions to Lewis. "You're not going with her?"

"There's no connecting bus from her stop to my place in the evenings," Lewis replies. "Is it cool if I hitch a ride with you?"

"Yeah, I'm already driving to your neighbor's house."

"If Yvie's going home, can we head off too?" I ask, pivoting between the boys. "I'm beat."

Lewis stands, grinning. "I've no doubt, daredevil."

I blush and mumble a laugh.

"Did I miss something?" Parker asks.

"Just something me and your girlfriend we're chatting about earlier," Lewis teases. He slings an arm around Yvette, leaving the table before us.

Parker sends me a wink, and I let the good feelings bubble inside me.

We wait for Yvette's bus and try not to look when the two cuddle and kiss, dragging out their goodbyes.

Parker breaks before I do. He turns around and says, "You want us to leave you behind, Lewy?"

Yvette finally relents and boards the bus.

Lewis jogs our way. "Coming."

Thankfully, driving by car is much faster than going by bus. Although, I wouldn't have minded if Lewis and I had to take a long bus ride home together.

As he drives past Main Street, Parker plucks my hand from my lap and intertwines our fingers. I smile as we hold hands above the center console. I can't help thinking about Lewis watching this and maybe—just maybe—he'll be jealous.

After parking in front of my house, Parker kisses my hand.

"Thanks for tonight," I say, opening the car door.

"Give Brandy a hug from me," Parker says, waving goodbye.

I smile, closing the door. "Will do."

Parker drives away, and Lewis and I move off the curb.

"Brandy?" Lewis questions.

"My dog. She and Parker have bonded."

"Oh, that's awesome. He was really cut up when his dog passed away."

"Yeah, he told me. I couldn't even imagine."

He slips his hands in his pockets. "So, tonight was fun."

"Yeah, it was."

"I got a text from Kai while we were driving back. We're gonna meet up tomorrow at Morton's Café."

A thrill jumpstarts my heart. "Cool. I'm working tomorrow morning."

"Nice. Kai's bringing Tabby and I texted Yvie to come along. We're trying to help the girls make up so it's not so awkward when we hang out."

I trip on the cement path, catching myself before I fall.

Lewis clutches my arm. "You okay?"

I blush. "Yeah. Thanks."

He lets me go. "It's cool you and Yvie are hanging out, but I think she really misses Tabitha."

"Mm-hmm."

"Anyway, I'll see you tomorrow when I order an extra-large pancake stack."

I fake a smile and wave. "See you then."

He waves and moves over to his yard.

Even though I've collapsed into a hunch, I speed toward the front door. When I get inside, I rest against the back of the door and pull out my phone.

I text Parker, *"You have to come to the café tomorrow morning."*

My fingers tap along the sides of the phone, impatiently waiting for his reply. I remind myself he's driving home, and pull myself off the door.

"Kikki?" Dad asks, moving out of the living room. "Hi, honey. How was your night out?"

"It was good. The burger was incredible, as per usual."

"Good to hear. And Parker? Was he a gentleman?"

A shiver runs down my spine as our kiss on the deck replays in my mind. I shake out of the thought and find a smile on my face.

"Yes, of course."

Dad beams. "Oh, Kikki, you look so happy."

I move in for one of Dad's bear hugs. "I am, it's just..."

Dad pulls me into his arms, waiting for me to continue. I lean my head against him, leaving the unfinished sentence to linger.

"What is it, honey?"

I sigh. "Everything's fine with Parker. It was the other couple that put a hitch in the night."

Dad unravels his arms, looking down as I lift my head. "Tell me what happened."

"Nothing bad. It's just..." I huff. "I like Lewis. You know, from next door?"

"Sure, he's a good kid." Dad's brow lowers. "That is, when he's not driving. He didn't, did he?"

I nod hurriedly, moving out of the hug. "No, of course not. It's his girlfriend."

Dad's expression softens. "Oh, I see. You two don't get along?"

I frown, nodding.

Dad brushes back my hair. "Oh, Kikki. I completely understand how this can feel awkward. You want to make nice for the sake of your new boyfriend. I think if you're honest with Parker about not being comfortable around this girl, the two of you can find another couple to hang out with."

How do I tell Dad that Parker is well aware of my feelings without blurting out every aspect of our arrangement?

"Or," Dad says with a hint of mischief in his eyes, "you two could try going on a date on your own. Just a thought."

I roll my eyes at the laughter in his tone, and cover with, "Parker likes hanging out with his friends."

Dad chuckles. "It was just a suggestion. Your mother's upstairs reading. Maybe you want to knock on the door and get her opinion."

"I'm just feeling down because Lewis told me he's bringing his girlfriend to the café tomorrow. It sucks because I'll be working and can't avoid them."

"Maybe they'll sit in Jamie's section."

I nod, feeling a twinge of optimism. "Yeah, hopefully."

Beep, beep. I check my phone, and there's a new text from Parker.

I kiss Dad on the cheek and tell him I'm heading upstairs. He wishes me a good night, and I move up the hallway.

In the back room, Brandy's curled up on her dog bed. I detour over to her and scratch her behind the ear, whispering, "Parker says hi."

She crooks her head and then sneakily licks my jaw.

I recoil, wiping the wet spot with the back of my hand. "Uh, thanks for the kiss, girl."

As I crouch by Brandy, I open the text message.

"Already missing me?"

Ugh. *"Lewis told me he's taking Yvette. Kai asked him because they're trying to patch things between her and Tabitha."*

"Crap. Okay, I'll be there."

I lower the phone, feeling the slither of optimism growing.

If anyone knows how to get in the middle of this reunion, it's Parker.

Thirteen

Whenever I work a Sunday morning shift at the café, I'm usually excited at the prospect of seeing Lewis. It's the highlight of a day that also includes early morning baking.

But today, all I feel is dread.

Last night was a disaster. Yvette was at her worst, and every chance I got to build on something with Lewis, it was destroyed.

Ugh, and I kissed Parker again.

I've really got to stop doing that.

I yawned my way through this morning's setup. Overnight, I was lucky to get a wink of sleep. I tossed and turned, imagining Yvette's shrill laughter echoing throughout the café. Whenever my mind replays last night's date, I jolt with shudders.

"Are you okay?" Jamie asks, readying the milkshake machines.

I wipe under my eye. "Just tired."

"Was yesterday at the lake more exercise than you usually do in a day?"

I frown. "Yes, actually. Plus, we went out to dinner last night."

"Who's we?"

"Parker, Lewis, Yvette, and me."

"Wow." Her eyes widen. "You guys are inseparable."

It's hard to hide the dissatisfaction from my face. "Mmm."

"Are you and Yvette actually becoming friends?"

I blow out a breath. "For the boys' sake, I'm trying."

Jamie nods as if a lightbulb's flashed inside her mind. "Ah, okay."

"She's coming here today."

Jamie almost snaps the jug against the base of the milkshake machine. "What was that?"

"Lewis is bringing her here."

"Yvette is coming to my café?" she says, growing red. "Why do these girls keep coming here? They're supposed to stay at Village Coffee."

"Can you seat them in your section?"

Jamie scoffs. "No way."

"They're coming with Kai and Tabitha."

At that, Jamie is livid. "Kai is behind this?"

I shrug sheepishly. "That's what Lewis said."

"That rat!" she yelps. "How could he not give me a head's up?"

"Maybe because you'd be mad?"

Jamie rolls her eyes. "Duh."

"What's with the raised voices?" Maddy asks, exiting the kitchen.

"Yvette Anderson is coming to the café today," Jamie says.

Maddy gives a blank expression. "Am I supposed to know who that is?"

"One of the Miss Perfects." Jamie huffs. "Tabitha's friend."

"Ex-friend," I clarify.

"Whatever." Jamie jams the milkshake jug into the machine. "Why do they need to have their reunion here?"

"Lay off the equipment," Maddy scolds. "Stop being so rough."

"You should've seen them yesterday," Jamie complains. "They fought over the dumbest stuff."

"I don't know how the boys think some pancakes will mend their relationship," I say in agreement.

Jamie moves to the back office and grabs her phone. "I'm texting Kai to call it off."

Yes!

"Jamie, put the phone down," Maddy says in a tired tone.

"I'm doing us all a favor," Jamie protests.

"Let your friends bring their girlfriends," Maddy replies.

Jamie drops the phone into the pocket of her apron and raises her palms. "It's sent."

I can't help grinning. I try to minimize it when I catch Maddy looking my way.

During the first hour of service, I'm shaky. Every time the door opens, and the chime rings, a bolt of anxiety ricochets throughout my body. But once the booths fill in the proceeding hour, my nervousness fizzles out.

Maybe Jamie's text worked? I look across the café floor to get a read on her. She's busy taking an order, fidgeting the way she does when she gets tongue-tied. Probably not the best time to ask her about the text to Kai when her jitters have taken over.

When the kitchen bell dings, I make my way to the food pass, choosing to take this as a win. My morning hasn't been ruined by Yvette. As I carry the plates to their destined table, the front door chimes. I place the plates down in front of the couple and grit my teeth as I peer over my shoulder. My back arches with curiosity as Parker and Tyler stroll in with their skateboards.

I leave the table to meet them in the aisle.

"Morning girlfriend," Parker says with a cheesy grin.

He leans in to peck my cheek and I use all my might not to recoil. "Hi."

"Ty and I met up after he finished training this morning," Parker says. "We thought we'd stop by and say hi."

I motion at the bustling tables. "None of your friends are here."

Parker nudges Tyler. "Wasn't your dad just talking to Kai's dad? Did he say anything about where Kai was?"

Tyler doesn't catch on. "No, why would he?"

"Because I thought Kai and the others were going to be here this morning."

"Oh, they're definitely going out for breakfast," Tyler says. "Kai told me I'd see him later."

"Just later?" Parker asks. "Or here?"

Tyler shrugs and moves away to chat with Jamie.

"Oh man," I mumble, trudging toward the counter.

"What?"

"Jamie texted Kai not to bring the girls here. She was going on about how they should stick to Village Coffee at the other end of Main Street." I purse my lips and brace myself against the glass display cabinet. "What if the four of them are hanging out over there?"

Parker's eyebrows raise. "We could be in the wrong place?"

I hug my middle. "I didn't think about them being someplace else. I just didn't want them here."

"But you texted me. You knew I'd be here to fix it."

"You being here wouldn't stop her shrill laugh."

Parker sniggers. "I like her laugh."

I smirk. "You would."

Parker peers into the glass display. "What did you bake today?"

Unintentionally, I yawn. "I was too tired, so I just made almond flour cookies, fudge brownies, and cinnamon rolls."

Parker smirks. "I love how you act like that's not a lot."

"It's simple stuff," I clarify. "I needed to make a few things because Sunday is such a busy day, but I'd usually put more effort in."

"Tired from your big night out?" Parker jokes.

"Yes," I say flatly. "And from staying up all night, thinking about today."

"Today?"

"The thought of Yvie being here was making me sick."

"You didn't have any faith in me?"

I sigh. "Actually, I'm so glad you got here before them. I feel less likely to faceplant."

Parker laughs, patting my back. "Please don't fall. Your parents are already waiting for me to do something that gets you hurt."

"You care about what they think?"

"Of course," he beams. "Your parents are cool. They sing and dance."

I laugh. "Some people would say that's what makes them lame."

"I don't think Lewis would."

I nod. "He doesn't seem put off whenever our parents chat. But that's usually by our fence where there's no music to encourage them."

Over Parker's shoulder, Kai and Milo walk into the café. I stare at the door, expecting the others to follow. When the twins walk further into the café, and the door stays closed, my brain malfunctions with possible scenarios.

Jamie moves up the aisle, fist-bumps Kai, and then passes him to throw her arms around Milo.

When Kai reaches us, Parker asks, "Where are the others?"

Kai grunts, rubbing his temples. "Don't even ask."

"Problem between Tabby and Yvette?"

Kai exhales hard, nodding.

"I could've told you getting those girls in the same place would be a disaster," Parker says. "Yesterday, the littlest things set them off."

"Well, I'm trying to fix that," Kai says bluntly. "I wouldn't care, but Lewis decided to date Yvie. If our girlfriends can't stand each other, it makes things awkward."

Parker pauses, and I see the cogs moving in his head. He'll need to deal with this issue when he's dating Yvette. I guess that's why he's banking on me and her becoming friends. It'll make things easier for him and Lewis to continue hanging out.

"So why isn't Tabby here?" Parker asks.

"Because I didn't want to fight with her," Kai says. "We were having a dumb argument about Lewis and Yvette, and she said she wanted some space. She said she'd meet up with us later at the skatepark."

"Maybe you should show up with flowers?" I suggest

Kai side-eyes me. "That'll work?"

I grin eagerly. "It would be so romantic."

"Thanks for the tip," Kai replies. "Anyway, I left Lewis at Yvette's house and took Tabby back home after she refused to wait for Yvie."

"Where was Yvie?" Parker and I ask at once.

Kai lifts his palms questioningly. "Asleep? I dunno. She wasn't ready and didn't seem to want to be quick about it."

I stifle my laugh. *Typical.*

"Lewis is at Yvie's house?" Parker asks through a tight mouth.

"Yep. I guess he's meeting her parents."

I whack Parker's arm. "I thought she wasn't allowed to be seen with a boy. She said her parents would flip out."

Kai *humphs* a laugh. "Lewis is a puppy. They probably see him as a dream guy compared to the meatheads she usually dates."

Kai moves over to the others, leaving me to stare dumbfoundedly at Parker.

Parker strains his neck, wincing as he massages his shoulder. "Lewis is meeting her parents."

My hands clench into fists. "How did this get worse? I hated the thought of her walking in here, but knowing they're spending time with her family..."

Parker's too stupefied to finish the sentence for me.

Rendering him speechless amplifies the magnitude of the situation. This boy can talk himself into seeing the positive of any situation. But he's got nothing.

"Kylie," Maddy says, walking out from behind the counter. "Can you clear the booths in your section?"

"Oh, yeah, sure," I say, forcing myself away from Parker.

As I clear away dirty plates, I can't help watching Parker join the others. Jamie has managed to stay glued to Milo despite the café floor being busy. Parker becomes more animated, getting caught up in Kai and Tyler's conversation.

I keep my gaze down as I pass them with my stack of dirty dishes.

My ears prick when I hear Tyler ask, "Is Kylie coming?"

I step into the kitchen and fidget by the stainless steel trough sink, confused about how to feel. Last weekend, if I heard Jamie's friends say my name, I'd assume they were setting up a prank or making a joke about me.

Now they see me as Parker's girlfriend. Are they happy about that? Or, do they wish I weren't hanging around? I am pretty lame compared to them. Yes, I jumped off the cliff, but they could be rolling their eyes and calling me names behind my back.

My mind rewinds to how annoyed Kai was about the drama between his girlfriend and Yvette. Am I just another hassle for him? For all of them?

"I'll take it from here, chicky," Jake says, moving toward the sink. "I'm done with all my orders. You can get back out on the floor."

I blink hard, taking in the reality around me. "Okay, thanks."

I move out of the kitchen and spot Jamie and her friends staring at me. Cautiously, I move out from behind the counter to join them.

"We were talking about our camping trip," Jamie says. "We go every year."

Kai nudges Parker. "Apparently, your boyfriend hasn't told you about it."

"First step was getting her to the lake with us," Parker says defensively. "Besides, you guys didn't lock down a date for ages."

"Well, we have one now," Tyler says. "Wednesday night."

"We're all going," Jamie says to me. "You should come too."

"Oh." I utter some syllables that don't make any words, and then clear my throat. "My parents will never greenlight me staying out all night without parental supervision."

"It's not just us," Kai says. "Mine and Tyler's parents are chaperoning."

Parker grins. "See, we've got it all covered."

My nerves don't settle as I pan around the group.

Parker grunts, throwing his arms around me. "Don't make me beg," he whines, resting his chin on the top of my head.

"I had to witness Jamie begging Milo to go," Tyler says flatly. "Don't make me go through it again."

"They promise it'll be fun," Milo says, almost convincingly.

I move my head to view Parker as he holds me. "Everyone's going?"

Parker takes the hint, asking Kai, "Lewis and Yvette coming?"

Kai nods. "Lewis said he'd bring her along."

Jamie groans. "What's a camping trip without a side of girl drama?"

"As long as Tabby and I get back on the same side," Kai says, lacking his usual confidence.

My jitters fizzle out as the image of Yvette and Lewis cozied up in front of a roaring campfire fills my mind. There's no way I'm not getting between that.

I hug Parker back. "Okay. I'll come."

Parker sways me in his arms as the group cheers.

"Good choice, Kylie," Kai says approvingly.

When the others nod along, a thrill of excitement rolls up my spine.

Whoa. They really want me to come with them?

I'm not an annoyance to them?

"Do I need to make a no-boyfriends rule so you girls keep working?" Maddy asks, passing us with a tray of coffees.

"You could, Aunty," Jamie says in a teasing tone, "but could you survive without your boyfriend stopping in?"

Maddy rolls her eyes and continues onto a table.

Milo runs a hand down Jamie's shoulder. "Do you want me to help you?"

Jamie bats her lashes, leading him behind the counter to help her with the clean up after making dozens of milkshakes and coffees.

"All right, I can be a good boyfriend," Parker says. "Put me to work."

I giggle at him. "You don't have to. You can take a seat with the boys and I'll bring you something to eat."

"No, it's cool," Parker says. "Should I wipe down a table?"

Kai and Tyler laugh, moving to an empty booth.

"Gotta see this," Kai comments. "We're in here all the time, and he's never once helped Jamie."

Parker ignores his friends and awaits my instructions.

I grab a cloth and spray bottle and move over to my section. "You know, you don't need to play it up. Lewis and Yvette aren't even here."

"Yeah, but I'm still your boyfriend to everyone else," Parker replies, following close behind. "And I don't mind helping."

"Not according to Kai."

"What would he know? Besides, Lewis and Ty never help either."

"You don't need to defend yourself. I'm really fine doing my own work."

"But isn't helping a romantic gesture?"

I hesitate, watching the genuineness softening his face. "You're trying to be romantic?"

"Yeah," he says with a blush. "I want to be good at being a boyfriend."

Aww. Why is he being so cute right now?

I lift the cloth and spray bottle for Parker to take. "Okay, boyfriend. Go for it."

He gives me a wink and then wipes down the table. I take delight in telling him where he's missed a spot.

He cleans the surface again. "How about now?"

"I guess it's fine for someone who's never worked a day in his life."

Parker turns to me and pretends to pull the trigger on the bottle, causing me to yelp and raise my hands.

He laughs, lowering the bottle. "I'd work if my parents let me."

I side-eye him skeptically. "They won't let you?"

"Nope. They say I don't need to. That I should focus on school."

"Well, my parents pay for things too. I just want to have savings for when it's time for college."

"How sensible of you."

"Well, there's that, and I like to splurge on baking supplies."

"Sounds more like it."

Parker moves onto the next empty booth and sprays the table surface. "So you're really joining us on the camping trip?"

"Sure." I shrug. "It'll be my first time camping."

"You really are an adventure newbie."

"Well, I need to try if I want Lewis's attention, right?"

"That's the spirit."

"But maybe Lewis and Yvette will be broken up by then, and I won't have to go."

"Green, you'll still have to go." Parker smirks. "You want to be Lewis's girlfriend, don't you? He'll want his girl on the trip with us."

I blow out a quick breath. "Oh, yeah, right."

He tugs on my ponytail. "Don't worry. You'll survive camping."

I whip my hair away, smoothing back the loose hairs.

He smiles, flicking the spray bottle around his finger by the trigger. "So, are you coming with us to the skatepark after your shift?"

"Is that a trick question?"

"No. Lewis and Yvie will be there. Aren't you dying to know what's been happening between them this morning?"

I hold my stomach and swallow hard. "I don't think I'll be able to handle the knowledge."

"Well, I need to know." He pats my arm. "And I need my girlfriend by my side."

I pinch the bridge of my nose, feeling a dizzy spell brewing.

Parker traces a finger under my chin. "Don't you want to see Lewis?"

I lower my hand. "Yes, I do."

"So you'll come?"

"I've got to be crazy, but yes. They've already spent too much uninterrupted time together."

He pulls a fist down in triumph. "*Yes.* Glad to have you on my team."

<h1 style="text-align:center">Fourteen</h1>

Maddy let Jamie and I clock out early because we got help from the boys. To everyone's surprise, Jamie opted out of coming with us to the skatepark. She and Milo were too wrapped up in each other, excitedly whispering about meeting up with his friends for a rematch in a game they play. Not even Kai could persuade her to stay.

On their skateboards, Kai and Tyler left us in their dust. Parker rode his skateboard, but at a snail's pace so I could walk beside him. I told him he could go ahead of me, but he said that wouldn't be a good look.

When we arrive at the skatepark, the boys are chatting with Lewis. Yvette stands off to the side, talking on her phone. As we approach, the boys ride their skateboards toward the obstacles.

Lewis skids his skateboard to a stop in front of us, his camera hanging by the strap over his shoulder. "Hey guys."

"Hey, we missed you this morning," Parker replies.

Lewis grins. "I know. There was a bit of a scene at Yvie's house. I stuck around to smooth things over with her family."

"You talked with Yvie's parents?" Parker asks. "I thought they didn't want to see her with any boys."

"None of her exes thought of talking to her parents before," Lewis says. "I think I'm the first guy they've met who's acted like a human being."

Parker's jaw flexes. "I guess they didn't leave a high bar to cross."

My heart hurts for Parker. He put in such a good effort with my parents, and it was all fake. He surely would've impressed Yvie's parents, but Lewis got in first.

My heart bounces higher, thinking about how it's just a test run. Sure, my parents like Parker, but they're gonna love Lewis. It'll be the same with Yvie's family.

Lewis sighs out in relief. "Feels so freaking good to get their approval. The rest of spring break would've been so tough if we had to keep tiptoeing around her parents."

"So you spent all morning at their house?"

"Yeah. Talked to her parents for a bit, but then they left me and Yvie alone." Lewis grins. "That was obviously the best part."

Parker goes a shade paler. "Totally."

"I'm sorry, I need to sit down," I murmur. "It was a long shift."

Parker brushes my hand. "Are you sure?"

I turn away, mumbling. "Very sure."

There's a shady tree a few feet away, and I'm in need of its sanctuary. As I flop onto the grass, Parker and Lewis continue to talk. The only thing that could lift my mood would be seeing Lewis in action with his camera.

Ahhh.

I already feel better just picturing it.

On the other side of the skatepark, Kai and Tyler slide their skateboards against rails and jump over ramps. That is until Tabitha walks across the grass toward them.

Kai speeds on his skateboard, dipping low on his knees to scoop up the bouquet of flowers he brought from the florist on Main Street. When he meets her on the footpath, her hands clasp over her face. Kai then says something, which makes her react with a lot of nodding. Her hands pull around his neck, and she pops a leg behind her as he lifts her up.

I can't help aweing when they kiss.

A light breeze swirls around me, and I relax in my cross-legged position. I look back up at the boys, and lose my relaxation when Yvette's off her phone and getting handsy with Lewis.

Obviously unable to stomach it either, Parker backs away from the couple. His mood lifts when Tyler coaxes him into skating with him. I try to focus on them, but Yvie's giggling keeps pulling me back.

Lewis attempts to get her on his board, but as per usual, she's dramatizing the whole experience. Changing his approach, Lewis then lifts his camera like he's Yvie's paparazzo. I rub the ache in my chest. How could he sully his camera with images of her?

Parker rides past them, and he strains not to watch. His board flicks up beneath him, and he almost misses when landing back on it. When he moves to another ramp, he gains air with his skateboard, but when he lands, he skids off the board.

"Parker, what's going on?" Tyler calls out. "I haven't seen you wreck it like that in ages."

Parker flicks up his board and rests it against the side of a ramp. "Yeah, I need a minute."

"*Eep.* Hold me up!" Yvette squeals, flapping her arms and reaching for Lewis.

Lewis laughs and grabs Yvette's waist. He hoists her off the skateboard and into a bear hug. My cheek sinks into my palm as I watch them laughing and hugging in a circle.

Parker walks toward me and takes a seat under the tree. We're silent as he also takes in the sight. Lewis coaxes Yvette back onto the skateboard, staying extra close as he gives her instructions.

"Do you want to be doing that with him?" Parker asks.

"No, I want to be doing *this* with him."

"What's this?"

"*This.*" I pat the grass. "Just sitting here."

"Oh, this is good for you?" Parker takes a beat, soaking up our immediate surroundings. "Yeah, I guess it's pretty nice."

"Taking in nature is like magic."

"Well, Lewis would agree with you when it comes to his photos." Parker hangs an elbow over his bent knee. "But he doesn't really sit still. Remember yesterday at the lake? He didn't join everyone else when we were sitting and eating cupcakes."

I frown. "Yeah, but he was with *her.*"

"Still, he's not one for sitting on the sidelines."

With determination, I don't lose my resolve. "That's because he's still waiting for me."

"*Ha.* I like your confidence."

"I've kept my crush on him for eighteen months because I have a tight hold on my beliefs."

"Okay, but you're not going to lure him over here." He lifts into a crouched position. "We're gonna have to get closer to everyone else."

I tilt my head, gazing at the skatepark's ramps and rails. "I'll play along until he realizes he's supposed to be with me."

"At a girl," Parker says, scooping his arms behind my back and underneath my knees.

Before I can ask what he's doing, he's standing with me in his arms. Moving towards the skatepark, he spins me in his arms. Squealing, I loop my arms around his neck and squint my eyes closed.

We stop spinning, and Parker throws his back with a laugh. As he cradles me in his arms, I can't help watching the sun dance in the brown of his eyes. Instinctively, my lips wet and then slightly part. He doesn't take another step, holding me and moving his gaze down to my mouth.

I clear my throat and look away. "Maybe you should put me down."

"They're looking," he whispers. "You can kiss me if you want."

I shiver against him.

Don't kiss him.

You need to stop kissing him.

I give him a smile, and suggest, "Maybe just spin me again."

He grins, spinning me faster, making the laughter spill out of me.

When we finally land in one place, Parker helps me to my feet. Still laughing, I lean against him until the dizziness wears off. As my vision clears, Tabitha comes into view.

"Is it possible for you two to be any cuter?" she jokes.

Yvie clicks her tongue. "They're just trying to catch up to me and Lewis."

Tabitha's lip upturns, turning her back on Yvie. "Yeah, sure."

From behind, Kai wraps his arms around Tabitha. "But seriously, stop being so cute. Now we all gotta step up our game."

Tabitha laughs, patting Kai's hands clasped against her stomach. "Don't worry, babe. You're already adorable, especially with those flowers."

Kai kisses Tabitha's cheek. "Thanks."

He releases Tabitha, and when she turns away, Kai sends me a wink.

I give him a thumbs up, and he follows Tabitha to a bench seat.

Parker grabs his skateboard and sets it on the ground between us. "You're up."

I splutter a laugh. "You're crazy."

"Come on, I can teach you." He gestures over his shoulder. "I bet you can master it before Yvie. Don't you want to impress Lewis?"

I cup a hand over my mouth, mumbling, "I'm scared."

Parker pulls on my wrist. "What was that?"

I don't let him pry my hand away, shaking my head. "I'm scared."

He tilts his head. "You're scared?"

I push my hand harder against my mouth, nodding.

Parker laughs, holding out his hands. "I'll hold you up."

I lower my hand and look down at the skateboard. Parker rests one foot against it, waiting for me to step onto it.

"Kikki, you jumped off a cliff."

"Don't call me that."

He smirks. "Is that all you heard? I'll repeat it. You. Jumped. Off. A. Cliff."

I shake out my hands, exhaling slowly. I clutch his hands and step one foot onto the board.

"Half your foot's hanging off the board," Parker says. "Slide it on further so you'll get better balance."

I scoot my foot across and lean my weight on Parker as I lift my other foot. With both feet on the board, it wobbles and makes me yelp.

Parker chuckles. "That's it. You're on the board."

I squeeze his hands. "When does it stop wobbling?"

"When you shift your weight."

"How do I do that?"

"Green, stop crushing my hands."

"No. I don't want to fall."

"Stop panicking. I'm right here. I'll catch you."

I stare into his sunlit brown eyes and release my grip on him. I wobble on the board until I leap off.

Parker throws his head back with laughter. "Okay, you lasted five seconds. Good start."

"It was longer than that."

Parker beckons me back on. "Come on, crush my hands again."

I take his hands, careful not to hold on so tight.

"See the bolt patterns," Parker says. "You want to have both your feet centered on them."

The bolts are fixed to the wheels, and I feel dumb for not realizing they'd help distribute my weight. I step my feet over the bolt patterns, but the board still rocks beneath me.

Parker bends his knees, taking my weight. "Your toes should hang a little off the board. And if your heels hang off a bit, that's okay too."

"Whoa." The board rocks harder as I try to keep my balance.

"You got it. Now bend your knees."

I lower on bended knees, and the board stabilizes.

"How does that feel?"

I grin. "Good."

"Awesome. Ready to let go?"

I squeeze his hands. "Don't you dare."

"*Ouch.*" He hisses. "I wasn't letting go. I was asking if you were ready."

"I'm not."

He smirks. "Clearly."

I concentrate on the placement of my feet, making sure my toes slip over the edge, but I overdo it. The skateboard tips toward Parker, and he changes position to catch me.

"*Oof.*" I bonk my head against his shoulder and trip over the skateboard.

Parker grunts, hopping on one foot after the skateboard flicks into his shin. "Dang it."

"I'm sorry!"

He sniggers, holding me against him. "It's okay. I'll have a bruise to commemorate the day."

I look down at his lower leg. "Does it really hurt?"

"No, not really. It's just a plank of wood that whacked into my bone," Parker jokes.

I pull out of his arms. "Be serious. Are you hurt?"

"I've walked off worse." He shakes out his leg. "Don't think you're getting out of your lesson that easily."

"Hurting the teacher isn't an automatic fail?"

He flicks the skateboard back onto its wheels. "No, it's a do-over."

"How do I do it without beefing it again?"

"Try getting back on the board. Your stance was really good. You just have to maintain your balance. So, lift your arms out to each side."

Over the bolt patterns, I ground my feet down. With bent knees, I gradually lift my arms. The board rocks, and my balance shifts. I squeak and lower my arms.

"It's okay. Try again," Parker encourages.

Steadying my nerves, I try the position again. My core contracts like it never has before. With my arms balancing out each side, I manage to stay on the skateboard.

"*Woo.* Go Kylie!" Kai and Tabitha cheer from their bench seats.

I smile at the ground, feeling a blush brightening my cheeks.

Parker gives me a thumbs up. "Wanna try moving?"

My airway constricts.

"I'm not asking you to pop an ollie," Parker teases. "Just point your left foot, and go that way."

"Left foot?"

He shrugs. "Or right. I'm left-handed, so I always opt left."

Because it feels more comfortable, I point out my right foot. With my arms out, I push my palms down as if balancing on an invisible railing. Slowly, the board edges to the right.

"Oh gosh, how do I stop?"

"You just started to roll. It's not like you're flying down a ramp."

"*Parker.*"

He grabs hold of my hips and anchors a foot against the side of the board, stopping it in place. "You good, daredevil?"

I cover my face with my hands, letting out a nervous laugh. "Oh my gosh, that was so scary."

"It barely moved."

I lower my hands. "But it moved."

He grins. "You moved it."

I giggle and place my hands on his shoulders. "Help me off."

He lifts me off the board, spinning me before letting my feet fit the ground. The laughter spills out of me as I stumble onto solid ground.

Parker cups the side of my face. "You did great."

"Do you think Lewis saw?" I whisper.

He lifts his hands away and nods.

My heart pitter patters and I peer over Parker's shoulder, finding Lewis and Yvette standing by the guardrail. Lewis lowers his camera and gives me an approving nod.

Oh my gosh. Lewis took a photo of me?

I grin like an idiot, my mood only souring when Yvie slides a hand behind Lewis's neck. She turns his gaze away from me and lays one heck of a kiss on him.

I shut my eyes and turn away.

Parker rubs a hand on my back, whispering, "I don't know how to get between them. It's like they're better than ever."

"Maybe we should just get out of here," I reply. "I don't know if I'll have any energy left for tonight."

"I hope they're not like this tonight, or I'd hate to think how intense they'll get on the camping trip."

I give Parker an apprehensive look.

He braces himself. "What?"

I wince. "What exactly do I need to bring for camping? I've never been. I've never even used a sleeping bag."

"Not even on a sleepover?"

"No, we had beds."

"Well, la-di-da," Parker jokes.

I nudge him. "C'mon, I'm serious. Do I need to buy a tent or a blow-up mattress? Geez, how would I even blow up a mattress?"

"Kylie, stop spiraling." He grabs my shoulders. "My whole family camps. We've got tons of gear. Why don't we stop by my place before I take you home?"

I give a hopeful smile. "That'd be okay?"

"Sure it would. I know no one else is camping this week, so all the gear will just be sitting there."

"Okay, then. Cool."

Parker cups his hands around his mouth, calling out to his friends. "Catch ya later. We're heading out."

Tabitha tugs on Kai's arms. "I'm not staying around with just *her*."

There's a shared glare between Tabitha and Yvette.

Lewis sends us a wave. "See ya tonight."

I wave back. "Can't wait."

Parker smirks. "Eager much?"

I shrug. "Yes."

He hitches his skateboard under his arm. "Okay, save up that energy. Let's get back to the car."

Fifteen

"Wow, your house is so nice," I say when we pull up on Parker's driveway.

"Thanks," he mutters, craning his neck to view the front door.

"Looking for someone?"

"More like hoping not to see someone." He opens his door and presses the clicker for the garage door. "Shall we?"

I follow him out of the car and into the garage. It has spaces for four cars, but only houses one at the moment. Parker pockets his keys and moves to the racking along the wall. There's five shelves filled with all kinds of sporting equipment. There are bicycles hanging on the back wall, and when I glance up I find kayaks tucked amongst the rafters.

"Wow. My garage has boxes of old school projects and our childhood toys. Your family is so sporty."

"Yeah, Dad wants us to stay active," Parker replies. "He used to do stuff with us, but he gets too busy these days."

"And your Mom?"

"She stopped working a few years ago, and now fills her days making sure my brothers get to all their activities."

"And what about you? Do you get free range?"

"Well, I can drive myself. And before then, I was always at Kai's and his parents always took our group everywhere."

I move over to the racking with him. "And I guess I'm now in this group too."

Parker pulls out three sleeping bags. "I know Lewis doesn't have extra stuff at home, so I'll pack for Yvie too. Just a guess, but I don't think she camps either."

"Did the perfect manicure tip you off?"

He wiggles his eyebrows. "You think she's perfect too?"

I retch, shoving him away.

He laughs, moving the sleeping bags to the side. He then pulls out two canvas duffle bags.

"These are two-person tents," he says, dropping them by the sleeping bags. "Maybe you and Lewis can share one."

All the blood rushes to my head and I gasp. "*What?*"

Parker presses into his stomach as he laughs. "Relax. I know you're not gonna jump his bones."

I fan my face, trying to ease my nervous system.

"But you and Yvie should bunk up."

"Oh, yay," I mumble.

He gives me side-eye as he neatens the pile against the racking. "You know it makes sense."

I huff. "I know. But it's easy for you. You and Lewis are already friends. Yvie and I couldn't be more opposite."

"Just try. I still want to hang out with Lewis when I'm finally dating Yvie."

I nod. "I am trying. I don't want to do anything that ruins your friendship."

He sends me a wink. "Thanks, Kikki."

My eyes roll back. "Ugh."

The side door, leading into the house, opens as someone begins talking. "Parker, why didn't you park in..." I turn around to see Mrs. Kelly with an exaggerated smile. "Oh my gosh, is this Kylie?"

"Uh, hi, Mom," Parker says in a flat tone.

"I was waiting for you to come inside the house," Mrs. Kelly says, walking further into the garage. "Why didn't you tell me you were bringing Kylie over?"

"Because we're not staying," Parker says, avoiding his mom's eyes.

Mrs. Kelly lifts a hand toward me. "Hi honey, I'm Parker's mom."

I shake her hand. "Hi Mrs. Kelly."

"I have a vague memory of you from when you were both in middle school," she says. "But I haven't heard about you since starting high school. I had no idea you two had gotten so close." She looks at Parker, batting a hand. "But then again, Parky never tells us anything."

I puff a laugh. "Parky?"

Parker's eyebrow raises as an air of irritation leaves him "Don't."

I give him my most mischievous look. "Why not, Parky? It's cute."

"Oh, aren't you two adorable," Mrs. Kelly gushes.

"Yeah, so cute," Parker's brother, Kurtis, says as he leans against the side doorway.

He's only a year younger than Parker, and he's the reason their parents know about me and Parker. Kurtis was sent the chem lab photo of us.

"We're just here to make sure we've got enough gear for the camping trip," Parker explains.

Mrs. Kelly eyes me with surprise. "You're going on the trip?"

"Mm-hmm. But I'm not the only girl."

Mrs. Kelly chuckles. "I can't believe all these boys have girlfriends now. Aww, you're all growing up so fast."

Parker's eyes roll. "*Mom.*"

I look across the racks of camping and sporting gear. "Are you guys going camping during spring break?"

"Afraid not," she replies. "My husband's busy with work and I have to wrangle Parker's brothers."

"Anyway, I need to take Kylie home," Parker says abruptly.

"No, you can't leave so soon," Mrs. Kelly says, clutching my shoulder. "Come inside for a glass of iced tea and we'll get to know you better."

"No, Mom, we really have to be going," Parker insists.

"Parker, you have a girlfriend, and I feel like I'm being left out," his mom complains.

"Yeah, Parker," Kurtis teases, "let Mom third wheel on your date."

Mrs. Kelly groans. "I don't want to go on one of their dates. I just want to get to know Kylie." She gives me a kind smile. "You must be special for Parker to slow down for you."

"Umm, yeah, maybe," I stammer.

She beckons me to follow. "So, you'll stay awhile?"

"Mom, do you ever quit?" Parker complains.

From his fidgety stance, tight expression, and agitated tone, the uncomfortableness pours off Parker.

"I really do have to go, Mrs. Kelly," I say. "But maybe I can come back another time? I just promised my parents I'd get back home in time to walk my dog."

Parker's eyes light up. "And you promised I could help walk her. Right?"

I grin. "Right."

"Mom, Kylie has a golden retriever," Parker says, becoming much more animated. "I almost thought it was Gus walking into the room."

Mrs. Kelly pouts, touching the side of his face. "Aww, honey."

Kurtis sniggers. "Is Kylie's dog a pity dog too?"

"*Kurtis*," Mrs. Kelly snaps while Parker's posture hunches.

I double take at Kurtis, unable to understand his question. "Huh?"

Mrs. Kelly waves a hand. "Don't mind him. He's being a brat. You kids have fun, okay."

Parker pecks his mom's cheek. "Thanks, Mom. We will."

"Bye Parky," Kurtis says in a mocking tone. "See you later, Kylie."

Parker ignores his brother, walking me out of the garage while I mumble my goodbyes.

On the drive to my place, Parker's body language is stiff, and I'm unnerved by his silence.

"Umm." I clear my throat of the choking awkwardness. "Back there, umm. What was that about?"

"What?" Parker grunts. "Nothing."

I swallow hard as the tension twists my stomach. "Okay."

He exhales hard, rubbing the side of his head. "My mom's just a bit much. I didn't want her to go overboard trying to get to know you. It'll be too hard after we break up. She'll have a million questions."

"Sure. That makes sense."

"And my brother." He fidgets in his seat. "Well, he's just a jerk."

"Has he been a pest about the photo?"

"Kurtis is a pain in the butt without needing to be provoked."

"Oh."

Parker glances my way and then back at the road. "I just didn't want them grilling us. I don't really tell them what's going on with me because they blow everything out of proportion."

"I'm sorry. It sucks that you can't just talk to them."

Parker eases in his seat. "They're no dancing family."

"I'm never going to live that down."

"I think it's cool."

I stare at him for a beat too long, waiting for a joke to land.

Unnerved by the silence, he turns his head. "What?"

I shrug. "Nothing. I was just waiting for you to make fun of me."

Parker lets out a nervous laugh. "I'm not joking. I like your parents."

My eyebrows push together with skepticism. "Okay."

"I'm not lying." His grin rises up the genuine-meter. "Anyway, now you can get the greenlight from your parents about the camping trip."

I wince. "You want me to ask them about it?"

"Ah, yeah. Wasn't that the point of me putting aside camping gear for you?"

I sigh heavily. "I guess."

"You need to go. It's non-negotiable. How else do we stop Lewis and Yvie from getting even more cuddly?"

Parker parks outside my house, and I unbuckle without confidence. "Okay."

"Perk up, Green." He pats my knee. "You're a good girl. They won't say no to you."

"It's a trip with my supposed boyfriend. I don't think they'll be down."

"Compared to Lewis, I'm a good boy." He steps out of the car. "I can drive without crashing."

I groan, moving out of the car. I move ahead of Parker to get inside the house. I search the hallway for Brandy, hoping to get her outside and bypass my parents. Asking about this camping trip is mortifying. How will they ever be okay with it? Until this week, Parker Kelly was a name I never brought up, and now I want to go into the mountains overnight with him.

I can't bear the humiliation of them saying no in front of Parker. It'll solidify just how lame I am.

"Huh?" Parker stops dead in the hallway, tilting his head as if listening for something. "There's no music playing."

"It's not on an eternal loop," I reply. "It's more of a mood thing."

Parker winces. "Is this a bad time? Are your parents in a bad mood?"

I puff a laugh. "No, they're just being chill."

"Oh, okay. *Phew.*"

We move along the hallway, finding my parents with a pitcher of iced tea in the kitchen.

"Parker," Dad cheers, lifting his glass. "Good to see you again."

Parker steps into the kitchen with a wave. "Hi Mr. Green. Mrs. Green."

"Hi Parker," Mom replies. "Hi honey, how was work?"

"Long," I reply.

Dad looks at the time on the microwave display. "Did you do overtime?"

"No, I went to the skatepark."

My parents share a baffled look.

Parker clutches my shoulders. "Kylie got on my skateboard."

Dad claps loudly. "That's amazing. Did someone take a video?"

"*Dad*," I groan.

"Next time," Parker says, letting me go. "I promise."

Dad points finger guns at him. "I'll hold you to it."

Mortifying.

"Actually, I think Lewis took a photo," I say, glancing at Parker.

Parker nods. "I'll ask him to send it to me."

"So, what are you guys up to?" Mom asks. "Here for another dance party?"

"Parker was worried because there was no music playing," I tease.

Dad snaps his fingers. "We can remedy that."

"No," I blurt, stopping him from asking the speaker to 'play Arnold's Hits.' "Don't worry about it. We're gonna take Brandy for a walk."

"Good idea," Mom says. "That lazy girl needs to get out of the house."

Parker nudges me. "Ask them about the trip."

Both my parents' ears prick, and Mom asks, "What trip?"

I suck in a hesitant breath. "What do you think about me going camping?"

My parents share a look, holding back laughter.

"*Guys*," I whine.

"Sorry, honey," Dad says, wiping under his eye. "It's just, it's you."

"Exactly," Mom agrees. "You and camping are not words that usually go in the same sentence."

"And usually Parker doesn't visit," I mumble. "Things change."

My parents' expressions brighten, looking at each other with hopefulness.

"Okay, Kikki, we'll take this seriously," Mom says. "Tell us what's happening."

"I don't exactly know the details," I say, looking at Parker for help. "Can you explain it to them?"

"Sure. It's a trip with my friends. We go every year."

Dad looks at Parker with scrutiny. "And they're parents?"

Parker is quick to nod. "Yes, sir. Tyler and Kai's parents camp with us."

Dad chuckles. "I love when this kid calls me sir."

Parker wiggles his eyebrows. "Does that mean Kylie can go?"

"We'll have to chat with the parents that are going," Mom says.

"Please don't be lame," I complain. "Will you say anything embarrassing to them?"

Mom gives me a puzzled look. "Like what?"

"I dunno. Just don't make me sound like a scaredy-cat who will be a total camping failure."

Parker smirks. "Don't worry. Milo's going, so he's got that covered."

"Just how many boys are going on this trip?" Dad asks, scrutiny squinting his eyes.

"Five," Parker replies. "Four girls."

"Maybe five girls if I can convince Josie to come," I add.

"That's a tall order," Mom says. "You getting adventurous is one thing, but Josie?"

I shrug. "She might like sitting by a campfire and making s'mores."

Mom smiles. "Yes, she might."

"Can you guys just say yes?" I ask, giving them my best puppy-dog eyes.

Mom and Dad both awe at me. Dad looks at Mom, saying, "There will be two sets of parents."

"Your parents aren't going, Parker?" Mom asks.

Parker shakes his head. "No, they're too busy."

"We'll have to take time to go over and visit them," Mom says to Dad. "Seeing as our kids are becoming so close."

I gulp. "No, you don't have to do that."

Mom sighs. "Kikki, will you stop panicking about us embarrassing you."

"It's not that," Parker cuts in. "It's just that they're so busy. Umm, maybe I'll get them to call you instead?"

"Okay, that's fine," Mom replies. "So when is this trip?"

"Wednesday night," I reply.

"And Thursday night," Parker adds.

"It's two nights?" I blurt at the same time as my parents.

Parker blinks. "Didn't I mention that?"

Dad tilts his head at me. "You want to go camping for two nights?"

I gulp. "I guess."

"We're heading out Wednesday afternoon, and coming back on Friday morning," Parker clarifies.

My jaw clenches as my gaze pivots between parents. "Is that cool?"

"I'll chat to the parents to make sure we have all the details straight." Mom gives Dad a look. "But, yes, Kikki. You can go camping."

I clap. "*Yay.* Thank you."

"Awesome," Parker cheers. "Now, can we take Brandy out?"

"Yes, kids, you're free to go," Dad says with a chuckle.

I get her leash while Parker coaxes Brandy off her comfy bed in the back room. Her tail swooshes from side to side as she follows Parker.

I giggle. "I think she thinks she's getting food."

Parker clips the leash to her collar, and I happily give him the reins. "Come on, girl. You can get food afterwards."

I scratch behind Brandy's ear. "Going for a walk won't be so bad."

"Is she like you?" Parker says with a teasing smile. "She'd prefer to just sit on the sidelines and watch the world go by?"

I open the front door. "Well, she does spend a lot of time watching me baking. She comes alive, waiting for me to drop some sugary goodness."

"That can't be good for dogs," Parker says, following me out of the house.

"It isn't. That's why she's always watching. I never drop anything on purpose."

As we set off on the footpath, which winds through my neighborhood, Parker asks, "So, is baking what you want to do for the rest of your life?"

"Maybe. It was one of the first things I realized I was good at," I reply. "So I kept practicing and trying more difficult recipes. I guess, maybe it's similar to you and skateboard tricks."

"Does that mean it's just a hobby?"

"I do have a dream to move to France and attend a patisserie school."

"Whoa. That'd be awesome."

"Sometimes, I think of baking as art. I like that people can look at it, smell it, and appreciate it. Eating it is sometimes just a bonus."

Parker mumbles a laugh. "I always just think about eating what you bake."

"That's perfectly fine. As long as you enjoy it."

"I don't think I've ever eaten a bad cake from Morton's Café. I can't believe I never knew you made them all."

"I don't make them all. And I don't bake for the café every day. It's just a little side gig for extra cash."

"Well, they're still amazing."

"Thanks, Parker."

Parker lifts the leash higher, grinning at Brandy. "She's got such a good pace. I was worried she was going to dawdle the whole way."

"She's fine once she's out of the house. It's just prompting her that's the issue."

Parker sniggers. "Just like her owner."

I nudge him. "*Hey.*"

Parker grins playfully, and I can't help smiling back.

My pocket vibrates and then my ringtone plays. I pull out my phone and see, *"Tessa Calling."*

Oh my gosh. I can just imagine her mind melting if she knew I was currently on a walk with a boy.

"Ah, call ya back, sis," I mumble and hit the decline button.

Parker side-eyes me. "Why are you ignoring your sister's call?"

I pocket my phone. "Oh no, you don't. You don't get to ask me that after being so weird at your house."

"What are you talking about? I wasn't acting weird."

"You couldn't wait to get out of there. Plus, you wouldn't give your mom or brother the time of day."

"Maybe I was just excited about getting back to your place?"

"Exactly. It doesn't make any sense why you'd prefer to be at my house than yours."

Parker motions with the leash. "Your house has Brandy."

I smile at the dog. "I'll give you that one."

Our conversation fades during the rest of our walk. Parker's laidback presence puts me at ease, and I love seeing his connection with Brandy. He praises her when she gets back on course after distractedly sniffing flowers, which hang over fences.

We make our way back to my home, and Parker's gaze drifts to the road. As his head tilts, his eyes widen when he focuses on something past my shoulder. Before I can turn to see what it is, his hand plants on my lower back, turning and dipping me. His other arm supports my neck and shoulders as his lips press onto mine. There's a small thud as Brandy's leash hits the pavement, and I hold Parker's shoulders out of sheer necessity.

In my reclined state, I don't kiss him back. As my confusion heightens, I hear a car slow beside us and turn onto Lewis's driveway.

All my questions are now answered. We're kissing for Lewis's benefit.

My arms tighten behind Parker's neck, I lower my eyelids, and finally kiss him back.

"Parker and Kylie," Mrs. Allen says, exiting the SUV. "Lewis told us you two were dating. I'm sorry to say I didn't believe it until now."

I wipe my mouth with the back of my hand. "I'm sorry. We shouldn't be kissing outside your house."

Parker lowers and grabs Brandy's leash, who pants as she sits near us. "Yeah, we were just taking the dog for a walk and, umm..."

Lewis's dad rounds the car with a chuckle. "Don't apologize for being young and in love."

"*Love?*" Parker and I both yelp.

As if on cue, we both start waving our arms in front.

"No, Mr. Allen, we're not that serious," Parker blurts.

Mrs. Allen laughs, linking arms with her husband. "Look what you did. You embarrassed them."

Parker motions to their car. "Lewis isn't with you?"

"No, he's staying in town with Tyler," Mrs. Allen replies. "He'll be out until tonight to take his girlfriend to the fair."

Parker flashes a smile. "Oh yeah, we'll be joining them tonight."

"Have fun, kids," Mr. Allen says, sending us a wave as he and his wife disappear inside their house.

I fan my face to rid the tomato redness.

"*Soooo*," Parker drags out the word. "Apparently we're really good at convincing people we're a couple."

"Well, you did dip me." I whack his arm. "Why did you dip me?"

"I thought Lewis was in the car."

I groan. "Well, he wasn't. Seriously, we need to stop kissing."

"It's fake with us."

"No one sees it as fake." My face grows hot again, and I snatch the leash from Parker. "And it doesn't feel fake."

"I was making a scene on purpose. I wanted him to take notice."

"Look, just stop kissing me," I say, backtracking with Brandy. "I mean it. Tonight at the fair, absolutely no kissing."

He steps forward. "But it's a date."

"I don't care. I don't want to kiss you."

Parker huffs, throwing his hand in the air. "Fine. I'll just ignore you and focus on complimenting Yvie all night."

I turn my back on him and tug Brandy down our front path. "Sounds perfect to me."

I hear the click of Parker's car locks and then the opening of the car door.

"Bye, Brandy," he calls out before closing the door behind him.

"Ugh." I pull on her leash as I turn the front door knob. "Come on, girl. Let's get inside."

Sixteen

Oh boy. It's time for the fair.

Ever since walking out on Parker, I've been left with a lingering bad feeling about tonight.

I fix my hair in front of the full-length mirror. I pin back the front, letting the rest fall in waves over my shoulders. I'm wearing a navy dress, which has spaghetti straps and falls above my knees. My chest felt bare, so I picked out a necklace with a circular sapphire pendant. I finish the outfit with a denim jacket and a pair of white sneakers.

With hope, I peer out my bedroom window in search of Lewis at his desk. Sadly, he hasn't returned home all day. My heart sinks with the heavy weight of knowing he's spent so much extra time with Yvie.

I leave my bedroom, descend the stairs, and say goodbye to my parents. I timed it so I'd make it out the door before Parker arrived. I close the door and see him walking toward me.

Parker stops dead on the path. "I was coming to the door."

"Don't bother," I say, pacing toward the car. "You don't need to make nice with my parents."

"But I like seeing your parents."

I brush past him. "You don't need to keep pretending. You can cool it when Lewis and Yvette aren't around."

Parker groans, following me to the car. "You're still mad at me?"

"Oh, good." I reef the passenger door open. "Your brain is still working."

"*Oof.* You're in a feisty mood." He rounds the car and gets into the driver's seat. "You're not really mad at me. You're only mad because Lewis wasn't there."

I scoff, folding my arms and turning my face away.

"I know because I felt you kissing me back."

"I'm mad that Lewis wasn't there, and I'm mad that you kissed me."

"That doesn't make any sense. I kissed you to make Lewis jealous. That's what you want."

"None of this is what I want. I don't want to be pretending with you. I want to do this for real with *him*."

Parker flops back on his seat, banging his head against the headrest. He scrunches his eyes closed, wincing. "This isn't how I wanted things to go either. But I think it's working."

"How is it working? He was at her house today, and they seemed closer than ever at the skatepark."

Parker opens his eyes, turning his head my way. "Kai and Tabby called us cute, and Yvie was quick to say we were copying them. Doesn't that sound insecure to you?"

"You still think they're putting on an act?"

"I don't think they're rock-solid."

"This whole thing is overwhelming. Can we make a deal? If things don't go our way tonight, we'll reconsider this fake relationship."

"You want to call it quits?"

"We said we'd do this until they break up. Well, what if they don't break up?"

He frowns. "Don't say that."

"Can you please promise me?" I press my palms together in front of my chest. "I promise to give things one more try tonight. But if Lewis and Yvette are the perfect couple, can you promise to break up with me?"

Parker exhales, looking up at the roof of his car. "*Kylie.*"

"Please?"

He slouches with a huff. "Okay. Fine."

I drop my hands, filling with sadness instead of my intended relief. "Thank you."

Parker turns on the ignition. "So, you'll still act like my girlfriend tonight?"

"Yes, but no more kissing."

He deadpans at me. "But this could be our last shot."

I purse my lips, shaking my head. "I don't want to kiss you anymore."

Parker rolls his eyes and puts his foot on the gas, pulling the car off the curb.

"Parker?"

His jaw flexes, ignoring me.

I lean forward. "Parker."

His eyebrows raise with an air of annoyance. "I don't think kissing should be off the table."

"I don't want to do it anymore."

"We'd both prefer to be kissing other people, but I see how it gets under their skin when we do it. It works."

"I hate manipulating him."

"Don't think of it like that. Just think of it as using me." He shrugs. "I'm fine with that."

I narrow my gaze. "How can you be fine with being used?"

"Because I'm getting what I want."

"Are you really aching that badly to be Yvie's plaything?"

His hands squeeze around the steering wheel. "Yes. Stop judging me."

I sit back. "That's not what I was doing."

His arms lock and his shoulders tighten.

"Are you okay?"

He flicks on the indicator and pulls the car curbside.

I hold on to the edge of my seat, startled. "What are you doing?"

Parker keeps a hold of the steering wheel, exhaling slowly.

"Parker?"

His eyes close as his chest rises and falls.

My teeth clench as I watch him shrink inward. Is he having an anxiety attack?

I unbuckle my seatbelt and sit forward. Gingerly, I raise my hand to touch his shoulder, but I second-guess myself. I pull back, worried he'll freak out if I touch him.

He shudders, releasing the steering wheel and opening his eyes.

"I'm okay. I just got a head rush."

My palms are slick with sweat. "Can I do anything?"

Parker rubs his eyes and grunts. "Can we stop arguing?"

"I was just trying to make sure we're on the same page."

"We are," he says. "We both want to be with other people."

"Yeah, but what about how we go about it?"

He massages the back of his neck, staring straight ahead. "I'm doing this because I'm willing to do anything to break them up. I thought you were too."

"I am, but..."

Parker pulls the car onto the road. "Then that's all there is to it."

Even though I want to keep stressing my point, I don't breathe another word. I don't want him to get another head rush and there not be enough time to pull over.

It doesn't matter, anyway. I'm not letting him kiss me, no matter how big a show he puts on.

We arrive at the fair, and once we're past the gates, my walk turns into a dawdle. The lights, music, and screams from the rides chaotically swirl around us.

Parker double-takes and waits for me to catch up. "What's happening?"

I press a hand into my stomach. "I don't do carnival rides."

He smirks. "Green, you recently jumped off a cliff."

"An impulsive action I don't intend to repeat."

Parker steps toward me, lifting one finger. "One. Just ride one."

I eye him skeptically. "One? You won't pressure me into more?"

"You might like it after you do one."

"Doubt it. After I rode a rollercoaster at age eleven, I swore off rides."

"Just ride the same one as Lewis. Isn't that enough incentive?"

My stomach flips. "I won't look attractive to him if I'm about to puke."

Parker laughs. "You won't puke. You'll have fun."

"Why are you acting like we've just met?"

"Why are you acting like you haven't nailed everything you've tried over the past few days?" He links arms with me. "Come on. You've got this."

I relent, letting him walk me toward the sideshow alley. Parker checks his phone, finding the location Lewis texted him. We find him and Yvette at a sideshow game, where he throws darts at moving targets.

As we approach the booth, Lewis groans, throwing his head back as the sideshow worker announces he's not a winner.

"*Oof.* Lewy, it's not your night," Parker teases.

Lewis sighs. "Hey, man. Great timing."

Parker snickers, patting Lewis's shoulder.

Yvette moves around Lewis and pulls me into a hug. "Hi, Kylie. So glad you're here."

"Oh, umm, hi," I say, taking a moment to hug her back.

She giggles, pulling out of the hug. "You got to see my boyfriend successfully *not* win me a prize."

"I tried," Lewis complains.

Yvette plants her hands on her hips. "Trying doesn't get me a teddy bear, does it."

Lewis presses a kiss on her pouty lips. "No, but I can give you better things than that."

Yvette drops her arms to her sides and leans against Lewis.

Parker rubs the back of his neck, averting his gaze. "So, have you guys been here long?"

"Only about twenty minutes," Lewis replies. "We were thinking about going on a ride next."

"Nice," Parker cheers.

Oh boy.

Parker hugs an arm around me. "What do you think?"

I chew my bottom lip. "Which ride are you going on?"

"Lewis and I were debating between the pirate ship and the tilt-a-whirl," Yvette says. "Pirate Ship is the closest."

"We could do both," Parker says. "Pirate Ship first?"

Yvette bats her lashes. "Exactly what I was thinking."

Parker shifts his stance. "Awesome."

Lewis takes Yvette by the hand, leading us away from the sideshow booth. "Let's go then."

Parker keeps his arm around me, forcing me forward. My anxiety is low as we walk down the aisle of sideshow games. However, we're now blasted with the shrieks and whirs of fast-moving rides.

When my feet scuff into the ground, Parker's force lessens. We stop and he points out something resembling a pirate ship that moves, forward and back, on an axis.

"That's the ride," he says.

My knees buckle. "It goes up so high."

"It looks worse than it is. It's pretty tame compared to the other rides."

My teeth grit. "If you say so."

Parker clutches my hand. "Are you up for it?"

Fear stains my eyes. "Do you not feel how sweaty my palms are?"

Parker laughs. "I wasn't going to say anything."

I look up at the ride and swallow hard. "At least it doesn't go completely upside down."

Parker squeezes my hand. "Is that a yes?"

I shiver, sending it up Parker's arm. "It'll check my quota of going on a carnival ride."

"That's the spirit," Parker cheers. "Plus, you'll be with Lewis."

Yvette lifts onto the balls of her feet, waving us over. "Come on, you two. Let's get in on the next round."

Parker steps forward, but my feet stay planted in place.

He jerks forward, clumsily regaining his balance. He turns to me with a wry smile. "I thought you were ready."

I shiver, holding onto his hand. "I'm sorry."

He stops closer with a sympathetic smile. "It's okay. But, you know, they're waiting."

"I just wish I didn't have to do this," I whisper. "I wish he wanted to sit this one out with me."

Parker nudges his shoulder toward the ride. "He's going on this ride with her, regardless if we tag along or not. Do you want to let them go alone?"

I press my lips into a line and shake my head.

Still holding my hand, Parker uses his other hand to pat my arm. "How about you use some of your Kikki confidence?"

"Kikki dances and sings in her kitchen. She doesn't get suspended in the air."

Parker winks. "I think she does now."

My mind flashes back to falling through the air and dropping into the water. I grow a smile, thinking about balancing and moving Parker's skateboard. His friends' cheers ring in my ears, like after they celebrated my achievements.

I squeeze Parker's hand and step forward. "Okay. We can do this."

Parker's pace increases, probably in case I chicken out again. He buys our ride tickets and swiftly weaves us through the line to catch up with Lewis and Yvette.

"What was the hold up?" Lewis asks.

"Oh, you know, Kylie had to tell me how handsome I am," Parker jokes.

Lewis laughs. "Umm, yeah, I'm sure."

I silently chuckle, sharing a look with Lewis.

The line moves swiftly, and we shuffle onto the ride.

"What the heck?" I utter.

Inside the pirate ship are bench seats.

Bench seats.

How is this safe? This thing lifts into the air!

Yvette latches onto my hand, dragging me into the row. "Come on, Kylie. We girls gotta stick together."

I sit next to her and gulp. "Aren't you scared?"

"This is manufactured scary," Yvette says. "Not like a freaking cliff at a lake. That's the real world where you could literally die."

I blink at her, remembering horror news articles about carnival rides malfunctioning with people on them. Ugh. Why am I thinking about that while aboard one?

"You can stop playing it up now, Kikki," Parker says playfully. "You don't have to act scared to make everyone else feel better."

I fake a laugh as a long guard rail is pulled over our row. It lands above our laps and leaves ample room for us to slip out. Umm. This doesn't come close to landing on my safety-meter. Then the music blares, competing with the whirring noises of the machinery firing up.

Parker nudges me. "Doesn't the music help boost your confidence?"

I'm too spooked to reply. Instead, inside my head, I play one of my favorite songs from my baking playlist. Simultaneously, I pray I get out of this without any injuries.

As the ride whooshes through the air, a scream shoots out of me. On the incline, my stomach rises into my throat. Searching for safety, I lean into Parker. He awes and reaches his arm across my front, acting as a second brace.

The ride descends backwards, and Yvie's scream wipes out the sound of mine. I lock my neck and shoulders, staring at our collective hands gripping the steel bar. Yvie's hand creeps over Parker's hand, and she claws at his fingers for support.

If I weren't scared stiff, I'd make an effort to look past Yvie and find Lewis. Can he see that his girlfriend is holding Parker's hand?

I look down as Parker intertwines his fingers with hers.

Okay, this officially got too weird. I'm leaning into him while he's trying to get closer to her. When I entered into this arrangement to get between a couple, I didn't think I'd literally be sandwiched between an intimate moment.

Thankfully, being totally weirded out distracts me from my fear. As the ride comes to a stop, the hands in front of me disentangle, and the bar is lifted from our laps.

We shuffle off the ride, and once we're off the platform, I get a glimpse of Lewis.

Whoa. He is not happy.

"Uh, what was that?" Lewis deadpans at Parker.

"What?" Parker says, unable to rid his smile.

If he wants to act dumb, this is a bad start. But I can't blame him. He got to hold Yvie's hand and get a step closer to being with her.

"You and my girlfriend," Lewis says, puffing out my chest. "Or did you not think I could see you holding her hand?"

Yvette laughs, wandering away as she scrolls on her phone. "Lighten up, Lewy. I just wanted something strong to hold on to."

Light pink colors Parker's cheeks as he watches Yvette saunter away.

Lewis groans. "Look, dude, it's not cool, and you know it."

"What did you expect me to do?" Parker argues. "Fling her hand off me?"

"You didn't need to hold her hand back."

Parker rolls his eyes. "You're being ridiculous. I wouldn't expect you to push Kylie away if she were scared."

Lewis glances at me, and then back at Parker. "I'm not saying you should've been mean to her. I just obviously wasn't cool with you holding my girlfriend's hand."

Parker shrugs. "What can I say? She grabbed my hand and thought I was a stronger choice than you."

Lewis smirks. "Dang, you're full of yourself."

"I'm just calling it how I see it."

Lewis looks at me, stifling a laugh. "How can you stand to be around him?"

I grin. "He can be a bit much."

Parker drapes his arm over my shoulder. "*See.* Only *a bit* much."

Lewis laughs. "Oh, man. You can take anything as a compliment."

Parker motions ahead. "Why don't you catch up with your girlfriend before she wanders away from the herd?"

Lewis quickens his pace toward Yvette, giving Parker and I space to talk.

"I told you not to worry about my friendship with Lewis," Parker says. "Anytime we have an argument, I make sure it ends with a joke. We'll be fine when this is all over."

"But you've never fought over a girl before."

Parker chucks my chin. "But, in the end, he'll have you as a prize."

A blush inflames my cheeks. "Oh, um, I…"

"You're so cute when you don't know what to do with compliments."

I clear my throat. "Maybe I need lessons from you on how to take them."

He smirks. "That can be arranged."

When we make it to the others, Lewis suggests we go back to sideshow alley. He mustn't want a repeat of Parker and Yvie holding hands.

Fine by me. One ride is more than enough.

Parker lets Lewis pick the game, and I can already see their competitiveness coming out. They race each other in a water pistol game. The goal is to aim the water into a clown's mouth, which then fills a balloon. Whoever fills their balloon the fastest, wins.

As Yvette and I cheer on the boys, my lips might cheer for Parker, but my heart is screaming for Lewis. I glance at Yvie, wondering if she's thinking about a different boy as well. It was, after all, her choice to grab onto Parker's hand on the pirate ship.

With a filled balloon, Parker puts down the water pistol and raises his fists in a cheer. I laugh at his wild competitiveness and applaud his achievement.

"Couldn't do it without my cheerleader," Parker says, stealing a look my way.

I gulp as he moves in closer. Parker presses his hand into the middle of my back, leaving little to no gap between us. When his lips pout, I'm quick to push him back.

"No."

"Come on," he whispers.

"No."

"But I won."

I wriggle away from him. "I said no, Parker."

Parker groans, backing away from me. He runs a hand through his hair and forces a smile. He steps around Lewis, sidling in close to Yvette.

"What do you think, Yvie?" Parker says with a flirtatious lilt. "Did I completely annihilate your man?"

Yvette giggles. "Yes, you were very manly with your little water gun."

Parker leans an elbow on her shoulder. "Well, I could move up to a paintball gun. Or, maybe an airsoft?"

Lewis scoffs. "So now you want to bruise me?"

Yvette twirls a piece of hair around her finger. "What's wrong, Lewy? You don't think you could beat him?"

"Maybe he knows he's too pretty to get bruised?" It comes out of my mouth before I finish the thought.

Lewis turns, grinning at me. He steps by my side and glances at Parker. "How about that? Your girlfriend thinks I'm prettier than you."

"She didn't exactly say that," Parker replies, as the carnival worker props a stuffed bunny on the counter.

Before Parker can offer it to Yvette, she moves in to claim Lewis.

Her hands move into Lewis's hair as she says in a breathy voice, "She's right. You'd have to be blind not to see how hot you are." Yvette hugs Lewis and views me with a smug expression. "Right, Kylie?"

I feel two feet tall. "Mm-hmm."

As I sink into awkwardness, a voice calls out to us.

"Oh, hi, guys," Kai calls out, walking toward us with his arm around Tabitha.

"Crap," Parker mumbles under his breath. Instantly, he flashes a smile and waves at them. "Hey guys."

"What's happening?" Lewis asks as the two join our group.

"Jamie and Milo went to meet up with Tyler," Kai says. "We were just walking around until they came back."

I can't help watching the face-off between Yvette and Tabitha. It soon morphs into both girls clinging to their boyfriends and doing their best to ignore the other's existence.

Tabitha smiles at me. "Hi Kylie. Having a good night?"

"Yes, thanks," I say with an unmistakable squeak. "You?"

She nods, wrapping an arm around Kai. "So much fun."

Yvette clears her throat in the most unsubtle way possible. "Umm, hello. I'm here too."

Tabitha doesn't look her way. Instead, inspecting her cuticles.

Lewis shifts by Yvette, searching for something to say. His silence only irritates Yvette, who huffs and glares at him.

Kai waits for his girlfriend to answer. When it's obvious she won't, he glances at Lewis and Yvette. "Anyone gone on the Tilt-a-Whirl yet?"

"It's our next choice," Lewis says, relieved at the subject change.

Kai pans around the group. "Should we head over?"

Tabitha frowns. "I'm not in the mood."

Kai's enthusiasm drops. "Oh. That's cool. We don't have to."

Yvette scoffs. "Doesn't mean we can't."

Tabitha doesn't look her way, but her eye roll registers.

Yvette leans forward to make sure I catch her grin. "I mean, we're all on a double date. Double means just two couples. Right, Kylie?"

Oh gosh. This is beyond awkward. Why does she have to bring me into this? I hug my middle, hoping someone else will chime in so I don't have to speak.

Noticing my anxious shifting beside him, Parker grabs everyone's attention. "Why not bumper cars? They're right over there."

I blink at him. Wait, what?

I pan around to all the faces, and they're onboard.

Everyone is into this idea.

Oh, crap. Do they expect me to drive one?

Seventeen

With everyone in approval, the dread seeping into my stomach gets even worse.

Parker pulls me close to him. "Why do you look worried again?"

"Bumper cars?" I wince. "That's literally getting into a tiny car for the sole purpose of being hit by other tiny cars."

Parker sniggers. "Exactly."

"Hey, kid," the sideshow worker grunts, lifting the stuffed bunny. "Are you taking this or not?"

Parker grabs the bunny and hands it to me.

I take it with a huff. "Getting hit is the opposite of my idea of fun."

"Don't be a wet blanket, Kikki."

Before I can protest, Parker lifts me into the air. I yelp as he hoists me against him, causing me to straddle my legs around his torso.

"Oh my gosh, put me down," I whine, dripping in embarrassment.

Parker chuckles, carrying me toward the bumper cars. "No. You're too adorable."

He looks up at me, smiling, as I look down at him. Without meaning to, I focus on the shine of his lips, and a thrill runs down my spine.

Stop it, Kylie.

I plant a hand over his lips and murmur, "It's still off the table."

His laughter vibrates against my hand, and then I feel his lips pucker. I fling my hand off after he presses a kiss against my palm.

He sends me a wink and lowers me to the ground at the ticket line.

Yvette and Lewis make their way onto the track first. Yvette practically skips as she drags Lewis to her car of choice.

Tabitha and Kai, on the other hand, are more casual in their approach. When Tabitha doesn't squeal or make an exaggerated fuss over the tiniest thing, it sucks even more that Parker doesn't want me to be friends with her.

After Parker buys our tickets, he guides me by the shoulders to our bumper car.

"You want to drive?" he asks.

I lift my palms. "Heck no."

He mumbles a laugh as he stretches the oversized seatbelt across both our bodies. The music pumps louder through the speakers, and the bumper car engines fire up. My head yanks backward when our car takes off.

"Whoa," I hum, holding onto the edge of the car.

"Hands in," Parker warns. "Someone will drive past and crush them."

I suck in a breath and swiftly plant my hands between my thighs.

Parker takes a wide berth around two cars and then steers our car like a missile toward Yvette and Lewis. I brace myself for imminent impact, but then we're struck from behind. We both grunt as the car spins out.

With his foot off the gas and steadying the steering wheel, Parker regains control of our car. Kai and Tabitha drive by, waving and laughing.

"Those rats," Parker mutters.

He slams on the gas, and we take off after them.

"Do you have to go so fast?" I complain.

"Ah, yes," he replies sarcastically. "I gotta get 'em back."

"I'm seriously getting motion sickness."

"I'm trying not to spin out again," Parker replies. "Believe me, I'm aiming to hit other people."

He doesn't gain on Kai and Tabitha, but Lewis and Yvette are nearby. Lewis drives and swerves to get away from us. Parker keeps on him, determined to smash into their car. But, when other cars get between us, Lewis and Yvette speed away.

Parker steers our car off the edge of the track. "Your turn to take the wheel."

"What?" I yelp. "No way."

Parker lifts his hands. "Take the wheel."

"*Parker*," I squeak as another car crashes into us. "You take the wheel."

A mischievous laugh rolls out of him. "It's your turn."

"I didn't sign up to drive a bumper car."

His face nestles by mine. "You also didn't sign up to kiss me, but you liked it."

"*Ick*." I shove his face away, making him laugh. "Fine. I'm only doing this to avoid being hit."

"Good luck," he teases as I take hold of the steering wheel.

I push my foot on the accelerator, and turn the bumper car too fast.

"Whoa," Parker chokes as we slam into a car on his side.

I bunch my shoulders high and wince. "Sorry."

He points ahead. "Just go forward. Avoid turning."

"But the other cars are coming straight at us."

"They'll turn. Haven't you ever played chicken?"

"Umm, no. That game sounds like a nightmare."

He nudges me. "Well, welcome to your nightmare."

I clench my jaw and straighten my arms. As Tabitha and Kai head straight for us, I scrunch my eyes closed.

Parker laughs and grabs the wheel. "Keep your eyes open, Kikki."

I squint them open and shake my head. "Nuh-uh."

He lets go, and I keep my arms locked, only steering when I near the tracks' edge.

"*Oof.*" I hiss as we're bumped on my side.

The familiar shriek of laughter passes us as Yvette and Lewis drive by.

"Step on it," Parker encourages. "Hit 'em back."

"I don't want to intentionally ram them."

"But that's the point of bumper cars."

"Also why I said I didn't want to do this."

Before Parker can make another argument, we're hit from behind.

"Ugh." I jerk forward, slamming myself against the steering wheel.

Parker looks behind us and smirks. "Nice one, Tabby."

"It was him, not me," she calls out.

They swerve around us, and Tabitha waves, but Kai gains too much speed for me to even smile back. There's no way I was waving back. My arms are cemented in this position.

"Are you good?" Parker asks.

"I'm hanging on."

"Do you want me to take over?"

"No," I say, surprising myself. "I prefer to have control. That way, the only surprises are what other cars do. I like not having your crazy driving in the mix."

I meander through the cars, avoiding being hit and hitting others, and soon our engine dies out.

"*Woo!*" Parker cheers, unbuckling. "You did it."

I giggle and joke, "We're still alive."

We leave the car and make our way off the rubber track.

"Okay, now it's time for the Tilt-a-Whirl," Lewis announces once we're all back on stable ground.

Yvette giggles, swinging Lewis by the hand. "You've been dying for that ride all night. Come on, baby, let's go."

The others head out toward the next ride, and I barely feel like I'm standing upright.

"Another ride?" I question warily. "Already?"

Parker hugs his arms around my shoulders, walking me behind the others. "Maybe they're will be a line and you'll have time to take a breather."

I grin. "You and your positive thinking."

We meander behind the others, and as the night sky grows darker, the rides area has become crowded. We line up behind the others, and the awkward tension rises as Yvette continually attempts to grab Tabitha's attention.

Tabitha clings to Kai, keeping her gaze well away from Yvette.

Yeesh. Why are they still hanging around us? If Tabitha wants nothing to do with Yvette, couldn't she make an excuse and leave and find Jamie and Milo?

I keep my gaze low as we wait in the immovable line. I sure don't want to be roped into the middle of the ugliness brewing between the girls. Beside me, Parker fidgets and then digs inside his pocket. He pulls out his phone, and I see the display reading, *"Kurtis Calling."*

Parker frowns at the screen. "What does he want?"

I nudge him. "Answer it. He might need help."

Parker groans, hitting the answer icon and raising the phone to his ear. "Hello?"

I watch him squint as he tries to hear his brother. He shakes his head and plants a finger over his ear. "Wait, what was that?"

He looks at the ground, trying harder to listen. "Dude, I can't hear anything you're saying." He lowers the phone and says to me, "Wait here. I'm just going to walk away so I can hear him."

"Okay."

It's a strange feeling as Parker walks away. Even though I have his friends around me, I feel alone. Like my security has been ripped away. I shift my weight, avoiding conversation with either girl. Kai and Lewis chat about something. I think it's a sports game, but I've really got no clue.

Come on, Parker. Hurry back.

The line moves forward, and I walk on tippy toes, searching for Parker.

Yvette grabs my wrist, tugging me forward. "Come with us. He'll catch up."

And just like that, terror vortexes in the pit of my stomach. A cold sweat coats my back and arms, and I grow light-headed. I fling Yvette off me, and stumble backwards.

She frowns at me. "What are you doing?"

I press my lips together as the nausea grows. Sickened to my core, I uncontrollably shake my head.

Yvette's expression sours, and she boards the ride with Lewis. I press my hands into my stomach, watching them get into the same car as Tabitha and Kai. I blink hard, thinking about how Parker would want me to get between them. I shudder, petrified at the idea of being up there.

As the ride begins, I hug the stuffed bunny close, but it doesn't give the same level of comfort as Parker's presence. On the ride, the group cheers with raised arms. Their car spins, seemingly out of control, as the base of the ride spins in a different direction. I swallow the second-hand queasiness, looking away as it starts tilting.

"Hey, why aren't you up there?" Parker asks, stepping toward me as he pockets his phone. "You didn't have to wait."

I open my mouth to speak to him, but the words clog in my throat.

Parker looks me up and down. "Kylie?"

Hugging the bunny, I wring my hands together. "I... I..."

Concern riddles Parker as he cups the sides of my face. "Hey, what happened?"

I shiver. "I don't know. I just couldn't do it."

Parker peers over his shoulder and then back at me with unease. "You've done tougher stuff than this."

My stomach flips, and I sniff hard. "I don't know. It felt different."

He tilts his head, moving his hands down to my shoulders and stroking my arms. "You're shivering. Are you okay?"

With the bunny between us, I hold on to his sides for stability. "Yeah. I feel better with you here."

A nervous laugh murmurs out of him. "Really?"

"Yeah. You weren't here to tell me I could do it."

He brushes back my hair. "But you can do it. You can do anything."

Tingles run down my spine. "I guess I still need to hear it from you."

He smiles. "Okay, I won't leave your side for the rest of the night."

"Unless you get a chance with Yvie."

"No, we'll stick to the four of us. I know all these lights and sounds can be overwhelming."

"Yeah, it's a bit manic compared to a speaker in my kitchen."

Parker's smile settles my nerves. Relief sets in, knowing I won't have to board another ride.

"What did your brother want?"

Parker rolls his eyes. "He wanted me to take William off his hands. You know, our younger brother. I said, no way, because my parents already roped me into babysitting him tomorrow."

"We're still taking a break tomorrow, right?" I ask. "I definitely need a recharge after all these activities."

He smirks. "Yes, daredevil. You can have a whole day without seeing me."

As the ride continues, I avoid watching at all costs. Parker, on the other hand, has no qualms about all the spinning.

It's funny how the rides feel shorter when you're not on them. Soon, everyone disembarks.

"That was so fun," Yvette cheers and grabs Tabitha's hand. "I'm so glad we could do this together. We're friends again, right?"

Tabitha flings her off. "You're not my friend."

"Whoa." Lewis gasps, leaning close to Yvette.

Parker takes half a step forward, intently watching the girls.

Yvette huffs. "You're so difficult. Why can't things just go back to how they were?"

"Because you never stuck up for me!" Tabitha shouts, the adrenaline from the ride surging through her body. "You were never a good friend."

Tabitha lunges at Yvette, causing the boys to act. Kai pulls his girlfriend back, while Lewis lifts an arm in front of Yvette.

Tabitha nudges her way forward as Kai's arms hug around her. "You never stuck up for me when Camila would say horrible things about me. How do you think I can forget that?"

"She did that to both of us," Yvette defends. "It's just how things were."

My heart hammers in my chest, watching the warring girls. Were things always coming to blows? Or, has the fact I've been hanging out with Yvie made things worse?

"I remember the things you said when I tried to put a stop to her," Tabitha says, eyes watering. "It wasn't the same for us."

"What do you want from me?" Yvette complains. "I'm trying to be better."

Tabitha breaks free of Kai, rushing at Yvette. Fearing the worst, I let the stuffed bunny hit the ground and move forward.

"Tabby, stop." I push my way between them. "You don't want to do this."

"You think you're so good, Tabitha," Yvette snipes. "You're the one who's pretending."

As I turn, Yvette lunges for Tabitha with her hand out to strike.

"*Ouch*," I hiss.

One of her perfectly manicured fingernails jabs my eye and scratches along my lash line, to the end of my brow bone. My vision instantly waters, and I press my palm against the stinging area. As I turn away from the girls, I run into something, and then arms wrap around me.

Recognizing his embrace instantly, I rest my head against Parker's shoulder. He strokes my hair while his other hand rubs my back. "Are you okay?"

I sniffle a response, scared I'll unleash a series of sobs.

"Kylie?" Tabitha's voice is wounded. "Oh my gosh, are you okay?"

Parker holds me tighter. "Maybe just give her some space."

"She's just checking she's okay," Kai says defensively.

"Kylie, I'm so sorry," Yvie yelps, breaking my personal space. "Are you okay?"

I whimper, scrunching Parker's T-shirt for comfort.

"You hit her," Tabitha lashes out. "She could be bleeding."

Parker rubs my back and rests his head by mine. "It's okay, Yvie. It was an accident."

Yvette exhales hard and backs away.

"You wouldn't have said that if it were Tabby," Kai accuses.

"Man, do we have to do this right now?" Parkers asks. "Kylie's hurt."

"I'm really sorry she got between us," Tabitha says.

I just want to hug her and tell her it's okay, but I'm too much of a mess to break away from Parker.

Tabitha lets out a shaky breath. "Kai, let's just get back to Jamie and Milo."

"Babe, give yourself a break," Kai says. "You're not the one who hit her."

"I didn't hit her," Yvette yelps. "It was an accident."

Parker clears his throat, gently swaying me. "Lewis, can you find some ice?"

"Yeah, sure," Lewis replies.

Parker brushes my hair back. "Okay, they're all gone," he whispers. "Do you want to show me the damage?"

I shake my head against the crook of his arm.

"Come on, Kikki," he coaxes. "I'm sure it's not that bad."

I sniff hard, lifting my head and rubbing my puffy, watering eyes. My left is much worse from Yvette's finger jab.

Parker's hand sneaks under my chin, lifting my head. "Move your hands," he whispers. "Let me see."

I sniff again, accidentally letting a sob break free. I lower my hands, and Parker angles my chin higher.

"Oh, it's not too bad," he says in an upbeat tone.

I swallow hard and croak, "Really?"

Parker runs a finger under my eye, trailing past my lash line. I suck in a breath as he reaches the tender area.

"Sorry," he murmurs.

I let out a shaky breath. "It's okay."

"You're not bleeding, if you were worried about that."

"It didn't feel like it was bleeding. It just stings so bad." I wipe my eyes. "And my dang eyes won't stop watering."

Parker mumbles a laugh, pulling at the shoulder of his T-shirt. "I know. You soaked me."

I slouch my shoulders. "Sorry."

He smiles, running his hands down my back. "Don't be. I'll hold you as long as you need."

I flinch. "Why?"

He tilts his head, looking into my eyes. "Because I…"

"Hey, it's kinda hard to find ice around here," Lewis says, jogging back to us.

Parker pulls his arms away from me, and I turn toward Lewis.

Lewis stands before me and lifts a paper cup of shaved ice. "But hopefully a snow cone will help."

I smile at the adorable gesture.

He lifts the paper cup, pressing it against the side of eye. "May I?"

I rub my lips, look up at him, and nod.

Yvette rushes beside us with her hands cupped over her nose and mouth. She drops her hands, exhaling with relief. "*Phew.* The way everyone was talking, I thought there'd be tons of blood."

Lewis lifts the paper cup. "Just a scratch."

Yvette winces. "*Oof.* It's really raised and red. Dang, Kylie, I didn't mean to get you like that."

"I know," I reply, steadying my tone. "I just hated seeing you two fighting."

Parker moves in beside Yvette. "Well, Tabby's gone now, and the four of us can get back to hanging out."

Lewis steadies the cup against my eye. "How's it feeling, Kylie? Are you up for more carnival fun?"

I chew my fingernail, giggling nervously from his attentive eye contact.

"She's tough," Parker answers. "Remember, she's the daredevil."

"That's true," Lewis says, running a thumb under my eye.

I clench my teeth. "Oops. Has my mascara run?"

"Don't sweat it," Lewis says, grinning. "You still look great."

"Okay, I think Kylie can hold the cup herself," Yvette blurts, curling her arm around Lewis's bicep. "Especially if you boys think she's so tough."

Lewis pulls the cup away from my face and shoves it at Parker. "Sorry, dude. She's your girl."

Parker takes the cup. "It's fine. I asked you to get ice."

Yvette tugs on Lewis's arm. "Come on. She's fine. I wanna go on the tango-tango."

Lewis relents and lets Yvette steal him away.

Parker gives me the paper cup. "Does it still sting?"

I lean the ice against the scratch. "Yes, but the ice is helping."

"I suppose you're not up for another ride."

"Oh my gosh, I'm really not."

Parker smiles. "It's okay. It looks like you already got your moment with Lewis."

A happy sigh whispers out of me. "It felt like he really wanted to be close to me."

Parker shifts his weight. "Yeah, it did."

"Did you get jealous?" I joke.

He coughs, clutching his elbows. "What? No."

I lower the snow cone. "I was joking."

He forces out a laugh. "Yeah, I know."

I give him a strange look. "Okay."

"The scratch is looking less red."

"Good."

Parker picks up the bunny and dawdles away from me. "Feel like going for a walk?"

I shrug, following him as I press the snow cone against my face again.

"Yvie was eager to get Lewis away from us," I mutter.

"From you," Parker clarifies. "She did not like her boyfriend being that close to you. Once she saw you weren't bleeding, she wanted out."

"Lewis almost dropped the snow cone. Like he felt guilty."

"Yeah, it seemed that way."

I watch Parker's side profile carefully. "Are you okay with talking about this?"

He double-takes at me. "Yeah. This is what we're here for. Aren't we?"

"Yes, but..."

"I'm fine. I think I'm just shaken up from you getting hurt."

I reach up and pinch his cheek. "Aww, Parky."

"Oh, no." He laughs, loosening up. "That's not starting, is it?"

"What? It's a cute nickname for your girlfriend to call you," I tease.

"Sure, sure." He slips his hands in his pockets as his smile grows. "Throw that back in my face."

The scratch is only a mild irritation now, and I toss the snow cone in a trash can.

"You good?" Parker asks, viewing the graze.

"As good as I can be."

Parker wanders toward the carousel. "Want to do something at an easy speed?"

I watch the leisurely, non-threatening ride, and my whole body mellows. My heart bounces to a happy beat, grateful he suggested something that doesn't spike my anxiety.

He probably just feels guilty about me getting hurt.

He gestures at the ride, growing a lop-sided grin. "What do you say?"

Eighteen

"The carousel?" I question. "It's not too kiddy?"

He shrugs, his smile sliding to the left. "It could be cute."

"It doesn't give me anxiety, so let's do it, Parky."

"Okay, you've hit your quota on the nickname," Parker says, moving to the ticket booth.

"As if," I complain, following behind him. "You've said my nickname an annoying amount of times."

"So?"

"So, if I have a quota, it applies to you too."

Parker wiggles his eyebrows. "No, I don't think so."

"Whatever." I step in front of him. "Can I buy our tickets? You've paid for everything since we've been together."

He pulls me back. "That's because I'm the boyfriend."

"But I'm the one with the job."

"Don't worry about it. This whole thing was my idea. I'll foot the bill."

"But I'm getting as much out of this as you. Just let me pay for the carousel."

"As long as it doesn't cut into your baking while we're together."

"Oh, I see. You don't want me to pay to ensure I'll keep baking?"

He winks. "You got it."

A space opens up at the ticket counter, and I step forward, buying two tickets.

I grab onto his hand. "Come on, Parky."

He chuckles, following behind me as we board the carousel. "You know, it's cute if I call you Kikki. But, can you imagine the crap I'll get if my friends hear you calling me Parky?"

I slide onto a plastic horse. "They'll think it's cute, Parky."

He holds onto the pole sticking out of my horse. "Is that so?"

I giggle, grabbing onto the collar of his shirt. He leans in, and I can't help noticing the shine of his lower lip. My hand smooths down his T-shirt and I feel the rise and fall of his chest. I suck in a breath as our eye contact intensifies.

He pulls away, moving to the adjacent horse. "Sorry."

"Don't be."

"It felt like one of those kissing moments, but no one was around."

My heart booms in agreement.

Leaving the bunny by his feet, Parker climbs onto his horse as it lifts into the air. The carousel begins to spin, and I can't take my eyes off him. He smooths back his hair and the lights of the ride brighten his pinkish face.

"I know kissing is off the table," he says. "I'm not going to try anything."

"You never actually agreed to it."

"But it makes you uncomfortable. I'd be a complete jerk if I kissed you when you're against it." He exhales hard. "I'm sorry for trying back at the sideshow game."

"I'm sorry too. I shouldn't have freaked out."

"No, you were right to say how you felt."

"But it's not like we haven't done it before." I hunch in embarrassment. "And it's not like it's not good."

He tilts his head in confusion. "So, do you want to put kissing back on the table?"

My heart pounds, pleading for a yes, but logic wins. "No. I want Lewis to be my next kiss."

Parker nods. "Okay, good."

Good? He doesn't want to kiss me anymore?

Ugh. Why am I acting disappointed?

This is a good thing!

Thankfully, the movement of the ride creates a breeze, cooling down my body heat. Parker sits back on his horse, seemingly cooling down too.

"This was a good idea," I say. "Much nicer pace."

He smiles. "I'm glad."

Once the ride comes to a stop, we disembark and find Yvette and Lewis strolling our way.

"Oh my gosh." Yvette giggles behind a cupped hand. "You guys were on the carousel?"

Parker leans into me. "She thought it'd be cute."

I playfully nudge him back. "Only because he suggested it."

Parker nods at Lewis. "Did you guys go on The Tango?"

"Yep," Lewis replies. "Gotta keep your lady happy, right?"

Parker bites his lip, and then mutters, "Absolutely."

The four of us meander around the fair until Yvette stops dead in front of us.

She tugs on Lewis's arm. "Oh, yay! I wanna go on the Ferris Wheel."

Parker snaps his fingers. "Yes, good idea. The fireworks are supposed to start soon, and the Ferris Wheel is the best place to see them."

Yvette squeals in delight and leads the way.

As we follow, Parker squeezes me in a one-armed hug. "Wanna have another moment with Lewis?"

"What do you mean?"

"Just leave it to me. I've got a plan."

"As long as it doesn't involve Yvie's finger in my eye again."

Parker sniggers. "Don't worry. If my plan works out, you and Lewis will be nowhere near Yvie."

My heart swells, and I shiver with tingles. "What's your plan?"

He taps his fingers to his lips. "*Shoosh*. We're almost there. Just hold tight while I buy our tickets."

I hang back with Yvette as the boys buy our tickets. She frowns at the bunny in my arms, clearly still peeved her boyfriend didn't win anything for her.

Lewis beckons us forward and clears a path through the crowd, who all want the best seats at the fair. Giddy to get on the ride, Yvette sticks close to Lewis as he guides us to the front to board the Ferris Wheel.

With quick thinking, Parker manages to get beside them. When Lewis boards their pod, he stops Yvie from following.

"Yvie, there's a spider on you," Parker blurts.

Before I can take in the scene, Parker shoves me forward. I launch into the Ferris Wheel pod with Lewis, who struggles to see what's going on.

Yvie rushes in a circle, screaming, as Parker crouches and swats at her legs. Yvie's dress billows out as she twirls, whipping Parker in the face.

"Okay, take your seats, kids," the Ferris Wheel operator says, pulling the brace over our laps.

Lewis and I sit, stunned, as Yvette continues to jump and yelp on the platform. The Ferris Wheel worker moves away from our compartment when the brace is fixed and locked.

"No, wait," Lewis says. "I'm with..."

He's cut off when our pod lifts into the air and moves to the next position on the wheel.

Lewis leans over me, trying to spy Parker and Yvette. "Is she okay?"

"Who knows," I murmur, "she overreacts about everything."

Lewis sits back, staring at me.

I let out a nervous laugh, lifting my palms. "That's Yvie."

"Hmm. I guess," he mumbles, looking ahead as we move onto the next space on the wheel.

Our pod keeps moving up positions as more people board the Ferris Wheel. Eventually, the wheel moves without any jerky stops.

Lewis slides down in the seat, relenting to the fact he's not with Yvie. My hands stay clasped over my lap because I have no idea how to react. It's easy to tell he wishes he weren't seated here with me.

Before I dwell in self-pity, the sky lights up in a dazzling display of fireworks.

"Whoa," it breathes out of me.

"Dang," Lewis murmurs. "We do have the best seats in the house."

I turn to him, and my heart swells as he mirrors my smile.

My gaze returns to the night sky, and I put on my fantasy goggles. In my head, Lewis is holding my hand and the words, "I love you," beg to leave his lips.

A chuckle escapes without me realizing it.

Lewis turns to me asking, "What's so funny?"

I clasp my chest, cringing. "Oh, nothing. Forget it."

He tilts his head, smiling. "You sure?"

I mumble a laugh, rubbing my lips together. "Mm-hmm."

"Wow, that's pretty," Lewis says, looking down at my chest.

He picks up the pendant hanging from my gold chain and inspects it against his palm.

Holy cow. Lewis's hand is so close to my chest. I can still feel where his fingers grazed my skin to grasp the pendant. He says something else about it, but I can't hear it against the heavy pounds of my heart echoing in my ears. It's literally drowning out the boom and crackle of the fireworks.

His voice breaks through. "Kylie?"

"Huh?"

Lewis chuckles with a ridiculously adorable smile. "I asked where you got it."

"Oh. My parents bought it for my birthday last year."

"Is it sapphire?"

"Yeah. I love how dark the blue is."

He lets go of the pendant, and it knocks against my chest. "Me too."

I keep hold of his eye contact, and his smile grows.

He's so close I feel his breath. Why is he so close? Did he do this purposefully?

Wait.

Does he want to kiss me?

Are we going to kiss?

I sit taller, arching my back.

He doesn't move.

Why didn't he move in?

Arching my back would've been enough for Parker to kiss me. Why doesn't it work with Lewis? Is a real kiss harder to conjure than a fake one?

Lewis sits back, and I exhale slowly.

Is Parker right about all our kisses being fake? Do I really have no idea what a real kiss will be like? Because, I swear, the kisses with Parker have felt as real as could be.

I'm not crazy, am I?

Lewis looks over the edge. "I don't see Yvie and Parker down there. Do you think they got on after us?"

"There's no screaming on the ground, so I guess so."

Lewis looks back at me with a grin. "Having a spider on you would be scary."

Although, I know it was a fake excuse made by Parker. I wring my hands together, stopping myself from blurting out something I'll regret. Parker's voice enters my head, reminding me about how to get Lewis's attention.

An easy smile spreads across my lips. "If it were me, I would've dealt with it. But I'm more adventurous than Yvie."

Lewis reclines on the seat, watching me with an impressed expression. "Is that so?"

I shrug casually, looking off to the side. "Some girls faint at the sight of danger." I look back at him with a mischievous grin. "Then there's me."

Lewis sits forward with interest. "So you're no damsel in distress? If this pod overturns, and you were clinging to the edge, you wouldn't need me to rescue you?"

"No. I'd hold myself up until you hoisted me to safety."

"Up to safety?" Lewis questions. "I think getting to the ground would be safer."

"But don't you have big strong arms to hold me?"

Lewis throws his head back, laughing.

I cup a hand over my mouth, giggling in disbelief that I'm flirting with Lewis Freaking Allen. With a large inhale of air, I lower my hands, one mistakenly landing on his thigh.

For a moment, my hand lingers as I take in the sight, but then my senses return.

I lift my hand, blushing and mumbling, "Sorry."

"No big deal," Lewis says, shifting on the seat.

As if the Ferris Wheel is mocking my chance at love, the ride slows and our pod comes to a stop at the platform. A worker opens our pod, and Lewis and I exit, searching for our dates in the surrounding area.

Lewis gestures up at the Ferris Wheel. "They were three pods behind us."

Above, Parker and Yvette share a pod. They're in deep discussion and haven't noticed us.

It doesn't take long before they hit the ground, and our group is reunited.

When they walk across the platform to meet us on the ground, Yvette has her arms crossed and a surly frown on her face.

"Oh, hi, Lewis," she says in a disgruntled tone.

"Hey, what's wrong?" Lewis asks with concern.

Yvette stamps a foot. "What's wrong? You freaking abandoned me! That's what's wrong!"

"Abandoned you?" he questions. "But I..."

Yvette cuts him off. "Who knows what would've happened if Parker wasn't there for me? I can't believe you left me."

Parker stands behind Yvette, trying to keep his expression blank.

Yvette shudders, smoothing down her dress. "He practically had to look up my skirt to get the spider off me."

Lewis's eyes enlarge when he looks at Parker in horror.

Parker recoils. "I didn't look up her skirt."

"But I would've let him if it meant saving my life." Yvette shoves Lewis. "How could you just leave me? I could've been bitten by a spider, and you didn't care."

Lewis stumbles, regaining his balance. "I was already on the Ferris Wheel. I thought you were behind me."

Yvette glares at him. "Well, I hope you enjoyed your time with Kylie, because you're not getting any more time with me."

My chin drops, and I snap my head in Parker's direction. Did he do it? Did he actually pull off breaking them up?

Lewis sighs, reaching for Yvette. "Yvie, what are you talking about?"

She bumps him off, stomping away from us.

Lewis chases after. "Yvie?"

I can't close my ajar mouth. As Parker closes the gap between us, I shake my head in disbelief.

Parker steps in close to me. "Are we good?"

I puff a silent laugh. "Umm, yeah. Despite Yvie being over-the-top *again*. I can't believe I rode the Ferris Wheel with Lewis. It was so romantic."

"Yeah?" he replies enthusiastically. "Did he put the moves on you?"

I cup a hand over my brow as a goofy smile lifts my cheeks. "Umm."

"Wait. He did?"

"You don't have to sound so shocked."

"No, I'm not. I mean... This is what we wanted to happen. I can't believe it did."

"It was just a little flirting," I reply. "Didn't things go according to plan with Yvie?"

Parker grits his teeth. "Kinda. We rode the Ferris Wheel together, but I wouldn't call it romantic."

"I figured since she was still complaining about the invisible spider." I give him an intense side-eye. "Just how handsy did you get with her legs?"

Parker smirks. "A gentleman never tells."

I laugh. "*Gross.*"

Parker nudges me. "So, give me the deets on what happened in your pod."

I rub my lips together, reminiscing about the way Lewis held my stare. "I swear, he was gonna kiss me."

"What happened?"

I lift my necklace pendant. "He touched my necklace, and when he let it go, we stared into each other's eyes. It felt the same as when you and I look at each other before we kiss. I don't know why he didn't keep leaning in."

"Oh, I don't know either."

I giggle, shying my face away. "And then I touched his thigh."

"Wow, and you call me handsy."

"Maybe I've been spending too much time with you," I joke.

"Hey, if it helped you get closer to Lewis, it's all worth it," Parker replies. "I really thought splitting them up on the Ferris Wheel would help break them up."

"There's still hope," I say. "They are fighting."

Parker grins. "Look who became the optimistic one."

I smirk, willing my blush away. "Oh, boy. I really am spending too much time with you."

"So, tonight has gone well?" Parker asks, bracing himself. "We're not gonna break up?"

I giggle at the ridiculousness. "We're not breaking up."

Parker lifts his fist in a cheer. "*Yes!*"

"You're such a goofball."

Parker grins. "Yeah, maybe."

Beep, beep.

I feel the vibration in my pocket, and pull out my phone. I double-take at the notification. "It's a text from Tabitha."

Parker leans over. "What's it say?"

I hand Parker the bunny and pull my phone away. "Give me a minute."

Out of Parker's view, I open the text. *"Sorry for what went down earlier. I feel so bad you got hurt, and I hate that I keep letting Yvie rile me up. I'm thinking about not going on the camping trip so you guys can have fun without me ruining it."*

I clasp my chest and pout. "Aww."

"What?" Parker asks, craning his neck.

I push him back. "Wait a minute."

I text Tabitha back. *"I feel so bad that you two are still fighting. Please don't ditch on the camping trip. Hopefully, we can all become friends by the end of it. We need to at least try for the sake of our boyfriends."*

She texts back. *"That's so sweet of you. I didn't tell Kai I was thinking about not going. I think he'd be super pissed."*

"Can you tell him Parker feels really bad about things going sour between them? He was just worried about me. He definitely doesn't want to ruin his friendship with Kai. I'd hate to come between them like that."

"I'll make sure he knows. I'm so glad Parker has you. I've never seen him this attentive before. He's better when he's with you."

I quickly lock the phone and slip it into my pocket.

He's better when he's with me?

Huh?

"Hey, what happened?" Parker asks. "What'd she say?"

"Oh, umm, she was thinking about not going on the camping trip."

"Oh, cool."

"No, not cool. Very uncool."

"But it'd be easier if she weren't there. Yvie gets too worked up when she's around."

I deadpan him. "Can you imagine Kai's reaction if his girlfriend says she's not coming? What if he takes it out on you? I told you, I don't want to be known as the reason you two aren't friends anymore."

Parker huffs, looking up at the stars. "Ugh. Okay, you're right."

"Plus, his parents are chaperoning. He could derail the whole trip by telling his family it's off."

He looks down at me with a defeated half-smile. "Okay, you've made your point."

Lewis strolls over to us, hands slung in pockets, and alone.

"Hey man," Parker says, handing me back the bunny. "Where's Yvie?"

"Yvie called her older brother to take her home."

Parker cranes his neck, looking for her. "I could give her a ride home."

"She doesn't want to get in the same car as me, and I was hoping to get a ride home with you."

Parker pats Lewis's shoulder. "Of course, bro. I've always got your back."

My stomach twists as shame writhes inside me. Parker is comforting his best friend after having a hand in putting him in this miserable situation.

My hands are dirty too.

We shouldn't be doing this to him. He's Parker's friend, and he's my longest ever crush. We should care more about him. There has to be a better way of breaking him up with this horrible girl.

Maybe I should say something? Tell him, point blank, she's no good for him. That I'd treat him better than she ever could. If only there were an easy way to explain my involvement with Parker. I can't claim to be in love with Lewis when he's watched me kiss another boy. It doesn't exactly come off as genuine if we haven't broken up yet.

"Are you sure Yvie has a ride home?" I ask. "Parker could take her home, and I could keep you company on the bus. I don't mind."

"It's fine with me," Parker adds.

Lewis sighs. "Honestly, I just want to get out of here. She yelled a lot, and my head is killing me. I think we both need some time apart."

Parker nods. "Okay, let's get out of here."

"It's okay?" Lewis asks, pivoting between us. "I don't want to ruin your date."

"It's fine," Parker and I blurt much too eagerly.

Lewis's eyes widen, and he smiles nervously. "Thanks, guys."

We leave the fairgrounds and make it back to Parker's car. The traffic in town is more congested than usual. Parker and I share glances, because all we want to do is discuss our one-on-one time with our crushes. Then there's the added hitch of my crush, sitting on the backseat in gloom.

I hate that he's so down. Do I need to remind him about our moment on the Ferris Wheel? Would that help him perk up?

Ugh. My heart couldn't take it if it didn't.

We reach the curb outside my house, and I unbuckle my seatbelt.

"Hey, man," Parker says, twisting to view the backseat. "I'm just going to walk Kylie to the door and then we can hang. If you want."

Lewis unbuckles. "Nah, man. I'm cool."

Worry wrinkles Parker's face. "Are you sure?"

"I'm good." Lewis opens the passenger door. "Thanks for the ride home."

"Okay, no problem," Parker mumbles. "See ya later."

Lewis waves, walking across to his front yard.

I rub my chest. "He's so down."

Parker rubs his forehead. "Ugh. I feel so bad."

"It's not your fault that Yvie treated him this way."

"I'm still getting between them. I wish he'd never gotten with her so I didn't have to break them up."

I cross my fingers. "It'll be worth it. Won't it?"

He smiles weakly. "Totally."

I reach for the door handle, watching Lewis open his front gate.

"Maybe he needs some perking up," Parker suggests and pats my knee. "This could be your cue to get even closer to him."

I chew my bottom lip.

"Go for it, Green. It'll make up for Yvie putting him in such a bad mood." Parker grins with encouragement. "Get your guy."

I suck in a breath. "Really?"

He nods emphatically.

I open the car door. "Wish me luck."

He winks. "You don't need it."

I leave the car and wave Parker off.

Without giving myself a chance to back out, I leave the bunny on the path to my house, and jog toward Lewis's front gate. "Hey, wait up."

Lewis stops on the path to his front door, turning my way.

I pace down the path and stop in front of him. "Umm." I awkwardly shift my weight. "I just wanted to check if you're okay."

His smile is minuscule. "Yeah, absolutely."

"It's okay not to be. I'm here to talk." I fidget, digging the toe of my sneakers into the stone. "You know, if you need it."

"Really?"

I clasp my hands together, standing taller. "Yes."

"You probably don't want to hear it."

"If that were true, I wouldn't be standing here."

His body language relaxes. "Okay, but I don't want to ruin your friendship with Yvie."

Umm, what? "It's okay. Tell me."

He sighs. "Yvie thinks me and Parker are fighting over you."

The wind is knocked out of me. "Me?"

"I know. It's crazy. I don't know how I'm supposed to convince her that I'm into her."

Is Parker right? Is there really a layer of insecurity to Yvette?

Lewis scratches the back of his head with nervous energy. "I shouldn't say this to you, but, umm, Parker and I were actually competing to get to Yvie first."

I hug my waist, looking down at my shoes. I hate how very aware I am of this.

"Maybe that's why Yvie's suspicious of my feelings," Lewis mutters. "She knows Parker and I were in competition, but she doesn't know she's the girl we want."

I hold myself tighter, hating these words coming from him.

"Did want," he blurts, causing me to look up. "*Did* want."

"Huh?"

"Parker is with you, not Yvie. I'm so sorry. The last thing you want to hear is that your boyfriend is into another girl."

Oh, Lewis, you have no idea the crazy stuff I've been hearing lately.

He winces. "Have I made you uncomfortable?"

"Uh, no, umm," I falter. "Why would Yvie think you want me?"

Lewis takes a step back, exhaling slowly. "I think because I was saying nice things about you."

I lift onto the balls of my feet. "You were?"

"You're a nice person, Kylie, and easy to talk to."

I plant my heels back on the ground. "Thanks. You too."

"Yvie was yelling at me about not protecting her from the spider, and I said..." He sighs, rubbing the side of his face. "I said, I was glad I got away from her because I had a nice time with you on the Ferris Wheel."

My heart throbs. "You said that?"

"I don't know why I did. She wouldn't stop talking. She was so loud and grumpy. I just realized how bad it would've been on the Ferris Wheel with her."

My mouth falls open, but I have no words to speak.

"Maybe if I were in the pod with her, it wouldn't have been so bad," Lewis reasons. "She just got worked up because I wasn't with her." He lets out a nervous laugh. "She said she thought you and I were kissing."

"Why..." My voice trembles. "Why would she think that?"

"Because apparently the Ferris Wheel is the most romantic carnival ride."

I swallow hard. "Oh."

"She said I wasn't very convincing when I denied it."

I wet my lips, feeling chapped. "But we didn't kiss."

"She was too mad to listen. Hopefully, she'll answer when I call her tonight."

I cross my fingers. "Maybe don't call her tonight."

"Huh?"

"She might need a night to sleep on it."

"You think?"

"She overreacts about most things. I can't see her calming down anytime soon."

Lewis nods. "You're probably right. Thanks so much for listening to me vent."

I lift onto the balls of my feet again. "It's no problem."

"I'm glad we're friends."

"Me too." I look to the ground bashfully. "Umm, did you take a photo of me at the skatepark?"

"Oh, yeah." He fidgets in his stance. "Of you and Parker."

I look up. "Oh."

"Did you want a copy?"

I grin. "I'd want a copy of any photo you take. You're so talented."

He puffs a laugh and rubs behind his neck. "Ah, thanks."

"I mean it. You're a true artist."

He runs a hand down my arm. "So are you with your baking."

"I've always thought of baking as art."

"Maybe I can photograph it one day," he suggests. "I bet I could get some cool macro shots of the action in your kitchen."

"Wow, that'd be incredible."

Before I can get out anymore gushing, Lewis pulls me into a hug. My head rests against his shoulder, and it takes a moment for the shock to wear off before I hug him back. We stay in the embrace for a long moment. It's not a tight hug, but I enjoy every second of being in his arms.

When he pulls away, he whispers, "That necklace is really pretty. How come I've never noticed it before?"

I run a finger over the pendant. "I don't wear it very often. Maybe I should change that?"

Lewis smiles. "Yeah, maybe you should."

Is he thinking about our almost-kiss on the Ferris Wheel? Is he upset because Yvie figured out he really does want to kiss me? Will he finally do it now?

"Thanks for being my friend," he says, lifting a hand to wave. "Good night."

My posture droops. "Good night, Lewis."

I practically float to my house. In the living room, when I hug my parents and say good night, I'm still in a dream-like state.

"Kikki, what happened to your eye?" Mom asks worriedly.

I grin like it's the best thing that's happened to me. "Don't worry. Lewis gave me ice, and I feel perfectly well."

Dad's eyes narrow. "Why are you acting like you're doped out?"

I giggle, backing out of the room. "I'm just happy, Dad."

I twirl by Brandy, scruffing her fur before gliding up the stairs.

In my bedroom, I set the stuffed bunny at the end of my bed, shed my denim jacket, and let out a blissful sigh.

Beep, beep.

It's a text from Parker. *"How'd it go?"*

I grin, letting out another swoon-filled exhale. *"Wonderfully."*

"Did you kiss him to make him feel better?"

"That sounds like something out of the Parker playbook. I'm much more subtle than you."

"Ha ha. That's why you need me."

I think about our hug. *"Then why did I leave him with a smile on his face?"*

There's a longer pause before I get the next reply. *"You're too good, Green."*

I move to the window and peer into the lamp-lit bedroom beyond the fence line.

Lewis leans against his desk and turns his head toward the window. His chin tilts upwards, and our eyes lock. A smile dashes across his face, and his hand lifts in a wave.

My heart swells, and I wave back.

He moves away from the window, and I collapse on my bed before my legs completely turn to jelly.

"Wow," I breathe. "What a night."

Nineteen

It's Monday afternoon at the café, and I'm still wiped after last night's events. I kept waking throughout the night with confusing thoughts about both boys. I'm so glad there's nothing real between me and Parker. I'm still convincing my brain all the lingering stares and hand holding are fake. My memories come through like he's my real boyfriend, and there's only so much I can take. Especially when things are turning around for me and Lewis.

We almost kissed. I'm sure of it. Yvette already thinks we've kissed. That has to mean there was a look in Lewis's eyes that said he wanted to be with me.

I need things to hurry up and end with Parker so my thoughts can stay on only one boy.

I place a milkshake on Josie's table and let out a loud huff. "I'm just so exhausted."

Josie stifles a laugh, sliding the tall glass toward her. "What have you been doing?"

I plonk onto the seat adjacent to Josie. "Ugh. Too much."

I wouldn't normally slack off, but Maddy is having the day off. Even though she's a chill boss, I don't like to push my luck. Today, I'm working with Laura, which is less pressure because she's not in charge of my paycheck.

"Don't leave me hanging." Josie twirls her straw through the whipped cream topping. "I only have twenty minutes until my writing workshop at the library. Catch me up on everything that's been happening with you."

I rest my elbows on the table. "Well, you know I was going to the lake."

"Yeah. Kylie Green got adventurous at Logan's Point. It's hard to believe it's non-fictional."

"I know. We went swimming, and it was super daunting. Everyone was doing back flips, trying to dunk each other, and just other chaos."

"*Oof.* I made the right call in not going."

"And then I jumped off a cliff."

Josie chokes on a mouthful of milkshake. "Excuse me?"

I fiddle with the end of my hair, avoiding her gaze.

"What the heck, Kylie?"

I shrug. "Everyone was doing it."

"You got peer pressured?"

"Essentially. Parker really wanted me to do it."

"Since when does Parker Kelly talk you into doing things?"

My teeth graze my bottom lip. "I guess, he's pretty persuasive."

"Oh my gosh. Don't tell me you're letting his kisses do the talking for you."

"No. Well..." My mind whirs. "No."

"So, you just jumped off a cliff?"

"Mm-hmm. It got me the seal of approval from his friends."

Hope shines in her eyes. "Especially Lewis?"

My posture droops. "Well, he kinda ran to Yvette instead."

Josie winces. "Sorry."

"It's okay. It was a lot easier to deal with than sitting through a double date with Lewis and Yvette."

"Why are you torturing yourself?" She reaches across and clutches my hand. "Is this really worth hanging around Lewis when he's with a girl who makes unattainable beauty standards look effortless?"

I swallow hard, urging my stomach to behave. "Parker says it'll work."

"I don't know how you can stomach it."

"I'll admit, it's hard."

"So, you said on the phone the double date was at Alto Burger."

"Yep. And the second one was at the fair."

"No wonder I've barely heard from you. You're running ragged."

"Mm-hmm. Plus, hanging out with Parker's friends at the skatepark." I flop my head back and sigh at the ceiling. "I'm beat."

"I've been worried about you. You used to write endless texts about seeing Lewis through your bedroom window. Now when we text, you're so vague. Is this not working? Is Lewis not noticing you?"

"No, it's just a balancing act," I say, forcing myself into optimism. "I mean, he sees me. We've talked. I even congratulated him on his newest photography nomination. He even offered to snap some photos of my baking."

"Wow. That could be so romantic."

I sigh. "But when Yvie's around..."

"Can your sanity really survive competing with her?"

"Parker distracts her."

Josie chuckles. "So, he actually has some charm?"

"He's a good guy." I motion to the scratch by my eye. "He was so amazing when I got hurt. He felt so strong as he held me. It was really kind."

Josie cups a hand over her mouth. "I just got goosebumps."

"Good goosebumps?"

"Very good."

"I just wanted you to know I'm safe with him," I say. "I mean, it's not all smooth sailing. But we're both working on being with our crushes."

"I'm worried about your heart. All I've heard, for a year and a half, is how Lewis is your soulmate."

"I never said soulmate."

She deadpans at me. "Kylie, who are you talking to right now?"

"My heart still belongs to Lewis."

"But you're dating Parker."

"Fake dating Parker."

"And your heart knows that?"

I pause, feeling the thump within my chest. "Of course."

"As long as he's still drooling over Yvette, I guess you're a step closer to Lewis."

"That's how this whole plan started." I reply. "Mid drool, Parker saw I was upset about Lewis and Yvette, and we started talking about it."

"That's weird," she says under her breath. She looks from side to side and then nods at me. "Yep. It's just weird."

I muffle a laugh. "I know."

"I just don't get how you could start kissing him right away."

I rub my forehead, fighting off my frown. "I don't know. To be honest, he took the reins on that."

"You weren't ready?"

I shake my head. "I wasn't expecting it. I agreed to date him, but I wasn't ready to kiss him. How could I be when I'd spent so long fantasizing about kissing Lewis?"

Josie gives me a sympathetic look. "Do you regret it?"

"It's been a really confusing few days. Sometimes, I wish things hadn't moved so fast. But, other times..." I pause, biting my lip. "Other times, I kiss him, and I like it."

Air puffs out of her in surprise. "Wow. Is he a good kisser?"

I rub my lips together. "The kisses are good. He keeps saying I'm good at kissing."

Josie tilts her head, her smile growing. "Wow. You look so happy."

It takes me by surprise. "Huh?"

"When you talked about kissing Parker, your tiredness went away. It's like he lights you up."

I cup a hand over my face. "Oh. Really?"

Josie sighs. "Dang. Your poor heart."

"My heart is fine."

"You enjoy kissing Parker while being hung up on Lewis."

"I want Lewis, not Parker."

"And he still wants Yvette?"

"Absolutely."

"I think you're both torturing yourselves. You've intensified your crushes to the point you're just picking at scabs."

"We're not." I huff, too tired to explain this. "This is working for us."

Josie purses her lips and shakes her head. "It's not healthy."

I fall into a hunch, picking at my fingernails. "It won't last much longer."

Josie reaches across and clutches my hand. "I hope not."

The door opens with a chime, and Josie chuckles as she watches who walks in. "What great timing. Now, I get both sides of the story."

I look over and instantly feel a twinge of pain between my shoulder blades. Parker walks into the café with his little brother, William.

"There goes that light in your eyes again," Josie says, her shoulders bobbing in a silent laugh.

"Huh?"

"You look like you wanna run over to him." Josie turns in her chair, waving. "Parker! Over here!"

"*Josie,*" I whisper, kicking her chair.

Parker waves back, steering his little brother toward the table.

"But I want a milkshake," William whines as Parker pushes him forward.

"We're literally walking over to a waitress," Parker says. He then tilts his head to meet my eyes. "Hi, girlfriend."

Josie snickers, scrutinizing my reaction.

Ugh. I can't deal with this right now.

I get up and motion to my empty seat. "William, you can take my seat and I'll take your order. I need to talk to your brother."

"Huh?" William double-takes at me. "You're Parker's girlfriend?"

"Umm, yeah."

"But you're not a goblin," he says.

I can't help but laugh at the random statement.

Parker grabs a clump of William's hair, forcing him to look up. "What does that mean?"

William raises his palms. "I just thought you couldn't do better than dating a goblin."

Bewilderment takes over Parker's face as he releases his brother.

Josie pats the space across from her. "You can sit with me, William. I already like you."

"Why wouldn't you?" he says, moving across to the seat. "I'm the best."

"Give it a rest," Parker complains. "Man, he's eight-years-old and already full of himself."

William sticks his tongue out at his older brother.

I push a hand onto Parker's chest and force him to step backwards. "Can we chat for a minute?"

"Ah, sure."

We move further up the aisle, and I quietly blurt, "What are you doing here? We agreed we were having a day off."

"I'm not here for you. This is my friend's café, remember. It's not abnormal for me to be here."

I fold my arms. "I know. It's just, Josie's been asking a million questions, and she's ready to interrogate you."

He curls a finger under my chin. "Well, when you stand like this, it looks like you're mad at me. Do you want to stage a fight?"

I drop my arms to my side. "No."

He leans in and presses a kiss on my forehead. "Then stop pouting."

"I'm just tired."

"Well, I have news that might perk you up."

"Really?"

Parker wiggles his eyebrows. "I was at Kai's house with the guys. Well, and Jamie, but she's one of the guys."

"Parker, get to the point."

"Anyway, I was chatting with Lewis and you came up."

"Me? What did you say?"

Parker grins, rubbing under his jaw. "Actually, Lewis was doing most of the talking."

"Lewis was talking about me?"

Parker nods. He glances at Josie's table and whispers out the side of his mouth. "I'll tell you about it later."

I grab his hand and tug on it. "No, you can't leave me hanging like that."

Parker chuckles. "Just the mention of him lifts your mood."

"At least tell me it was good stuff."

"Very good stuff."

"And you and Kai are okay? Last night, the two of you didn't leave things on the best terms."

He holds my hand tighter. "I apologized and said I was just being overprotective."

"I hope he understood. It's how he is with Tabitha."

"Exactly." He tugs on my hand and walks me to Josie's table. "Come on, let's not abandon your friend. Plus, my brother needs to be reined in."

"I dunno. I like that he says what's on his mind."

Parker pulls an arm around my shoulders. "Because you're not the target of his insults."

William grimaces at us. "How could you let him kiss you?"

I snigger. "I know. I must be outta my mind."

Josie gestures at William. "He was just asking about Brandy."

Parker sighs, letting his arm fall off me. "Mom told him about your dog, and I have not stopped hearing about it. He's relentless."

William leans on the table. "I would give up the milkshake if I could meet the dog."

My heart swells as I pout. "Aww. Well, you can do both. I can get you a milkshake, and you can meet Brandy."

"Now?" William blurts.

"No, not now," Parker quickly answers, pulling a chair over to the table. "We've got to get home after this."

"But we can visit the dog first," William argues.

"No, we can't," Parker replies. "Kylie's still working, and we're not seeing each other again until the camping trip."

"Camping trip?" Josie questions.

Parker looks at me. "You haven't told her?"

"We've had a lot to catch up on," I reply.

Josie deadpans at me. "*You're* going camping?"

I grin and bat my lashes. "Wanna come with?"

Josie recoils. "*Eww.* No way."

"I can pack extra camping gear," Parker offers. "It's no problem."

She side-eyes him. "I don't do camping. And until recently, my best friend didn't either."

Parker looks up at me, his smile twitching. "There's a lot of new things your best friend now does."

"Oh my gosh, you have the same look in your eyes that she does," Josie says.

Parker blinks, shifting his gaze to Josie. "Huh?"

Josie gestures at the two of us. "You two look at each other like lovesick puppies."

Parker sits back in his chair, smirking as he folds his arms.

William raises his hand. "Umm, Miss Kylie, can I order a cookies and cream milkshake?"

I nod, happy for an excuse to leave the table. "Coming right up." I clear my throat, and look at Parker. "Anything for you?"

"Make it the same," Parker says, smiling.

A tingle slithers down my spine, and I hurriedly turn away from the table and move to the counter. Never have I been happier to work the milkshake machine in my life. I let the loud mechanical sounds drown out my thoughts. However, I can't help peering over my shoulder at the table. Josie's shoulders jiggle as she watches the brothers interact. She's not grilling Parker, but it still feels like there's a warning sign flashing.

I finish making the milkshakes and carry them to the table.

"Yum, thanks," Parker says, eyes glued to the Oreo-flaked whipped cream topping.

William mumbles, "Thank you," before hurriedly shoving the straw into his puckered mouth.

"You're welcome." I lean in close to Josie and clutch her shoulder. "Are you okay?"

"Oh sure," Josie replies. "I've had fun scrutinizing your boyfriend."

My jaw clenches. "Scrutinizing?"

"You've had so many more dates since we were at the smoothie bar," Josie says. "I'm just making sure he's still good enough to escort you on further dates."

"I tried to deflect with the camping trip, but she wasn't buying it," Parker says. "Not even when I suggested a setup for her and Tyler."

I squeeze Josie's shoulder. "That could be so cute."

"Umm, excuse me, you know who my heart belongs to," Josie defends.

"Yeah, a Hollywood star," Parker jokes.

Josie clicks her tongue. "I knew him before that."

"So did a bunch of us. Doesn't mean we hear from him now," Parker says.

I lift my hand. "Don't bother, Parker. You'll never win this argument."

"I guess I'm not like the two of you. I can't switch out my crush for someone else."

Parker's Adam's apple bobs, and he glances at his brother to check if he caught on. Oblivious, William continues sucking up his milkshake.

Josie narrows her eyes at Parker. "You still have that crush, don't you?"

Parker also narrows his eyes. "Yes. We still have the same game plan."

"Are you sure?" she doubles down. "Because I wasn't making a joke when I mentioned how you two look at each other."

"We're just really good at this kind of relationship," I reply, omitting the word 'fake' for the sake of William's ears.

Parker nods, slouching in his seat.

"It's weird," Josie says, "but you two seem to be making things work. I just wish this relationship didn't involve letting this wound fester."

"When we're in the right relationship, the wound will be healed," Parker replies.

William spits out his straw, and his lip upturns. "What the heck are you guys talking about?"

"Nothing," we all reply at once.

When William returns to his milkshake, Parker says, "You don't have to worry, Josie. Kylie and I are on the same page."

"I know," she replies. "And the page is toxic."

"Okay, Josie, lay off," I say gently. "We're doing our best."

Josie nods. "I'm sorry. I didn't mean to sound rude. Honestly, Parker, you seem like a really great guy, and I'm so glad you took care of Kylie when she got hurt."

Parker grins. "I told you I'd protect her."

Josie nudges me. "Your boyfriend is super cute with his little brother, by the way. It's adorable."

My hand presses on my chest. "Really?"

William rolls his eyes, swallowing a mouthful of milkshake. "Ugh. We're not cute."

Josie glances at Parker. "It's a good sign when a guy is good with little kids. I wouldn't have pegged you for it."

"Well, he needs someone with him," Parker says, trying not to blush at the praise. "And Kurtis won't do it."

William winces. "If Kurtis has to babysit, we'll all be dead."

I laugh. "Wow. Not dramatic at all."

William taps the milkshake glass. "This is really good. Thanks, Kylie."

My heart swells. "You're welcome."

Parker motions to the glass display by the counter. "You think that's good. You know all the cakes we get from here? Kylie makes them."

William's mouth falls open. "Wow. You *are* good."

I smile proudly. "Thanks."

"You have a golden retriever," William says, bluntly changing the subject back to dogs.

I pull over a chair to stop fidgeting. "Yes, that's right."

Willian leans in. "Kurtis told me Parker cried when he saw your dog."

"Will, what the heck?" Parker yelps.

"When Gus died, Parker felt like it was when his…" William doesn't end the sentence because Parker slaps a hand over William's mouth.

Parker retches, removing his hand. "Yuck. You licked my hand, you little monster."

Parker wipes his palm down the side of William's face, who flinches and laughs.

"What is going on?" I ask cautiously.

Parker glares at his brother. "Nothing. Right, Will? You're zipping it."

William huffs and returns to sucking up the remainder of his milkshake.

Sharing a look with Josie, and feeling tension between the brothers, I promptly decide it's best not to ask any more questions.

Josie slides her chair back. "Umm, I have to get going."

"Right, your workshop," I say, standing with her.

Josie leans in and hugs me. "Keep me posted. I'm still getting used to you hanging out with all these sporty people."

I giggle as we pull out of the hug. "I promise I'm not changing into a different person."

Josie waves at Parker. "Keep her safe, or else."

Parker gives her a salute. "Not a problem."

Josie smiles, backing away from the table. "Bye, guys."

I sit back down when Josie leaves.

"When does your shift end?" Parker asks. "Do you want a ride home?"

Laura ambles past our table. "If you clean behind the counter, you can sign off. It doesn't look to get any busier here."

"Okay, thanks," I reply.

I leave the boys to finish their milkshakes, taking Parker up on his offer to drive me home.

Twenty

When I'm almost through with cleaning, Parker joins me behind the counter with two empty milkshake glasses.

"Thanks," I say, taking them and placing them in the sink.

"I just realized I won't be able to tell you about Lewis with my little brother hanging around."

My muscles tighten, unwilling to go without the information. "Tell me now."

Parker glances at the kitchen door. "Is it okay?"

I beckon him closer. "Sure it is. Spill."

"He said he's surprised by how much Yvie makes a big deal out of everything."

I smirk. "Has he just met her?"

Parker nudges me. "He also said, Yvie left him in such a bad mood last night, but after talking to you, he felt so much better."

I clasp my hands over my chest and rise on the balls of my feet. "He said that?"

"You texted me that you left him with a smile on his face."

I squeal in delight.

"That's not the best part."

I plant my hands on the counter for support.

"Lewis said you seem much more chill." Parker grins, holding back a laugh. "I tried so hard not to laugh, because of how much I've witnessed you panic."

I deadpan him. "This is the best part?"

He waves his hands, swallowing his budding laughter. "No, he said you seemed like a more relaxed girlfriend. He told me, when he got to Yvie first, he thought he'd won. But now, he's not so sure."

I almost slip against the counter. "What does that mean?"

"I think it means I won, because I have you."

I tap my chest. "Does Lewis want me?"

Parker shrugs. "He's been thinking about you."

"Whoa. This is big. I knew there was something romantic behind him wanting to take photos in my kitchen."

Parker flinches. "Take photos of what?"

"My baking. Macro shots."

"Oh, okay. I thought maybe he wanted you to model."

I wince at him. "Why would your mind go there?"

Parker shrugs. "I don't know, because he was rambling about you. He kept talking about how you're more adventurous. Like, you're a better fit for our group than Yvie."

"Wait, he wants me to be this active person?" I say with doubt demolishing my excitement. "Someone always ready for an adventure?"

"Yeah. You can do that."

"No, I can't. You know how much I hesitate."

"That's why you're practicing with me. You won't hesitate with him."

"I'm just doing this stuff to get him to notice me. My goal is for him to want to slow down with me. At least, that's how I always pictured it happening for us."

Parker shrugs. "Just be this active person for this week and keep his attention. Once you're together, I'm sure he'll be happy to slow down with you."

My stomach sloshes with doubt. "Do you think so?"

"Sure. He's already thinking of you as more than the girl next door. You have him on the hook."

I sigh. "I just don't want to lead him into thinking I'm something I'm not."

"It's not like you've completely changed your personality because you've gotten more adventurous. Besides, I've gotten to know you while we've hung out. You're cool, and I find myself slowing down just because I like being around you."

Tingles run down my arms. "Really?"

He rubs the back of his neck, looking away. "Yeah. Just think about how hard Lewis will fall for you."

"I just feel like I'm putting on an act around him. It's easier with you because you're well aware I'm pretending."

"Just have a little faith."

"Did Lewis tell you that Yvie thought he kissed me on the Ferris Wheel?"

Parker's mouth hangs open.

"I swear he wanted to kiss me outside his house. It felt like it could've happened."

"Man, you're getting so much closer to him than I am with Yvie."

I shake my head. "I wouldn't be so sure. Yvie was mad at Lewis for not being as attentive as you are. I wouldn't be surprised if he only started thinking about me to make Yvie jealous."

"No way."

"Yes way. Lewis was so annoyed because Yvie said he wasn't as good a boyfriend as you."

Parker's eyes enliven. "She said that?"

"It's what they were fighting about before Yvie left the fairgrounds."

Parker leans back on the counter. "Whoa."

"You'll need to keep up the good work if she's still going on the camping trip."

Parker's eyebrows lift. "She needs to go on the camping trip."

I nod. "It'll be your time to shine. You can make sure there are no spiders."

Parker laughs. "Oh, man. I can't believe that worked."

"*Parker*," William whines, approaching the counter. "Are we going or what?"

I untie my apron. "I'm just about done. I'll punch out, and then we can go."

After I say goodbye to Laura, I follow the boys out to Parker's car. As we leave the parking lot, William rambles on about wanting to meet Brandy. When we turn off Main Street, the car's media display lights up with the notification, *"Mom calling."*

Parker hits the green answer button. "Hello?"

"Hi honey," his mother replies. "Can you go to the grocery store before coming home?"

"Sure, we're already on our way home."

"No, we're not," William blurts. "We're going to Kylie's house."

"Oh, hi Kylie," his mother says in a higher octave.

My mouth runs dry. "Hi, Mrs. Kelly."

"I'm making tacos for dinner," she says through the speakers. "Why don't you join us?"

"Oh, umm," I stammer.

"She can't," Parker says matter-of-factly.

"Oh, come on," Mrs. Kelly insists. "We'd love to have you over. What about tomorrow night?"

Parker groans. "*Mom.*"

"What? I want to get to know your girlfriend. It's not a crime."

I chew my lip, hearing the genuineness in his mother's voice. I can understand her excitement. My parents have enjoyed having Parker over. It's been a good stepping stone before I have my real boyfriend.

"Okay," I blurt. "I can make it tomorrow."

Parker's eyebrows push together as his mother cheers through the speakers.

I mouth to Parker, "Practice."

"Any requests, Kylie?" Mrs. Kelly asks.

"No, thank you. Just let me bring dessert."

"Splendid! Can't wait."

Parker rubs his temples. "Mom, what did you need from the grocery store?"

His mother laughs. "Oh, yes, that's right. Can you get hot sauce, a head of lettuce, and a can of black beans?"

Parker's finger hovers over the red icon on the display. "Okay. We'll be home soon."

"Thanks, honey," she replies. "Bye, Kylie."

Parker ends the call before I get a chance to respond. We turn onto my street, and Parker's body language stays stiff. When he stops outside my house, I open the door and say goodbye.

Parker opens his door. "I'll walk you to your door. William, stay in the car."

"But what about Brandy?" William whines.

"Another time," Parker says bluntly, getting out of the car.

Parker closes the door, and William replies by blowing a raspberry against his passenger window.

I cup a hand over my laughter as Parker rounds the car.

"Before you say it," Parker says, "no, he's not cute."

I hold my thumb and index finger an inch apart. "He's just a little bit cute."

Parker smiles, shaking his head as we move away from the curb.

"You know, he could've come in to meet my dog."

Parker shakes his head. "He'll live. Besides, I'd rather get him home. He gets a little manic when over-stimulated."

"Oh, okay then." We wander down my front path, and I can't help glancing next door. "So, Lewis isn't spending today with Yvie?"

"No. They're having a break."

My jaw drops. "A break?"

Parker sucks in a breath. "Sounds dire, doesn't it?"

"Ah, yeah. Break is the first word in break up."

Parker pats my back. "Are you ready to pick up the pieces of his shattered heart?"

I blow out a breath. "It's a big call." I bite my lip, eyeing him. "Are you going to be okay with Yvie overreacting to everything?"

"I think it's cute when she does that. Besides, it'll prove I'll make a better boyfriend than him. I don't get why Lewis doesn't hold her and ask if she's okay. I'm certain I'll be able to calm her down."

My mouth dries, remembering all the times Parker has done that for me.

Parker's eyes widen, and he's quick to add, "But I'm sure Lewis will be good to you. He'll be a better boyfriend because the two of you will be better suited."

The way he blurts it out fills me with doubt. "You think?"

"Yeah, because *you* think you're suited. I trust your instincts."

I smirk. "Except when I say I don't want to do anything adventurous."

"I wouldn't have pushed you if there hadn't been curiosity in your eyes."

"Maybe that's why we're not suited. You see fear as curiosity."

"No way. It's not fear. You get scared of people calling you names, or actually getting hurt. But I saw you having fun when you got out of your comfort zone."

I hug my middle, fighting my bashful smile as we near my door.

"Umm." He clears his throat. "That's why you and Lewis will have so much fun. You'll be ready to dive off cliffs with him."

"Or, this week will wear him out and he'll be ready to relax on the sidelines with me."

Parker chuckles. "Sure. That's an option too."

"Well, I have my fingers crossed for you and Yvie. If anyone can calm her down, it'll be you."

"Thanks." He glances back at his car. "You can make an excuse to get out of dinner tomorrow night."

"No, it's fine. Besides, it'll be good practice for you. You're obviously freaked out about bringing a girl home. If they meet me first, they can get out all their crazy before meeting Yvette."

He blows out an uneasy breath. "You really want to take on their crazy?"

"How bad could it be? Your family seems pretty normal."

"Mmm," he mumbles, slipping his hands in his pockets.

I open the door, and 'Arnold's Hits' echoes through the hallway. I grin at Parker. "Do you have your dancing shoes on?"

Parker frowns, checking his watch. "I've gotta get Will home."

"Uh-oh. My dad will be so disappointed," I say sarcastically.

"Ah, you're killing me." Parker leans against the doorway. "If I don't cross the threshold, can I skip out on the dance party without tarnishing my rep with your parents?"

I mumble a laugh. "Yes, I'll let you off the hook."

He straightens, raising a thumbs up. "You're the best, Kikki. I'll see you tomorrow."

I nod as he backs down the path. "Yes, you will."

Inside, I pull my hair out of my ponytail and bop my way along the hallway. "I'm home."

Dad moves out of the back room, toward the kitchen. "Hi honey. How was work?"

"Slow."

"That's good, isn't it?" he replies, boogying on the spot. "You said you were tired before you left."

Instinctively, I yawn.

Dad chuckles. "Come on, let's get something to eat."

"I'll just get changed first." Before I venture further up the hall, there's a knock at the door. "I'll get it."

I backtrack, suspecting it's Parker, reminding me I can back out of dinner with his family.

I pull the door open and almost keel over.

Lewis stands on the front step with his adorable smile lighting up his baby-blue eyes.

"Uh, Lewis, hi," I say, unable to rid the shock from my tone.

Is this the day? Does he want to take photos of me baking already?

My eyes pan up and down. Nope, no camera in sight.

"Hey, Kylie. We've got a bit of a home repair issue," Lewis says, hanging a thumb in the direction of his home. "Does your dad have a torque wrench we can borrow?"

I step out of the doorway and beckon him inside. "I have no idea, but you can ask him."

He steps inside. "Thanks."

I grin, holding out an arm to stop him. "Wait. You have to dance your way there."

His eyebrow raises. "I have to do what?"

A giggle spills out of me. "It's house rules. When the music's playing, you must dance your way around the house."

He winces. "Umm, no. That's definitely not happening."

My heart sinks, and embarrassment cramps my muscles. "Oh, yeah. Don't worry, it's dumb."

Lewis points up the hallway. "Is your dad this way?"

I lead the way. "Yeah, in the kitchen. Follow me."

I pinch the bridge of my nose, feeling like a total idiot.

Ugh. Parker was immediately up for dancing. I assumed Lewis would be as carefree about it. Maybe Parker only did it because he wanted something from me. He needed my parents' approval for me to go to Logan's Point.

I'm so dumb. I knew he didn't actually like my house and my family. *Gah*! Now Lewis thinks I'm a loser.

"Dad, can you help Lewis?" I ask, leading Lewis into the kitchen.

Dad closes the fridge door, grinning. "Lewis! Why, hello there. What brings you by?"

Lewis hangs a thumb toward his house. "I came home and found my dad fixing a burst pipe. We can't find our torque wrench. Do you have one we can borrow?"

Dad moves to the cupboard under the sink and pulls out his red toolbox.

"I should be able to help with that," Dad says, searching the array of well-organized tools.

"Wow," Lewis says, leaning in. "Is there anything you don't have in there?"

Dad pulls out what I assume is the desired tool. "Always be prepared. That's my motto."

"Thanks," Lewis says when Dad hands him the tool.

Dad gives Lewis a second glance. "Does your old man need a hand?"

"Well, he has me," Lewis says hesitantly.

Dad dusts his hands. "I'll come over."

Lewis exhales. "Thanks, Mr. Green. I'm not really much help."

"Can I do anything to help?" I blurt, pulling at my black T-shirt. "I'm already dirty from work, so I don't mind getting in there."

Dad grins. "Maybe you can hold a flashlight."

Lewis smirks. "Saves me a job."

My heart sinks. He's not going to ditch because I'm there to help, is he? I'm volunteering so I can be near him.

We walk over to Lewis's house, and Dad goes straight into action. He gets down on the kitchen tiles, helping Mr. Allen with the leaky pipe under the sink.

I wince at the water spilled all over the floor and turn to Lewis. "Where's your mop?"

Lewis backs out of the kitchen, showing me to the cleaning cupboard by the laundry.

"Thanks," I say, grabbing the mop. "At least this way I can be useful."

"Suit yourself," Lewis says with a yawn. "It looks like they've got it covered."

"They still might need a hand with something."

"Hopefully not," Lewis says, dawdling toward the kitchen. "I'm kinda sick of my dad badgering me."

"Oh. Maybe he's just stressed about the leak?"

"Yeah, but that's not my problem. I didn't bust it."

A nervous laugh murmurs out of me as I follow him. "I don't think he'd say you did."

"I'm just not in the mood today."

I frown as we stop in the hallway. "Because of you and Yvette?"

"She's ignoring my texts."

I gulp. "I'm sorry. That sucks."

"I don't even know why we're fighting. It's not like I said I didn't want to be with her."

"And you still do?"

He throws up his palms. "Of course, I do. She's freaking gorgeous."

I hug my middle. "There's more to relationships than looks."

Lewis huffs. "I know that. But everyone wants Yvie for her looks. I just want to show her I'm the guy for her."

I chew my fingernail, feeling every pin prickle of awkward discomfort in the small space.

He told Parker I might be a better girlfriend than her.

Why isn't he telling me that?

We could put an end to this charade, right here, right now.

"I have to make it work with Yvette," he says decisively. "I have to."

I nod slowly. "Okay."

Lewis moves back into the kitchen. "Dad? You good?"

"Yeah. We've got this," his dad replies.

Lewis moves further into the hallway. "I've got a killer headache. I need to lie down. See ya round, Kylie."

I swallow hard and force myself to look happy. "Okay. Hope you feel better."

I mop the excess water on the kitchen floor, getting a thank you from Lewis's dad. The gratitude feels hollow, knowing Lewis couldn't care less about my help.

After I wring out the mop and put it back in the cupboard, I make sure the men don't need any more help. When they thank me again, and tell me I'm free to go, I trudge my way home.

I've never felt more confused.

Was Lewis just lying about me? Is he using me to make Yvette jealous?

Is that all I'm good for?

All these boys keep using me just so they can turn the head of one vapid, self-centered girl.

Twenty-One

All night I tossed and turned. I rewrote several messages to Parker, calling this whole thing off. The only thing stopping me was remembering the way Lewis looked at me the night of the fair. It's undeniable something was between us. And then Parker's voice circled through my mind, telling me to have faith.

I put the phone down and escaped into fantasyland. Imagining my perfect relationship with Lewis. The giddiness warmed my soul. I soon lulled back to sleep.

Beep, beep.

I blink myself awake, rubbing the sleep from my eyes. I lift the phone and squint at the time.

10:30 a.m.

I squint again, seeing a notification. A text from Parker.

I put the phone down, not awake enough to read whatever he wants.

Beep, beep.

"Ugh." I groan. "If that's you again, Parker, I'm throwing the phone across the room."

I fling my arm across my eyes, hoping to drift back to sleep.

No such luck. My ringtone buzzes beside me.

"Ugh!" I grizzle. I reef the phone into the air, and see, *"Tessa Calling."*

"Oh," I mutter, hitting the answer button. "Hello?"

"Whoa. You sound croaky."

I pinch the bridge of my nose. "Just woke up."

She sniggers. "Late night?"

"I kept waking up. Stupid thoughts clogging my brain."

"Wanna talk about it? Could help to purge."

"Thanks, but I'm too groggy. Besides, I managed to think happy thoughts and got back to sleep."

"Let me guess. You went into fantasyland with that boy."

"I'm too predictable."

"Isn't it too hard to think about him now that he has a girlfriend?"

Oh, sis, you have no idea. "No, because in fantasyland, I'm his girlfriend."

"Oh, Kikki, that's not healthy."

I hug my pillow. "Oh, *shoosh*. It soothes me."

"Fine. As long as it's just in your head, you can't get hurt. Although, I'm worried about your emotions. I don't think you guard yourself enough."

"I'm plenty guarded. You have no idea how big my comfort zone is."

"No need to get defensive."

"Sorry. I'm just sleepy."

"Okay, I'll let you wake up properly and call you later."

"Sounds great. See ya, Tess."

"Bye, Kikki."

I lower the phone and see the notifications from Parker's text messages. I open the message chain and sit up as I read his words.

"What do you mean this is over? What happened? We can fix this."

I rub the heel of my palm against my forehead. What the heck?

I scroll up, and my chin drops. I didn't erase the text I was writing to him. When I dropped the phone in the middle of the night, I must've hit the send button.

At 3 a.m. my text pinged on Parker's phone, saying, *"I'm done. Lewis thinks I'm a massive loser. I'll never be good enough, except when it comes to being used."*

Oh no.

Could I have been more dramatic?

I scroll down to Parker's second text message.

"I'm sorry if something didn't go well with Lewis. He's just sour because Yvie's giving him the brush off. Please don't give up. I hate that you feel used. I'm sorry."

My heart hurts. I exhale a steadying breath and type a reply. *"Is there any way you can forget I sent that text? I was spiraling."*

He texts back immediately. *"You're not quitting?"*

"I thought about being with Lewis, and I got in a better mood."

"That's a relief."

"I never meant to send that text. I thought I deleted it."

"It wasn't the best thing to see when I woke up this morning."

"My bad."

"It's all good. As long as you're okay."

"I am."

"Good. This only works if you're happy. And remember, everything could change on the camping trip."

I send him a thumbs up emoji because my positive mood is waning.

Do I really want to see Lewis winning over Yvette in a place I can't leave? I'll be stuck in the wilderness, watching him smooch and cuddle her.

My stomach flips, and I force myself out of bed. I make my way downstairs because only waffles can lift my mood.

"Why hello there, sleepy head," Mom says, smirking as I make my way down the hallway.

"Most kids, during spring break, don't get up before midday," I say, wiping my eyes. "This is early for a high schooler."

"Except, you're a high schooler who voluntarily gets up before dawn to bake."

I wave her off. "Whatever. I'm making waffles. You want some?"

"*Mmm*," she purrs. "Would love some, but I've already had breakfast. Plus, I'm about to go into town and meet up with Mrs. Nelson."

The statement jolts through me. "Kai's mom?"

"Yes. We were talking on the phone about the camping trip and decided to meet up for coffee."

I deadpan her. "With Kai's mom?"

"Why do you look so shell-shocked? It's just coffee. And it's making me feel better about you spending two nights in the wilderness."

"Okay, have fun."

"I'm just going upstairs to get my handbag and then I'll head out," Mom says. "Do you need anything from the store?"

I wander into the kitchen. "Nope."

I busy myself with getting the mixing bowl and spoon, and then laying out all the necessary ingredients. Above, I hear Mom's heels clicking and thudding on the second floor. I'm mostly done mixing my ingredients by the time she walks down the stairs. Her handbag must've been hidden somewhere completely covert.

The doorbell rings, and Mom calls out, "I'll get it."

Good, because nothing's pulling me away from these waffles.

"Kikki," Mom calls out. "Parker's here."

I drop the mixing spoon into the batter. "Huh?"

"Okay, I'm off, honey," Mom calls out, and the front door closes.

Footsteps enter the hall, and Parker shimmies into the kitchen. "Hi Kikki."

"What are you doing here?"

He points his fingers to the sides as he does the twist. "Here for the baking dance party."

"No, really. Why are you here?"

He moves closer to the counter. "You've never sent emojis before."

My brow furrows. "Huh?"

He slips his phone out of his pocket. "You replied with an emoji. That was a bad sign."

"Oh." I blink as he pockets his phone. "You're here because I sent you a thumbs up?'"

"None of your texts have emojis. Even when you're raving about Lewis. You're wordy, Green. A single emoji is a cry for help."

I chew my lip. "I had no idea I had a tell."

Parker laughs under his breath. "I dunno if it's a tell, but I was worried about you."

I tilt the mixing bowl in his direction. "You don't have to be. I'm about to have waffles."

His eyes light up.

I grin. "You want some?"

He clasps his hands behind his back. "Well, seeing as I'm here."

"I'm glad you're here. My parents already ate, and it feels kinda sad to have waffles alone."

Parker steps around the counter. "Is there anything I can do to help?"

I'm suddenly reminded of being inside Lewis's house yesterday. When I suggested our dads might need help, Lewis couldn't have backed away fast enough.

"Umm, you want to help?"

"It feels rude to expect you to serve them up to me."

I point at a cupboard. "Can you pull the waffle maker out of there? I still have a few ingredients to add, but it'll need to heat up in the meantime."

Parker crouches, opening the cupboard. He lingers before looking up at me. "There's a lot of machines in here."

I stifle a laugh. "It's the round one that has a picture of a waffle on top."

Parker rummages inside the cupboard, eventually pulling out the right appliance.

"Good, you didn't pick the blender," I tease.

He sets the waffle maker on the counter. "Sorry, I'm not a kitchen whiz. At home, my mom makes the food and I help by eating it."

"Wow. So helpful."

He nudges me. "See. You should feel special that I've offered to help."

I rub my lips, hoping to minimize my smile. "I do appreciate it."

"Anything else I can do?"

I pour the vanilla into the mixing bowl and nod at the power socket. "Wanna plug it in?"

Parker moves the waffle maker closer to the power socket while craning his neck to view the mixing bowl. "What's in the waffles?"

"I just followed a classic recipe, but I added choc chips for good measure."

Parker tilts his head back, salivating. "Oh my gosh, you're the best."

I giggle. "You're practically drooling."

He slides close to me, hugging an arm around me. "Because I've already learned, anything you make is automatically good."

I shiver at his touch, and it exhilarates my heart.

He removes his hand. "Sorry, I got excited. I shouldn't have gotten so close."

I mumble at the bowl, "No, it's okay."

"So, I can't help noticing this playlist doesn't sound like 'Arnold's hits.'"

I gesture at my phone. "No, it's 'Kikki's Bake Time.'"

Parker grabs my phone. "Can I check it out?"

"Sure."

"Your phone is locked."

"Put it in front of my face."

As I pour the batter into the waffle maker, I stare at my phone as he holds it by my side. The batter makes a satisfying sizzle as Parker scrolls through my playlist.

"Looks like a lot of pop," he remarks.

"Nothing better to put you in a good mood."

"Oh, wait. Here's some interesting tracks." He lowers the phone. "You like Frontier Leaders?"

I shy away with a coy smile. "I learned to like them. I saw the album cover on Lewis's phone one day at the café. When I got home after that shift, I streamed the album. I didn't love them at first, but now I can't go a morning without listening to at least one of their songs." I huff over the mixing bowl. "If only my playlist had been playing when Lewis came over yesterday."

Parker puts my phone down on the counter. "Why do you say that?"

"Because he was completely mortified at the prospect of dancing in my house."

Parker lets out a hearty laugh. "He wouldn't dance?"

My hands press into the sides of my face. "It was completely embarrassing. I never should've told him about these stupid house rules. He looked at me like I was a total loser."

Parker plucks my hands off my face. "Kikki, you're not a loser."

My eyes water as I pout. "Yes, I am."

His eyes droop. "No, you're not. You're fun and cool. Maybe Lewis was too embarrassed to show off his lame moves." Parker points and sways his hips in a goofy disco fashion. "Not everyone can be as awesome as me."

I giggle, wiping my eyes. "This is what I mean, though. You danced the minute you walked through the door. Lewis didn't look embarrassed for himself. He was embarrassed for me."

"Aww." Parker pulls an arm around me. "Don't say that. You look so sad. He was just in a mood because of Yvie. It wasn't about you."

His arm slides off me as I open the waffle maker. The divine smell lifts my sullen mood.

Parker gasps. "Oh my gosh, that looks amazing."

I plate up the waffle, drizzle it with maple syrup and slide the plate toward him. "All yours."

"I'll wait to eat with you."

I pour in the batter for the next waffle. "Okay, thanks."

While the next waffle sizzles, we don't speak. In our silence, we bob along to a catchy pop song. I even catch Parker mumbling the words when he thinks I'm not looking.

When we move over to the table, which is tucked in the corner, I happily announce, "Bon appétit."

Parker gives a thumbs up after his first mouthful. "Thanks, Kylie. This is delicious."

"I'm glad you're here to eat it with me. I hate having good food without anyone to share it with."

"Girl, you can text me anytime you're in the kitchen. I'll always be down to eat your food."

I wink, lifting my fork for another bite. "Noted."

"Are you feeling better? I'm sorry that seeing Lewis yesterday left you in such a crappy mood."

"I'm better. Nothing a good waffle can't fix." I tilt my head, looking out the window at Lewis's house. "Although, Lewis didn't sound very confident yesterday. Maybe Yvie won't go on the camping trip."

"That would suck. Then we would be dealing with a mopey Lewis."

"Dancing doesn't fix anything for him, but I could bake something to cheer him up."

"Now, that's being positive." Parker lifts his fork. "Lewis is such a dope. Have you noticed every time Yvie and Tabby argue, Lewis stands there and does nothing? It always leaves me arguing with Kai, while Lewis hangs back."

I shovel in a mouthful, waiting for him to make his point.

"If I were with Yvie, she and Tabitha would be friends already."

I raise my eyebrow because my mouth's too full to comment.

"I'm serious," he says. "You can tell Yvie wants her friend back. She was so excited when they got off that ride. Lewis just let it escalate to the point you got hurt. And then he annoyed Yvie by getting more concerned over your cut than how she was feeling."

I swallow. "Isn't that the point? He's supposed to be more into me than her?"

Parker sits taller. "Yeah, totally. I'm just saying, he's not suited to be with Yvie."

"Compared to you, who'd make everything magically better?"

"I'm just saying, I'd step up and help make Yvette feel better. And if I could help mediate between the girls, I would."

"No offense, but you're kinda the reason they haven't been given a chance to make up. You've gone out of your way to put us between them."

"And just think about if I use those powers for good."

I sit back, puffing out a laugh. "You're too much."

"You don't think I could do it?"

"No, I think you can. But how about you step up now? During the camping trip, you should help Yvette and Tabitha make up. You'll be fixing your karma, and Yvie will see how diligent and sweet you can be."

He winces. "You want me to do it before we break up?"

I nudge him. "It'll help you get with Yvie. At some point, we have to call an end to all this pretending."

He sighs. "Yeah. I guess you're right."

"Of course, I'm right."

"Are you baking for the camping trip?"

I side-eye him. "Who are you talking to?"

"*Yes.* I am so fake dating the right girl."

I smirk. "Why are you getting so excited? My baking will be for Lewis."

"I'm driving you out there. Doesn't your driver get a treat?"

"Okay, I'll bake some for you." I chew my fingernail, giggling. "You know, seeing as you're here, you could help me bake something for dinner tonight."

He winces. "We're still doing that?"

"Of course."

"We can blow it off and get one-on-one time with our crushes instead."

"Parker, it's dinner with your family. It's not a brutal punishment."

"Maybe for you," he grumbles.

I place a hand on his wrist. "Do you really not want to do it? Because I won't go if you really don't want me to."

He stares at my hand on him, and after coming to my senses, I swiftly remove it.

"No, we'll do it," he says. "Like you said. It's good practice."

We finish eating in silence, except for the music. I brought my phone over so Parker could stream the new Frontier Leaders album. Brandy sneaks into the kitchen and sits by Parker's side, happily awaiting a chunk of waffle.

Wow. Why does this feel so easy?

Yesterday, when Lewis entered my house, he acted like I was a freak at the mere suggestion of dancing. Now, sitting with Parker feels effortless and uncomplicated. And it's always fun, bopping to some of my favorite songs.

I scroll through my favorite recipes website on my phone. "So what do you want to make for your family?"

"Something chewy so they can't speak," Parker jokes.

"Be serious."

"I am."

I click my tongue, watching his growing grin. "Is there a crowd favorite? Or, maybe something they haven't had in a long time?"

Parker leans over to view my phone. "Are you saying you can make anything?"

"Sure. As long as I have a recipe."

Parker takes control of my phone, scrolling through the dessert images. "Oh my gosh, chocolate cherry layer cake. My parents would love that."

"Sold!" I cheer.

"But look at the layers. It looks difficult."

I wink. "But I love a challenge."

"Since when?"

"Since it comes to baking."

Parker sits back, holding my phone. "Ah, I see."

Before I can ask to see the recipe, my ringtone buzzes.

"It's Tessa," Parker says, flipping my phone around and simultaneously hitting the answer button.

My eyes widen as I hear Tess's voice calling out, "Hello? Hello?"

Parker laughs. "Aren't you going to talk to her?"

"Kylie?" Tess's voice questions. "Who is that?"

"It's Parker," he says, drawing the phone closer to his lips.

"Umm, is Kylie there?"

I wipe the loose hair off my face and swiftly grab hold of my phone. "Hey sis."

"Umm, why is a boy answering your phone?"

"It's Parker. We were just talking about chem lab," I lie.

Parker's eyebrows raise.

"During spring break?" Tess questions.

I force myself to sound as upbeat as possible. "Yeah, why not?"

"Kikki, what's going on? This morning, you sounded miserable. And now you're talking with a boy? I'm worried about you."

"There's nothing to worry about. And you especially don't have to worry about Parker."

"How come I've never heard about him before?"

"Because he's just a boy from school. I bumped into him." I keep my head down, careful not to catch Parker's gaze. "Anyway, I've got to go. Sorry, sis, I'll call you back."

"Okay, but..."

"Bye, Tess," I blurt and hit the end call button.

"What was that?" Parker asks.

I blow out a breath, tossing my phone onto the table.

Parker shifts in his seat. "Do you want to talk about it?"

"No. It's just better that Tess doesn't know what's happening between us."

"Because it'll be easier when you start dating Lewis?"

Definitely not. "Plus, she's not living here. There's no need to mess with her head."

"Sure. I wish my brothers were in another town."

"Don't get me wrong. Tess and I get along great. I just don't think she'd approve."

"Your parents don't know we're a fake couple. She wouldn't have to know either."

"It's complicated." I get up and move toward the fridge. "I'll check if we have any cherries, or I'll text Mom to get some from the store."

"You can pick another recipe, if you want," Parker says, bringing my phone to the kitchen counter.

"No, it's okay," I say, moving to the pantry. "I'd like to wow your parents."

Parker mumbles a laugh. "Why?"

"It's practice for me meeting a boyfriend's parents."

"You already know Lewis's parents."

"Not as a girlfriend. It's different stakes." I pull out a jar of maraschino cherries. "*Eureka.*"

After skimming the ingredients list, I arrange all my supplies on the kitchen counter. Parker keeps commenting on how I don't need to worry about the cake turning out perfect, but I refuse to listen. Even if we're pretending, I'm determined to make a good impression with his family. Plus, there's no way I'm letting rumors circulate that I brought them a sub-par cake.

I ask Parker to help measure out ingredients, and he does so heavy-handedly.

"I've seen you in chemistry," I say. "You're usually so precise. Why are you making such a mess?"

"Maybe I care about the class more than I care about a cake for my family."

I take possession of the measuring cups. "Well, I care."

I measure out the rest of the ingredients and let Parker add them into the mixing machine. I ask him to turn it on a low setting, and then the machine emits a loud buzz. Flour erupts from the mixing bowl, dusting the countertop.

I deadpan him. "I said low."

He laughs, turning off the machine. "Oh man. Your face."

"Do I literally have to do everything?"

"Hey, I'm helping," he says, sweeping the flour off the counter with his hands.

"Oh my gosh. You're just making more of a mess."

He cups the flour, spilling it because he's laughing more.

I turn him toward the kitchen sink. "Can you at least get some of the flour in there?"

He dusts off his hands. "I'm sorry, Kylie. I'll get it together."

"Why are you sabotaging this?"

He turns to me. "I'm not."

"You clearly are. You're never this clumsy."

"I'm just lightening the mood."

"I'm baking, so the mood is light. You're the one making things weird."

He sighs, moving back to the mixing machine. "I'm just in my head about tonight. That's all."

I grab his hand before he can touch the power settings on the mixer. His fingers fold around mine, and for a moment, my brain malfunctions. The moment lingers, and I can't seem to pull away.

There's a slight tremble in his hand, and I jolt back into my thoughts.

I drop his hand. "Maybe you can prep the cherries instead of mixing?"

Parker opens the jar with a pop as I pull a knife from a nearby drawer. I hold the knife with the blade facing downward and lift it in his direction. He doesn't lift his right hand for the knife, instead twisting and grabbing the knife from another angle with his left.

"*Arghh*," he yelps, pulling his left hand away.

"What just happened?" I ask, dropping the knife onto the cutting board.

Parker clamps his right hand over the tips of his fingers. "I touched the blade."

Warning signals blare inside my head as I witness a red streak seeping between his fingers.

"What?" I yelp. "How did that happen?"

"I'm left-handed, but you held it towards my right."

"Doesn't mean you needed to grab the blade."

"I didn't know you held it at such a weird angle."

"It's a safe angle," I argue. "Oh my gosh, let me see."

"I don't want to take the pressure off."

I wince. "Was it one finger, or..." I swallow hard. "Or, all of them?"

Parker's face falls. "I think you sliced through bone."

I jerk backwards. "*What?*"

Parker's grin gives him a way. "Relax. It just grazed my index finger."

I grab the edge of the counter, steadying my breath. "Huh?"

"It stings, and is definitely bleeding, but I've done way worse when I've fallen off my skateboard."

I blink at him. "So, you're fine?"

He laughs. "I'm fine."

I whack his arm. "Oh my gosh, you scared me."

"It was too easy."

I huff and move to the doorway. "I'll get bandages from the bathroom."

As I get the first-aid kit from under the bathroom sink, I can't help feeling a wash of relief. He might just be a fake boyfriend, but through all this, he's genuinely become a friend. And, I never want to see any of my friends hurt.

When I get back to the kitchen, Parker has moved over to the sink.

"It's not a deep cut, is it?" I ask, clenching my jaw. "Like, in need of stitches?"

"Relax, Green. You didn't cut me that badly. It looks as bad as a paper cut."

I put the first-aid kit on the counter by the sink. "Since when did I cut you? You're the one who shifted and came at the knife in the most awkward way possible."

"Well, it wouldn't have happened if you right-handed people didn't think everyone should conform to your ways."

"Shut up," I laugh, pulling the backing off a band-aid. "Show me the damage."

Parker lifts his hand toward me, and I frown at the slice along the side of his index finger.

"It's not that bad," he insists as I wrap the bandage around his finger.

For good measure, I wrap a second band-aid over the first. "How's that?"

"Nice and tight," Parker replies. "It's great. Thanks, Kylie."

"You're welcome."

As I trash the backing of the band-aids, Parker says, "I'll stick to mixing from now on."

"Considering you cut yourself before you even started, I'd say that's a good call. I can deal with some flour and chocolate spilling instead of bloodshed."

Parker wiggles his bandaged finger. "This wasn't another effort at self-sabotage. I swear."

I nod. "I didn't think it was."

While we mix the cake batter, I'm so grateful Parker is a good listener. On so many occasions, my dad has tried to help, and I find myself constantly repeating instructions because he doesn't pay attention. Once he got out of his head, Parker's a super cute helper.

"You can leave once the cakes are in the oven," I say after prepping the cake pans. "They need a while to bake and then cooling time before I can frost and layer them."

"I don't mind staying," Parker replies.

"I also don't mind if you don't see the decorations. Then I can surprise you as much as your family."

An infectious smile brightens his face. "Okay."

"Do you want to help me get the batter into the cake pans?" I ask. "It's always easier with someone's help when I have to divide the layers."

"Sure. Just tell me what to do."

I have Parker pour the batter into the cake pans so I can make sure they're even. On the third pan, I can tell there's too much batter left in the mixing bowl, so I touch Parker's hand to stop him from pouring.

He tilts the bowl up, and I can't seem to move my hand. We both stare at our hands, and I swear, I've forgotten how to breathe.

Parker clears his throat. "Where do you want me to pour it?"

I blink hard, pulling my hand away from his. "Just evenly into the first two."

When Parker finishes pouring the batter, I check the oven's temperature is ready for the cakes. I get his help loading the three cake pans into the oven, careful not to touch his hand again.

"Do you need help with the frosting?" Parker asks when I close the oven door.

My mind conjures an image of myself making the frosting. I see myself whisking and my arm getting tired. Parker moves in to take over. He grasps the mixing bowl while my hand is still there. His fingers meld over mine in a moment that stretches out time.

I jitter out of my thoughts and wipe the sweat off my brow. "No, it's okay. I've got loads of time."

"Well, thanks for letting me help. It was fun, besides the war wound."

"You're a good baking assistant."

Parker smiles, finding Brandy sneaking back into the kitchen. He leans over to pat her. "Better than Brandy?"

"You didn't try to lick the uncooked batter, so yes."

Parker scratches behind Brandy's ear. "Don't let her talk smack about you, girl. You eat all the batter you want."

"*Hey*," I squeak. "That's bad dog-owning. Batter's not good for them. It's not even good for us when it's uncooked."

Parker swats a hand. "Whatever. It's delicious."

"I know. That's why the cookie dough cups are always a hit."

"Lemme guess," Parker says, "you'll be making them for the camping trip to keep winning over Lewy-boy?"

A confusing niggle hits my stomach, giving me the ick. I smile to cover the slimy feeling. "No, I think I'll do something more creative."

Parker grins. "That sounds like Kikki. Always gotta up the ante."

"Well, I can't just rehash day one of this scheme."

Parker laughs and then digs into his pocket, pulling out a buzzing phone. He double-takes at the screen. "Whoa. It's Yvie."

I almost lose my balance. "Huh?"

He reads the text. "She wants to meet up."

"Why?" I cough, shaking my head. "I mean, is she still not talking to Lewis?"

"I don't think so." He lowers the phone, looking me dead in the eyes. "I should go. Shouldn't I?"

"Yeah," I say with a layer of fake enthusiasm. "This is big for you and her."

"She probably wants dirt on Lewis."

"Or she woke up and realized she's deeply in love with you."

Parker grins, brushing a hand through his hair. "She's only human."

"So, where are you meeting up?" I swear I hear a crack splintering in my heart. "Her house?"

Parker taps on his phone and stares at the screen, awaiting her reply. "No, apparently her brother's watching her like a hawk. She wants me to pick her up in the alley behind her house and take her to Main Street."

"Good luck."

He lowers the phone and gives me a sympathetic look. "Are you okay with this? I know you're still down about what happened between you and Lewis."

I shake my head, faking a smile. "No, I'm fine. You go and soak up Yvie's attention."

"You're sure?"

No. "Of course."

"You're the best." He gives Brandy another pat, telling her, "Wish me luck, girl."

"We're both sending you good vibes."

Parker sends me a wink. "At least you know Lewis won't be with her. Maybe you can go next door and try again with him."

I hug my middle. "I don't think I'm up for that. Besides, I need to stay here and make sure the cakes are perfect."

"Good luck with them, dessert queen."

Parker leaves, and I lean against the kitchen counter with a heavy sigh.

Why does the notion of him leaving to see her hurt so much? It's what I want. If he can be with Yvie, it frees Lewis to be with me.

I remember Lewis's attitude from yesterday. Not only in how he acted toward me, but in his gruffness toward his dad. It wasn't exactly attractive that Lewis didn't get down on the kitchen floor and help his dad fix the plumbing issue.

I sigh again and glance at the oven.

At least I have baking to concentrate on.

It's the only part of this day that makes any sense.

Twenty-Two

"So what happened with Yvie?"

He still hasn't replied to this text message. Every time I check the text chain, my stomach clenches harder. It's not like him to ignore my messages.

Did it not go well?

Did it go *too* well?

Oh my gosh. Did Yvette see my text message and force him not to reply? Are they now *together* together?

Or, did she see my text, and it caused a fight? Did I ruin Parker's shot at being with her, and now he's mad at me?

I pace my bedroom floor and struggle for a regular intake of air as my chest constricts. I can't go to his house tonight if he's mad at me. What if he's expecting me not to turn up? What if I get there and he yells at me in front of his family?

"Kikki, are you okay in there?" Mom calls from the second-floor landing.

"I don't think I can go tonight," I call back.

"Why not, honey?"

"Parker hasn't replied to my text, and I think he's mad at me."

Mom's laughter hums through my closed bedroom door. "Honey, he's having you meet his parents. He's probably a nervous wreck. Don't let an unanswered text throw you off your game. They're going to love you." The doorknob turns. "Do you need a hug?"

"I'm still getting dressed," I answer. "Afterwards, yes."

"Well, don't be too long. We'll need to get going soon."

"Yep. Thanks, Mom."

I blow out a long exhale and move toward the full-length mirror. I can't believe I spiraled like that. Especially after an entire afternoon of fixating on our lingering touches.

I can't believe it happened more than once.

We've held hands so many times this week. But that was always to put on a show. This was at my house. In privacy. No one was watching us. But there it was. A lingering touch. I swear, I still feel it now.

Why is that? Why won't it get out of my head?

Was it fueled by the fact I helped him with the cut on his finger?

The worst part is, I can't replace the memory with Lewis in Parker's place. Before this week, I could put Lewis into any situation to get the maximum romantic enjoyment out of it. But this time, it's like fantasyland is shut down.

Ugh. I can't stop picturing Parker's stupid, enthusiastic, energetic face.

Needless to say, I've been splashing cold water on my face all afternoon. The only thing slightly distracting me was decorating the cake. It's exquisite, if I do say so myself.

I get dressed in a yellow tank top and floral skirt. It's nice not to have to thumb through my wardrobe for blue outfits.

"Ready to go, Kikki?" Mom calls from the bottom of the stairs.

I slip into a pair of beige wedge sandals and leave my bedroom. "Coming."

"Aww, don't you look adorable," Dad says by the staircase.

I move in so he can kiss my cheek. "Thanks, Dad."

"Have a nice time, honey," he says, rubbing a circle on my back.

"I will. Hopefully, they like me."

He pinches my cheek. "How could they not?"

I move down the stairs and meet Mom, who holds the Tupperware containing the layer cake.

"This looks fabulous, honey," Mom says, handing the container over to me.

"Thanks. I was a bit nervous that it was going to slide."

"Don't fret. I checked it before taking it out of the kitchen. There's no lean on it."

I breathe out slowly and follow Mom to the car.

On the drive over to Parker's house, Mom keeps yammering about how cute it is that I'm having dinner with my boyfriend's family.

"You're not going to embarrass me, are you?" Knots twist between my shoulders. "Can you please stay in the car?"

"Oh my gosh, let me say hello to his parents."

"Parker's probably going to answer the door. You already saw him today. His mother didn't hold his hand at our front door."

Mom huffs. "Okay, okay. I won't walk you to the house. But I want to organize a joint dinner after this."

"No problem," I agree, knowing there's no chance of that happening because we'll be broken up soon enough.

Mom parks outside Parker's house and gives me a good luck hug. When I leave the car, my stomach somersaults. I find myself wishing Mom hadn't agreed to let me walk to the door alone.

Hugging the cake container close, I press the doorbell, fidgeting in my stance. Extra nerves glitch inside me as Mom's car waits idly for me to go inside. If she's not standing here with me, I wish she'd drive away. Knowing she's staring is making me so self-conscious.

But what if I'm right? What if Parker doesn't want me here?

Oh no. What if Yvette's inside the house, and the family looks at me like an invader?

Finally, the door opens, and my chest rises with nauseous anticipation. Kurtis stands before me, causing my head to spin.

He smirks, looking me up and down. "I can't believe you turned up."

Crap. I was right?

"So, you and Parker are really doing this?"

My brow furrows. "Excuse me?"

"Dude, get away from her," Parker calls out.

My anticipation rises as he comes into view over his brother's shoulder.

Parker shoves Kurtis out of the way, telling him to go back into the living room.

Parker wipes his brow and turns back to me with a nervous grin. "Hi. Wow, you look really pretty."

My nerves dissolve, and exhilaration tingles in their place. "Really?"

"I've never seen you in yellow before."

I hug the cake container, worried I'll drop it mid-blush. "It's okay?"

"Yeah, you look like sunshine. It suits you better than blue."

"Yellow is my favorite color." I look away with a mixture of worry and hope. "I'll just keep the blue for Lewis."

"Good call." Parker takes the cake container from me. "Shall we?"

"Sure," I reply. "Umm, how did..."

He tilts his head, waiting for me to finish. "How did what?"

I cup a hand over my reddening nose. "Uh, no, nevermind. Are you nervous about tonight?"

"More like irritated," Parker says in a joking tone as he walks me into the house. "Mom keeps asking me if you'll like what she cooked, if you'll like what she's wearing, and if you'll like our family."

I giggle in surprise. "Wait. She's nervous about me liking her?"

"Wild, isn't it?"

I walk inside with him. The foyer has large white and black marble tiles and off-white walls. Overstuffed hooks run across the wall with coats, sports team uniforms, and an array of baseball caps. A mound of shoes are stacked below it.

Past the foyer on the right is the living room, where a wrestling match plays on the TV at a bellowing volume. Kurtis lounges on a couch, while William sits cross-legged on the carpet, glued to the screen.

"I'll take you into the kitchen," Parker says. "It might lower Mom's stress levels."

"I don't understand why she's nervous. She's a parent. Aren't things like this supposed to be easier when you're an adult?"

"Maybe it's because I'm the first one to bring a girlfriend home," Parker suggests as we round a corner.

A rush of high heel clicks echo from a nearby room. Mrs. Kelly emerges into the hallway, smoothing back her lush, sandy blonde hair.

"Hi, Kylie, welcome to our home," she says, opening her arms wide.

"Hi, Mrs. Kelly," I say as she swoops her arms around me.

"Geez, let her breathe, Mom," Parker mutters.

Hurriedly, Mrs. Kelly pulls out of the hug, clutching my upper arms. "Sorry, did I hurt you?"

I blink at her. "No, you're good."

Parker lifts the cake container. "Check out what she baked for us."

"Parker helped," I blurt.

"Oh yum," his mom says, beckoning us to follow her into the kitchen. "Bring it in here so I can take a look."

I follow them into the kitchen and almost stumble on my footing. My mouth falls open. "Oh my gosh!"

Mrs. Kelly flinches. "What is it?"

I cup a hand over my mouth, grinning. "Your kitchen. It's stunning."

Mrs. Kelly places a hand on her chest. "Thank you, sweetheart."

The room is massive. Three pendant lights hang over the large island counter, which is marbled in forest green. They have a large stainless steel double oven and a sparkling six-burner range. The top cabinets have glass doors, and the internal lighting showcases the glassware inside. The splashback is glossy, without a single fingerprint, and lit with hidden backlighting.

The kitchen flows into a spacious dining area. The far wall has floor to ceiling windows, showcasing their impeccably landscaped backyard, which is highlighted by garden lights.

Parker places the cake on the counter. "Should this go in the fridge?"

"No, it's fine to stay out," I say, walking into the room and ogling the deep cabinet drawers, the walk-in pantry, and the six high stools on the other side of the island counter.

Parker laughs. "You look more in awe here than at the fair."

"You didn't tell me you had the most perfect kitchen in town."

Mrs. Kelly laughs, batting a hand. "I wouldn't go that far. I just enjoy cleaning, which I do far more than cooking."

My eyes wander over the two pots on the stovetop. Despite the cooking, there isn't a drop of food spillage anywhere.

"You obviously didn't get Parker to help cook," I joke, gesturing at the cake. "He dusted the counter with flour instead of getting it into the mixing bowl."

"Aww, Parky. I think it's so cute you helped Kylie bake," his mom gushes, pinching his cheek.

"*Mom*," he grumbles, pulling his face away.

"Parky was very cute," I tease, leaning against a stool.

Parker gives me an unimpressed look, but it's ignored when his mom opens the cake container.

She lifts the top cover, and her mouth falls open. "Oh, Kylie, this is sublime. You shouldn't have gone to so much trouble for us."

"It's no problem," I insist. "I enjoy baking for other people."

She places the lid back on. "I already can't wait for dessert."

"Is there anything I can do to help with dinner?" I offer.

"No, you're our guest," she replies. "You two can watch TV with the boys."

Parker smirks. "Hard pass."

When Parker wanders into the dining area, I follow and notice the gallery-style wall of photos adjacent to the head of the table.

"Oh, wow," I murmur, zeroing in on a particular photo. "Was that your dog?"

Parker moves to the photo wall with me. He smiles, tapping the framed photo of him and Kurtis, sitting on either side of a golden retriever. "Yeah, that's Gus."

"He's a gorgeous dog. I can see why seeing Brandy gave you a jolt."

"Yeah, it was surreal."

I pan across the array of family photos. Some are clearly professional photo shoots, like the holiday-themed images, and others are candid, like ski trips and birthday parties.

"It's so nice you have all these photos on display," I say in awe.

Parker shrugs. "Yeah, I guess."

"Hello everyone," Mr. Kelly announces, moving into the dining room from the rear.

"Hi honey," Mrs. Kelly calls from the island counter. "How was work?"

Mr. Kelly huffs, smiling as he sets his briefcase on a dining chair and flicks his keys onto the table. "It was work," he jokes, and then double-takes at me. "Oh, Kylie. Hello there. I almost didn't recognize you."

"Hi, Mr. Kelly."

He looks me up and down. "How are you?"

"I'm good, thank you. And you?"

Mr. Kelly grins. "Very well. Wow, Parker, how'd you manage to land such a stunner?"

I hope he's ready to totally trip when Parker's with Yvette.

Parker smirks. "It took a lot of convincing."

Mr. Kelly chuckles. "And what'd he do to win you over, Kylie?"

"Just by promising a spring break that would change both our lives," I say, stifling a laugh.

"Big call, son," Mr. Kelly says. "Hope you're putting in your best effort."

Parker folds his arms. "Trying to."

Mr. Kelly brushes back Parker's hair and kisses his forehead. "That's all you can do."

Parker leans into his dad, and I could just melt.

When Mr. Kelly moves on to greet his wife, I whisper, "That was really sweet. It's nice to see how close you and your dad are."

Parker's eyes drift to the photos on the wall. "Is it?"

"I thought so." I shift beside him as his parents chat in the kitchen. "I just haven't seen your dad around. I didn't know what to expect."

"Sometimes he's like my mom," Parker whispers. "Trying too hard. I dunno. Sometimes it feels forced."

My eyebrows push together. "Are you serious?"

"It's fine. It's just how my family is."

"Oh."

"I'm ready to serve dinner," Mrs. Kelly announces. "Honey, can you get the boys ready?"

Unraveling his tie, Mr. Kelly wanders out of the kitchen.

As Parker and I take our seats at the dining table, we overhear his dad greeting his brothers in the living room. Their voices are boisterous and laced with fun. I can't help stealing a glance at Parker, who's still fidgety.

Why is he so stressed out? Listening to his dad and brothers, nothing seems forced. Is he just on edge because his family might embarrass him? That's something I can completely understand.

"Your home is so nice, Mrs. Kelly," I say from the table. "At least, what I've seen of it."

She mumbles a laugh. "Just stick to the first floor. The boys have exploded upstairs."

"Does it drive you crazy?"

"Oh, gosh, it does. They all try to blame my nursing background for my love of cleanliness, but they'd hate it if I didn't clean up after them." She chuckles to herself. "This place would be like a sty."

"Are you talking about your OCD?" Kurtis asks, moving into the room and toward the dining table.

She clicks her tongue. "I'm not that bad."

Parker leans forward and teases, "Mom quit her job so she could clean the house full time."

"Oh, Parker," his mom complains. "I hope you boys see me as more than your cleaner."

"Yeah, our cook," Kurtis blurts, cracking himself up.

She frowns. "*Kurtis.*"

"How long has it been since you stopped nursing?" I ask.

"Since William was born," she says. "I always felt like I was running behind while I was working. I wanted to attend all of Parker and Kurtis's school events, and their sports games. With another one so much younger, I was too stressed out to work and stay on top of being a mom."

Mr. Kelly walks back into the room. "My promotion came at the perfect time to let Tasha retire."

"That's awesome it worked out," I say.

"Of course, I would've kept working if we'd needed it to survive. I just feel so privileged to be able to look after my boys full-time."

Mrs. Kelly serves our dinner, and then she and Mr. Kelly bring the plates over to the dining table.

"Being a nurse must've been fulfilling," I say as everyone takes their seats.

"William," Mr. Kelly calls. "What's the hold up?"

"Coming," his little voice calls back.

Mrs. Kelly gestures at Parker. "Kylie, looks like you'd make a great nurse. You bandaged him up so well."

Kurtis peers at his brother's hand. "What happened, Parker?"

Parker lifts his hand. "I grazed a knife when we were cutting cherries to go in the cake."

"Wait, what happened?" William asks, dawdling into the kitchen.

"It's not a big deal," Parker says flatly. "I just cut my finger."

William's eyes bug. "Did you need stitches?"

Parker deadpans at his brother. "No. It was a graze."

Kurtis snickers, folding his arms. "Good thing you didn't slice off your hand and need a blood transfusion."

"*Kurtis*," his dad says in a warning tone.

Mrs. Kelly slams cutlery down. "Why would you say something like that?"

Kurtis shrugs, laughing to himself.

My gaze pivots around the family members. Clearly, there's a piece of information I'm missing. I land on Parker, who has a green tinge and averts his eyes.

"What have I told you about pushing buttons, Kurtis?" Mr. Kelly says.

Kurtis smirks. "Shouldn't Kylie know what she's getting herself into?"

Their mom huffs. "This dinner is for us to get to know Kylie. She doesn't need to know how much of a brat you are."

Their dad gains my attention. "I hear you work at Morton's Café. Do they treat you well down there?"

I smile and nod. "Very well. Plus, they allow me to perfect my baking skills."

He gestures at the cake on the counter. "Looks like you're doing well for yourself."

"She won't be a nurse," Parker says. "She's too incredible at baking."

"We should skip dinner and go straight to dessert," William pipes up.

Their parents chuckle, settling into the light-hearted vibe.

Mr. Kelly nods at William. "You eat your dinner and then you can have cake."

William pouts, scraping his fork across his plate.

"I still can't believe all the detail you put into decorating the cake," Mrs. Kelly says in awe. "I'd almost given in to William and skipped dinner."

My shoulders bounce with my laugh.

"Aren't we worried there's Parker's blood in the cake?" Kurtis blurts.

Parker rolls his eyes. "I didn't bleed on the cake."

Kurtis's lip upturns. "I'm not risking it."

"*Eww.*" William grimaces. "Did Parker really ruin the cake?"

Mrs. Kelly rubs her forehead. "Can we have dinner without you boys going at it?"

"Boys, cool it," their dad warns. "Don't get your mother worked up."

I sit back in my seat, unnerved by the growing hostility at the table.

"You know you picked a lemon, don't you?" Kurtis says to me, leaning forward in his seat. "He's been a nonstarter since day one."

Recoiling, I glance at Parker, and then back at his brother.

"Kurtis," his dad fires up. "What did I just say?"

Kurtis sniggers. "I'm just making conversation."

Parker glares at his brother. "You're being a jackass."

Kurtis ignores him and smirks at me. "Don't you want to know more about your boyfriend?"

I swallow the distaste rising in my throat. "Why do I get the feeling I don't want to know?"

"I'm guessing no girl wants to realize she's with a reject," Kurtis says with a mocking tone. "You know, someone you might be better off pressing the abort button on."

At that, Parker pushes back his chair with a screech and is quick to leave the table.

Mrs. Kelly stands as Parker storms out of the room. She calls out to him as we hear his footsteps hurrying up the staircase.

I stand and step ahead of his mother. "Can I?"

Mrs. Kelly swallows hard and nods in approval.

On shaky legs, I leave the dining room and move toward the staircase.

Twenty-Three

On the second floor, I crane my neck for signs of Parker.

At my house, the second floor landing is tiny. Just enough room to walk past the bedroom and bathroom doors. Here, there's a large living area, hosting a huge flatscreen TV and littered with gaming consoles. Teenage boys' clothing is flung over the couches and shoes are strewn across the floor.

How does their neat freak mother stand it?

I pan around at the numerous doors, and softly call out, "Parker?"

I edge across the carpet, peering into the open doorways. I pass a room that's clearly William's, and another that's devoid of personality and likely a guest room. When I pass his parents' bedroom, I hear a toilet flush. A few moments later, Parker emerges from a bathroom.

He slouches against the door frame. "Hey."

"Hey. Are you okay?"

He points below us. "That, down there, is the reason I didn't want to do this."

"I'm sorry if me being here made things worse."

Parker steps across the hall, opens a door, and gestures for me to follow him inside.

I press a hand into my fragile stomach and follow behind.

Parker plonks on his bed, running a hand over his brow. "Don't apologize," he mumbles. "You never make anything worse."

Inside his bedroom, a wave of calm washes over me. I can't explain it, but this room manifests Parker's personality. He has a knack of pulling me out of anxiety, and so does this room. It has light green walls, plastered with band posters and a collage of images of him and his friends. His desk is littered with textbooks, a gaming PC, and a dissected skateboard. The open closet has one neat side, and the other is piled with washed and unwashed clothes.

It just feels like him.

It feels safe.

I edge closer to him. "So, what was all that down there?"

"I'll tell you, but you have to promise you won't tell anyone else."

I nod hurriedly. "I won't."

Parker shifts to pull something out from under the bed.

"Wait," I blurt.

He sits up tall again, waiting for me to say more.

I swallow dryly. "You don't have to tell me. I mean, why would you tell me if none of your friends know?"

"You've already kept a secret," he replies, gesturing between us. "You haven't told your family or my friends that we're not really dating."

"That's it? You trust me?"

"And, you're looking at me like I'm weird. I don't think I can hang out with you on the camping trip if you're looking at me like I'm a martian."

I sit back. "I'm sorry, Parker. I didn't mean to act strange. There's just an off vibe around here."

Parker smirks. "I tried to warn you. I told you to make an excuse to get out of tonight."

"I thought you were exaggerating."

Parker takes a deep breath in and out. "Okay. So, you know how Kurtis wouldn't lay off the whole blood thing?"

I hug my waist, sitting cross-legged on his bed. "Why was he being such a jerk?"

He shrugs. "Because that's what my brother does."

"Okay. So what's his fascination with blood?"

Parker rubs the heel of palm across his chest, wincing. "When I was seven-years-old, I was in a really bad accident. There was a lot of blood, and I needed to go to the hospital."

I gasp. "Oh my gosh."

"It was so bad I needed a blood transfusion. The doctors asked my parents to donate, but neither was a match." He takes another deep breath. "Obviously, that raised some questions. It was soon after that I learned I was adopted."

My jaw drops, and I can't even utter a syllable to describe my shock.

Parker chews his lip, apprehensively waiting to continue.

"So..." I falter as the fog lifts from my mind. "Umm, is it just you? I mean, are all your brothers adopted?"

He shakes his head. "We all have the same dad. I just have another mom."

I gulp, feeling an ache deep in the pit of my stomach. My forehead builds with sweat as I fathom the part where he didn't know about this.

Parker tilts his head. "Are you okay?"

I sit back, wide-eyed as I wipe my brow. "Yeah. Why?"

"Because you look ready to puke."

"No," I rush. "Oh my gosh, no. Parker, I'm sorry. I just... I don't understand what this means."

Parker sits back on the bed and exhales slowly. "My real mom died after I was born." He averts his eyes as he adds, "And I mean, straight after I was born."

My hands raise, trembling, to cover my nose and mouth.

Parker leans forward and pulls a framed photo out from under the bed. "This was her. I still can't believe I went years without knowing she existed."

I lower my hands, taking in the striking eyes and familiar smile of the woman in the photo.

"She has your smile," I murmur.

Parker sets the photo down between us.

I shut my eyes tight, trying to make sense of this. "How did you not know about her?"

"My parents said it was too hard."

I stare at him with a mixture of confusion and simmering anger.

Parker draws a finger around the frame. "I dunno. They said they tried, but it was always too hard. When we were kids, Kurtis and I always wanted to be the same. Apparently, anytime they sat me down to tell me about my mom, I'd get upset. Either that, or Kurtis would want to be part of the conversation too."

I clench my fists, keeping my anger in check. I need to be calm so Parker can tell his story, no matter how outraged I am at his parents.

"They said they wanted to tell me when I got older." Parker shifts, looking away from the photo. "I know it really hurt my mom to admit I wasn't really hers."

"I get that this is a tough topic," I say, my resolve crumbling, "but you have a right to know your own history. Why didn't they tell you sooner?"

"I guess they didn't want to confuse me." Parker stares at the photo. "But it would've been easier, seeing this face as I grew up, and knowing she existed."

I clutch my chest, feeling a break in my heart. "Of course, it would've been. I'm so sorry. I had no idea you were struggling with something like this."

Parker shakes his head. "Don't feel sorry for me. I'm fine."

"You can feel bad. It's okay. You don't need to put on a front."

He hikes a knee on the edge on the bed and rests his elbow on top. "I hated finding out in the hospital. It was like I instantly didn't belong. And then the next year, William was born. No one said it, but it felt like I wasn't allowed to bring it up. They didn't want to hear about what I was going through because there was a new baby to look after."

"No way," it puffs out of me.

"And me and Kurtis have never been the same. We used to be so close, like best friends. Then when Mom and Dad told him about my real mom, he acted like I was different. Like I was a freak that didn't belong. Now, our rift is too big to fix."

"You shouldn't be made to feel like the black sheep just because you have a different mom."

"I have a good family," he says. "Like, I know this. I'm just different from everyone else."

I plant my hand on his thigh. "You're not abnormal. You didn't choose how you were born."

"I know. It's just this thing, hovering over our family, that no one wants to talk about." He drops his foot off the bed and leans forward, pulling two more framed photos out from underneath. "I just wish it was easy to see her face."

"Oh my gosh." It tumbles out of me, shattered. "Downstairs, they have all those photos on the wall, and you have to store these under your bed."

I trace a finger down the side of a photo. Between two golden retrievers, sits his bio mom. I sniff hard, fighting the bulging sob lodged in my throat. With a grunt, the urge breaks and my throat clears.

"You said you had a golden retriever because your mom had them," I murmur, fixated on the dogs. "But it wasn't your mom who's downstairs."

He rubs the back of his neck, frowning. "I just remember being so confused and upset when I found out I had a different mom. It was hard, dealing with who I am. So, my dad would tell me stories about my bio mom, like how she was dog-obsessed. Those were the stories I liked the most, so Mom and Dad agreed to get me a dog of my own. It was like having a piece of her with me once we got Gus."

"Oh my gosh," I rush. "That's what Kurtis meant about a 'pity dog.' Ugh. He's such a jerk!"

Parker smirks. "That's what I've been telling you all along." He pushes the photos away. "Ugh. It hurt so bad when Gus died."

My soul crushes, now knowing how linked his pet was to the memory of his mother.

I wrap my arms around him and rest my head on his shoulder. "Thank you for sharing this with me. It couldn't have been easy."

He rests his head by mine. "It's actually nice to finally tell someone."

"No one knows about your bio mom outside of your family?"

He smirks, lifting his head. "Except you."

"But how is that possible? The gossip trains run fast in this town."

He sits back, putting a gap between us. "It's because I wasn't born here. Mom and Dad got together after my bio mom died." He swallows hard, staring at the opposite corner of the room. "A year later, Kurtis was born, and news about them was already running hot. They didn't want our lives to be overshadowed by scandal, so we moved here to Victoria Falls to start over."

"Oh."

"I just didn't know why we moved until I found out about the adoption."

"Makes sense as to why this was all hidden so well."

"Yeah. Mom couldn't exactly keep her job at her old hospital after falling in love with a man whose wife had just died."

"Was your mom a nurse at the hospital where you were born?"

He nods. "She was in the room when I was delivered."

"Whoa."

"I almost died," he whispers. "I wasn't supposed to make it."

My jaw clenches, and my hands bundle into fists, bracing myself as I listen to his words.

"There's this thing mothers do with premature babies to help them gain strength," he says. "They put them on their chests so they can hear their mother's heartbeats, because it's the only thing a newborn will recognize. Anyway, my birth mom was already gone, but as a nurse, Mom couldn't give up on me. She sat for hours with me lying on her chest, and that's how she saved my life."

I clutch the space over my heart. "And that's when your parents fell in love?"

Parker smiles and nods.

I grasp his hand. "Oh, Parker. You brought your parents together. That's incredible. Oh my gosh, your bratty brother should be thanking you, not teasing you. Without you, neither him or William would exist."

Parker mumbles a laugh. "Maybe you're right."

I deadpan him. "I'm one-hundred percent right."

He shifts away, folding his arms across his middle.

I chew my lip and ask, "And you really don't want anyone else to know about this?"

"No way. I'm keeping this locked down."

"But it's nothing to be ashamed of. Won't it be easier if it's not a secret anymore?" I shift away, letting awkwardness consume my posture. "What about Jamie? I don't know all the details, but I know she's had hardships with her mom. Haven't you ever thought about talking about this with her?"

Parker shudders. "Ah, no. Jamie's never directly talked to me about that stuff. When we hang out, it's to play video games or head to the skatepark." He stretches his back with a long exhale. "Honestly, that's the way I want to keep it. At least while I'm living in this house." He glances at the photos. "Maybe when I'm in college, I'll hang these on the wall."

I take one of the photos and move over to his desk. "Would it be so bad if you had these on display?"

He frowns. "My mom wouldn't like it."

"Your mom has to suck it up," I blurt. "She's lucky because she has you. Your other mom shouldn't be forgotten."

I rest the photo frame on his desk, and he chews his lip as he stares at it. He then lifts the other two frames, handing them to me. I take them and stand them on his desk.

I smile at the display. "Perfect."

"It might only last a night."

"It's a start," I reply. "So long as you're sharing, how was she kept a secret? Didn't you have another set of grandparents?"

He shakes his head. "Dad said she didn't have any family but him. Like, they were alive, but she didn't talk to them."

"You've never met them?"

"No. Dad said she didn't want them in our lives."

"Oh. Okay."

"I don't feel the need to meet them. She cut them out for a reason." He looks off to the side. "There's just one thing I wish I could ask my parents."

"What is it?"

His shoulders droop. "I want to visit her grave. Maybe it's dumb, but it just feels like I'll find a missing part if I do that."

I clutch my chest. "That's not dumb."

"I'm too scared to ask. What if they don't want me to go?"

"I'm sure that's not it. They probably think you're too weirded out to go there." I look down at his birth mother's photo. "You know, if you needed someone to go with you, I'd be there."

"Really?"

I look back at him and hold his gaze. "Definitely."

"Wow. Thank you."

I lean against his desk. "So, this secret is why you wanted me to stay away from your home?"

"Pretty much."

I move and sit beside him. "I never would've known. You always seem so confident at school and with your friends."

"You have your Kikki power at home. Mine is away from home."

My shoulders hunch forward as I slouch in sadness.

"Don't look sad. This is why I'm always looking for the positives in life," he says. "After finding out this stuff about my life, nothing else seems bad in comparison. You know, I could dwell on all the negative feelings. Or, I can see all the good things my parents do for me and how lucky I am to have them."

I nod, keeping my eyes downcast as if I can see his family downstairs.

Parker smirks. "And now you know why they overdo it."

"Do you think it's because they feel guilty?"

He nods. "They fell in love so soon after my bio mom passed away. How could they not look at me and only feel guilt?"

"No way," I perk up. "I've seen how they both look and act around you. They love you so much."

"I know. But this is why I like to keep all this family baggage out of my social life. I don't need to feel like crap when I leave the house."

My heart hurts. "You feel like crap?"

He shrugs. "It's just this deep cut I'm never allowed to talk about, so it just festers."

I clutch my elbows, pleading with my eyes not to well.

"Don't get me wrong," he blurts, "it's not like this all the time. I'm not constantly thinking about it. It's only if something triggers it, like Kurtis making a stupid remark. Usually, everyone just avoids the subject, and tip-toes around me like I might break."

"That sounds so hard."

"I think it's my parents who are afraid of breaking."

"Maybe they don't know how to talk about it. Perhaps they should think about putting you all in family therapy."

"*Yikes.* That would be so awkward."

"Only at first."

His eyebrow crooks. "You've been in therapy?"

There's a knock at the door. "Parker?"

Parker huffs, slouching on his bed. "Go away, Kurtis."

"Mom told me to come and get you," Kurtis says through the door.

I suck in a breath and protectively shield the framed photos on the desk behind my back.

"I'm not going back down there with you," Parker replies bluntly.

Kurtis grunts, and the door knob twists. "Can I come in?"

Parker stands from the bed, his hands resting on his hips, as his brother enters the room.

Kurtis opens his mouth to speak, but when he glances my way, he falters.

Something inside me snaps.

All I see is red.

"You should apologize to your brother," I order. "He does so much for you, and you just treat him like crap."

Kurtis rolls his eyes, muttering, "I know."

Parker tilts his head. "You know what?"

"I know I shouldn't have said those things," Kurtis mumbles at the carpet. "But I couldn't stop myself."

"You used the word abort," I blurt, disgusted, "about your own brother."

Kurtis's expression is tight, and there's pain in his eyes when he looks at Parker. "Obviously, I didn't mean that. I want you around, Parker."

Parker folds his arms. "Uh-huh."

Kurtis rolls his eyes. "Don't make me say something stupid like I love you."

Parker winces, holding up a hand. "No, don't do that."

"I just couldn't stand one more thing going your way," Kurtis admits.

Parker's head jerks back. "What does that mean?"

"Everything is always working out for you," Kurtis says, disgruntled. "Now you have a girlfriend who actually likes you, and Mom and Dad are still bending over backwards to applaud you."

Parker recoils, about to question his brother before being cut off.

"You're treated like royalty around here, Parker," Kurtis continues. "Everyone has to be so careful of what they say, because we're not supposed to upset you."

Parker points a thumb at his chest. "I'm the one who has to walk around on eggshells."

Kurtis scoffs. "Get real. Everything revolves around making sure you're happy. It's like I'm the only one who sees through it. Every day, I want to snap. But I'm given a lecture about what I can't say to you."

With a sigh, Parker turns away. "Look, man. I'm sorry if you feel cheated, but I'm the one who had his life changed."

"But I still wanted you to be my brother."

Parker turns back to face Kurtis.

Kurtis eyes the photo frames on the desk and exhales hard. "Everything changed for me too when we found out about *her*. Man, I didn't want us to be different."

"Then why do you act like we are?" Parker questions.

He shrugs. "Because I don't know how to deal with this."

Parker steps closer to his brother and holds one arm out. "Come here, you idiot."

The brothers side-hug, and Kurtis mumbles into Parker's shoulder. "I'm sorry, bro."

"Thanks." They pull away from each other, and Parker motions to the door. "Do me a favor? Go back downstairs and put the brakes on Mom and Dad?"

"I'll try, but they don't want to hear from me. I'm grounded again."

Parker smirks. "You'll never learn."

Kurtis looks at me with a guilty smile. "Sorry for making your introduction to our family so awkward."

I chew on my lip, pivoting my gaze between the boys. "I'm just glad you two are actually talking about this stuff."

Kurtis fidgets in his stance, and then backtracks out of the room. "Uh, I'll leave you guys to it."

Parker nods and then Kurtis's hurried footsteps descend the staircase.

I step closer to Parker. "Are you doing okay?"

Parker huffs, rubbing his hands over his face. "I'm done pretending for the night."

I flinch. "Oh, okay. I can call my mom to pick me up."

He grasps my hand. "No, I still want to spend time with you. Just not around people we have to put on a show for."

My shoulders relax. "What are you thinking?"

He nods at the door. "Let's go for a drive."

Twenty-Four

"Parky," Mrs. Kelly rushes to meet us at the bottom of the staircase. "Honey, I'm so sorry for what happened. Will you both come back to the table?"

"No, Mom," Parker says flatly. "Kylie and I are heading out."

Mrs. Kelly's eyes water, and her face elongates. "Oh, please. We can wipe the slate clean and try again."

"Not tonight," Parker replies.

"But we still have cake," she pleads.

Parker moves toward a door, which leads into the garage. "It's okay. You guys eat it."

I hesitate to follow Parker. His mother looks so broken. Even though I'm so mad at her past actions, it's undeniable how much she truly loves Parker. She is his mother in every way that counts.

I take her hands and give her a kind smile. "My mom wants to have you and Mr. Kelly over for dinner. Or, perhaps, we'll go to a restaurant. It could be a do-over."

She smiles, sniffing back her tears. "Really? That would be wonderful."

I release her hands. "Umm, just so you know, Parker showed me a photo of, umm, his other mom."

She jerks back with surprise. "He did?"

I nod. "I set the photos on his desk. I hope you're not mad."

She clutches her chest. "Mad? I'd never be upset about that. I just didn't think he wanted to talk about her."

I blow out a painful breath. "Your family has to get better at communication."

Her shoulders slouch. "We suck at it."

I step past her and rub her arm. "I hope you enjoy the cake."

"Thanks, sweetheart."

I move into the garage as warmth spreads through my heart. Parker and I might not be together for much longer, but it doesn't hurt to give Mrs. Kelly a shred of hope. It's better than her spending the rest of the evening wallowing in despair.

"What were you doing?" Parker asks when I join him inside his car.

"Just trying to make your mom feel a little better."

He starts the ignition and smiles. "Thanks."

"So, where are we headed?"

"Usually, in times like these, I'd head over to Kai's and play video games with the boys." His wrist drapes over the steering wheel as he gently turns my way. "But I'd much rather hang out with just you."

I let out a nervous laugh as a tingle runs down my spine. "So, what's the alternative?"

"Wanna go to the arcade?"

I wince. "The arcade?"

He nudges me. "Come on. It'll be fun."

I raise my hands. "Okay, let's do it. We do quiet stuff when I'm upset. We'll do loud stuff with flashing lights to perk you up."

He sniggers. "That's the spirit."

When we get to the arcade, I try my best to mask my apprehension. I'm happy to be here to lift Parker's mood, but it's not exactly my speed.

We start with a duck shooting game. Parker insists I play with him, but I hardly put in any effort. The thought of shooting ducks, video games or not, just isn't something I'm into. Also not helped by the fact we're holding plastic rifles.

"Okay, maybe that wasn't the best place to start," Parker says, collecting our tokens. "What about a street fighter game instead?"

"Umm, do I look like a worthy adversary for that?"

Parker laughs. "Kikki, you've continued to surprise me all week. So, yes, you could be."

His enthusiasm lights me up and I agree to play.

However, it doesn't work out well for my character. I hold my own better than I expected, but Parker knows the control better than me. There was no chance of this going my way.

Parker makes me high five him when the game ends. "You did well, Green."

"I need more practice so I can beat you."

"Oh, them's fighting words."

I wink. "Don't you know it?"

We amble around the aisles, but Parker is too distracted to suggest another game.

I watch his expression, unable to read it, and ask, "So, did you end up hanging out with Yvie today?"

Parker's eyes widen. "Oh, I never replied to your text. Sorry, Mom was driving me nuts, and I got distracted. But yes, we hung out for about an hour."

I tap my fingers against a game machine and let my gaze wander along the adjacent machines to seem casual. "So, what happened?"

"She wanted to know if I suspect something is happening between you and Lewis."

An uncontrollable laugh tumbles out of me. I hold on to the arcade machine for support as I reply, "Are you serious?"

He nods. "She can't get it out of her head. She's obsessed with the fact you two live next door to each other," Parker explains. "Her exact words were, 'How could they help it from happening?'"

"Umm, maybe from me never telling Lewis how I feel, and Lewis being oblivious to my existence."

"I think, because she and Lewis are continually having this same argument, she's started panicking and thinking up scenarios between you and him."

"Is this part of your theory that Yvette is just a poor insecure girl?"

"Don't make fun. Everyone has issues."

I frown. "You're right. I never would've guessed anything was messing with you."

"At least seeing Yvie was a bright spot in my fiasco of a day."

I fake a smile, nodding along.

He tucks a piece of hair behind my ear and lets his hand rest on my shoulder. "But it doesn't compare to having you by my side."

My chin drops. "What?"

"I can't imagine anyone else finding out about that stuff with my family. I feel so lucky to have you as a friend."

Feeling an imminent blush happening, I cough and cover with, "So, did you and Yvie discuss anything else?"

"I pushed for her to go on the camping trip."

"Did she say she was going?"

"She was still cagey. I hinted at helping her mend her friendship with Tabitha, and it seemed to make her happier."

I push off the arcade machine and move past the race car simulators. "I'm glad."

"You know, I'll still help you with Lewis too."

"I know," I reply. "But right now, I'm not really thinking about him. That was huge back at your house. All I care about is making sure you have a good time to make up for it."

"Sounds great," Parker says, slinging an arm around me. "No more talk about Yvie and Lewis."

"Oh, I didn't mean you couldn't talk about her. If it makes you happy, talk about her all you want."

"Why would I talk about her when I'm out with you?"

"*Uhhh... Uhhh...*" I want to say, because you're in love with her. Because I'm nothing compared to her. But the way he stares into my eyes with those delicate smile lines crinkling in his expression, I can't get out the words circulating through my mind.

Parker gestures ahead to a game called Pop-A-Shot. "How's your basketball skills?"

"If you mean as a spectator, they are on point."

Parker laughs. "Okay, you can play cheerleader this time around."

Watching Parker is a ton of fun. His aim is impressive, and the score keeps growing higher. More astounding is the fact he can throw himself into fun and laughter when something so ugly happened at his home. I understand it's his life, and he's known this history for a long time, but this also means he's been masking this pain with fun and competition for just as long.

After the basketball arcade game, he makes me play Whack-A-Mole with him. This is one Tess and I played a lot as kids. My reaction time is something to be desired, but I can't help drowning in laughter as I smash my foam mallet against the fast critters.

We then wander around the arcade some more, watching people mingling around the games. When we near the photo booth, Parker pulls me to a stop.

He hangs a thumb at the machine, asking, "Wanna commemorate tonight?"

"You really want to remember this?"

He slings an arm around me. "Yes. I want to remember the relief I felt at finally sharing the truth with someone."

I rub my lips together and release them with a smile. "Okay. I'm up for that."

We nestle on the bench seat inside, and to my surprise, Parker presses a kiss on my cheek as the first photo snaps. I turn toward him, looping my arms around him as I gaze into his big brown eyes for the second photo. When it's time for the third, Parker makes the strangest yet funniest face at me, and I throw my head back with laughter as the photo snaps.

Parker collects the line of three photos and hands it to me. "Pretty cute, Kikki."

"You're not so bad yourself, Parky."

He grunts, getting off the booth seat. "*Eww.*"

I laugh, following him out of the booth. "You really hate the name Parky, don't you."

"It's cutesy, and I don't do cutesy."

I smirk, grabbing his hand. "I don't know. I think you're pretty cute."

He laughs, tugging on my hand as he takes a few steps backward. "Come on. Let's get out of here."

"Where are we going?"

"I think we need ice-cream."

My taste buds light up in anticipation. "I think you're a genius."

We leave the arcade and walk the pavement behind the strip mall to get to the ice-creamery.

"What flavor are you getting?" Parker asks, tapping his fingers against the glass display.

"I need one scoop of butter pecan, and one scoop of mint chocolate chip."

Parker grins as the server scoops out my order. "You *need* it, do you?"

I grin back. "Yes. Yes, I do. What are you getting?"

"I can't decide," he says, continuing to tap on the glass despite it irritating the server on the other side. "Is rocky road good?"

"It's marshmallow and chocolate. Can't go wrong."

"Hmm. I think I'll eat my weight in marshmallows and chocolate on the camping trip." When the server puts my ice-cream cup on the counter, Parker says to her, "Okay, one scoop of pistachio, and one scoop of..."

The server starts to scoop the pistachio as Parker's half sentence ligers in the air.

I nudge him. "Are you going to finish ordering?"

"I told you, I can't decide."

"There's a cherry one."

"No, I don't really like cherries."

"But you told me to make a cherry chocolate cake?"

"Yeah, because my mom likes cherries."

"Oh. Well, what do you like?"

"I like pistachio flavored things." He nods at the server. "Screw it. Make it two scoops of pistachio."

I giggle, saving that information for later.

I get in first to pay for the ice-creams, and we take our cups outside to eat on the deck under the hanging twinkle lights.

"Mmm, so good," I purr after the mixture of flavors hits my tongue.

"That's a very weird combination you put together."

"I know," I reply. "In my brain, I'm so aware of these things not working together. But there's just something about it that lights me up. Call it childhood nostalgia."

"I get that," he says. "It's like when you get unlimited refills at a diner and start mixing all the different soda flavors together. Somehow, it still tastes awesome."

"Until it inevitably doesn't when you take it too far," I reply with a chuckle. "Tessa and I used to do it all the time on road trips."

Parker points at my selections with his small plastic spoon. "If you're into the combination, it must work. You know your sweets."

I lift the cup toward him. "Wanna try?"

He lifts his cup. "Trade?"

"Sure?"

We swap cups, and I take a spoonful of pistachio. It melts on my tongue with a satisfying nutty flavor. "Mmm. Good choice."

We switch cups again after Parker tries both ice-creams. "The butter pecan rules, but I don't love the mint choc chip. I would pair it with cookies and cream instead."

"Fair enough," I say, digging my spoon back into my selections. "If anyone at French patisserie school found out I put these flavors together, they'd kick me out. It's definitely a selection that stays in my hometown."

"You think you'll go to Paris for school?"

"Maybe. I can't imagine being that far away from my family. But surely the experience would be worth it."

Parker chews his lip, and I notice a pinkish hue highlighting his cheeks. He gestures between us with his spoon. "Has this experience been worth it?"

"I've done a lot of things this week I never would've dreamed of doing," I reply. "But getting to know you, Parker, has been more than worth it."

He looks at me with surprise. "Really?"

"Truly. I never thought of you as someone I'd want to hang out with. Now I can't imagine not spending a day with you."

He nudges me. "Ditto."

I giggle, tucking a piece of hair behind my ear. "Who knew Parker Kelly wasn't just a skater boy who backflips off cliffs? He's actually a down to earth human being."

"Shocking, I know," he jokes.

"The number of layers to you is surprising. I had such a hard time working out why you were so cagey about your home life," I say. "If I had never gone to your house, I would've thought you were confident twenty-four-seven."

"I guess I've hidden things pretty well."

"I'll say. I still stand by therapy helping your family. You and Kurtis may have had a heart-to-heart back at the house, but it was only scratching the surface."

"That's where we got interrupted earlier. Have you been in therapy?"

"Not me," I reply. "But my sister. I joined a few of her sessions, and her therapist was really nice."

"What's the deal with your sister?" Parker asks. "Why do you ignore her calls?"

I chew on my fingernail, averting my gaze.

"Oh, come on, Green. I told you a bunch of messed up stuff about my family. You've gotta give me something."

"Okay." I sigh. "She made me promise not to date or spend time with anyone with popularity."

"Doesn't she know about your crush on Lewis?"

"She knows, but she doesn't want me to take it any further than my daydreams."

"Why?"

"Because of how much she got bullied when she was at Ashworth Academy."

Parker frowns. "What happened?"

"She had a huge crush on this guy named Hugh Smith," I explain. "He was super popular, on the football team, and Tess thought he was a total hunk."

"Why do I feel like this story has a nightmare ending?"

I inhale deeply before continuing. "Somehow, Hugh found out about Tess's crush. There was a school formal coming up, and he asked Tess to be his date. She thought it was a joke and shied away from him. To her surprise, he kept asking. She said he was really sweet about the whole thing."

Parker grunts, pinching the bridge of his nose as his eyes scrunch closed. "This was a prank?"

I swallow hard and nod. "She was ridiculed and humiliated. She thought her dream guy was asking her out, and that he might be in love with her. Instead, he picked her up in a limousine but didn't take her to the dance. They went to the old quarry on the south-side of town. Hugh met up with his cheerleader girlfriend, and his friends said the most horrible things to my sister. After they were all in a fit of laughter, they left her there and went to the formal."

"What the actual heck?" Parker asks, floored. Outrage lights in his eyes, and his mouth hangs open.

"It completely broke her. She sat there for almost two hours before calling Dad to pick her up."

"Oh man. I see why she's so scared of anything happening to you."

I press a hand into my stomach. "I never want to upset Tess. But I don't want to be scared all the time. I want a boyfriend, and I want to be happy."

"That will happen for you. You're smart, and you're caring. Any guy would be lucky to be with you."

"I still can't shake how turned off Lewis was yesterday," I admit. "There was nothing appealing to him about me or my life."

"Don't put yourself down just because Lewis is too uptight to dance in your hallway."

"No, I'm a loser. He'll never want to be with a loser."

"Kylie, don't say that. It's not true."

I hug my middle, looking down at the ground. "If only I were beautiful like Yvette, then a boy would want me."

Parker lifts my chin. "Kylie, you are beautiful."

I retch, pulling my face away. "You don't have to pretend with me."

He grasps my shoulder, turning me back. "I'm not lying. You are beautiful."

I blink hard, taking in the kind creases in his face, and gulp. "Why are you saying that?"

"Because I don't want you thinking you're not good enough. You're more beautiful inside than any other girl is on the outside."

I pull away, rolling my eyes. "Thanks. I know what a great personality is code for."

Parker sighs, shifting his weight. "That's not what I mean. You're beautiful inside and out. Any guy would be lucky to be with you. I would..."

He trails off, forcing me to look back at him.

Parker chews his bottom lip, hesitating on his words.

I search deeply into the eyes. "You, what?"

He clutches my hand and whispers, "I'd be lucky to be with you."

My hand trembles in his, sending a shiver up my arm and coursing through the rest of my body.

"I told you," he murmurs, "I'm done pretending today."

"What..." I stammer. "What are you saying?"

He drops my hand. "That I'm not lying about you being beautiful."

"Oh, okay. Umm, thank you."

He smiles as the twinkle lights dazzle in his eyes. "You're welcome."

Somehow more confused, I rest my elbows against the railing, looking out at the view. He fidgets beside me, and I find myself wishing Lewis and Yvette were here. At least if we were on a fake date, I'd know where we stand. Him, saying wonderful things to me, just to be nice, has my head and heart in a scramble.

"At least you and your sister go into things by listening to your hearts," Parker says. "I'm the one who's messed up. I wanted to be with Yvette to prove I'm winning at high school."

"What do you mean?"

"Come on, you've already figured this out. I work so hard at making sure everyone sees me as fun, adventurous, happy-go-lucky, so they never see me the way I am at home. I just figured, if I could get a girl like Yvette, then it'd prove I've got everything going for me at school."

My expression is stiff. "That's why you want to be with Yvette?"

He folds his arms, resting on the railing. "I thought we'd make a good couple."

"No wonder you only called her hot. You just want to use her too."

"That's not true. I really do think I could help her. If she were with me, she wouldn't be so nasty to other girls."

"You think so?" I ask skeptically.

He huffs, looking ahead at nothing in particular. "I just don't know what I want anymore."

"Well, Yvette is a grade-A moron if she can't see what a wonderful boyfriend you'd make."

Parker puffs out a laugh. "Is that so?"

I smirk. "But maybe she is too dumb to see it. Perhaps on the camping trip, I'll have to literally explain it to her."

"What do you mean?"

"I'll tell her about all the nice things you've done for me."

He looks down, a blush brewing on his cheeks. "Like what?"

"You always sit with me when I'm alone, even when I say I'm fine."

He shrugs. "I just think everyone should have company."

"Then there's all the encouragement and positivity you give me."

"Well, a negative attitude gets you nowhere."

"And there's making sure no one says anything hurtful to me." I run a finger across my lash line. "And I can't thank you enough for holding me at the fair when I was hurt."

He scratches the top of his head. "It was nothing."

"It was comforting. It stung so dang much, and everyone was arguing, and I just wanted to disappear." I place my hand on his arm. "And you did that for me. It's like I got put on pause. Thank you for that."

"Why wouldn't I do it for you? You're such a good person, and I like being around you." He lifts his hand toward mine, but doesn't touch it. "It's all good. I'd do it for you again anytime you needed it."

I remove my hand, shifting awkwardly. I clear my throat as I look away, ready to change the subject, but Parker clutches my wrist. I look up at him, my lips parting in surprise. Parker gazes into my eyes, and his hand caresses the side of my face.

"I want to kiss you," he whispers. "But I know you don't want that."

A tingle races down my spine. Feeling slightly dizzy, I clutch his bicep for the support I need.

"I only said kissing was off the table on double dates," I say with my mouth rapidly drying. "I don't see anyone else here."

Parker's Adam's apple bobs, and he wets his lips. "Are you sure about this?"

I smile. "Do you still want to kiss me?"

His hands slip behind my back, and I love feeling every digit press against the material of my tank top. "Yes."

I bite my lip and raise onto my tippy toes. "Then kiss me."

Parker leans in, but he hesitates.

"It's okay," I breathe.

He shakes his head, pulling away. "No. You told me you want your next kiss to be from Lewis."

My heart sinks, and my head can't work out why. "But I want…"

"What?" he murmurs. "What do you want?"

"I don't really know," I mumble. "But, at this moment, I have a growing urge to kiss you."

"But we're not meant to be together."

I shake my head. "I don't care about that right now."

He smiles, leaning back in. "Good. Me either."

Before I'm able to take a breath, Parker's lips are on mine, giving me all the life I need. I snake my arms behind his neck and lean my body against his. His heartbeat patters against my chest, and I tilt my head to get more out of his kiss. When my back arches, his hands press more firmly against it. A cool breeze whirls around us, helpfully lowering my elevated body temperature.

When we pull out of the kiss, Parker pants as his face rests by mine. "I can't get enough of that," he whispers. "You're so dang good at it."

A silent giggle shakes my shoulders as he holds me. "I don't know how," I whisper as he brushes loose hair off my face. "All I do is put my lips on yours."

"Well, it's working," he says with a chuckle. "You must have a natural talent for it."

"Why don't you stop talking and kiss me again?"

He smiles and angles his head. "With pleasure."

This time, my toes curl so tightly I can't stand on tippy toes. Parker notices me struggling and leans me against the railing without breaking away from the kiss. He leans over me, kissing as I'm supported by the rails. I squeeze his shoulder as he rocks my world, and accidentally bite his bottom lip.

He pulls back with a laugh. "What was that?"

"*Oops.* Sorry. I got caught up."

"Don't be sorry," he says, kissing my nose. "I was into it."

I press on the back of his neck, pulling him back into the kiss. I don't know what this means. I don't know if I'm setting myself up for heartbreak when tomorrow I watch him getting Yvette's attention. And I don't know why I don't care.

Right now, kissing Parker is bliss.

I feel wanted.

I feel validated.

I feel safe.

Who cares what tomorrow brings, because nothing can take away what is happening tonight.

After a considerable head rush, Parker takes me home. We hold hands for the entire drive.

"Thank you for listening to me tonight," Parker says, walking me to my door. "Despite the drama at my house, I had so much fun hanging out with you."

"Tonight was incredible," I reply, stepping onto my front porch. "I'll always be here to listen to you. I'm so glad I know you better."

He smiles and caresses the side of my face. "You're the only one that does, Kikki."

I rub my lips together and lean in for one more firework-inspiring kiss. As my head tilts for maximum enjoyment, the front door opens.

"Okay, kids," my dad says. "Time to call it a night."

We break apart, and my face burns tomato red as I brush a hand over my wet lips.

Parker scratches the back of his head, looking sheepishly at my dad. "Ah, hi, Mr. Green. We were just saying good night."

"Uh-huh," Dad says, crooking an eyebrow. "It's nice to see you two are so infatuated with each other, but let's keep it PG. Okay?"

My face is at molten lava level. "Okay, I'm officially mortified." I clutch Parker's hand and give it a gentle squeeze. "Thanks for tonight. I'll see you tomorrow?"

"I'll text you when I'm ready to pick you up." He pecks my cheek. "Good night, Kylie."

I release his hand, and my dad steps out of the doorway to let me inside.

"Good night, Parker," Dad says with a wry smile.

"Good night, Mr. Green." Parker waves and moves down the path toward his car.

I move inside, and hurry along the hallway so I don't make eye contact with my dad.

"How was your evening, Kikki?" Mom calls out.

I hurry up the staircase. "Good, thanks. I just need a shower."

Never have I needed to cool off faster.

Twenty-Five

I just couldn't help myself. I made a batch of pistachio macarons to take on the camping trip. After last night, I can't get Parker out of my head, and just want to see him happy. I also made lemon bars and blueberry muffins. I can practically do them in my sleep, which allowed me to put the majority of my effort into the macarons.

When the baked goods are on cooling racks, and I'm almost finished cleaning up, the doorbell rings.

"Mom?" I call out. "You got that?"

Mom doesn't reply, so I dry my hands with a dish towel, and move toward the front door.

I open the door and almost lose my balance. "Lewis?"

"Hi," he says with a small smile. "Do you have a minute to talk?"

"Umm," I falter. "Yeah, sure. Do you want to come in?"

"Thanks."

Lewis comes inside as Brandy scampers up the hallway. She skids to a halt, looking up at Lewis. She cries, lowering her head as her tail dips between her legs.

"What's with her?" Lewis asks.

I look between them and my heart sinks. "I think she thought you were Parker."

Lewis puffs out his chest. "Hey, girl, I'm better than Parker."

He moves forward, reaching out his hand to pet Brandy. She whimpers again and retreats to the back room.

"Is Parker over here a lot?" Lewis asks.

How am I supposed to answer that? Parker is supposed to be my boyfriend. But how much do I admit to the boy who I've always wanted to be my boyfriend?

"Just before or after dates," I say awkwardly. "You know, nothing too serious."

"And is it nothing too serious that he was over at my girlfriend's house too?"

I bite into my lip and clutch my elbows, shifting my weight between feet.

Lewis sighs. "Sorry. You probably don't want to hear this."

I shrug. "Parker told me he spent time with Yvie."

Lewis's eyebrow raises. "He did?"

"Yeah. On our date last night."

"You still went out with him? After he was with Yvie?"

"Yeah. We were having dinner with his family."

"Whoa. You met his family? I can't even get in the door at Yvie's."

I show Lewis into the living room and we share a couch. "I thought you hung out at Yvie's house on Sunday when you didn't come for pancakes."

"Yeah, but after she complained about me to her brother, he's roaming their house like a bodyguard."

"Oh. She's really put a wall between you two."

"I've barely spoken to Yvie since the night of the fair. And I can't even drive over there."

"Maybe it wouldn't be the best idea to drive when you're upset, anyway."

His eyebrow lifts. "You think I'm a bad driver? That accident wasn't my fault. Not that anyone believes me."

I raise my palms. "I wasn't saying you were a bad driver. Just that the situation is tense."

Lewis checks his phone, sighing. "I've been texting her, but she still hasn't replied. I just want her to call me back."

"So you don't know if she's going on the trip today?"

He shakes his head. "No idea. Man, if you saw my texts, you'd totally call me a beggar."

"You've been begging her to go?"

A nervous laugh whispers out of him. "Yeah. The digital version of getting on my knees."

I press my hand into my uneasy stomach. "Does she still think something happened between you and me?"

"Maybe. That's what caused this whole problem."

"But we haven't been hanging out."

"Hasn't stopped her from ignoring me." Lewis huffs, hanging his head in his hands. "Do you know what she and Parker talked about?"

"Us." I swallow hard. "She wanted to know if Parker suspected anything was happening between you and me."

"Whoa. Parker told you that?" He sits back in awe. "You two must have good communication. How do I get that with Yvie?"

Maybe start a fake relationship so all your cards are on the table from the beginning. "I don't know. I'm no relationship expert."

"I don't know about that. You seem to have entranced Parker. It's like all his thoughts are about you."

"No way."

"Yes way. He's always defending you to our friends and making sure you're included. He's nuts about you."

"I dunno. He might still think about Yvie."

"He makes me think that maybe all my thoughts shouldn't be on Yvie."

I sit back. "What do you mean?"

"It's driving me crazy," he whispers. "Why didn't I notice you before? How did Parker see something in you, and I didn't?"

My gulp is mortifyingly loud. "I don't know."

"Me and him are usually in sync. That's why we competed to get Yvie's attention. I don't understand how I never noticed him wanting to be with you."

"I wouldn't think about it too hard. I'm only the second choice."

Lewis smiles, leaning forward. "I wouldn't count yourself out."

Dang it, my mouth is so dry.

He sits back, blurting, "Oh, I don't have that photo of you and Parker anymore."

It takes me off guard. "Huh?"

He shakes his head, casually looking off to the side. "Yeah, the one I took at the skatepark. I accidentally deleted it. Sorry, I know you wanted a copy."

"Oh, umm, no problem."

He looks back at me with a half-smile. "Do you have any last-minute advice about getting back into Yvie's good books?"

"I don't know if I'd be much help," I croak.

"Kai said it was your idea to give Tabby flowers when she was upset."

"You could try that with Yvie, but she seems more like a jewelry girl."

Lewis winces. "Sounds expensive."

"I guess it depends on how much you want to be with her." I lean forward, a wave of confidence washing over me. "Maybe if it feels too hard, it's not worth it."

Lewis stares into my eyes, but then his brow furrows, and he stands from the couch. "No, she's worth it. I mean, it's Yvette Anderson, for goodness's sake. I'd be crazy to give her up."

"That's what every guy says, but she keeps ending up single."

"Not this time," Lewis says, tapping on his phone. "I'm not leaving her. We're gonna stay together."

Is he lying to himself? Am I crazy, or was he just suggesting he should pay attention to me instead?

Lewis puts the phone to his ear, and shocked excitement lights up his face. "Yvie? Yes! Thank you for answering."

He listens intently, and then replies, "No, I'm at Kylie's." There's more silence as he waits for her reply. "What's the big deal? She's my neighbor?"

Oof. Wrong thing to say. She literally thinks something is happening because we're neighbors. Somehow, she's oblivious to the fact he's never looked my way in eighteen months.

"You weren't answering the phone," Lewis says, heat seeping into his tone. "I needed to talk to someone. You can ask her yourself. I'm over here getting advice on how to win you back."

Oh my gosh. Do not put me on the phone with her.

"I thought you two were friends." He listens to her, periodically shaking his head. He then lowers the phone, sliding his hand over it as he whispers, "I've gotta finish this conversation."

I stand, nodding. "Okay."

He smiles and mouths, "Thanks," and leaves the living room and heads out the front door.

I huff a loud breath, confused by the whole interaction.

Why did he tell Yvette he was here? Did he want their fight to escalate? Besides, he wasn't taking any words of wisdom from me. I barely said anything he didn't already know. Was he just here to make Yvette jealous?

Lewis was already annoyed that Parker was hanging out with her.

Was this just tit for tat?

Ugh. I'm so over being used as a prop to get that girl's attention.

I go back into the kitchen to take out my frustrations by cleaning the counters. Once I'm finished cleaning, have packed up my baked goods, and brought my overnight bag downstairs, it's time for Parker to pick me up.

"Hey," he says with a happy smile. "How are you?"

"Good, now that I get to see you."

He takes my bag for me. "You're not sick of me?"

"Not yet." I say, stepping onto the porch with him.

"So, I have no idea if I'm supposed to pick up Yvie or not."

My mood sinks. "Lewis was over here before, complaining that he still hadn't heard from her."

"He talked to you about that?"

I nod. "He said he wanted my advice, but I don't think I told him anything helpful. He managed to get her to answer the phone, and then totally sabotaged it by telling her he was with me."

"Whoa. Is he trying to make Yvie jealous, or you?"

"All he did was successfully give me a headache."

Parker stops on the footpath and lowers his voice. "Hey, if Yvette's not coming, do you want to tell Lewis we're broken up? I don't want to hold you back from taking your shot."

My mouth opens to answer, but nothing comes out. I stare up into his sunlit brown eyes, and I'm paralyzed.

Do I want this to be over?

Something deep inside me says no.

Lewis's front door bursts open, and he calls out, "The world's not over."

Parker gives him a quizzical look. "What's that, man?"

Lewis hikes his bag over his shoulder, moving toward the curb with us. "Yvie's still coming. Her brother's driving her to the camping spot."

"She doesn't want to come with us?" Parker asks.

"She said she'd meet us there," Lewis replies. "I don't want to push it. I'm just relieved she's agreed to come."

Me too.

Whoa.

Whose voice is that in my head?

Regardless, I find myself smiling.

At least the trip into the mountains will be peaceful without Yvette around.

On the drive, Parker turns on the stereo and skips the tracks until a Frontier Leaders song plays. We share a glance with mirrored smiles, and I settle into my seat.

Behind me, Lewis retches. "Dude, why do you keep listening to this band? I'm so sick of them."

My smile flips into a frown, and I catch a flex in Parker's jaw as he winces.

I turn in my seat and ask Lewis, "You don't like this band?"

Lewis shrugs. "They're okay. I listen to them only when Parker controls the music."

I turn around and eye Parker. "Was it your phone I saw that day in the café?"

Lewis laughs. "Don't tell me you like this band too, Kylie?"

"She does," Parker replies, eyeing his friend in the rearview mirror. "Because she's cool."

"Oh, man. Have you two been bonding over this lame band?"

Lame?

Ouch. My heart.

Parker's hand sneaks across the center console and grasps mine. I look up and find him smiling.

"We've bonded over more than that," Parker says. "It was just the cherry on top."

My limp hand is secure in his. Memories of yesterday flash in my mind. Parker and I, sitting at my kitchen table, bobbing to the latest Frontier Leaders' album. It was one of the best moments of the entire spring break.

Besides kissing outside the ice-creamery.

I smile back, interlacing my fingers with his.

When we arrive at the campsite, there are already three cars parked.

"Who's car is that?" I ask, gesturing at the SUV with a speedboat hooked up to the back.

"That's Tyler's parents," Parker replies. "They bring the boat every year. Are you into water skiing?"

My eyes bug. "Water skiing? That's a big yikes."

Parker smirks. "Yikes isn't a no."

"It's past a no," I say, getting out of the car. "It's past heck no."

Parker laughs, rounding the car to meet me. "I bet I can coax you onto the skis."

Instinctively, I back away. "No way."

"Relax, Green. They haven't even gotten the boat onto the water yet."

"Hi guys," Kai says, walking over to us. "Where's Yvie?"

Tabitha follows, looking hopeful Yvette won't show up.

"Her brother's driving her out," Lewis says.

"Did you two make up?" Kai asks.

"We're on the way," Lewis replies.

"Have you guys been here long?" Parker asks.

"Only ten minutes," Tabitha answers.

"Okay, kids, let's set up the tents before we do anything else," Kai's dad says. "I want boys on this side, and girls on the other side. That's right; the parents will be in the middle."

"You think that's going to stop your son?" Tyler jokes, carrying a duffle bag.

Mr. Nelson raises an eyebrow. "Which son?"

Hearing the comments, Jamie and Milo emerge from behind an SUV.

Tyler sniggers. "Either one."

"You're just jealous, Ty," Kai says, moving toward the back of his parent's SUV.

"Oh, sure," Tyler says, dumping his duffle bag in the tent area. "I'm dying to have my parents spy on me when I'm making out with my girlfriend."

"Ugh," his mother revolts. "I would never want to spy on you."

"You don't have to worry about that," Jamie cuts in. "Ty's girlfriend is imaginary."

"Kylie's best friend is single," Parker adds, teasing Tyler. "We could put in a good word for you."

I stifle a laugh, knowing how mortified Josie would be if she knew she was brought up in this conversation.

Tyler groans, rolling his eyes. "Guys, if I wanted a girlfriend, I'd have a girlfriend."

Kai chucks another bag at Tyler. "You know the rules. You give someone crap, you get it back."

"*Ha ha*," Tyler mumbles, unzipping the bags with the tent supplies inside.

I help carry bags from Parker's car, and to my surprise, Lewis stops me and takes the bags.

"Oh, thank you," I say, blushing from the gentlemanly act.

"No sweat," Lewis says with a grin. "They looked heavy."

As I take in the smile lines on his face, and glimpse his baby blues, I get a flash of the night after the fair.

The moment we almost kissed.

Our second almost-kiss.

"You okay?" he whispers.

"Mm-hmm." I nod, moving out of the way so he can carry the bags over to the girls' section.

"What happened?" Parker asks, moving beside me.

I jolt as my thoughts dissolve around me. "Huh? Nothing."

Parker smiles. "Okay?"

I awkwardly fiddle with the hair near my face. "Umm, Yvie's on her way here. You mentioned breaking up. Did you want to do that because she and Lewis have been on a break?"

Parker's eyes widen. "You want to break up?"

"No," I blurt. I then cough and cover with, "I mean, I don't want to hold you back."

"Umm," he stammers. "Maybe we should see how things play out when she gets here. Unless you don't want to?"

"No, I want to," I mumble and fidget in my stance. "I just, umm. No, nevermind. We're good. Right?"

Parker's eyebrows raise. "Yeah, we're good. I think."

I swallow hard and nod, turning away from him. I listen to his footsteps moving over to the boys' area. Oh boy. Or, should I say, oh boys.

On the girls' side of the camping spot, Tabitha and Jamie get to work, setting up their tent. Jamie is such a pro. She basically does the whole setup herself, only asking Milo for help when she can't reach the top of the tent to secure the last clips.

Parker and Lewis help with my tent. With Tabitha and Jamie sharing, I guess I'm officially bunking with Yvette. Geez, I really hope she doesn't turn up. Not that I love the idea of sleeping in a tent, by myself, in the wilderness, but it has to be better than being in close proximity to Yvette's complaints.

I follow Parker's lead, clipping together pieces of a plastic pole that curves over the tent to create the structure. When we're about to put the pole into place, a black sedan nears our campsite.

"Yvie," Lewis breathes. "Thank goodness."

I suck in my bottom lip, glancing at Parker. He moves away, letting the pole tilt idly in my grip.

Yvette gets out of the car, and I glimpse her brother's sour disposition. From what I've heard, he's not thrilled about his sister camping with her boyfriend.

Lewis moves in to hug Yvette, but she turns her body away. Her brother asks if she's okay, and when she waves him off, his black sedan drives away.

"What are we all doing?" Yvette asks, slinging her dusty pink backpack over her shoulder and walking toward our side of the campsite.

"Setting up the tents," Lewis says, following closely behind her. "You don't have to worry about doing anything. We got this."

With their tent already set up, and Yvette moving closer, Jamie and Tabitha leave for the boys' side of the campsite.

"Why don't you leave this to Kylie and me?" Yvette says, standing at the opposite side of the tent from me.

"Have you ever set up a tent before?" Lewis asks.

"It can't be that hard," she replies, tossing her bag to the ground and gripping the other end of the flexible pole.

"I think it can be," I pipe up. "I've got no idea what to do next."

"Just let me help you," Lewis says to Yvette.

She groans. "You don't need to hover over me."

"What if I help you?" Parker offers. "It's better than struggling with the setup. And it means we all get to chill out sooner."

Yvette shrugs, nudging Lewis away from her. It's tough work, keeping my mouth from falling open. She's actually pushing Lewis away. A guy she should be on her knees, praying with thanks for getting him in the first place.

Parker steps in close to help Yvette, and my grip on the pole intensifies. Why does seeing them so close cause such stress to my muscles?

"You want to do it like this," Parker says, taking the pole from Yvette. "You bend it toward you and then pull it down so it connects with the fastener at the bottom."

Yvette giggles, leaning into Parker. "I'm so bad at this. You totally gotta do it for me."

"Don't you want me to teach you?" Parker asks, struggling to hold on to the pole as she leans her weight against him.

When Yvette's index finger grazes Parker's chin, my hands drench with sweat.

Yvette giggles. "No, I'd much rather watch you do it."

Parker clears his throat and asks Lewis, "Can you get on the other end and help Kylie?"

Lewis moves over to me. When he grabs the pole, his hands brush over mine. Normally, something like that would send a thrill of tingles down my spine. But it's like I'm numb to his touch.

Yvette moves away from Parker, crossing her arms as she stares us down. "He didn't say to hold her hands."

"Yvie, you know I'd much rather hold your hands. I'm just trying to help."

It's nothing compared to what you just did to my boyfriend.

Whoa.

Oh, geez, I'm glad that didn't come out of my mouth.

What is happening? Why am I getting so protective of Parker? We're literally in the positions we've both been dreaming about.

The boys rush through, connecting the flexible poles to the bottom fasteners. Once all four ends are connected, I meet Lewis's eyes, and he winks.

As if we pinged on Yvette's radar, she lets out a squeaky grunt.

Lewis gulps and turns to her.

"Just admit it," Yvette says, stomping her foot against the dirt. "You'd rather be with Kylie."

"What?" it puffs out of me with shock.

Lewis moves away from me, hurrying toward her. "Why do you think that? Can't you see I'm crazy about you?"

Her eyes narrow. "I've seen you watch her when she's with Parker."

He watches me?

"Only because I couldn't work out why they were together." Lewis takes hold of her hands. "Doesn't change the fact that you're the girl I want."

Yvette shakes her head, backing away. "Why don't I believe you?"

Lewis points at Parker. "Ask him. We've been competing to get your attention since your last three boyfriends."

Yvette looks at Parker. "You liked me too?"

"*Ahhh... Ahhh...*" Parker stammers.

Yvette clicks her tongue, frowning. "Just another story, Lewis. Stop pretending it's not Kylie you're both competing over."

"Yvie, you're talking crazy," Lewis says, following as she backs away.

"Crazy?" Her eyes water. "You promised you wouldn't be like my exes. But, here you are, calling me crazy, just like them."

"Yvie," Lewis yelps as Yvette runs from the campsite.

He calls after her again, chasing her into the mess of bushes by the hiking trail.

"Holy cow," Parker murmurs, moving closer to me.

I stumble backwards. "I don't think I can do this."

He reaches for me. "Can't do what?"

I recoil from him. "I hate being used in their arguments. I hate not knowing if my feelings are wrong."

I blink the water from my eyes and stare up at him.

Most of all, I hate that I don't know how I feel about him.

"It's almost over," he whispers.

"I don't want to be put in the middle of more fights while we're out here. This isn't fun."

"We'll have fun on this trip. I promise."

I tilt my head, hating the jealousy festering inside me. "What exactly happened when you saw Yvie yesterday?"

"I told you what happened."

"Everything?" I ask bluntly. "She was touching you a lot. Was that the first time? Or is there more you haven't told me about?"

Parker grunts, averting his gaze. "I didn't think there was any point in telling you. We were having such a nice time at the arcade."

My heart sinks. "Oh my gosh. What happened? Did you two kiss?"

"What? No. I wouldn't do that to Lewis. When Yvie and I kiss, she and Lewis will already be broken up."

"So, what really happened?"

"She just touched my thigh when we were talking. And then my arm. And my shoulder." He sighs, wiping his brow. "And we hugged a few times. I mean, it's not a big deal. You and Lewis have done similar things, right?"

"Yeah, but I told you about it right away."

"I'm sorry. I didn't purposefully keep anything from you."

"And our kisses last night," I murmur, holding my waist, "were they just more practice?"

"What's happening? You're acting so differently."

I brush my hair back, blinking away my tears. "I don't know. Everything feels different."

Parker clasps my shoulders. "Last night, I kissed you because I wanted to kiss you. I wasn't thinking about anybody else."

I look up at him with hope. "Really?"

He nods. "Yes. But maybe you were right. Maybe kissing should stay off the table. It seems to be confusing the situation."

My heart sinks. He thinks I'm crushing on him, and he wants it to stop.

Parker's hands rub down my arms. "Look, it's intense with those two. Why don't we take advantage of this moment away from them and regroup?"

I plant a hand over my thumping heart. "I hate to admit it, but part of me wishes they hadn't come back to camp."

"Only because we're so close to the end of this. Sometimes getting what you want is scary."

"Yeah, maybe."

He tilts my chin up. "You still want to be with Lewis, don't you?"

Do I? I forced myself into becoming a fan of a band he doesn't even like. Now, everything feels like it's falling apart.

"Kylie?"

I sigh out. "Of course. I guess you're right. It's the thought of finally being with him that's sending me into panic."

Parker smiles. "We got this."

I smile and lower my voice. "No one said creating a fake relationship to break up another couple would be easy."

"Ain't that the truth. Anyway, I hope nothing they said hurt your feelings."

"I'll be okay. I just hate being a pawn."

"But this is the game."

"I know. It's just hard."

"Who knew it'd be easier when we spent time alone together."

"My parents kept questioning why we didn't go on solo dates. I couldn't exactly tell them our plan."

"No, our parents would think we're crazy. Speaking of parents, I'm so glad we practiced last night," he says, resting his arms on my shoulders. "I can't imagine how it would've gone down if Yvie had been at that table with my family."

"Ah, yeah," I stammer. "Hopefully, she'll be understanding when you tell her about your family history."

Parker sucks in a breath as his arms fall off my shoulders. "I'm never telling her. You finding out is as far as it's gonna go."

"But don't you want to be with her?"

"Yeah, but I don't want to bring the baggage."

I bite my lip, careful not to say anything that'll upset him. But how can he think he'll have a meaningful relationship with her if he keeps her in the dark? Will he never take her home to meet his family?

I can't keep talking about this. I gesture at the tent and suggest, "Wanna help me finish this?"

Parker smiles, grabbing the canvas material. "Sure. Shouldn't take too long."

Twenty-Six

Besides Parker's instructions, we mostly put together the tent in silence. It's a more peaceful process than Yvette's brief 'help.'

"Hey guys," Tyler calls out once we've placed the camp beds and sleeping bags inside the tent. "We're checking out the hiking trail. Wanna come?"

Parker clutches my hand. "Wanna go?"

"Is it hard?"

Parker shakes his head. "We'll just dawdle behind."

I grin. "I can handle that."

"Coming," Parker calls out as the others head out.

As we move toward the trail, I can't help glancing over at the bushes where Lewis and Yvette disappeared. "Do you think they'll come back to camp soon?"

"They're either breaking up or making up," Parker says. "Do you want to find them?"

I shake my head. "No way. If they're fighting, I don't want Yvette to accuse me and Lewis of secretly being in love."

"Why does that bother you? Don't you want Lewis thinking about you like that?"

"It feels wrong. Plus, it puts Lewis on the defensive. It reminds him why he wants Yvette instead of me."

Parker squeezes my hand. "Let's just chill before they come back on the scene. Hopefully, when they're back, they separate and the vibe is better."

"I think you'll have to work overtime on the positivity. It's just not soaking in."

He gestures ahead. "Or we could just soak up nature. Doesn't that do it for you?"

I smile and my shoulders ease. "Ah, yeah. This could totally work."

Parker doesn't drop my hand as we wander the trail behind Tyler, Jamie, and Milo.

The others are more lively, talking and joking between themselves. Sometimes Parker joins in, but mostly we walk in silence. The foliage framing the hiking trail lulls me into serenity, my mind doesn't even need to meld into fantasyland.

"Wow," I murmur as we reach a peak with a view of the setting sun.

Tyler checks his smartwatch. "We'd better turn around. Dad said he'd be getting the grill on soon."

Jamie pats her stomach. "Good. This thing's starting to growl."

The walk back is downhill, seemingly much faster. My mood lifts as we approach the campsite. That is, until Yvette stands in our view.

"Umm, Kylie," Yvette says, digging her shoe into the dirt. "Can I talk to you for a minute?"

"Me?" I point at my chest. "Alone?"

Jamie tugs Milo out of the way, and Tyler gives us a double take before following them.

"Please?" Yvette's eyes round. "It's important."

Parker nudges me. "Go on. You're roomies, aren't you?"

I groan. Unfortunately, yes.

I nod at Yvette and, with delight, she leads me into our tent. We crouch on our sleeping bags and sit across from each other.

"I just wanted to clear the air," Yvette says, clutching her elbows.

My bottom lip quivers as I search for any shred of confidence. "Why do you think something is going on between Lewis and me?"

"Because there has to be a reason he's not interested in me."

I'm floored. "What? Of course, he's into you."

She shakes her head. "He's interested in being seen with me, but he doesn't really like me."

"What makes you say that?"

"When he came to my house on Sunday, I thought things were different," she says. "He waited all morning to see me. Even my parents relaxed after talking to him. We hung out and watched TV, and I thought it'd be super cute and romantic. But he just scrolled on his phone and didn't say much. He didn't even have his arm around me."

"Maybe he was nervous?"

"Honestly, he seemed bored. It was like if his friends weren't around to see us together, he didn't want to put any effort in. When I hung out with Parker, it was a completely different story."

My stomach flips. "How so?"

"Umm, he actually listened," Yvette says dryly. "And it was nice to have eye contact while his arms were around me. Shouldn't that be how my boyfriend acts?"

As far as Yvette's aware, Parker is my boyfriend. Does she really think it's okay to tell me my boyfriend had his arms around her?

"Communication just comes easier to Parker," I reply. "Lewis can be really sweet."

Yvette huffs. "Yeah, right."

"Well, the times Lewis and I have hugged, we've made a lot of eye contact. I also felt like he was listening to me."

Yvette glares at me. "How many times have you hugged my boyfriend?"

I flinch. "Just a few. He was mostly upset about being apart from you."

"So he just went running to you?"

"Didn't you do the same thing when you asked Parker to meet up?"

She rolls her eyes, turning away from me. "Whatever."

"Didn't you say you wanted to clear the air?" I ask, sitting forward with growing confidence. "How exactly is this helping?"

Her eyes roll again, and she faces me. "I just didn't want you to think I'd been making out with your boyfriend behind your back."

I retch as something flies up from my stomach and hits the back of my throat. I swallow hard, wincing. "I didn't think that. Why would you say that?"

She deadpans me. "Because, obviously, I've been picturing you and Lewis doing that since the night of the fair."

My face screws up. "Why?"

"Because I spent that day with him, and he was bored out of his mind. You and Parker turn up, and suddenly he's full of life again." She groans. "And then he had this smug look on his face after leaving the Ferris Wheel with you. I watched him put in all this care to make sure your eye was okay. He barely cared enough to give me eye contact. Ugh. It was the last straw."

"It can't have been the last straw. You're still with him. Aren't you?"

"Technically."

"Lewis and I haven't been hanging out. I've been spending too much time with Parker. The only times I've seen Lewis, he's been miserable about not seeing you. Like, too grumpy to be nice to me. Whatever you think has been going on, has been in your head."

I don't know why I'm trying to make her feel better. I want her and Lewis to break up. I don't think they're good together. But if that happens, she and Parker will get together. And the thought of that... I can't. I just can't stand the thought of it.

Yvette stares at me hard. When she finally blinks, she lets out a loud sigh. She leans forward and flings her arms around me. "You're not messing with me? You haven't been getting between us?"

"Huh?"

How am I supposed to answer that? I want to say no, because I haven't kissed him. But getting between them? That's a big, fat yes.

Yvette squeezes me tighter, squishing my head against her shoulder. "Seriously, you're not stealing my boyfriend, are you? We're friends, right?"

"Umm... I..."

A shattered sigh rolls out of her. "Oh, I'm sorry, Kylie," she whimpers. "I wanted to be with Parker to make you jealous. And to make Lewis jealous, of course, but... Oh, I really wanted to hurt you."

We pull out of the non-consensual hug and my muscles cramp. "You were that convinced I was with Lewis?"

Her eyes water. "He doesn't love me."

I bite my lip, remembering all the months I wished for Lewis to fall for me. "I don't think he loves me either."

Crap. That hurts. That really freaking hurts.

She grabs my hands and pouts. "I'm sorry I've taken this out on you. I'm just so scared. I've ruined all my friendships, and I keep replacing my boyfriends so I'm never alone. It would be nice if I just had one friendship that worked."

My eyebrow raises. "With me?"

A nervous smile twitches her lips. "Would that be so bad?"

"Not if you're honest and kind." My hands go limp in hers. "And I'm sorry, Yvie, I just don't know if you can be."

Her shoulders slump. "Me either. I don't know what's wrong with me."

"There's nothing wrong with you," I say, sliding my hands out of her grip. "You're just prone to overreact. But hey, what girl isn't tied to her emotions?"

She sniffs and pats under her eyes. "Do you forgive me?"

Considering I am trying to get between her and her boyfriend, and I'm unwilling to admit it, what choice do I have? "Sure, Yvie. You're forgiven."

She squeals and pulls me back into a tight hug. I grunt in her grip, struggling to breathe.

"Thank you, Kylie," she whispers. "I promise to be a better friend."

Remembering I can't do anything to jeopardize Parker and Lewis's friendship, I nod against Yvie's shoulder. "Me too."

"So, do you think I should patch things up with Lewis?"

No. "Are you actually mad at him? Or are you just feeling insecure?"

Dang, Parker's getting in my head.

Yvie sits back. "Hmm. I hadn't thought of it like that before."

"Besides thinking he's into me, is there any other reason you don't want to be with him?"

Yvie sighs. "It's not that I don't want to be with him. It's that, I'm scared he doesn't want to be with me."

"So, insecurity is at play?"

Dang it, Parker.

She shrugs. "I guess. I thought I had my stuff together better than this."

"We all have our stuff."

Intrigue lights up her eyes. "What's yours?"

I gulp. There's no way I'm telling the gossip queen about my Kikki alter ego or my fantasyland with Lewis.

I fake a smile. "Oh, you know, I'm always afraid my hair is a mess when I'm at school."

Yvette brushes a hand over my hair. "You always look good. You're just too mousy for your own good."

I flinch. "You think?"

"Sure. It's your personality holding you back. Everyone forgets about you because you're too quiet and shy." She giggles to herself. "That is until you came out of your shell for spring break. Who knew Kylie Green could be so much fun?"

I smirk. "Certainly not me."

"Do you feel better about yourself when you're with Parker?"

I sigh and admit, "Yeah, I do."

"That's what I want," Yvette murmurs and then moves off the sleeping bag. She unzips the canvas door and leaves the tent.

Panic fills my veins. What does that mean? Does she want to feel more secure when she's with Lewis? Or, does she want to feel better by getting with my fake boyfriend?

A boost of adrenaline fires within me, and I leave the tent after her.

I don't have to move far to reach Yvie. She's stopped in the middle of the campsite, staring ahead. I move next to her and find Parker and Lewis sitting on a log. Parker rests an elbow on Lewis's shoulder as they both stare out into the distance. Their closeness is so sweet.

"Aww." Yvie pouts and clutches my hand. "Look, our boyfriends are best buddies. That's why I want us to be close too."

My heart swells. "Me too."

It's the truth. Even though I wish we'd swapped boyfriends.

My heart misses a beat.

I do want that. Don't I?

Yvie tugs me forward, and the boys watch us and smile.

"Aren't you two just the cutest?" Yvie says on our approach.

Parker drops his arm off Lewis and fixates on my hand in Yvie's. "You two look like you're getting along."

Yvie drops my hand and sits by Lewis. "Kylie and I want to get closer. I mean, how else will we survive our future double dates?"

Lewis's eyes light up. "Future dates? So, we're okay?"

Yvie leans in and pecks his lips. "We're okay."

Parker's chin drops, and he turns my way. He may as well have crushed up my heart like a wad of paper. Disappointment cuts through his stare, and I see all the questions running through his head. Why didn't I feed into Yvie's insecurities? Why didn't I encourage her to end the relationship with Lewis for good?

Yvie brushes the side of Lewis's face. "Kylie said some really nice things back there. It's the kind of stuff I want for us. I want us to be better."

Lewis grins, muttering, "Wow."

The wonder and gratitude on Lewis's face is too much. Coupled with the disapproving sting from Parker, I'm about to shatter into a million pieces.

I back away, mumbling, "I need a minute."

"Kylie," Parker says in a low tone.

When he pushes off the log, I turn and run.

I dart away from the tents and weave behind the cars.

"Hey," Parker says, grabbing onto my elbow as I flee behind his car. "What's going on?"

"I'm not okay with this," I yelp. "I've been trying to tell you."

"Look, I know it's…"

I cut him off. "I want to come clean and end all this pretending."

He frowns. "But neither of us has a shot if we do that."

"It's better than lying."

He rubs his forehead, pacing three steps to the left. He drops his hand with a grunt. "I don't want everyone to know I'm a liar. I'll be a bigger loser than I am at home."

"Is it really worth becoming a big shot if it's all based on a ruse?"

"Don't make me out to be the bad guy. You thought it was worth it to be with Lewis."

"Yvette and Lewis are real people with real feelings. We're messing with them, and it's not cool."

"They're a trainwreck together. They want what we have, and what we have is fake." He huffs, adjusting his T-shirt collar. "They have no idea what they're doing because they're with the wrong people. We're doing this so they can be happy with us."

My hands clasp against my chest. "I want them to break up, but I don't want to be the cause of it."

"Whatever happens won't be your fault. They'll break up because they're not a good fit."

"What if they were a good fit, but we never gave them a chance?"

Sympathy fills Parker's expression. "Man, the guilt is really getting to you."

"How is it not affecting you?"

He winces as he presses a hand into his stomach. "It is when I see the sadness on your face."

"But what about when you were talking to Lewis? Don't you feel bad when he says he's messed things up with Yvie?"

"I didn't cause that. He's the one who didn't pay attention to her. He didn't comfort her when she needed it."

"But you would've helped him figure this stuff out if you weren't into her too."

He tilts his head pensively. "Is that what you did with Yvie? You gave her advice about Lewis because you felt bad?"

"I hate that she's with him, but I saw another side to her." I sigh and roll my eyes. "I saw the insecure side you were so sure was there."

Parker grins. "You should know better than to doubt me."

I click my tongue. "Whatever."

He puts an arm around me. "Just, next time she's feeling insecure, maybe encourage her to cuddle with me, not him."

I shiver against him and remember the adrenaline coursing through me when Yvie left the tent. How I was cramped with jealousy at the thought of her making a move on Parker.

Parker rubs my arm. "You have goosebumps."

I flash a smile and clutch my elbows. "It's okay. I'm good."

His eyes search mine. "Are you sure?"

My mouth runs dry. "Uh-huh."

His arms pull around me in a warm hug, and my back knots with confusion. As I look up at him, my heart begs him to stay close. His hand traces my jaw, and his thumb grazes my lower lip.

"I'm sorry if I was harsh," he whispers. "You were just being caring towards Yvie, even though she drives you nuts. It's one of the reasons I like you so much."

My heartbeat pounds in my ears, leaving me overwhelmed. I fixate on the shine of his lips, and when I lift my gaze to his big, brown eyes, my knees weaken.

"I need the bathroom," I blurt.

He flinches at the abruptness, dropping his arms from around me. "Okay. I'll show you where it's set up at the back of the campsite."

I pace away from him. "It's cool. I'll find it."

Before he can follow, I make my way behind the line of tents. With my head down, I scurry toward two tall and slim canvas tents, standing a few feet away from the rest. One is for the camp shower; the other is for the camp toilet.

I close myself inside the toilet stall just as my eyes pool with water. I sit on the closed lid of the camp toilet as my throat clogs with ugly sobs. My palms press against my eyelids in an attempt to stop the tears.

How can he do this to me? He can't keep telling me how much he wants Yvie and then act like he wants to kiss me again. It's not fair.

Last night replays over and over in my mind. The kisses under the twinkle lights that were just for us and not for show.

I smear the tears under my eyes and scrunch my hands into my hair. Gritting my teeth as I hunch forward, I force the sobs into submission. Maybe I'm just imagining that Parker wants to kiss me. I'm just so confused about my feelings for him, as well as the history of emotions I have for Lewis. Let's face it, I'm good at conjuring illusions.

I pull at the toilet paper and wipe my eyes. I realize I'm most afraid of being alone at the end of spring break. I've already experienced the turmoil of Lewis not wanting me. And when this scheme ends, I'll lose Parker. Even if it's fake, even if it's not romantic, I enjoy being around him. When he becomes Yvie's boyfriend, I know she won't want me around him.

I slump forward with a huff. It's what makes me the saddest. The notion of losing someone I never expected to bond with.

After a very shaky exhale, I stand and exit the makeshift bathroom.

"Whoa," Tabitha blurts, standing in front of me. "Kylie, what's wrong?"

I hurriedly pat my face dry and fake a smile. "Nothing. Just a bad case of allergies."

Her forehead creases as she frowns. "Are you sure?"

"Yeah. I'm just a homebody. Nature is getting to me."

"So, you and Parker weren't arguing?" Her tone implies she knows something.

"Arguing?" My tone couldn't have lacked less assertion.

She gestures behind her. "Kai and I heard some raised voices. We didn't know if you were fighting or not?"

I fidget in my stance. "You didn't hear what we said?"

She shakes her head. "We weren't that close. But the vibe felt off."

"We did argue about something," I admit, "but we're not fighting. Believe me, Parker and I are cool."

She winces as she tilts her head. "So, you weren't crying?"

I blow out a breath and fake a laugh. "No. Oh my gosh, I'm on a trip with my boyfriend. Why would I be crying?"

Tabitha smiles. "Okay. If everything's chill, I'll stop questioning you."

I grin. "Everything's chill."

"Well, in that case, can I get past you? I really need the bathroom."

"Oh, sure," I squeak, happy to end this conversation.

"Everyone's moving down to the lake to toss the frisbee around," she says, stepping into the tall, slim tent. "I think they're also setting up the volleyball net."

"Of course they are," I mutter under my breath. Not only am I camping, but I'm camping with a bunch of sporty people. "Okay, Tabby, see you over there."

I leave Tabitha in privacy and make my way through the campsite and toward the lake.

"Hey," Parker says, standing from a log. "How are you feeling?"

I slow my pace as I near him. "I'm fine."

"You ran off fast," he says. "I wanted to make sure you're okay."

I can't help but smile. "I'm totally fine. I promise."

He smiles back. "Good. I can't survive this trip without my partner in crime."

I giggle. "That's what I am?"

Parker steps closer and links his arm with mine. "You keep pointing out that what we're doing is shady, so I think the title fits."

I playfully nudge him. "I hear we're playing Frisbee."

"Does the daredevil want to get her frisbee on?"

"I have terrible aim and my throws lack anything resembling power, but I'm happy to cheer on my fake boyfriend." I give him a wink. "But maybe I'll cheer on my crush just a little harder."

He laughs, leading me toward the lake. "That's the spirit. Do you think Yvie will cheer for me?"

"Yvie thinks you're boyfriend material," I say, secretly loving how much it makes him blush. "If Lewis doesn't up his game, she will definitely cheer you on."

"But she kissed him after the two of you left your tent."

"It was a peck. Pecks lack passion."

The possibilities send a flurry of emotions across Parker's face. His dang infectious smile fills me with excitement. But it's not excitement for me and Lewis. If crying on a camp toilet taught me anything, it's that Parker means a great deal to me. If he wants to be with Yvie, then I'll do my best to show her what a wonderful guy he can be.

Twenty-Seven

While the parents got dinner ready, everyone gathered by the lake to toss the frisbee around. Tabitha sat by my side as I watched. We didn't talk much. She mostly cheered on Kai, while I watched Yvie and Parker. Shamelessly, she used a baby-voice to coax him into teaching her the best frisbee-throwing technique.

I kept my distance throughout dinner. I'd gone easy on Yvette because of my guilt, but that doesn't mean I think she's genuine. I still don't believe her feelings for Lewis are real, and I can't say it's any different with Parker. Before I can let him go, I need to know she can be trusted with his heart. I can't end this fake relationship to later find out she put him through a nightmare.

From across the campfire, I watch Yvette snuggle into Lewis while keeping her eyes on Parker. These boys aren't dumb. They have to realize she has a foot in one relationship, while the other foot sneaks into another. Parker might say he doesn't mind being used if he's getting what he wants, but he can't feel good about this.

After dinner, I keep my eyes on Lewis. He's aware Parker and Yvie have feelings for each other. Whether they're genuine or not is beside the point. I just hate the idea of Lewis feeling bad.

"Hey Lewis," I say after rinsing off my plate. "How are you doing?"

His eyes twinkle against the nearby blaze. "Yeah, all right. This trip is always the highlight of spring break. Are you enjoying yourself?"

I nod. "Yeah. It's my first time camping, and so far so good."

"We have so many camping newbies this year. Should make it a trip to remember."

I lift onto the balls of my feet. "All in good ways, I hope."

Lewis looks around the campfire. "I hope so too."

I plant my heels on the ground. "Everything okay with you and Yvie?"

He sighs, rubbing the back of his neck. "I really don't know. She doesn't seem to want to spend time with me."

"She was sitting pretty close to you."

"But not talking to me. I'm a glorified couch cushion."

I let out a nervous laugh. "You're more than that."

He smiles. "At least you see that."

My voice lowers. "I've always seen there's more to you."

"Lewis!" Yvette calls from her log by the fire. "I'm getting cold. Come back and snuggle with me."

Lewis mumbles a laugh. "Back to couch cushion duties."

Without thinking, I grab onto his arm. "You don't have to go running back to her."

"Huh?"

I let him go. "She's making you jump through hoops."

"I told you, Kylie, I'm not letting her go."

I nod as he moves toward her. Over his shoulder, I catch her smirk and wicked glance my way. Just how much more obvious must she be before he wakes up?

After all the dishes are cleaned, the parents take a cooler of drinks down to the boat, leaving us kids at the campfire.

"Hey Milo," Kai calls out from the log he shares with Tabitha. "Truth or dare?"

Milo frowns, waving a hand. "No way."

"Go on. It's a camping tradition," his brother encourages. "Pick. Truth or dare?"

When Jamie nudges him, Milo rolls his eyes and says, "Truth."

Kai grins, rubbing his hands together. "When was the first time you fantasized about Jamie?"

My gut tightens with second-hand fear. Sweat builds on my forehead, scared someone will ask me the same thing about Lewis.

How freaking embarrassing.

Milo glances at Jamie and then the rest of the group. "I dunno. It was so long ago. I just thought I'd stay invisible to her, so I didn't really count the days."

Murmured laughter rounds the group. Kai looks slightly disappointed, like he was expecting something juicier.

Interesting that Milo doesn't count the months like I do.

"Okay, Milo, it's your turn to pick someone else," Tabitha says.

He glances around the group, and I dip my gaze to avoid being picked.

"Lewis," Milo says, and my stomach drops. "Truth or dare."

Lewis is quick to reply. "Dare."

I look up, smiling at his confidence.

Milo grins. "Talk in a British accent until your next turn."

Everyone erupts in laughter.

"What?" Lewis puffs. "I was expecting to hang off a tree limb or to steal something from the parents."

Yvette nudges him. "Do it. British accents are sexy."

"If I can do it," Lewis says in a terrible attempt at an accent.

More laughter spills out of the group.

Tyler smirks. "Hey, Hugh Grant, pick someone."

Lewis sighs, and then gets his British on. "Okay then, chaps. Uh, erhm, ladies too, that is."

My eyes water and I hold my belly, laughing.

"Tyler, truth or dare?"

"Dare."

In his phony British accent, Lewis says, "I dare you to smell and lick the bottom of Kai's foot."

A bunch of retches, grimaces, and complaints of, "Yuck," "*eww*," and "gross," circle around the group.

"Why my foot?" Kai complains.

Lewis laughs. "Because, my good man, you're always running around barefoot."

Tabitha giggles. "They do stink, babe."

Kai rolls his eyes and throws his foot up. "Get over here, Ty."

Tyler is green. He slinks over to Kai, wincing as he lowers to his foot.

"*Eww.*" I wince and cover my face as soon as Tyler's tongue pokes out.

Parker throws his head back and laughs. "That was so gross."

Tyler shudders as he snakes around to the seat beside me.

"Umm, has anyone got sanitizer for my foot?" Kai asks.

"Your foot?" Tyler complains. "What about my tongue?"

"*Eww.*" I wince again. "Can you pick someone else so we can stop talking about this?"

Tyler laughs. "Okay, Yvie."

Ugh. Couldn't you have picked better?

"I was going to pick dare," Yvie says, "but after that display, I'm gonna have to say truth."

"Okay," Tyler sits back, ready to fire. "How does Lewis compare to your other boyfriends?"

"*Dude*," Lewis hisses.

Milo points at him. "British accent."

Lewis rolls his eyes, shifting awkwardly as Yvie gets ready to answer.

She looks Lewis up and down, and then clears her throat. "Well, he's hit some nerves. There's a word you used that I won't repeat. But, my parents let him into the house. That hasn't happened since Chase McIntyre, who I dated last year. So, he's an improvement from the last few."

Kai smirks. "Geez. How many boyfriends have there been?"

Yvie grins. "I believe I already answered my question."

Tyler winks. "We know our question for the next round."

Yvie rolls her eyes. "I get to pick someone now, right?" She zeroes in on me. "Kylie. Truth or dare?"

Even though it was inevitable I'd get picked, my stomach still clamps down. I'm way too scared to do a dare. What if it's streaking? Or, I'm asked to kiss someone? Or, I have to do something impossible like a handstand?

But can I handle answering her question?

What if she asks if I have feelings for Lewis? Am I ready to blurt it out before they're broken up? Or, what if she suspects Parker and I are fake dating? That would be so embarrassing *and* ruin everything.

I grunt and slouch in defeat. "Dare."

"I dare you to sing karaoke, but acapella," Yvie says, grinning. "That means no music. Just you."

The blood drains from my face and pools in my feet.

Everyone claps in encouragement, but I sink lower in my seat.

Parker rubs a circle on my back. "You can do this," he whispers. "It's time to use your Kikki confidence outside of the house."

I deadpan him. "But I have music then."

"I know you've memorized all the words from your baking playlist," Parker replies. "Just close your eyes and listen to the song play in your head."

"Come on, Kylie!" Tabitha cheers. "*Woo.*"

I stand up and do my best not to let my hands tremble. As everyone's eyes fixate on me, I close my eyes. A Frontier Leaders song plays in my head, and I can't help smiling at the beat. As I sing along out loud, my knees dip and my hips sway. There's a round of cheers, causing me to laugh, and I manage to sing my way through the rest of the chorus.

When I open my eyes, I promptly sit back down. I giggle at the round of applause and lean into Parker as he gives me a side-hug.

He kisses the side of my head. "Knew you could do it."

I bite my lip, feeling a surge of adrenaline. "Thanks."

He lets me go, saying, "Now you gotta pick someone."

I glance around the group and then shrug. "Parker, truth or dare?"

He sits back. "Truth."

As *oohs* and *ahhs* float around the group, all I can do is blink at him.

Truth?

And he wants me to ask the question?

Me, who knows the biggest truth about his past.

I look away, panning around the group. When I land on Lewis and Yvie, there's a niggle between my shoulder blades.

I turn back to Parker and ask, "What's your biggest regret?"

Tyler whistles. "Whoa. Good one."

Parker sits forward, thinking about it. "Umm, I dunno. Maybe not asking the girl I liked out sooner."

I can't help feeling second-best.

Slouching, I stare at my lap and am surprised when Parker lifts my hand. I sit taller as he kisses the back of it. Tabitha awes, while Tyler and Kai call him sappy. But I don't buy it. He wasn't talking about me. He doesn't need to put on a show.

"You think I'm sappy, Kai?" Parker says. "Truth or dare?"

Kai sits up. "Dare."

"I dare you to serenade Tabitha for one minute in front of all of us."

What happens next, has me in stitches. After initial reservations, and being under everyone's looming stares, Kai stands and holds Tabitha's hand. He tells her she's beautiful, awesome, and sweet. The surprising part is, he begins singing to her like he's in a movie from the sixties.

After Kai's turn, we all need a break. My throat hurts so much from laughing that I chug a bottle of water.

Parker sidles over to me, simmering with laughter. "I never expected that from Kai."

"No one can say he doesn't really love Tabitha," I say, turning my back on him.

He touches my shoulder. "Did you like my answer?"

I bump him off. "You don't need to keep putting on an act."

"I wasn't," he says in a small voice. "I was really talking about..."

"Yvie," I cut him off.

He turns me toward him. "No, you."

I roll my eyes so I don't have to look at him. "You wanted to date me sooner so you could be with *her* sooner."

Parker scoffs. "That doesn't even make sense."

"You're the one who said last night was a mistake."

Fury lights his eyes. "I never said that. I just said our kissing has confused things."

"Exactly," I bite back. "You're saying it shouldn't have happened."

Parker grunts, turning away. "I don't know why you're being like this. I'll just give you some space."

"Fine," I mumble as he walks back toward the campfire.

Now I need to chug water for a completely different reason. The confrontation has left my heart pounding like it's run a mile.

When I return to the campfire, Parker pats the empty space beside him. I shake my head, instead sitting by Tabitha. Parker scoffs, getting up and moving closer to Yvette. Even with Lewis on her other side, Yvette listens to Parker like he's the most fascinating person at the campsite.

Like me, does she suspect his game answer was about her?

Ugh. Why would Parker lie to my face and say he was talking about me? I thought we were supposed to be honest with each other. Although, he did keep details of his time alone with Yvette from me. And then he kissed me when no one was watching.

Ugh. This is so confusing.

The game comes to a close as we get distracted by other conversations. Soon, everyone starts heading off to bed. When Lewis yawns, I can't help feeling sleepy, and I'm happy to retreat to my sleeping bag.

Yvette sits beside Parker. "I'm not tired yet."

Parker smiles at her. "Me neither."

I'm already two steps away from the campfire. Can I pivot without being super embarrassing about it?

"Umm," I mutter, turning back to the campfire as Lewis sits back down.

"I definitely won't fall asleep yet," Lewis says.

Yvette pats the space beside her. "Are you staying, Kylie?"

There's space by Lewis. This could be my best shot. Snuggling up to him while everyone else has turned in for the night.

When Yvette creeps closer to Parker, my stomach flips.

"Umm, no," I mumble. "I'm too tired."

"Okay, good night," Yvette blurts.

"Night, Kylie," Lewis says.

I smile and wave at him. When I glance at Parker, he barely smiles at me.

Is this him giving me space? Or, is he mad I'm not taking this opportunity?

Of course, he's mad at me. He wants Lewis distracted so he can have Yvie all to himself.

My stomach flips again. I can't watch Parker and Yvie cuddling by the fire. I escape into my tent and shimmy into the sleeping bag, feeling more awake than ever. How could I possibly sleep when my imagination can conjure up the worst things going on by the fire?

I lie on the camp bed, listening to the muffled voices outside. The only thing coming out clearly is Yvette's laugh.

Ugh.

The conversation pivots between the boys, and my heart warms as they joke around. When their voices die out, Yvie basically begs for their attention. The conversation seemingly revolves around her until I hear footsteps.

"Yeah, I gotta head in," Lewis says. "I can't keep my eyes open."

"Okay, good night, babe," Yvette says, much more loudly than anything else she's said.

She's still marking her territory with him.

Maybe she doesn't want Parker?

Maybe she doesn't want either of them and enjoys getting them to fight over her.

There's no good night from Parker, so I assume he's still sitting with her. I sit up, squinting as if it'll help me listen better. I do catch the hummed words shared between Yvie and Parker. Their faint whispering is so much worse. It's more intimate.

Just how close are they?

Apparently, they've already been hugging and touching each other behind my back.

I throw my legs out of the sleeping bag.

Ugh. Could they be kissing?

I can't stand this. I need to know.

I creep out of the tent to get a closer look. They sit only an inch apart, and Yvette dreamily stares into his eyes as the campfire glows against their complexions. A giggle bubbles out of her as she walks two fingers up Parker's arm. My stomach sloshes when her arms snake around his neck.

As apprehension seizes Parker's expression, and he leans away from her, a stick breaks under my foot.

Parker's eyes flick in my direction, but Yvie's quick to turn him back to face her. She leans into him and pecks his cheek.

My gut cramps as she giggles and leaves the log they share, sauntering toward our tent. Hurriedly, I B-line for the camp toilet. I don't want her catching me gawking and making this ten times more awkward. I close myself in the tall, slim tent and wait a few moments before reemerging.

When I step out, Parker's making his way over.

He gives me a small wave. "Hey."

My heart pounds, and I smile. "Hi."

He hangs a thumb over his shoulder. "Uh, you saw that?"

I bat a hand like it's nothing. "You're just a step closer to what you want."

He holds his thumb and index finger half an inch apart. "So close," he whispers in disbelief. "I'm so close to being with her."

My chest deflates, and there's a cramp in my lower back. "Oh, cool."

"This is what you wanted me to do, right?"

"Huh?"

"You pushed me away, so I'd get closer to her."

Umm. "Yeah, of course."

He gestures in the direction of his tent. "Do you wanna hang out and talk to Lewis? He only just went in."

I swallow hard, and my voice grows hoarse. "Uh, no. It's cool. I'll see him in the morning."

Parker nods, moving toward his tent. "Okay. Good night, Green."

"Yeah, night, Parker."

I make my way back to my tent, scuffing against the patchy grass.

Dang it. Why does this hurt so much?

Parker was never my end game. After this, the guy of my dreams will be free.

Why aren't I ecstatic?

Twenty-Eight

"Huh?" I wake up, blinking at the empty camp bed. "Yvie?"

I sit up, rubbing my eyes awake. My ears prick to the voices outside my tent. Yvette's giggle is easy to pick out. So is Parker's laugh.

Since when did Yvette Anderson get up early? Did she set an alarm to get extra Parker time?

I gulp. Did they plan this last night?

I rub my temples. Why do I care? I've put so much effort in to make sure this happens. Shouldn't I be thinking about Lewis instead?

I leave the tent and am hit with the delicious scent and crackles of bacon and eggs.

"Morning, Kylie," Kai's dad says by the grill. "Hungry?"

I smile and pat my stomach. "I am, now that I smell what's cooking."

"Oh my gosh, Kylie will probably eat her body weight," Yvette jokes, sitting by Parker. "You should've seen her at Alto Burger. She couldn't stop shoveling food into her mouth. It was so gross."

"There's nothing wrong with a girl who can eat," Mr. Nelson says, serving up my breakfast.

I give him a weak smile as I take the plate. "Thanks."

Sitting on another side of the campsite is Tabitha, Jamie, and Milo. Are none of them questioning why Parker and Yvie are acting like best friends? Or, why do they stare at each other like Lewis and I don't exist?

I pan around for Lewis and find him crouched down in front of where Kai and Tyler sit. My heart swells with a boost of joy as I watch him focus his camera on foliage on the ground.

I take my plate and wave to the girls and Milo as I walk past them. I move toward Lewis and the boys, and can't help grinning at the happiness on Lewis's face as he snaps the shot.

I take a seat as Lewis moves over to the boys. "Hi guys." When they reply, I'm giddy as Lewis sits beside me. "Get the perfect shot?"

"Took a few duds, but the last one's definitely a keeper," he replies.

"I love seeing how quiet and patient you get with your photography," I gush. "Do you like feeling that way?"

He nods. "For the right shot, but it's way too boring for the rest of life."

I slouch in disappointment. "Really?"

Lewis grins. "For sure. I'm much happier when I'm active and living in the moment."

"Oh."

He nudges me. "How was your first night at camp? Did you sleep well?"

"Like a log."

"So, does camping agree with you?" Tyler asks.

"It must," I reply. "I always enjoy sitting out in nature, so it has some big pluses for me."

"What about hiking and rock climbing?" Kai asks with a smirk.

"I can leave that to you boys," I say.

Lewis nudges me. "I dunno. A girl who can jump off a cliff on her first attempt can probably scale a mountain."

I giggle. "You might not want to put that much faith in me."

Tyler points to the water. "Dad's getting the boat ready. Are you gonna come out with us?"

I nod, swallowing a mouthful of breakfast. "I think I can deal with that."

After some more small talk, we finish our breakfast and help clean the plates and cooking utensils.

"Hey," Parker says, sidling up to me. "Haven't had the chance to say good morning to you yet."

I shrug. "You and Yvette looked cozy. I didn't want to impose."

"At least you got time with Lewis."

I smile. "Yeah, and your other friends. I can't believe I was scared to hang out with them. Everyone's been so welcoming."

"That's because you're awesome." He gestures at the lake. "Did Ty tell you about the boat? What do you say? Are you gonna try water skiing?"

I suck in a breath. "I already know I'll be bad at it, and falling into the water doesn't help my confidence."

Parker smirks. "You already drank the lake after jumping off the cliff."

"Thanks for reminding me."

"Do you want to come out on the boat, anyway?"

"I'd totally be up for being a passenger."

"Cool. Afterwards, we're going rappelling."

I flinch. "What's that?"

"It's where you scale down a mountain or cliff face with a rope."

I wince. "Hard pass."

Parker laughs. "That's what you always say."

"Don't try to talk me into it by saying Lewis will be there."

"Well, he will be. And Yvie's ready to go. She already asked me to spot her."

My eyebrow raises. "Not Lewis?"

He grows a mischievous grin. "Nope. He's all yours."

I look around. "Where is Yvie, anyways?"

"Getting changed. She wanted to wear her bikini on the boat."

My eyebrow raises. "Does she plan on getting in the water?"

Parker chuckles, clutching his elbows. "I don't think so. But, heck, I'm not complaining."

Yvie races out of our tent in her hot-pink bikini. "*Woo*! Let's go!"

She runs past us, pumping her arms into the air, and I couldn't feel more uncomfortable. It's just too much bare skin for this early in the morning.

Tabitha nudges Kai. "I'm not going on the boat at the same time as her."

Kai shrugs. "Fine by me. We'll go on the second trip. That way we get double the time without her."

They catch me staring, and Tabitha winces. "Sorry. You and Yvie are friends now, right?"

I shake my head, very ready to say no, but I zip my lips. I don't know what would happen to the group dynamics if I denied being friends with Yvette.

"Are you going out on the boat?" Kai asks.

I nod. "I guess I should get my bikini on."

I don't plan on getting in the water, but it's an excuse to walk away from this awkwardness. Plus, Parker would be disappointed if I didn't wear my blue bikini in front of Lewis again.

I hurriedly change in the tent, wearing a short yellow dress over the bikini, and then meet the others near the boat.

Parker smiles as I approach. "Hey there, sunshine."

I smooth a hand down the dress. "Oh, yeah, I forgot that you like me in yellow."

"Why are you even wearing a dress?" Yvie blurts from aboard the boat. "Are you shy?"

I don't give her eye contact as Tyler's dad helps me onto the boat.

Onboard, Yvette nudges Lewis. "Isn't Kylie just the cutest? It's like having a little kid around."

Lewis mumbles a laugh. "I wouldn't say that. She doesn't look like a little kid to me."

I look up and share a smile with Lewis.

Parker boards behind me. "Ah, Kylie's not a little kid. Trust me, that's not how she acts in private."

I hide my face with a cupped hand and take a seat. "Okay, that's enough."

Yvette *humphs*, sitting on the opposite side of the boat, folding her arms across her bare midsection.

As Tyler gets set up on the water skis, his dad says to Yvie, "You should have something on over your swimsuit if you're getting out on the skis. You know, in case of any wardrobe malfunctions."

Sitting next to Yvie, Lewis's eyes light up and he stifles a laugh.

Yvette swats a hand. "I'm not getting on any skis. I'm not breaking my neck."

"I could teach you," Parker says, sitting by me.

Lewis puts a hand on Yvie's bare thigh. "She's gonna want a lesson from a real pro."

As Yvie giggles, I have to look away. Seriously, put some clothing on.

The boat roars into action, and Tyler hangs on the back by the tow rope. He glides through the water, pushing waves of water to each side of the skis. I can't help joining in with the other's hoots and hollers, because I'm downright impressed.

When the boat swerves by the shoreline, Tyler glides to the edge, never losing his balance.

"Okay, who's up next?" Tyler's dad asks over our raucous applause.

Parker is quick to get up. "Me."

He pulls off his shirt, clips on the lifejacket, and disembarks the boat. For a moment, Lewis and Yvie disappear. I'm focused on Parker attaching himself to the skis and giving Tyler's dad a wave when he has the tow rope in his grip.

I grip the edge of the boat as we take off. My heart pounds to a low beat as I watch him glide across the water. My muscles tense as one of his hands loses grip on the rope. I sit on my knees as he regains control of the rope. As the boat swerves, Parker gains air, flicking the skis to the left before hitting the water again.

"*Woo*, Parker!" Yvie cheers through cupped hands.

Parker glides across the water, seemingly making 'S' patterns with his skis. As the boat swerves again, he pulls up the skis for more air, but something goes wrong. As if he miscalculated, he stumbles and loses grip on the rope.

He falls backwards into the water, and I emit a shriek. With my hands planted over my mouth, I rush to the back of the boat.

"Is he okay?" Yvie yelps.

"Parker?" Lewis calls out.

Parker bounces up in the water, waving at the boat.

My hands fall over the space above my heart. "Thank goodness."

"We needed our first wipeout of the day," Tyler's dad says with a laugh. "Can you reach the rope, Parker?"

Parker gives another wave, gesturing with the rope.

"Here we go!" our skipper calls out.

The boat takes off again, and Parker lifts into the water. He keeps his grip on the rope the entire time until the boat nears the shore and he skids to the edge.

While the boat idles, I jump off the back and wade my way back to shore. I don't care about staying close to Lewis. I want to hug Parker and make sure he's okay.

Kai and Tabitha meet Parker on the shoreline as he unbuckles his lifejacket.

"Parker!" I call out, my dress sticking to my thighs as I bound through the water.

He turns and double-takes at me. "Hey. What are you doing? You jumped off the boat?"

I wring out the bottom of my dress as I hit the shore. "I wanted to make sure you're okay."

He sheds the life jacket. "Oh, that was nothing. I've smacked into the water worse than that."

Kai laughs. "I can vouch for that."

I shift awkwardly. "Oh. Okay then."

Parker looks out at the boat. "You didn't want to stay with the others?"

I bite my lip, knowing he means Lewis.

Tabitha huffs and rolls her eyes. "*Dude.* Your girlfriend is obviously dying to hug you."

"Oh." Parker laughs, stepping close to me with arms out. "Come here."

Despite the awkwardness wreaking havoc within me, I melt into him. The lake water dripping off us gives the hug an unsettling weird feeling. Then there's the fact he's not wearing a shirt. I'm so glad the dip in the water has cooled me off.

"Are you guys coming back?" Yvette calls out, hanging off the side of the boat.

Parker waves them off. "Go on without us."

I pull away from him, rubbing the excess water off my arms.

"Or did you want to go back on the boat?" he asks me.

I shake my head. "I'm good. I already got a show."

When Tyler boards the boat, and Lewis is on the skis, the boat takes off. Parker grabs our towels, and we sit on a patch of grass that isn't too shady. We gaze out as Lewis hangs on behind the boat. He gets air and tries some kind of flip, but doesn't make it all the way.

Parker reclines on his elbows. "Good try, Lewy."

"I'm surprised you didn't try any flips."

He flops onto his back. "I was off my game."

"No way. Not the great Parker Kelly."

He chuckles as I lie down next to him. "What can I say? I've never felt like I had to impress like this before."

"But you're always competing with your friends."

"Yeah, but, I've never had two gorgeous girls on the boat before."

I blush, even though I know Yvie is consuming his thoughts.

"Anyway," he says, brushing it off. "I just got too in my head."

"About impressing Yvie?"

He shrugs. "I knew she was watching me." He nudges me. "But I really wanted to impress you."

I mumble a nervous laugh. "Me? Why?"

He frowns and folds his arms across his chest. "I don't know anymore."

My back cramps, and I turn my face away. Why do I get the feeling I'm the one who keeps saying the wrong thing?

I clear my throat and murmur, "Well, you still did better than I ever could."

He smirks. "Maybe, but I haven't seen you on the skis yet."

"Keep dreaming."

"Dreaming about you, on skis, in a bikini?" Parker questions. "I can manage that."

My breath catches in my throat as my blush increases. Both last night and this morning, he's had excessive time with Yvie. He should be raving about her non-stop. So, why is he flirting with me?

I turn my face back and smile at his big brown eyes.

Parker brushes back my hair. "You know, I just thought of something. A week ago, I walked into the café where you work and convinced you to date me."

I puff a laugh. "Oh my gosh, that was a week ago? *Ha*, happy anniversary."

"Would it be our one-week anniversary today, or tomorrow?" Parker questions. "Last Friday at school was when we convinced our friends."

"But last Thursday you convinced my boss this was for real."

"True." Parker smirks. "Happy anniversary, Kikki."

I giggle. "Happy anniversary, Parky."

He twirls my hair around his finger as his eyes fixate on mine. There's a magnetic pull compelling me to lean in to him.

"Aw, cute," a voice calls out as footsteps move toward us.

Parker and I sit up, viewing the intruders. Tabitha and Kai grin and nudge each other as they take us in.

"Do you mind?" Parker asks sarcastically.

"We just like you two together," Tabitha says.

"Yeah," Kai agrees. "You're less annoying when you're with Kylie."

Parker scoffs. "Thanks."

Kai takes Tabitha's hand, and they continue on their walk past us, despite whispering and glancing our way.

I clear my throat and sit cross-legged. "Well, that wasn't awkward."

Parker reclines on his arms and laughs. "Not at all."

"Parker!" Yvette calls out, waving in the air from the boat. "Come here. I need you."

"You're being summoned," I comment dryly.

He sits up. "I don't know what's happened. She can't get enough of me today."

"Your plan worked." I hold my breath. "I'm happy for you."

"I don't have to go, though," Parker says, pulling his knees to his chest. "I don't want to leave you alone."

"I'm hardly alone. Kai and Tabby, plus Jamie and Milo, aren't on the boat."

"Yeah, but I'm supposed to stay with you."

I click my tongue. "I don't want you doing anything out of obligation."

"That's not what I meant. Geez, are you going to misunderstand everything I say to you on this trip?"

I sit back. "What's that supposed to mean?"

"Look, all I'm saying is, I've spent plenty of time with Yvie." His hand lifts to touch my arm, but then retreats. "Since truth or dare last night, it feels like we've spent a month apart."

I fake a smile so I don't get a replay of the ugly jealousy I felt last night. "Don't be silly. You want more time with Yvie. I don't need babysitting like when we were at the lake."

"It's not babysitting. I like hanging out with you," Parker insists. "I'm starting to miss you."

"Parker!" Yvette calls from the boat.

I nudge him. "Go. I can't stand it when she yells."

With a grunt, he stands up. "Fine. Are you going to hang out with Lewis? He's getting off the skis."

"Yeah, I'm just not going to be as obvious as Barbie."

Parker smirks. "What'd I tell you, Green? Subtly doesn't always go in your favor."

"And I told you, I'll be with Lewis by being myself."

"Well, who can argue with that? Yourself is more than awesome."

He walks away, and I'm left feeling hollow. In private, we're cutesy and talk about silly stuff like our anniversary. How am I supposed to change gears and go after Lewis? My heart's too fragile to transition between both boys.

I get up and walk away toward the campsite. I need space, or I'm literally going to explode.

"Hey, is Yvie getting off the boat?" Jamie asks as I approach her and Milo by the tents.

"I think so. She asked Parker for help, which I assume was for disembarking the boat."

"She can't use her own legs?" Milo jokes.

Jamie squints at me. "Why is she asking your boyfriend for help instead of her own?"

A wave of ugliness scrambles in my gut. "Probably because Lewis was still on the skis."

"Mm-hmm." She doesn't buy it.

"I think I need to lie down," I say, moving past them.

"Are you going rappelling later?" she asks.

I frown. "Probably not."

I can't keep watching Yvie flirt with my fake boyfriend. Even if it means I have Lewis all to myself, there's only so much I can stomach.

Twenty-Nine

I went with the others to the rappelling location, but I hung back. Yvette's flirtatious remarks to Parker are still torture. Like every group activity, she chickened out of this one too. I think it was just an excuse to get Parker to hold her as she wailed.

Once Lewis finished his descent, I walked back to camp with Tabitha and Milo. Milo was quick to stick his head in a book, and Tabitha and I helped the moms prep dinner. Soon after Jamie, the boys, and the dads make their way back to camp. Along with a lot of mocking and teasing thrown back and forth. I crane my neck, but I can't spot Yvette and Lewis anywhere.

Parker moves over to me as I toss the salad. "I really thought you'd give rappelling a go," he says.

I shrug. "I think I've had my fill of being adventurous for one week."

His eyebrows wiggle. "It's been quite a week, huh?"

"Mm-hmm." I glance over his shoulder. "Where's Yvette and Lewis? When I left, she seemed to be glued to your side."

Parker chews his lip and looks away. "Well, as you can probably guess, Lewis didn't love the fact she was showing me more attention." He sighs and gestures at the trail. "They fell behind when the arguing set in."

My chest constricts as I laser focus on the trail. "They're fighting?"

"It's almost over," Parker whispers.

I look back at him as he slinks away.

Once everything's ready for dinner, we place the platters on a plastic folding table and everyone serves themselves. As we eat, Yvette and Lewis still haven't returned.

"Should someone go looking for them?" Tyler's mom asks, nudging her husband. "It's getting dark."

"Finish up eating, boys," Kai's dad says, "and then we'll search for them."

Once the boys dump their plates, I help with cleaning up. When we're almost done, Tyler and Kai hurry back to camp.

"Umm, we found them," Kai says in a low tone.

"What is it?" Tabitha asks. "Are they okay?"

Kai bursts out laughing. "Ah, yeah. They were, uh, making up."

"*Eww*," Tabitha retches.

Tyler laughs, patting Tabitha's shoulder. "At least you didn't walk in on it."

It? What does *it* mean?

I shake it off and move toward a log by the fire. On the way, I pass Milo, who's lying in a sleeping bag and reading.

"Good book?" I ask, taking a seat.

He lowers it and fixes his glasses. "It's all right. It's the third in the series, and I don't particularly like the change to the main character. It's jarring."

"Oh, that's a shame."

Before we can continue the conversation, Jamie makes her way over and slides herself into Milo's sleeping bag. The two giggle as they cuddle up together, and I can't help becoming goo.

So dang cute.

As the others make their way over to the fire, Jamie's head rests on Milo's chest as he continues to read.

"Only my brother could have his head in a book while we're out here," Kai says, walking over with Tabitha.

"He's avoiding the new round of truth or dare," Tyler adds, taking a seat near me.

Parker laughs, sitting on my other side. "Reading a book ain't gonna save him."

I smile and pat Parker's knee. "Give him a break."

Parker smiles, slouching beside me.

Yvette's giggle reaches the group before she does. Emerging from the darkness, she hurries forward, arms linked with Lewis. His face is pinkish and there's mischief in his grin.

Oh boy. What were they doing in those bushes?

Everyone settles in around the fire and Kai's mom drops off the ingredients for s'mores.

As she walks away, she frowns at the sleeping bag. "Jamie, how about you get your own sleeping bag?"

Jamie groans and shimmies out of Milo's sleeping bag.

The group laughs as she plonks on a log with Kai and Tabitha.

"Milo," Kai says, reaching out to whack his brother's sleeping bag. "Put the book down and join the humans."

He grunts and sits up. "Fine. But only because I want to be near Jamie."

Parker nudges me. "So, is there any technique for making the perfect s'more?"

Tabitha leans forward. "Yeah, Kylie. You'd have some tricks up your sleeve."

I giggle. "No, you can't really mess them up. I'd just say, be generous with your layers."

As everyone gets underway with their s'more making, conversation circles around Jamie and Milo.

"Who knew they'd end up being the cutest couple on this trip?" Tabitha says with a giggle.

Jamie grimaces. "Don't make me barf."

Milo's shoulders bounce as he laughs. "Nice."

Jamie laughs and leans against him.

Yvette smirks and shifts closer to Lewis. "How are they cute together?"

Tabitha rolls her eyes, and no one answers the question. I let my gaze stay low so I can avoid her vapid comments.

Yvette clears her throat, clearly wanting attention. "Hey, Jamie. It's funny how you never dated anyone, and then you randomly ended up with a guy like Milo."

"How is..." Jamie stutters, losing her cool. "How is that funny?"

Yvette shrugs. "Because of your mom."

Jamie sucks in a breath, sitting back.

Milo sits forward, protectively putting an arm out in front of her.

"It's funny how you didn't turn out like her," Yvie babbles. "I mean, didn't she have a bunch of boyfriends? Isn't that why you didn't know who your dad was?"

Jamie's eyes grow wide as her face pales.

"Yvie!" Tabitha snaps. "How could you say something like that?"

Yvette flinches, shrinking inward. "What? It was just a question."

"You were calling her mom a slut," Kai blurts.

Jamie sniffs hard and pushes Milo's hand away, getting up from her seat.

"I don't get why everyone's upset," Yvette says, launching into victim mode. "It's not like everyone doesn't know her mom's past."

"Stop talking about her mom," Milo orders, standing up. "You don't know anything about her."

Milo walks Jamie away, as everyone's stares intensify at Yvette. That is, everyone but Lewis and Parker.

"*Dude,*" Tyles hisses, nudging Lewis. "Aren't you gonna say something?"

"You're unbelievable, Yvie," Tabitha says, getting up and following in the direction of Jamie and Milo.

Kai stays put, staring down Lewis. "We're waiting."

"Stop acting like he has to say something," Yvette defends. "I didn't say anything wrong."

I scoff and find myself standing. "How can you say that? What's wrong with you?"

Yvette's mouth falls open. "Kylie! I thought you were my friend."

"No friend of mine would ever treat people this horribly and think it's okay."

Unable to stand another moment around her, I storm off in a different direction to the others.

"Kylie," Parker's voice follows me.

As I make my way away from the campsite, I turn to his nearing footsteps.

"Yvie could have used a friend standing up for her," Parker says.

In outrage, I pull at my hair. "What are you saying? Are you seriously okay with her talking to your friend like that?"

"Of course not. But she can learn that talking like that isn't okay."

"She's fifteen. She should already know that."

"But her home life doesn't sound as easy as ours."

"So that makes it okay for her to rag on other peoples' families?" I throw my hands in the air as shock pours out of me. "What about you? How would you react if she found out about your bio mom and then told everyone?"

"*Shoosh.*" He hisses, looking over his shoulders.

"And she wouldn't just tell people. No. She'd put her Yvie spin on it, and make it sound like the most scandalous situation on the planet."

He folds his arms, averting his eyes. "She won't find out."

"Do you really want to be with her and live in fear of her finding out the truth about you?" I step to the side to gain his eye contact. "Parker, you deserve better than that."

He huffs and turns away. "Kylie, don't start."

I grab his shoulder and turn him back. "No, I mean it. You deserve better than her."

"Why would you say that?"

"Because it's true. You can do better."

"Well, excuse me if I don't trust your judgment," he says in a sarcastic tone.

I flinch. "What's that supposed to mean?"

"You went into this like your imaginary boyfriend was gonna come to life," Parker replies. "The fake Lewis in your head might be your perfect guy, but he isn't the real Lewis."

I clutch my elbows and dig my shoes into the earth. This morning, Lewis told me he hates being patient and still, outside of his photography. My heart still won't let me believe it.

"I went into this arrangement not caring if you and Lewis would end up together. All that mattered was that you thought it could happen."

I exhale hard in shock. "Are you saying you've been lying to me?"

He shrugs. "I'd call them pep talks to keep you motivated."

There's a sting in my eyes. "I can't believe you."

"I never lied about what I think of you," he's quick to add. "I do think you're awesome, talented, funny," he pauses, swallowing hard, "and beautiful. I just knew you weren't the girl for Lewis."

I frown and take a step back. "Why are you being so mean?"

He looks away. "He's not the guy for you either. You're not a good match."

"Why should I believe anything you say? Your whole persona is based on a lie."

He recoils. "That's what you took from me telling you about my family?"

"I just wish you didn't feel like you had to put on an act to be accepted. How can I not start doubting everything you've said to me?"

"I lied when I said you and Lewis would end up together." He fidgets in his stance. "But I'm not lying about you. I care about you too much to let you pine after someone who'll never be interested in you."

"You're just saying this because of what I said about Yvie."

"No, I've thought this all along. You need more than Lewis is willing to give."

"No, it'll work with us."

"Kylie, I know my best friend. And throughout this past week, I've gotten to know you too." He shrugs it off. "You're not compatible."

I shove him backwards. "He does want me. He's told me he wishes he'd noticed me before you."

"I didn't notice you. I noticed an opportunity."

I retch and turn away from him. As I move away, my vision blurs.

He curses behind me and then hurries to grab my arm. "I'm sorry," he whispers.

I fling him off. "No, you're not."

"Yes, I am. I don't want you to be upset."

I half turn. "Because you've been lying to me this whole time?"

"No. Because you're my friend."

I retch again and turn my back on him.

"Kylie, I'd give up on Yvie if it meant keeping you as my friend."

I fold my arms and peer over my shoulder. "Why would you say that?"

"Because it's true. I don't want you out of my life."

"Yvie's made it clear she doesn't want me around her boyfriend, whoever it ends up being."

"I'd make both work."

I scoff and turn to face him. "Now who's deluding themselves? You'd be her little lap dog, just like Lewis. You wouldn't have time for me."

His expression drops. "I don't want to lose what we have. Especially after..."

I roll my eyes and cut him off. "Don't fret. I won't broadcast your secret."

He groans. "I know you won't. That's not what I was saying."

I fold my arms. "Why are you clinging to this crush on Yvie? She'll make you miserable."

He shakes his head and opens his mouth for rebuttal, but is distracted by others yelling back at the campfire.

I shudder. "What was that?"

He gulps, growing pale. "That's Yvie."

We run back to the group just as Yvie yells, "I'm so over this! How much work does it take for you to love me?"

"We've been together a week," Lewis complains. "I thought this was supposed to start out fun."

Yvette groans, walking off. "All I am to you is some fun."

She stomps her way to our tent, zipping herself inside.

"Are you okay, man?" Parker asks.

Lewis rolls his eyes, escaping into his tent.

"He finally gave it to her," Kai says in a low tone. "And so he should. She can't go saying stuff like that to Jamie, or anyone else."

Parker nods. "I agree. She needs to cool it. And I think she will."

"What is with your rose-colored glasses when it comes to Yvie?" Tyler questions. "Why do you think she'll magically change?"

Parker shrugs. "Because I know she wants to."

I put distance between me and Parker, and ask Kai, "Where is Jamie?"

Kai throws a thumb in their direction. "Down there. I think she's okay."

I wander down to them and find Tabitha and Milo sitting on either side of her.

I crouch in front of her. "Are you okay?"

Jamie sighs. "Yeah. She's said much worse stuff over the years."

"It's like it's her first day on earth," I say in a hushed tone. "She has to know saying that stuff isn't okay."

"It's how people act when they're fighting their own insecurities and are terrified of being a target," Tabitha says. "When I was friends with her and Camila, every day was a fight not to be broken down to my tiniest flaw. With the three of us, if we saw a weak target, we attacked." She squeezes Jamie's shoulder. "What she said to Jamie was a cheap shot."

I roll my eyes. "She's so obsessed with being part of the cutest couple. Now, it's blown up in her face. She and Lewis have stormed off to their own tents."

Jamie smiles and gets up. "So, it's safe to go back to the campfire?"

We stand with her, and I reply, "Only if you're up for going back."

Jamie pans around us. "This is my trip with my friends. I'm not going to let Miss Perfect ruin this for me."

Milo kisses her cheek. "You're so strong."

Jamie clutches his hand and nods toward the campsite. "Shall we?"

We join the others, and the night is much more subdued than the previous. We return to making s'mores, and Kai, Tyler, and Jamie force dares upon each other.

My stomach ties another knot every time I catch Parker staring at my tent. At this point, I should just swap camp beds with him, and he can share with whimpering Yvie. When his melancholy eyes land on me, I'm quick to look away.

Once I'm completely worn out, I go to bed. I creep inside the tent, and Yvie doesn't make a sound.

Thank goodness.

My heavy eyelids need no encouragement, and soon I drift to sleep. That is, until a car pulls up and honks at our campsite. I jolt awake and blink at Yvette, who's struggling to get her bag out of our tent.

"What are you doing?" I croak.

"I texted my brother," she whispers. "I'm going home."

I blink at her, and she disappears out of the tent.

I scramble out of bed, and follow her to the black sedan. Everyone else is crawling out of their tents, awakened by this sudden arrival.

"Yvie?" Lewis calls out. "What are you doing?"

"Leaving," she blurts.

The parents race out of their tents in major protective mode.

"What's happening?" Kai's dad asks.

Tabitha gestures at Yvette. "She's leaving."

"With who?" Tyler's mom asks in panic.

"My brother," Yvie says, tossing her bag into the car.

"If you leave right now," Lewis says in a warning tone, "we're through."

Yvette nods. "I'm well aware."

Lewis lifts his hands and backs away. "Fine, Yvie. We're done."

Yvette seemingly ignores Lewis, instead turning toward Parker. She flings her arms forward and pops a heel behind her as she melts into him.

"I'll miss you," she says into the nape of his neck. "Call me when you get home."

Jamie and Tabitha share shocked looks. I look away when they turn my way.

Yvette gets in the car, and Lewis's friends circle around him.

"Are you okay, man?" Tyler asks, slinging an arm around Lewis's shoulders.

"That can't have been easy," Kai adds.

Tabitha edges closer to me with her eyes on Parker. "Why didn't Yvie seem cut up about leaving?"

Jamie folds her arms. "Parker, why was she hugging you?"

He shrugs. "I dunno. I'm not in her head."

"She wants you to call her," Tabitha says.

"We've been hanging out a lot and become friends," Parker says nonchalantly. "Anyway, she's gone. Can we just focus on Lewis right now?"

Parker moves into the boys' huddle, and I avoid the girls' questioning glances. This situation leaves my head plagued with questions. I rub my temples and turn back to my tent.

I mumble, "I need to go to bed," and get inside before anyone can stop me.

"Come on, kids," the parents' voices blur together outside my tent. "Time to get back to bed."

They coax everyone back inside their tents after some mild protests. My gut spasms as I stare at the empty bed beside me. I shut my eyes before I conjure up ugly scenes happening in Parker and Lewis's tent.

Are they talking things out?

Is Parker admitting any fault?

Is Lewis regretting walking away from Yvie?

I roll over, sweating in my sleeping bag.

Jamie and Tabitha's faces come to mind. They already had so many questions for me.

Ugh.

I hate that everyone will be talking about this in the morning.

Thirty

Oof. My head.

I sit up, groggily waking up, with the worst headache.

I leave the tent and zombie my way to the camp bathroom to feel more alive.

Before I reach for the zippered door, Lewis walks out.

"Oh, Lewis," I say, stumbling backward. "How are you?"

He blows out a breath, rubbing his forehead. "Okay, I guess. Would've been better if I didn't spend last night breaking up with my girlfriend in front of everyone."

"Was that really it? You and Yvette are over?"

He nods. "It's too much work. I can't keep doing it."

I nod, searching his eyes as Yvie's voice circles in my mind. Her complaints of him not paying enough attention and not doing anything romantic for her.

He tilts his head, taking me in. "Maybe she was the wrong girl. Maybe with the right girl it wouldn't feel so hard."

I wet my chapped lips. "Yeah, maybe."

He steps aside, rubbing my arm. "I'll get out of the way so you can use the bathroom."

"Thanks," I mumble and step inside.

I take a while to collect myself. My head is clogged with heavy thoughts, and my heart wants to shut down entirely. By the time I join the others, most have finished breakfast and are talking about playing volleyball.

"Hey," Parker whispers, pulling me to the side. "Lewis said, you and he almost had a moment."

My brow furrows. "He told you that?"

Parker chews his lip, nodding.

Did they talk about swapping girlfriends last night? Was Parker expecting this news?

I shrug. "He just wanted comfort."

"Then you should give it to him. I don't want to stand in your way."

I swallow hard. "Are you sure?"

"They're broken up, aren't they?"

"That's what he said."

"Then there's no reason for us to keep up the charade. If he's the guy you want, you should go after him."

I nod slowly, my head and heart glitching out.

"We're breaking up?" he asks with mild hesitation.

I bite into my bottom lip, hoping his hesitancy takes over, stopping me from saying this. "Yes."

Parker blows out a hard breath and there's a tremble in his hands. "No time like the present."

"Wait. You want to do it here?"

Parker increases his volume. "That's it, we're through."

My hands clench into fists, and dread tightens the knots in my back. "Now?"

Parker's eyebrows raise, and he gives a slight nod. As his friends gather around, he becomes someone I don't recognize. "You know this isn't working. We need to stop kidding ourselves."

"I... I..." My words disappear as the faces of Kai, Tabitha, Jamie, Milo and Tyler blur around me.

Kai steps beside Parker and plants a hand on his shoulder. "You sure you wanna be doing this, man?"

Tabitha and Jamie get on either side of me.

"How did this happen?" Tabitha asks.

Confusion creases Jamie's face as she looks at me. "I thought everything was sweet between you two."

Parker nudges Kai's hand off him and then gestures at me. "Kylie agrees. It's not just me."

"No way," Tabitha murmurs.

My face burns and my eyes water from sheer embarrassment. I cup my cheeks and shake my head as I back away. "No, he's right," I mutter. "We're through."

Milo fiddles with his glasses as he pivots between me and Parker. "Guys, I know you don't have everything in common, but that doesn't mean…"

He doesn't finish the sentence. He's as dumbfounded as everyone else.

We wanted this relationship to be believable so we could infiltrate Lewis and Yvette's relationship. But, evidently, we did too good a job.

I look around at everyone, and I'm officially done. It was fine to pretend when I had Parker by my side. There's no way I'm faking my way through a breakup when I won't have him around anymore.

I huff and back away from the group. "I gotta get out of here."

"I don't blame you," Tabitha says, glaring at Parker. "You shouldn't be forced to be around him anymore."

"No, Kylie, I can still take you home," Parker says.

"You can't make her get in the car with you after you dumped her," Tabitha says, aggression heating her words.

"But I'm taking Lewis home," he replies. "He's right next door."

His eyebrows lift as if there's a hint I'm not taking. But I get it. It's my time to strike with Lewis.

I just can't right now.

I link my arm with Tabitha. "I'm exhausted. I need to go home."

Jamie snaps her fingers at Kai. "Gimme your keys. Me and the girls are gonna go home now. You guys can pack up everything."

Kai hands her the keys. "Since when weren't you part of the guys?"

"Since there are girls who need me," Jamie replies. She turns to us. "Shall we?"

Tabitha hugs an arm around me. "Come on. Let's get our bags and go."

As we step away, Parker takes a few steps closer. "Kylie, I..."

Tabitha steps in front of me. "Can you leave her alone?"

Parker huffs. "I still want to know she's okay."

Tabitha turns me away, telling Parker, "You don't get it both ways."

"Dude, just give her some space," Jamie says, following Tabitha and me to our tents.

With our packed bags, the three of us escape into Kai's car, and Jamie zooms away from the campsite.

"What the heck was that?" Jamie asks with a sigh. "If anyone was going to break up, I didn't think..."

I cut her off. "I don't want to talk about it."

Tabitha leans forward from the backseat. "But it just doesn't make any sense."

I cup a hand around my eyes as they water. "Yes, it does," I croak.

Jamie double-takes from the driver's seat. "What does that mean?"

When a tear drops, my shoulders shake, and it's impossible to keep the sobs at bay. "He likes Yvette," I say in a garbled mess.

"Oh, honey," Tabitha mourns, clutching my shoulder from behind.

"He's a freaking idiot," Jamie says through gritted teeth. Through the blur of tears, I notice her grip on the steering wheel exponentially increasing.

"How can you be sure?" Tabitha asks. "I know Yvie can be a total flirt, but..."

I cut her off with another sorrow-drowning sob. I wipe a hand under my nose and mumble. "I just know."

"Why would he date you if he was still into her?" Jamie asks, squinting at the road. "That's the dumbest idea. Of course, someone was going to get hurt."

I want to tell them that I was also into Lewis so Parker doesn't take all the heat. I hate the idea of his friends seeing him as the bad guy. After all, this was a mutual partnership. But with the tears stuffing my nose and throat, getting my point across is near impossible.

Tabitha leans further forward, angling her head at Jamie. "You think Parker still had a crush on Yvie?"

"He and Lewis practically drooled over her," Jamie replies. "I thought for sure World War Three would begin when Lewis and Yvette kissed in the cafeteria. Imagine my shock when Parker doesn't continue the competition and instead tells us he's with Kylie."

Tabitha sits back with a thud. "It was quick."

"It came out of the blue," Jamie continues, "but then I started thinking, once Lewis and Yvette hooked up, maybe Parker felt like he got permission to be with Kylie. I just really believed he liked you all along."

I deadpan her. "You did?"

She shrugs. "You just always seemed to be on the same page."

I frown. "It was an act."

Tabitha huffs her frustration. "No one's that good of an actor."

"Maybe you guys just wanted to believe it badly enough and didn't see the cracks."

"I didn't think I saw any cracks," Tabitha concedes.

I rest my head against the window with a sigh. "My head hurts too much to talk about this."

The girls stop hounding me, and soon I'm home. With my bag slung over my shoulder, I dawdle into my home.

"Hi Kikki," a familiar voice calls out.

I move into the living room and almost fall backward. "Tess?"

"I came home to spend the weekend with everyone," she says. "Imagine my shock when Mom and Dad told me you were on a two-day trip with your boyfriend."

"Tess, I…"

"You're dating Parker Kelly?" Her hands plant on her hips as she strides toward me. "You said he was just a boy from school. Even though it sounded fishy, I believed you. Do you know why?"

Guilt slithers through my gut as I hug myself and turn away. "Tess, don't…"

"We don't lie to each other, Kikki. What the heck?"

As tears pool in my eyes, I hurriedly wipe them away. "Well, it's not something you have to worry about, anyway. We broke up."

Mom gasps in the hallway. "You did *what*?"

"Can everyone just back off?" I say, raising my hands. "I just want to be alone."

"Kikki, I'm so sorry," Mom says with a pout.

I push past her and rush upstairs.

In my bedroom, I flop onto the bed and reef the covers over me.

Beep, beep.

I fumble inside my pocket and pull out my phone.

I frown at a text from Parker. *"So, everyone really bought that we broke up."*

No kidding. You yelled, 'We're through,' so everyone would crowd around us.

But I can't type the reply. I just don't want to talk to him right now.

I lower my phone, but another text comes through.

"I know this fake breakup is awkward, but you should've stayed and talked to Lewis. I would've given you space on the drive home."

Ugh. He's so worried about me missing a chance with Lewis so he has a clear path to Yvette.

I lock the screen, but another text comes through.

"Can you just reply so I know you're okay?"

I drop the phone on my nightstand. I'm not okay, so that's my permission not to reply.

There's a knock at my door. "Kikki?" Tessa's voice breaks through. "Can I come in?"

I squeeze the pillow over my head and grunt an answer.

There's a click as the door knob turns.

I grunt again, keeping my face planted against the mattress.

"Kikki," Tessa says, creeping toward the bed. "Please talk to me."

"You don't want to hear it," I sob into the sheets.

"Yes, I do." She sits beside me. "I'm so sorry I haven't been supportive of you wanting a boyfriend. I've never wanted you to get hurt."

"You're just here to call me an idiot," I whine. "That I should've listened to you, and then my heart never would've been broken."

Tess gently rubs my back. "You're not an idiot. You're fierce and passionate. You'll pick yourself up like I never could."

I lift my head and turn toward her. My sister's kind smile helps my tears dry up.

She leans forward. "Oh, sis, can I give you a hug?"

I nod and collapse against her, letting her arms wrap me up.

"I'm so sorry," she whispers. "Mom and Dad told me how great Parker has been. He's nothing like Nightmare Hugh. Do you want to talk about what happened?"

"No, I'm too tired."

"I really wish I hadn't come down on you so harshly."

A silent giggle shakes me against her. "Isn't that what big sisters are for?"

"So, you're not mad at me?"

I pull out of the hug and pat my eyes dry. "No. I kept Parker a secret from you. I get why you felt cheated."

"I just want you to be safe."

"Parker made me feel safe." And at that, another avalanche of tears falls.

I hang my head as I hiccup through my cries. Tess holds me close, cooing that everything will be okay.

Will it though? I knew this day was coming. Parker and I always had an expiration date. If I'm this crushed by a fake relationship ending, how will I ever survive the collapse of a real one?

Thirty-One

I've hidden in my bedroom since Friday morning. It's nearing midday on Saturday, and I'm now refreshed after a shower. Tess has been badgering me to take one since last night, but I was too broken to get up. Now that she and my parents have left for a day at the mall, it felt safe to leave the sanctuary of my bedroom.

This is what I feared most. After all this was done, I'd be alone.

I sit on the edge of my bed, clutching the bunny Parker won at the fair.

A day when I was so mad at Parker for kissing me. A night when I was so sure I'd won Lewis's heart.

I get up and walk to my window. I look down at the fence line and air hitches in my throat.

Lewis.

He tosses a black plastic bag into his trash can and then wanders along the fence line. The melancholy is evident in his walk and his head hangs low.

My eyes close as I think back to the last morning of the camping trip. Lewis's words replay in my mind. *"Maybe with the right girl it wouldn't feel so hard."*

He was signaling to me. He wanted me to know that being with him was an option.

I toss the stuffed bunny across the room and pace toward my wardrobe. This isn't going to be all for nothing. Dang it, I did this to be with Lewis. And there he is. Newly single and in the front yard. I'm done living in fantasy. I'm not watching him from afar for another year and a half.

It's time to make my move.

If Parker's not going to be alone at the end of this, neither am I.

I check my hair in front of the full-length mirror and hurriedly change out of my sweats. I find my cutest blue outfit and clasp my sapphire necklace around my neck. After a flick of mascara, I race out of my bedroom and downstairs to the front door.

"Lewis!" I call out, sprinting toward his yard.

As I make it into his yard, he pans around to find me. "Kylie, hey. What's going on?"

I pant, standing before him, realizing I don't know my next move.

Can't it be like a movie, where he dips me with a passionate kiss?

"We're both single," I blurt.

He blinks at me.

Geez. Am I completely without game?

He sighs. "Yeah, I was with the guys at the campsite. I really thought you and Parker had things figured out."

"It was only a week-long relationship," I brush it off.

"So was mine," Lewis replies, "and it still hurts."

My shoulders slump. "I know. I'm just trying to forget it. It feels easier."

Lewis smiles. "I'm down for the easier option."

I'm the easier option. Ugh. Why can't I say it? Is my tongue literally tied?

Lewis chuckles, folding his arms. "I hate to think my dad might be right. He says, 'Being single is the easiest option.'"

"*Oof.*" My hand rests on my chest. "Your dad doesn't sound super romantic."

"Not exactly. But he might have a point."

"Don't be down on love just because you were with the wrong girl."

Lewis rubs the back of his neck. "You think she was the wrong girl?"

"It's not up to me. You practically told me she was the wrong girl on the camping trip."

Lewis huffs. "In my head, she's been the perfect girl for so long."

I purse my lips and nod along. "I totally get that."

"Parker?"

This is the time to stop lying. "No, not Parker."

"But, you and he..."

We stare at each other for a long beat, awkwardness soaking up the surrounding space.

He takes a step forward. "Who?"

My heart pounds so hard that my chest rises higher than it ever has. When I catch my breath, I whisper, "You."

His bottom lip lowers, and there's confusion in his expression.

I suck in air, compensating for the marathon my heart's undertaking.

"Me?" His brows knit together. "You're into me?"

Even though the blush covers my entire face, I still tell him, "I have been since the day we met."

His smile twitches with nervousness. "You mean, when I moved here?"

I nod. "You probably never noticed."

"Well, no, but I... I just didn't know."

"I kept it all inside," I whisper. "But that doesn't mean my feelings weren't real."

Lewis swallows hard and then takes another step closer. He looks down at my chest and smiles.

"Did you wear this for me?"

He runs his finger across my necklace and picks up the sapphire pendant.

I shiver. "I remembered how much you liked it."

Lewis drops the pendant, and his hand brushes back my hair and caresses my neck. There's only a sliver of air between us, and after many practice kisses with Parker, I know what this means.

The air shifts, and there's shared heat between us. I lower my eyelids, and my heart pounds in anticipation.

I'm going to kiss Lewis Freaking Allen!

They weren't practice kisses.

Huh?

It wasn't fake.

The small voice in the back of my head doesn't sound familiar. But with every word it whispers, my heart strums like I'm listening to an old friend.

Parker's dang infectious smile crowds my mind just as Lewis's lips creep over mine.

I pull back, and my eyes spring open. "I'm sorry. I can't."

His pout eases and his eyes open. "Huh?"

"It's... It's..."

He clicks his tongue. "It's Parker."

"Yes." I take a step back. "I'm sorry. I have to tell him how I feel."

He steps forward. "But you just told me you've had a crush on me for over a year."

"I know. I'm sorry for confusing things, but this has been my whole week. I've been confused about my feelings for both you and Parker. And I'm sorry, I just figured it out."

"And it's Parker?"

"Yes. I want to be with him." I step around Lewis. "I've gotta go."

Lewis grabs my wrist. "Wait. Both girls want him more than me?"

My heart leaps into my throat. "I sure hope Yvie doesn't want him."

"Well, considering she told me I need dating tips from him, I think she's into him."

I pull my arm away, but he doesn't loosen his grip. "Lewis, please let me go. I need to see Parker."

"Only after you tell me there's nothing between us."

"Please don't act like you like me."

He flinches. "Huh?"

"Yes, I've had a crush on you forever, but you didn't care," I say candidly. "You only want me because I was with Parker. You had a year and a half to make a move, and you ignored me. I'm not another trophy in your silly competition. Either Parker wants me, or I'm walking away from both of you."

He releases my wrist. "I don't see you as a trophy."

"You don't see me as girlfriend material."

"I care about you. I've liked the time we've spent together. Like after the fair or just hanging at your house." He rubs his neck, averting his gaze. "But, no, I don't see you as my girlfriend. Part of me wants to be with you just so my breakup doesn't hurt. And, maybe, to get under Parker's skin."

"I don't want to do that stuff anymore."

He crosses his fingers over his heart. "I promise to never use you."

I sigh, relieved. "Thank you."

"If you want to see Parker," Lewis says as if the words are painful, "I'll drive you over."

"You'll drive?" My body locks with apprehension. "But I thought you were still on your ban?"

He bats a hand. "The month will be over soon enough."

"No, I'll find my own way over there."

"It takes two buses to get there, and there's always a long wait between them."

"I can find someone else to drive me."

"Just let me give you a ride," he insists. "I don't want you thinking I'm a jerk."

"I don't think that."

"My car is still in the shop, and my parents are inside. Any chance you have a car we can take?"

"Well, there's my sister's car," I hesitate. "She's at the mall with my parents."

Lewis snaps his fingers. "Perfect. Get the keys."

"I gotta be crazy."

"Don't worry, you won't get into trouble. My parents will hardly blame the quiet girl next door."

"What about my parents?"

He shrugs. "I corrupted you."

So that's my reputation, is it? "Okay. I'll get the keys."

I have goosebumps on the drive over. One, I'm about to tell Parker that my feelings were never fake. Two, I'm in the car with Lewis Allen, who has a reputation as a terrible driver.

Lewis slows down the car, but we're not on Parker's street.

"What are you doing?"

He points to the left. "Don't you recognize that car?"

I gulp when I see it. Parker's car.

"He's at Yvie's house," Lewis says. "Guess that answers that."

"No, it doesn't," I blurt, unbuckling my seatbelt. "Stop the car."

A warning sound blares from me not wearing a seatbelt while the car is in motion.

"Kylie, buckle up. I don't wanna get caught doing another thing wrong while driving."

"It's not you. Your mousy neighbor is in the wrong. Now stop the car."

As I reach for the door handle, there's a locking sound. I yank on the door handle, but there's no give. "Lewis, unlock the door."

"Why do you want to hurt yourself?" Lewis says, keeping the car moving along the street. "Seeing those two together won't give you closure. It'll only make you feel worse."

"He doesn't love her," I protest. "You silly boys put her on a pedestal and think your lives will be better because she agreed to be with you. Parker's smarter than that. One moment with her, when they're both single, he'll realize what a mistake he's made."

Lewis parks the car a few houses away from Yvette's. "I'm not unlocking the doors until you listen to me."

"Ugh. Then spit it out."

"You might have a fantasy of rushing in there and tearing them apart, but this is real life. Maybe he will figure out Yvette is wrong for him, but let him work it out."

I sit back in the seat, taking in the sincerity in his eyes. "You really care about him, don't you?"

Lewis smiles. "He's my best friend."

"But how is your friendship not trashed after you've both gone after the same girl?"

"Because that's not how our friendship works. Besides, didn't you realize how much I loved our double dates? It was too much fun making Parker jealous. It's one of my favorite things to do."

"Ugh. I'll never understand boys."

"The best was making him squirm when I kissed Yvette under the waterfall."

"That wasn't fun for either of us."

Lewis smirks. "Hey, I already gave you an opportunity to kiss me."

I laugh at the ridiculousness and buckle my seatbelt.

"Can I buy you a burger?" Lewis asks.

"Sure. Sounds like a great way to mask my sorrows."

Lewis drives us to Alto Burger. He orders himself a double sizzler and me a whadda burger.

He sends me a wink. "I remember your favorite."

We sit out on the deck, waiting for our orders to arrive.

"So, you really had a crush on me for a year and a half?"

I sigh, covering my face. "Am I going to regret telling you that?"

"No, I was just wondering what changed," he replies. "If you still felt the same way about me while you were with Parker, why didn't you kiss me back at the house?"

I frown, sitting back as my stomach twists.

Lewis smirks. "Don't tell me the thought of kissing me broke your crush on me."

"Umm, no. That's something I've thought about doing a lot." I shy my face away. "It was something else."

He leans forward. "What was it?"

"I can't say. It's stupid."

"Come on. It could help me. Despite my dad's lame advice, I don't want to be single forever."

"Well, I don't know how much it'll help you. I think it's a very me-specific issue."

"Just tell me. It's starting to freak me out."

I exhale hard. "You didn't dance."

He sits back, flabbergasted. "Huh?"

"At my house. You didn't dance."

"At your house?" he questions. "When?"

A server brings over our burgers, and I thank her before telling Lewis, "When you needed a wrench because there was a leak in your kitchen."

He squints. "You're not making any sense."

"How can you not remember this?"

"I remember getting the wrench, but I have no idea what dancing has to do with anything."

I flatten my hands on the table. "I told you it was the house rules. To dance when the music is playing."

He shakes his head. "Your crush on me ended because I didn't dance in your house?"

"I know it sounds crazy, but Parker danced right away. It just felt like a bad omen that you wouldn't even humor me."

His expression softens. "And that's what made things complicated? Parker did something you wanted, but you thought you liked me more?"

"Exactly."

"I thought maybe it'd be when I made fun of the band you and Parker like."

I smirk. "That was strike two."

I don't need to tell him strike three was when he shattered my illusion of him being my quiet, patient, and sensitive guy.

"Well, I'm sorry if I made you feel bad because I didn't dance with you. I remember that day. I was miserable because Yvie wasn't talking to me. I had zero capacity to pay attention to another girl."

My gut sinks. "Dang. You really liked her. I'm sorry it didn't work out."

"It's okay. We didn't really get to know each other. I'm not so sure we were the right fit."

"Could Parker and Yvie be the right fit?"

Lewis shrugs. "They might find something in common."

I hug my middle and stare at my lap. "I just can't see it happening."

"If they get together, will you tell Parker how you feel?"

I blow out a hard breath. "No, I couldn't do that to him. Whatever happens, I want him to be happy."

"Even if it's with her?"

I nod. "Even if it's with her. Geez, I can't imagine walking into school and seeing them together."

"Okay, this is a bit out there," Lewis says, shifting in his seat. "But, it could help save face."

"What do you mean?"

"Well, if you're worried about school on Monday, I could walk in with you."

"Why would you do that?"

"If we walk in together, and I have my arm around you, they might think we got together."

I push back in my seat. "Like, faking we're together?"

Lewis smirks. "I know, it sounds ridiculous. But it might give us some confidence to go back to school."

My nerves ease, and I sit forward. "You're nervous about it?"

"Ah, yeah," he says, folding his arms. "I left for spring break with Yvette Anderson on my arm. Now I'm going back single. It's not exactly a boost to my ego."

"No one would think badly of you. Everyone knows Yvie jumps from guy to guy."

"Yeah, but it would help shift focus if I had a new girl by my side."

"I'll walk into school with you, but I'm not faking that we're together."

Lewis mumbles a laugh. "Yeah, that's fair. It's probably not something that's easy to make believable."

I avert my eyes. "*Ha*, yeah."

"Are you cool to hang by my side, anyways?"

I look back at him, and there's pleading in his eyes. "I'm so sorry you got hurt."

He sits back in surprise. "It's not your fault."

Those words hit me like a semi-truck.

I rub the space over my heart and say, "I see no reason we can't walk into school together. We're neighbors after all."

Lewis pulls a fist toward himself in triumph. "*Yes*!"

I give him a guilty smile. "Can I be honest with you about something?"

His eyebrows lift. "Sure."

"I hate the Wasteland Gang movies. I watched them so I'd have something to talk to you about, but I think they're really dumb."

Lewis laughs, clasping a hand over his chest. "Ouch. Kick a guy when he's down."

"I'm sorry. I just felt like I needed to confess." I giggle behind a cupped hand. "I also got into Frontier Leaders because I thought you liked him."

"*Oof*. Now, I'm sorry." Lewis smirks. "Does Parker know?"

I nod. "He didn't tell me you didn't like them."

"Because then you'd really know they weren't a cool band."

If I couldn't tell Lewis the whole truth about me and Parker, at least I came clean about something. It feels good to have told him. Now, my obsession with the boy next door has come to an end.

"As long as we're confessing," Lewis says. "Remember how I told you I accidentally deleted the photo of you and Parker?"

"Yeah?"

"Well," he draws out the word. "It wasn't an accident. I did it on purpose."

"Why?"

"Because you two looked so happy, and it made me jealous."

I laugh out of shock. "Really?"

"He was holding the sides of your face, and you were both staring into each other's eyes and smiling. Me and Yvie were in a bad place, and part of me really wanted to be with you." He huffs, slouching in his seat. "I just got into a bit of a rage. Forgive me?"

I shrug. "It's already forgotten. Besides, Parker and I took some really cute photos in the arcade photo booth."

Lewis grins. "But did it have my composition and perfect lighting?"

"No. It was grainy and off-center. But I love it."

Lewis rests his chin in his palm. "You two really did have a good thing going, huh?"

"Not the whole time. We were both hung up on different people."

"Give him time. He'll see clearly."

I nod. "I hope so."

After lunch, Lewis drives me home, and when I take the keys from him, my front door opens.

"Get away from my daughter!" Dad's voice booms.

Lewis and I jolt apart.

"Kylie," Dad says in a lower tone. "Get inside."

"Dad, we just…"

"Now," he orders.

Lewis waves goodbye and sheepishly nods at my dad. "Bye, Mr. Green."

Dad beckons me over as Lewis rushes into his own house.

Inside, Mom closes in beside Dad, and my sister lingers by the living room doorway.

Ugh.

"How could you do something so irresponsible?" my dad yells, swiping Tess's keys from me. "I told you, I don't want you anywhere near that boy when he's driving."

I grunt, folding my arms. "What's the big deal?"

Dad's forehead creases. "The big deal? I told you how dangerous that crash was. How could you put yourself in danger like that?"

I huff and throw my hands up. "I guess I'm not the goody goody you thought I was."

Mom clutches Dad's arm. "Kikki, honey, no one's saying you're a bad girl. We're just surprised you'd do something like this."

I stomp my foot. "I'm capable of more things than you give me credit for."

Tess fidgets. "Mom and Dad are just saying to stay away from that boy."

I curl my fist as I turn to my sister. "Don't you start."

Tess pouts. "Kikki, I just…"

"I don't care about being with Lewis. I just used him for a ride."

Dad tenses. "A ride to where?"

My throat tickles and my eyes itch. "To Parker's."

"Oh, honey," Mom breathes.

Before the pity party sets in, I fly past them, down the hallway.

"Kikki, wait," Tess calls out.

I rush up the stairs and toward my bedroom. Before I can slam the door, Tess juts out a hand, keeping the door open.

"Leave me alone," I whine.

"Talk to me," she whispers, following me to the bed.

I sit on the edge, wiping my eyes dry. "I want him back, Tess."

She sits beside me, rubbing a circle on my back. "I know."

I shake my head, swallowing a sob. "No, you don't."

"Yes, I can see how he..."

"No, you don't understand," I cut her off. "You don't know the whole truth."

Her hand falls off my back. "What do you mean?"

My vision blurs until I blink it clear. "I kept my relationship from you because I know you don't want me to date."

"I just didn't want you..."

"To get hurt. I know. Just let me finish."

"I'm sorry. Go on."

I blow out a long breath. "Mom and Dad don't know this, but my relationship with Parker was never real."

She squints. "But they said he was over here and got their approval."

"I guess we put on a good act."

"This doesn't make any sense."

"I never meant the lie to get out of control."

She recoils. "You were lying to Mom and Dad?"

"Not about where we were going and what we were doing. Just that our relationship was fake."

She gasps. "Huh?"

"We got together because our crushes were dating." I swallow hard, humiliation weighing me down. "We were trying to break them up."

"There's no way."

I nod. "It's the truth. I wanted to pretend because I was into Lewis, but he had a girlfriend."

"So you fabricated your feelings for Parker to mend your broken heart?"

"Pretty much. It was a stupid idea. Now I feel like I lost something so great, even though we made it all up. We weren't really in love. It's just hard to remember that it was all fake."

"Are you sure it was all fake?"

"Yes," I rush. "Josie told me what I was doing was toxic, and she was right. It blew up in my face."

"I'm so sorry you felt like you couldn't tell me this." Tess's eyes water. "Now I feel like this secrecy has hurt you even worse than a night in the quarry ever could."

I wrap an arm around her. "Don't do that. Your pain was real."

"But I always cut you off when you spoke about your crush. I haven't been here for you."

"It's okay. I was such a mess when I tried to explain this fake relationship to Josie. I don't think I could've ever gotten it across to you." I sigh. "Besides, the plan was to end the relationship as soon as possible. Then he could be with Yvie, and I could be with Lewis."

"Okay, so you and Parker agreed to do this for mutual gain?" she asks, piecing this together. "But you don't want to be with Lewis despite spending time with him today?"

"It just didn't feel right. My heart doesn't belong to him."

Sadness droops her face. "But it does to Parker?"

I nod. "And he's already with another girl."

"You saw them together?"

"No. His car was parked outside her house."

Tess sniffs back her tears and pulls me into a hug. "Oh, Kikki, your poor heart. I'm so sorry."

I hug her back. "I'm sorry for keeping this from you. I want to be able to talk to you about this stuff."

"I'm always going to be protective of you," Tess whispers. "But I want us to be open. I want to know when you're hurting and when you're giddy, no matter who the guy is."

"Right now, I'm hurting and giddy over the same guy."

She pulls out of the hug and wipes under my eyes. "How are you feeling about going back to school?"

"Dreading it," I mutter. "And I'm insanely scared about tomorrow. Parker usually comes into the café during my Sunday shift."

"Can you text him not to come?" Tess suggests.

I shake my head. "I can't reply to his text. Not when I know he's currently with Yvette."

Determination narrows Tess's gaze. "He'd be a fool to walk into the café with *her* on his arm."

I press a hand into my churning stomach. "The thought of his hands anywhere near her is sickening enough."

Tess squeezes me into another hug. "Are you going to be okay? You're not turning into a rebellious teen, are you?"

I mumble a laugh. "No, I swear I haven't changed my personality."

"Good, because you're awesome just how you are."

I sigh, staring at the stuffed bunny lying on its side on the carpet. "That's what Parker would say."

Thirty-Two

With each passing hour of my Sunday morning shift at the café, my health declines. Whenever I take a pancake stack to a table, my stomach does somersaults. Now, standing at the counter, my nerves frazzle every time the door opens. My forehead is slick with sweat and my back aches with the torture of anticipation.

Jamie sidles up to me. "Umm, hey. So, umm, how are you, ah…"

I give her a dubious look. "Why are you being so awkward?"

She huffs, hunching forward. "The breakup. How are you doing?"

Good, blunt Jamie is back. "I'm hanging in there."

"You don't need to keep watching the door," Jamie says. "I've given the boys strict instructions not to come here today."

"You did?"

She nods. "Kai had them all go over to his place, and they're having a video game marathon. I'm heading over after work."

I exhale hard. "Okay, good. I don't know what I'd do if I saw any of them today. I'm a bit embarrassed that they all witnessed the breakup."

"Don't be embarrassed. No one thinks badly of you. It's Parker who's the grade-A moron." Her frown is tight as she shakes her head. "I always knew

Parker was an idiot. Lewis and Yvette ending their relationship was easy to see coming, but you and Parker... Nope. It makes zero sense."

"Well, you didn't know everything that happened between us. With full context, it makes sense."

"Well, I know about his stupid crush on Yvette, and that's enough for me to label him an idiot."

I laugh, which eases my nerves. "Well, thanks, Jamie."

"Milo was telling me he and the guys tried to talk sense into Parker after we left the campsite," Jamie says. "Apparently, he was being super vague and cagey. Makes sense to me, because he has no good reason to break up with you."

"That's sweet, but I don't want everyone treating him differently. Me and him just didn't work out, and that's fine. I don't want anyone to stop being friends with him."

"You're sticking up for him?"

"Sure. I still think he's a good guy."

"Well, it's not like he's kicked out of the group, but we will give him a hard time. That's just how things roll with us."

"Yeah, so I've seen."

She pats my shoulder as she leaves the counter. "Glad you're doing okay."

The next time the café door opens, my nerves don't spike.

Phew.

It's Josie.

She edges her way over to me, her head shaking with disbelief.

I walk her to an empty table, and she flops down with a huff. "You and Parker broke up?"

I lower myself beside her, careful not to sit during such a busy shift. "Mm-hmm."

"So, what does this mean? Are you and Lewis a thing?"

I shake my head. "No, but I think Parker and Yvie are."

Rage boils in Josie's eyes. "He didn't."

I shrug. "It was the plan."

Josie pivots left to right, and then she asks, "So, Lewis is single?"

I raise a hand. "Don't go there. It's not happening."

She winces. "Did he reject you?"

I click my tongue. "Ugh. I rejected him."

She splutters a laugh. "No way."

"Yes way. He wanted to kiss me, and I pulled away."

Josie pulls at her hair. "How can this be? That was your dream. *The* fantasy!"

"I just don't feel the same way anymore."

"How come?"

I sigh. "Because of Parker."

"Oh, Kylie. I'm sorry."

"I feel so stupid for catching feelings. I knew what we were doing and where it was leading."

"Well, I tried to tell you, you had the feels."

I scoff. "When?"

"The other day when he brought his little brother into the café," Josie replies. "You both lit up around each other. I swear, he was into you too. How the heck could he leave you for Yvette?"

"Because he wants her."

"Baloney."

"Ex-excuse me?"

She watches me with steady eyes. "Who does your heart belong to?"

"Parker." I rub the heel of my palm across my chest. "I wish it didn't, but it does. Ugh, Josie, I'm so in love with him."

She slams a fist on the table. "Then fight for him."

"*Josie*," I hiss, looking around at the nearby tables. "Keep it down."

"You two started this because you were willing to fight for someone. Turns out, it wasn't the correct endpoint. If Parker's your guy, you gotta let him know."

"He wants Yvie."

"That's what Lewis thought. Yvie will break both their hearts."

"Parker has the qualities she's looking for. I think he's her endgame."

"*Bull*," Josie splutters. "Yvette Anderson doesn't deserve him."

"I can't compete with her."

"Didn't Lewis try to kiss you?"

"Only to make Parker jealous. He admitted as much."

"Look, you know I'm infatuated with Wyatt. If I had another chance to fight for him, I'd do it, no question. Don't leave this in regret."

"I don't want to put myself out there just to be rejected."

"I've seen the way he looks at you. It's more special than the hubba-hubba looks Yvette gets."

"I was crazy jealous when Yvette touched him while I was fake dating him. It'll kill me to see them touching, or worse, kissing in front of me."

Josie grabs my hand. "I'll be with you. I won't let them hurt you."

"Do you know how to bandage a heart?"

"Yes. I believe it's called pints of ice-cream."

I giggle, letting myself breathe more freely. "Thanks, Josie. I can't believe you saw through all our pretending."

"I was just watching him to find out how much of a player he is. Who knew I'd detect real feelings?"

"I hope you're right."

I leave Josie's table, getting back to work, and she sticks around until the end of my shift. We leave Morton's Café together, and Tessa's car is out front to take us home.

"Did he come in today?" Tess is quick to ask.

"No." I breathe out in relief. "Jamie made the boys stay away."

Tess smiles. "Nice. I'm glad she has your back."

I launch forward and wrap my arms around my sister. "I'm so glad I have you. I'm sorry for lying to you, and I'm sorry for acting so bratty. I love you so much."

Tess hugs me back, resting her head by mine. "All I want is for you to be happy and safe. Mom and Dad said Parker fit in so well. I mean, if the boy can disco dance to 'Arnold's Hits,' he has to be a good egg."

I giggle, pulling out of the hug. "I'm sorry you never got the chance to meet him."

Josie sits forward from the backseat. "She will. You're going to get him back."

Tess turns to the back. "How can you be so sure?"

"Because I have spent time with Parker," she replies. "He's infatuated with our girl. Anytime he spends with Yvette Anderson will only make him see clearly."

Tess gives me a hopeful smile. "I want to wish you all the luck, but I'm scared about your heart getting broken."

"It already broke," I admit. "If it's smashed again, it can't hurt any worse."

Tess winces. "It can if you see them kiss."

Josie groans. "Who let Miss Negative behind the wheel?"

It makes me giggle. "That's why I need Parker. He's Mr. Positivity."

Tess sighs. "I'm so sorry that I have to go back to the dorms tonight."

"Don't be. I'll be okay."

Josie clutches my shoulder. "I won't leave our girl alone."

Thirty-Three

Lewis's parents gave him back his driving privileges for the first day back at school. Before spring break started, if anyone told me I'd be riding in Lewis Freaking Allen's car, it'd be the equivalent of winning the lottery. Now, as we pull into the student parking lot, it feels like we're two wounded soldiers, coming back from the battle of broken hearts.

"Ready to do this?" Lewis asks, opening his car door.

"Nope."

I exit the car and we wander toward the school gate.

I glance around the surrounding cars. "So, you haven't seen Parker since the camping trip?"

"No, it's weird. He didn't turn up at Kai's on Sunday, and he hasn't been returning my texts."

"Does he think everyone's mad at him?"

"He shouldn't. Tyler and Kai were texting him too."

I grimace. "Ugh. You don't think he was too wrapped up in Yvie to reply, do you?"

He frowns. "It's a possibility."

I dip my hand into my pocket and clutch my phone. "Well, he texted me on Friday, but I never replied."

"Even though you want to be with him?"

"Well, I only figured that out on Saturday." I gulp. "Then we saw his car at Yvie's place."

"Yeah. Makes things awkward."

We move through the school gates and into the foyer. My stomach flips and my heart swells. So many mornings, I'd picture myself walking into school with Lewis. Now it's happening, and I can't stop thinking about another guy.

Ugh. Am I destined to never be happy?

Lewis exhales slowly. "Thank you so much for walking in with me. This would be so hard to do alone."

I smile and pat his arm. "It's no problem."

He smiles. "You're such a great person, Kylie. I'm an idiot for never noticing how awesome you are."

"As long as we can be friends now, the slate is wiped clean."

He slings an arm around my shoulders. "Deal."

A grin spreads across my face and I let my eyes wander the crowded hallway. I almost trip when I land on Parker.

He lifts his hand in a mediocre wave. "Hey, guys."

Lewis tugs his arm around me tighter. "Hey, man. We missed you on Sunday."

Recognition fills his eyes as he nods at me. "Oh. Sorry I couldn't make it."

My heart thunders in my chest as I stare at the only boy I want to be with.

"I'll walk you to your locker," Lewis says, forcing me to move past Parker.

I don't answer because all the words I want to say to Parker are clogged in my throat.

When we turn into another hallway, Lewis drops his arm from around me. "You're welcome."

"Excuse me?"

Lewis gestures to the prior hallway. "For getting you away from Parker."

"I didn't even get to say hi to him."

"Did you really want to hear him admit he spent Sunday with Yvette?"

I grunt and step away from him. "Thanks for walking me, Lewis. I need to find Josie."

He waves me off. "No problem."

I keep my head down as I walk through the hallway. I avoid eye contact with those around me, and stuff my bag into my locker. At Josie's locker, I can't even admit to her that I saw Parker. I know she wants me to fight for him, but what if Lewis is right? What if Parker spent Sunday with Yvette?

I zombie my way through my first two classes. When I leave social studies, I trudge behind my peers, in no rush to get to my next class on time.

"Kylie," Josie's voice calls out.

I look up and see her waving from the opposite direction. I hug the wall and wait for her to reach me.

Josie clutches her elbows on her approach. "I'm so sorry."

I flinch at the dread in her tone.

Josie flings her arms around me, and my chin whacks her shoulder.

I cringe. "Why are you commiserating with me?"

Josie pulls back, wincing. "Because I saw Yvette and Parker together."

All my internal organs freeze. "Together?"

She nods glumly.

"So, that's it?" There's a tremble in my voice. "You saw them kissing?"

"No," she blurts. "They were just talking. But..."

I impatiently wait her out. "But what?"

"They were really close," she whispers. "Like, intimately close. He was holding her hands on the desk and they were whispering."

I swallow the ugliness at the back of my mouth and nod. "Okay, I knew this was happening. They were close and whispering throughout the camping trip. Now, they're both single and can choose to be together."

Josie's bottom lip quivers. "I'm so sorry, Kylie."

I shake my head, forcing my eyes not to well. "Don't be. It's okay, as long as he's happy."

"You're allowed to be sad."

"Not at school. I don't want anyone, especially Yvette, seeing me cry."

Josie nods. "Okay. We'll keep a low profile."

"Library at lunch?"

"Absolutely."

I get through the next two periods, and when I leave art class, Parker exits Spanish from across the hall.

He fumbles with his stance, and then summons the courage to get closer. "Hey," he whispers.

I fold my arms, leaning against the wall. "Hey."

"How are you?" he asks, shifting awkwardly. "You never returned my texts."

"Well, we were done playing make-believe."

"But I thought we would still be friends."

I hold my resolve, watching his Adam's apple bob and a sweat bead down the side of his forehead.

I push off the wall and step away. "I don't think I can."

He grabs onto my shoulder. "Why?"

I fling him off. "It's too hard Parker. I can't be around you."

"But I miss..."

"Back off!" Josie yells, running down the hallway.

Parker lifts his hands in surrender.

Josie shoves him away. "Don't you think you've messed with her heart enough?"

Parker's mouth hangs open as he stumbles to get his balance. He blinks hard as he pivots between me and Josie. "Josie, I'm not..."

Josie steps in front of me, her hands planted on her hips. "Don't start, Parker. You just stay away from my best friend."

I tap her shoulder. "Josie, let's go."

"Kylie," Parker pleads. "Can't I just..."

"No, you can't," Josie blurts, and then turns away with me.

As we pace up the hallway, I say mid-pant, "Josie, you didn't have to do that."

"No, I did. He doesn't get to toy with your emotions."

"I was already walking away from him."

Josie sighs. "He was pulling you back in."

"Ugh. My head hurts. When will this day be over?"

"We could play hooky?"

I splutter a laugh. "This is us we're talking about."

Josie and I spend lunch in the library, and I psyche myself up for my next class.

Chemistry.

The class that started this whole mess in the first place.

I was just a girl, lusting after the boy next door. It was innocent and safe because I had the protection of fantasyland. Now, the real world has made everything ugly and my heart is bruised and battered.

"Welcome back, class," Mr. Thompson says as we file into the science lab. "At the request of some students, today you can switch lab partners if you wish."

I hug my books close, feeling a vortex of sickness swirling in my gut.

Before I step further into the aisle, I duck behind the workstation in the front row. I sit behind the desk and lower my head so I don't make eye contact with anyone walking into the classroom.

If only I could click *mute* on my ears. Within the mass of footsteps moving into the room and between the desks, I hear two distinct voices.

Parker and Lewis.

On instinct, I hold my breath. My shoulder hunch forward, and I hope by making myself small, I somehow become invisible.

When their voices trail off close by, I slowly raise my head. From the corner of my eye, I spy Helen Redfern making her way into the classroom. She's a diligent student who usually sits somewhere close to the front. I wave at her and she happily takes the seat next to me.

I breathe out in a hurry, glad I haven't made eye contact with either boy.

"How was your spring break?" Helen asks.

Oh boy. Where would I even begin? "Eventful."

"Did you go to the fair?"

"Yeah. But I wish I didn't."

Helen chuckles to herself. "Me too."

"What happened?"

"My little brother puked on me after eating a bucket of cotton candy and riding the tilt-a-whirl."

I grimace. "*Eww.* That does not sound fun."

Helen pats her textbook. "Getting back into this sounds like a whole lot more fun."

I smile. "Well, I'm really glad we can be lab partners."

"Why aren't you sitting up the back anymore?"

The truth is, I fought hard for my last workstation. I wanted to sit as close to Lewis as possible. The fact I got stuck with Yvette as a lab partner was worth the close proximity to my crush. Although, I remember being annoyed when Parker took the aisle seat, making Lewis another position away from me.

"I need to focus better in this class."

Helen cups a hand around her mouth. "Your grade level can only be improved by not being stuck with Yvette Anderson."

I nod. "Everything improves when you get away from her."

I keep my head down in class, and I never turn around. I don't need proof of Parker and Yvette being together. Seeing them cuddled up at my former workstation would be the last straw to break me.

At the sound of the bell, I quickly pack up after our theory lesson and hightail it out of the lab.

"Hey, you! Wait up!" a voice yells in the hallway.

I stop dead, listening hard. Is that... Is that Yvie?

"Yes, Kylie, I'm talking to you!" her voice booms as I slowly turn around.

Dread consumes my body as she storms toward me.

"You miserable cow!" she yells. "You just couldn't help yourself, could you?"

The fury in her eyes shakes me to my core. "Huh?"

Yvette lands in front of me with a mighty shove. "You just couldn't help stealing him, could you?"

I grunt, fumbling for balance.

Her shrillness intensifies as she stands over me. "Is it your mission to take every potential boyfriend away from me?"

All I want to do is ask what she's talking about, but the wind is knocked out of me.

"Do you want me to be single forever?" Fire burns in her gaze as her arm lifts to strike. "Huh? Is that what you want?"

Her fingers lock together, ready to cut through the air like a blade. Her arm swings forward, aiming a slap at my face.

Without a second to spare, I brace myself, squinting my eyes closed.

The air hits me, but Yvette's hand doesn't connect.

Two hands land on my shoulders, and I open my eyes to see another hand holding back Yvette's arm.

I blink as Lewis holds Yvette's arm. She stomps her foot in protest.

Before I can look behind me, whoever's holding my shoulders pulls me to the side. I pant my breaths as I turn to see Parker moving me to a safe distance.

"It's not Kylie's fault you're single," Lewis says to Yvette. "It's not my fault, or your exes' fault. You're the reason you jump from boyfriend to boyfriend. It's because no one can stand to get to know the real you."

Yvette gasps at the brutality of his words. Her eyes water, and her bottom lip throbs. She emits a whimper and then turns on her heels and bolts up the hallway.

My panting causes my chest to rapidly rise and fall. "She was about to slap me."

"She was hurt to hear about you and Lewis," Parker says.

I glance at Lewis and then back at Parker. "What about me and Lewis?"

Parker gestures between us. "How you and he…"

My eyebrow raises and I stare at Lewis with my hands on my hips. "What exactly did you tell them?"

Guilt colors Lewis's face. "I told you I wanted to save face."

"Wait," Parker draws out the word. "You two aren't…"

I turn to him with all the sincerity I can muster. "No. Never."

Parker's eyebrows raise as Lewis slinks away. "Why not?"

My mouth runs dry. "Because… Because…."

I look away, hating myself for not being braver.

Parker hooks a finger under my chin and lifts my gaze. "Why not?"

I swallow hard and sniff. "Because I'm in love with you."

His eyes lift up, and a smile spreads across his lips. "You are?"

"Mm-hmm."

His hands cup the sides of my face. "Oh, thank goodness."

"Huh?"

"When I told Yvie I couldn't be with her, I was hoping and praying that you…"

"*What?*" I blurt. "You and Yvie aren't together?"

He grins, running his hands down to my shoulders and giving them a squeeze. "Kylie Green, I can't stop thinking about you. You're the only person who sees me as I really am. I am so freaking in love with you."

My heart practically explodes into confetti.

My brain catches up, taking in the magnitude of his words.

From the corner of my eye, I spy Josie in the crowd of onlookers. Her hands clasp over her chest, and her mouth pouts in awe.

"I've been so scared," Parker whispers. "When you didn't reply to any of my texts, I thought I'd lost you as a friend. That hurt the most."

"I just couldn't stand the idea of seeing you with another girl. My heart couldn't take it."

He pulls his arms around me. "That's never gonna happen. I'm a one-woman man."

I giggle and lift onto my tippy toes. "Good. You're a keeper," I whisper and peck his lips.

Mocking *oohs* and *ahhs* come from the onlookers, who are soon shooed away by teachers trying to clear the halls.

I don't budge an inch. I stay wrapped in Parker's arms, happily listening to the thrum of his heartbeat.

"So you and Lewis never kissed?"

I look up at him. "I leaned in to kiss him and could only think about you. If I couldn't have you, I didn't want to be with anyone."

"He's so annoying," Parker complains. "I totally thought you two were together. You looked so close this morning."

I groan. "Lewis promised to never use me, and on the first day of school, he broke it. I guess he proved he's not the guy for me."

Parker smiles, caressing the side of my face. "I want to be the only guy for you."

"You and Yvie..."

He frowns. "I was so sure you wanted Lewis. For the entire camping trip, I was preparing for when Lewis finally woke up and saw how amazing you are." He exhales slowly. "Camping was the worst. I just wanted to be with you, but kept forcing myself closer to Yvie. I hated it. Then I cracked when we were playing truth or dare."

"What do you mean, you cracked?"

"When you asked me about my biggest regret," he replies. "I regretted I hadn't asked you out sooner. That I didn't notice you before we hatched this scheme. I regretted that we weren't a real couple from the start."

My hands plaster over the space above my heart. "You really felt like that?"

"Yes, but you didn't believe me."

"I didn't believe I could compete with Yvette."

"Anytime I tried to tell you how I really felt, you cut me off. I hate that you didn't feel good enough."

I fidget in my stance, letting myself really hear him this time.

"All I want is for you to be happy, even if you're with a different guy." He looks off to the side, shaking his head. "Man, I wiped out on the water skis because of how hard I was crushing on you. At the same time, I was watching Yvie and knew I had to pretend I still had a crush on her."

My mouth hangs open. "Your crush had ended?"

"How could I still like her after all the time I'd spent with you?"

An airy sigh drifts out of me. "Oh, Parker."

"After the trip, I felt like I had led Yvie on, so I went to her house on Saturday. I told her I couldn't be with her, and that I was in love with you."

I blink hard. "You told her that on Saturday?"

He nods.

"And you didn't see your friends on Sunday?"

"I was too miserable to hear Lewis gloat about being with you."

"We're such idiots. We could've been together this whole time."

Parker grins. "At least we're both sure now."

"Wait. Josie told me she saw you and Yvie getting close in class."

Parker shakes his head. "I was just being nice because I don't want her to be sad. But she was trying to get me to reconsider, while also wanting advice on getting Lewis back. She's kinda a mess."

I tap his forehead. "*Duh.* I've been trying to tell you that."

He chuckles. "What can I say? I've been fighting my feelings for you since the first time we kissed."

"You mean, in the cafeteria?"

He nods.

I lift onto the balls of my feet. "Me too. That was one heck of a kiss."

He cups the back of my head. "All your kisses are amazing."

I pout as my lids lower. Our lips meld together as his arm snakes around my waist. I tilt my head, getting the most out of the kiss. As he holds me tighter, my back arches, and I giggle at what's coming next.

Parker dips me, laying more pressure into the kiss.

Wolf whistles and cheers surround us, and Parker pulls me back up. We separate, hurriedly wiping our mouths.

Kai, Tabitha, Tyler, and Jamie ogle us.

"Do you guys need to watch?" Parker jokingly complains.

Tabitha nudges Jamie, and says, "We needed proof that you're not an idiot, Parker."

"Lewis told us you two were making up," Tyler says as Kai snickers beside him.

Parker shoos them away. "Okay, you've seen. Now give us some privacy."

They laugh and disperse toward their designated classrooms.

Parker grabs onto my hips. "I guess it's only right that they saw our official couple kiss. They did witness our first fake couple kiss."

I cup the sides of his face. "Yeah, but our kisses are so much better when we're not putting on a show for other people."

Parker pulls me closer. "Yeah, like outside the ice-creamery."

"Mm-hmm." I pull on his school tie, and lay another kiss on him. "I love you so much, Parker Kelly."

He grins. "I love you, Kikki."

Epilogue

Four Weeks Later...

Parker and I have been together for a month in an official relationship. Well, most people think we've been official since that kiss in the cafeteria. We kinda count that first week, anyway. Every touch, every kiss, and every truth revealed, brought us to this place.

Absolute bliss.

Tonight, we're doing something we've both been dreading. Dinner with both our parents at Fratelli's. It's one of the fanciest restaurants in Victoria Falls. My parents would've been happy with Alto Burger, but as Parker says, his parents like to overdo it.

Parker spends a lot of afternoons at our house. For some reason, he really does love my parents. Tess has yet to meet him in person, but they've chatted on the phone when my parents have her calls on speakerphone. Parker feels so comfortable with my parents, he's shared with them about his birth mother. This was huge. He's been keeping such a big secret for so long, and now he's letting it out. He's still not ready to tell his friends, but I'm so proud of the growth he's shown.

I haven't spent a lot of time with his family. We're doing baby steps. But I didn't want his family to feel excluded, so I nudged Parker to make tonight happen. We both cringe anytime one of our parents threatens to tell an embarrassing baby story.

I roll my eyes and lift my phone as my mom yammers away. I open my message chain with Josie for any latest updates I might've missed. Her long-term crush and Hollywood celebrity, Wyatt Hayes, is currently in hospital. The rumors online are that he's suffering from amnesia. It's blown all our minds, especially Josie's. When I'm not with Parker, I'm by her side, comforting her as we wait for more news to drop about her special guy.

"Anything yet?" Parker asks beside me.

I place the phone on the table and frown. "Not yet."

He kisses my cheek. "Josie will be okay. She has you to lean on."

"*Eww*," William complains from across the table. "Can we have one dinner where you two don't kiss?"

Kurtis then chucks up a wadded piece of bread at Parker.

As the brothers bicker, I sit back and let my eyes wander around the restaurant. I find Yvette having dinner with her family. Her jaw drops at the sight of Parker and I and our respective families. With a screech, she flies off her chair and books it to the bathroom.

As guilt writhes inside me, I excuse myself from the table and make my way to the restaurant bathroom.

"Yvie?" I say softly, approaching her at the sinks.

She grunts, tearing at the paper towel. "Go away."

"I just wanted to reach out. I haven't seen much of you at school."

"Well, loners don't exactly want to be seen."

"I'm so sorry your heart got broken over the break," I say. "But, to be honest, I think you'll benefit from being single."

She retches. "You would. You stole both boys who were interested in me."

"Yvie, you jump from guy to guy, but never figure out who you are as an individual. Don't you want to feel happy without a boyfriend?"

"If I don't have a boyfriend, I'm a loser."

"Who told you that?"

She sniffs and wipes under her nose. "It's the truth."

I turn her towards me. "No, it's not. Why should you let a guy define your self-worth?"

She frowns. "What if I don't like the person I find?"

"Not possible. I know there's a good person under there somewhere. You just need to learn to think before you speak."

"My friends used to reward me for saying mean things. Now I don't have them, and I don't know what I'm supposed to do."

I clasp her hand. "I know I said you should be single, but I don't want you to be alone. I couldn't live with myself if you became isolated in your misery."

"I deserve to be alone. I almost slapped you for goodness's sake."

"No one deserves to be alone," I whisper. "If you let me, I'd like to help you and Tabitha mend your friendship."

"I've tried and failed so many times. She'd never want that."

"At least let me help you figure out your own interests. Maybe there's a club you can join to make new friends."

A hopeful smile emerges. "Yeah, maybe."

I give her a quick hug. "I just want you to feel better. However that looks for you."

"Thank you, Kylie. Dang. Parker is so lucky to have you." She glances at the bathroom door. "Are you here with your families?"

"Yeah, it's the big meeting."

"That's so cute. I've never had that before."

"Find a guy who values you. Someone you truly, deeply love."

She smiles and nods.

"I gotta get back out there. Will you be okay?"

"I will be." As I leave, she adds, "Oh, Kylie, I promise to never try to slap you again."

I hold on to the door handle, tugging it open. "If you can promise never to say mean things to other people, that'd be a great start too."

"I'll do my very best."

I walk back to the table, and Parker's eyes are locked onto me.

"What just happened?" he asks as I take my seat beside him.

"I was just checking to see if Yvette was okay."

Nervousness creases his brow. "There was no slapping?"

"No, of course not. Although, she did apologize for that."

"So, everything's good?" he asks hesitantly.

I nod. "She just needs to find herself."

Parker interlaces his fingers with mine. "I'm so lucky to have met a girl who has already found herself." He kisses the back of my hand. "I just had to pull Kikki out of the house."

"You were the missing piece that helped me get my confidence."

"No way. It was all you."

"What if we needed each other?" I compromise. "I can't imagine you having this dinner if you never opened up about your birth mother. And we definitely wouldn't be taking this trip tomorrow."

Parker shifts in his chair. "I know. I don't know why I'm so nervous about it."

I squeeze his hand. "Because it's a big moment. You've wanted to visit her grave for so long, and now we're gonna do it."

He smiles. "There's no one I'd rather go with than you, Kikki."

"I'm glad."

"And you're sure you're not weirded out by visiting a cemetery?"

"Not in the slightest. Besides, I'm not letting you go alone."

"My family said they'd go with me. At least they did in our last family therapy session." He leans closer to me. "But, I have to admit, I'd much rather go with you."

"Parky, I'll be with you through anything."

He chuckles. "Ugh. That nickname."

I nuzzle my nose against his. "It's cute, boyfriend."

He wraps his arm around me and kisses my cheek. "You're just lucky you're cute."

Beep, beep. Parker and I lean forward, viewing a text from Josie. *"Wyatt's manager just called and said Wyatt wants to see me. They're arranging a flight."*

I swallow hard and blink at Parker.

A nervous laugh spills out of him. "Umm, okay. That blows our trip out of the water."

I utter some garbled nonsense before finally spitting out, "She's meeting up with a celebrity?"

"Well, the girl is head over heels for him."

I nod, still not comprehending the magnitude of the situation. "Well, we know what love looks like."

He hugs me close. "It looks like me never letting you go."

Thank you

Scan the QR code and get a FREE chapter from Parker's perspective.

Kylie thought Parker was at Yvette's house to proclaim his love to her. Turns out, he was revealing his deep love for Kylie to Yvette.

How did Yvette take it, and why did it stop Parker from expressing his feelings to Kylie?

SCAN ME!

About The Author

Milly Rose is an animal-loving romance enthusiast with a swoon-inducing book formula. Shy girl + hot guy + first kisses. Her YA sweet romance books will have you falling in love every instalment. Milly Rose is the quintessential shy girl, who you can contact via her mailing list and reply to her monthly email blasts! Milly spends her days vying for her cat's affection, dreaming up her next book boyfriend, and writing a fun meet-cute under candlelight with a lovely brewed cup of tea.

Join Milly Rose's Mailing List
millyrosebooks.com
Follow on Instagram @shy.author.milly.rose
Follow on Tiktok @shy.author.milly.rose

Also By

ALL BOOKS SET IN ASHWORTH ACADEMY

Shy Girls Can't Date Billionaires (Christie & Ash)
Shy Girls Can't Date Bullies (Ava & Beau)
Shy Girls Can't Date Frenemies (Jamie & Milo)
Shy Girls Can't Date Bad Boys (Vanessa & Dax)
Shy Girls Can't Fake Date (Kylie & Parker)
Shy Girls Can't Date Celebrities (Josie & Wyatt)
We Shouldn't Be Together (Tabitha & Kai)

www.ingramcontent.com/pod-product-compliance
Lightning Source LLC
Chambersburg PA
CBHW010337170726
48283CB00009B/2851